THE REST OF THE NOAH STORY

PALESTINE - 2014

To RENEE -

May this story touch you heart the way it touched mine!

[illegible signature]

And the waters prevailed, and were increased greatly upon the earth; and the Ark went upon the face of the waters.

Genesis 7:18

THE REST OF THE NOAH STORY

Upon the Face of the Waters

BY KEVIN J. TODESCHI

Yazdan Publishing • Virginia Beach • Virginia

Printed in the U.S.A.

Published by:

Yazdan Publishing
P.O. Box 4604
Virginia Beach, VA 23454

ISBN 13: 978-0-9845672-6-3

Available at bookstores and Amazon.com

Cover art: "Noah's Ark" by Edward Hicks (1780-1849)

Cover design by Richard Boyle

Text and design layout by Cathy Merchand

Contents

There is an ancient Armenian legend which states that a gopher-wood craft, enormous in proportions, rests high upon the mountain of Aghri Dagh—just waiting until the moment is right for its discovery.

According to the tale, God—in His omnipotent wisdom—hid the craft, for He knew a time would come in the history of humankind when all the peoples of the world would need the chance to believe.

And if the legend is true, that moment approaches.

In Greece, he is Deucalion . . .

In Mexico, he is Tezpi . . .

In the Babylonian Epic of Gilgamesh, he is Utnapishtim . . .

In rabbinical folklore, he is Menahem . . .

In the Bible and the Koran, he is Noah . . .

His tale is known by more than 200 cultures on every continent of this planet. There are verbal traditions about him that claim to be older than recorded history; written accounts are traceable at least as far back as the third millennium B.C.

Since 1840 alone, there have been more than twenty recorded sightings of his craft, by ten times as many people—all insisting that his story is true.

And yet, critics maintain the story is nothing more than a legend.

Some state that humankind could not possibly have lived as long as legend records—that life spans nearing a thousand years are utter fantasy.

Others contend that such an alleged history would have more visible geographic evidence of authenticity.

Many point out that there isn't enough moisture in the entire atmosphere to initiate a worldwide deluge.

For these reasons, and many, many more, today individuals all over the world believe that the account of the gathering of the animals, of the Ark, of Noah, and of his family, is simply the remnants of a long-forgotten fable.

This story is for them.

Imagine . . .

That humanity has been on this planet much longer than we suppose.

That the earth was once a tropical paradise, completely surrounded by a water vapor canopy.

That the vapor provided a mist that watered the planet's life every moment of every day and prohibited the sun's radiation from reaching the ground, allowing life spans of mythic duration.

That a greenhouse effect about the planet prevented temperature fluctuations, so that:

> It was just as warm all over the earth;
>
> There was no such thing as wind;
>
> All the waters of the planet were stable at seventy degrees;
>
> There was no such thing as snow;
>
> The earth was filled with lush vegetation and an abundance of trees.

And then, close your eyes and imagine this earth of very long ago . . .

A place where there is no such thing as rain.

Author's Prologue

It is difficult to pinpoint exactly what awakened my interest in Noah and the Ark. I know that as a child one of my favorite pop-up picture books detailed the story of the Flood, the animals, and Noah's family. I also know that my interest was reawakened years later as an adult while reading the book of Genesis when I realized something that had never been pointed out to me before: Methuselah was Noah's grandfather, and the dating suggested by scripture implied that the oldest man in the Bible had died the same year as the Flood. In spite of the fact that this information was easily deduced from the Genesis account, most individuals with whom I discussed my findings were not aware of either detail.

My fascination with the story was further heightened when I began researching the topic from various unrelated perspectives. That process led to the amazing discovery that a number of source materials described complementary aspects of Noah's tale that expanded the story; however, most authors of these materials seemed totally unfamiliar with many of the other references. The appeal of Noah's story continued to grow for me and eventually I would scour dozens of sources, thousands of pages of reference materials, and eventually write my graduate thesis on the topic.

Perhaps more than any other Old Testament tale, it is the story of Noah and the Flood with which individuals of all ages and religious backgrounds are most familiar. In Christian, Jewish, and Islamic literature, the story of the Deluge plays an important role. However, tales of a global flood are not limited to the Bible or the Koran. In addition to the story of Noah, there are actually more than two hundred Flood traditions scattered throughout the world. Next to the Genesis tale, the most well known account was not even discovered until the latter half of the nineteenth century when twelve tablets were unearthed at Nineveh. These tablets detailed the Gilgamesh Epic and the adventures of Utnapishtim—a Babylonian Noah—and created a worldwide fascination with the Flood, while lending further credence to the possibility of a deluge of mythic proportions.

In the Christian world, the story of Noah has played an important role for two thousand years. At one time the tale was even more important in the lives of individuals than it is today. It was once seen as a story that perfectly embodied the potential that humankind had for degeneration and evil—a story that Jesus brought to mind in the hopes that Christians would ever be watchful of their ways (Matthew 24:37-39). Between the Middle Ages and the nineteenth century the fact that fossilized bones of sea creatures could be found on mountain ranges throughout the world was generally believed to be proof that the Flood had occurred. In Christian medieval towns while Biblical mystery-moral plays were making the circuit the story of Noah and his family was a frequent favorite. Even with the discovery of plate tectonics in the 1800s and the knowledge that ice sheets had once covered much of the Northern Hemisphere—challenging the medieval belief that "fish bones on mountaintops equals world-wide deluge"—the belief in Noah's Flood was never doubted by those faithful to scripture.

Further confirmation of the existence of the Ark even after the nineteenth century came in the form of eyewitness accounts of the craft upon Mount Ararat in Turkey near the borders of Armenia and Iran by many reputable investigators, scholars, military professionals, and theologians. In fact, there have been more recorded sightings of Noah's Ark since 1840 than during any other period of recorded history! These sightings, however, have not been limited to the modern world. Historical references to the discovery of the Ark are traceable at least as far back as the third century B.C.E.

These personal sightings of Noah's Ark by literally hundreds of people over the last twenty-four-hundred years is especially amazing considering that any ascent of the mountain has not been an easy undertaking. Mount Ararat's base covers approximately 500 square miles, and its highest peak soars to almost 17,000 feet. At various places on the mountain, ice accumulation has been measured at more than 250 feet! Generally, reports of the Ark's sighting have occurred only after an unusually warm period of months when the ice has had a chance to thaw. Even then the mountain peaks are perpetually covered with snow. Nighttime temperatures during the summer can drop to twenty degrees below zero, and winds at the summit of the mountain sometimes reach a velocity of 150 miles per hour. It is not uncommon for a storm to occur daily on Ararat, not to mention the fact that the mountain is infested with poisonous snakes at lower levels and mountain lions and bears that roam the ravines.

Essentially, the biblical account of Noah and the Ark is contained in Genesis 5-9. It is the story of an old man, singled out from among the corrupt and wicked of the rest of the world, who found favor in the eyes of God. God told Noah that He had decided to destroy man's evilness. He gave Noah instructions to build an enormous craft and to enter into it with his wife, his sons, and his son's wives, as well as two of every kind of creature (birds, mammals and reptiles), and enough food for him to keep all of the Ark's inhabitants alive for the duration of the flood that was coming to destroy the earth.

According to the Old Testament, the Ark's incredible dimensions measured three hundred cubits long, fifty cubits wide, and thirty cubits high. Historically, a cubit is thought to be the length of a man's forearm, or somewhere between eighteen and twenty-two inches. It is interesting to note that the Ark's dimensions of six to one (length to width) were considered so seaworthy that Marine architect George W. Dickie purposefully used the same ratio when constructing the U.S.S. Oregon, which was launched in 1898. For a time, the Oregon was considered the flagship of the American fleet and was one of the most stable vessels ever constructed.

Noah followed the instructions, and when his task was complete—and the Ark's inhabitants were sealed safely inside—it rained for forty days and forty nights: water rose to cover even the mountains of the earth. Approximately seven months later, the Ark became lodged atop the mountains of Ararat (sometimes referred to by locals as Aghri Dagh). For several more months the waters evaporated while the Ark remained lodged upon the mountain until Noah finally decided to release first a raven and then a dove. After several attempts, eventually the dove returned with an olive leaf in its beak, signaling that the waters had dried from much of the land and that life had returned to the earth.

More than one year after Noah and his family first entered the Ark, the craft's inhabitants disembarked. Noah offered a sacrifice of burnt offerings in thanksgiving for having survived the Deluge and God set a rainbow in the sky as promise that He would never again destroy the earth by flood. From a literal approach to the traditional story, all of humanity is credited with having descended from one of Noah's three sons: Shem, Ham, and Japheth.

Because of the reference in Genesis 6:3: "And the Lord said, My spirit shall not always strive with man, for that he also is flesh: yet his days shall be an hundred and twenty years," it has often been surmised that Noah received the Ark instructions 120 years before the Flood, which was how long it took him to build the craft. During his spare time, Noah would have preached repentance to any that might listen. Others have speculated that Noah may have even used construction crews, thereby greatly decreasing the amount of time necessary to construct the Ark.

To be on the safe side, however, Tim LaHaye (a Baptist minister and president of Christian College) and John Morris (a member of the Institute for Creation Research) proposed in *The Ark on Ararat* (1977) that a literal interpretation of the Bible regarding the Ark's construction by Noah and his three sons was indeed possible. Based upon the Ark's dimensions and estimated volume, they calculated that the Ark contained 1,520,000 cubic feet of lumber. Assuming that four men working six days a week could install a minimum of 15 cubic feet per day, the Ark could have been built in as little as eighty-one years. Since "gopher-wood"—the lumber used for the Ark's construction—is not mentioned elsewhere in the Bible, it is often assumed that gopher-wood refers to a durable and decay-resistant lumber from the region such as cypress or white oak.

Perhaps the most exhaustive mainstream attempt to examine every imaginable detail of Noah's story from a Judeo-Christian perspective came in the form of Dave Balsiger and Charles Sellier's *In Search of Noah's Ark* (1972). Their book sold more than one million copies and resulted in a documentary movie released the following year. Among the details examined by Balsiger and Sellier are such things as the total number of animals aboard the Ark, which they surmise included between twenty-four and sixty-six "clean" animals (two of each times seven pairs) plus between 604 and 734 "unclean" animals (two of each), placing the total as being somewhere between 1,544 and 2,392 creatures. Essentially, a "clean" animal is a non-flesh eater that biblically chews a cud and has a divided hoof. The Ark would require more than one pair of each of these creatures since some would inevitably become prey to those that were unclean.

In terms of scientific proof regarding a catastrophic Flood, in 1998 geophysicists William Ryan and Walter Pitman of Columbia University presented a fascinating scientific examination of a flood in the Black Sea region that occurred in the sixth millennium B.C.E. Their work, *Noah's Flood*, suggests that an immense flood of mythic proportions forever changed the history of a continent by prompting a migration of its people, who took with them oral traditions of a Mesopotamian catastrophe that—in all likelihood—became the basis of the Epic of Gilgamesh. Whether their findings suggest that the root of Noah's biblical Flood is the same event remains an unknown. Other sources involved in Flood "arkaeology" suggest that more than one massive flood may be at the impetus for so many diluvial traditions around the world.

In terms of the biblical account, what may come as a surprise to many individuals familiar with the Genesis story is that there is more to the tale than is generally gleamed from a simple reading of the text. In fact, what is not generally known by the modern world is that Genesis contains not one account of the Flood story but two! Over the years theologians and religious scholars have isolated at least three major sources within the book of Genesis: the J source, the P source, and the E source, standing for Jehovah, the Priestly document, and Elohim, respectively. Both the J source and the P source have their own accounts of the Deluge.

Originally, the different sources of Genesis were discovered because of the way in which the sources referred to God. The J source uses only the name "Yahweh" (Lord) when referring to the Deity; the P source uses the names "Elohim" (God) and "El Shaddai" (God Almighty), and the E source uses both "Yahweh" and "Elohim."

The Jehovistic source dates from the eighth or ninth century B.C. J is concerned with thorough descriptions, the personality of the characters, and the care and involvement of a loving God with His creation. The P document dates from the period after 586 B.C. (when Jerusalem was taken by King Nebuchadnezzar and the Jews were carried into captivity). P is most interested in the literal interpretation of the Law, tradition, and the manner in which God guides his chosen people. Perhaps the most distinctive element in P is the author's interest in family genealogies and a seemingly endless number of "begettings," through which can be documented the purity of the line that God used to direct His activities in the earth. However, because of the merging of the independent narratives, we are faced with certain duplicities within the Genesis account, including:

> For behold, I will bring a flood of waters upon the earth, to destroy all flesh in which is the breath of life from under heaven; everything that is on the earth shall die . . . Noah did this; he did all that God commanded him. (P Source, Genesis 6:17 & 22)

And,

> . . . I will send rain upon the earth forty days and forty nights; and every living thing that I have made I will blot out from the face of the ground. And Noah did all that the Lord had commanded him. (J Source, Genesis 7:4-5)

Major differences between these two sources also include the number of animals Noah was instructed to take upon the Ark, and the length of the Deluge:

> ***J Source:***
> Seven pairs of birds and clean animals and one pair of unclean (Genesis 7:2)
>
> The rain lasted 40 days and 40 nights and the water evaporated after three seven-day intervals of Noah releasing the dove; total=61 days (Genesis 7:4, 7:12, 8:6-8, 8:10, 8:12)
>
> ***P Source:***
> Only one pair of each creature came into the Ark (Genesis 6:19)
>
> The water lasted 150 days and remained on the earth for a total of one year and eleven days (Genesis 7:11, 8:14)
>
> *Anchor Bible*

Historically, the separate narratives of the J and P sources were combined by a redactor (compiler) whose job was to bring the two accounts carefully together, discarding superfluous material in the process. As one example of the redactor's work, there is only one account of the Ark's construction (Genesis 6: 14-16).

In addition to the Old Testament, an analysis of the Great Flood story has also been a frequent favorite of rabbinical scholarship for more than a thousand years. According to Jewish legend, Noah was recognized as being special from birth. His father, Lamech, was so overcome by the child's appearance that he believed the baby to be the offspring of angels. The child was called Menahem at birth and only later would be called Noah, a name that came to mean "rest," because he assisted his cousin Tubalcain in the invention of iron and brass, from which laborsaving tools were created (Genesis 4:22).

There are various arguments among Jewish scholars as to why Noah may have waited until the ripe old age of 500 to father any children. Some rabbis claim that Noah foresaw the Flood and then refused to have any children because they would drown. Others contend that Noah was unable to father offspring until the age of 500 as a precaution against his having more righteous children than would have been able to fit into the Ark. In any event, approximately 120 years before the Deluge, Noah had a vision in which he saw what was to come. Enoch, one of his ancestors who had previously been "taken up" by God (Genesis 5:24) appeared and announced the end of the world. Noah's three sons (Ham, Shem, and Japheth) assisted their father in constructing the Ark.

In Islam, Noah is seen as one of Mohammed's favorite characters because the patriarch is mentioned more than a dozen times in the Koran and is regarded as one of the principal prophets sent to save humankind. According to Arab scholars, Noah is also said to have written more than ten books, all of which are now lost. In the Islamic version, it was the angel Gabriel who showed Noah how to build the craft, and a total of eighty individuals was allowed on board.

In addition to theological debates detailing every imaginable aspect of the story and eyewitness accounts of the Ark itself, many modern-day researchers have devoted their time, their resources, even their lives to explorations searching for the physical remains of the Ark. Perhaps the best collection of modern-day quests for the Ark is B.J. Corbin's *The Explorers of Ararat* (1999), which contains first-hand experiences of expeditions searching for the fabled craft.

What may be most amazing about the story of Noah's Ark is the many ways in which seemingly unrelated sources often draw similar conclusions from the tale. For example, because of the information contained in Genesis 2:5-6, a number of Christian authors believe that rain was absent from pre-deluge earth and that the planet received moisture from a water vapor canopy that engulfed it: " . . . for the Lord God had not caused it to rain upon the earth . . . But there went up a mist from the earth, and watered the whole face of the ground." This same premise was also advanced by Austrian-born philosopher, educator and clairvoyant, Rudolf Steiner (1861-1925), the founder of the Anthroposophical Society.

Steiner reportedly possessed the ability to perceive information beyond the material world, from a "spiritual world" that was just as real to him as the physical world was to others. In describing the pre-deluge earth, Steiner stated:

> . . . at that time the air was saturated with water mist vapors. Man lived in the water mist, which in certain regions never lifted to the point where the air was completely clear. Sun and moon could not be seen as they are today, but were surrounded by colored coronas. A distribution of rain and sunshine, such as occurs at present, did not exist at that time. It only appeared in the post-Atlantean period. Our ancestors lived in a country of mist . . .
>
> (Steiner, "Cosmic Memory," pg. 253)

Some individuals contend that it was the disappearance of the water vapor canopy and the resulting influx of solar radiation that became responsible for the tremendous decrease in humankind's longevity—from almost 1,000 years to the present span of seven to ten decades. Scripture further supports this premise in that, immediately after the Flood, life spans begin to decrease with each subsequent generation. In addition, the absence of rain suggests that the earth had no system of winds until after the Flood. A proposition that is supported, interestingly enough, by a literal reading of Genesis 8:1 with the first biblical mention of wind occurring after the Deluge: " . . . And God made a wind blow over the earth . . . " Steiner's reference to the continent of Atlantis also places the timing for the Great Flood as occurring long before the traditional date of occurring somewhere between 2,350 and 2,500 B.C.E. In fact, Steiner pointed out:

> Nearly all the peoples who have left reliable records or legends refer to the Flood as having taking place about three thousand years before the Mystery of Golgotha [the crucifixion and resurrection of Jesus]; that is the period indicated by the legends . . . Obviously it does not refer to the Atlantean catastrophe, for that took place very much earlier. (Steiner, "Earthly," pgs. 128-129)

Another intuitive, Christian mystic Edgar Cayce (1877-1945), provided independent confirmation of Steiner's timetable. Cayce's information on ancient civilizations suggests that Noah's Flood occurred at a time corresponding to one of three destructions that would eventually annihilate the continent of Atlantis. Cayce also provided detailed information about Noah's family, including the names of Noah's daughters-in-law (Rezepatha, Maran, and Shelobothe), whose names are not mentioned in scripture. According to Edgar Cayce, Rudolf Steiner, and others, Noah and his family were not the only individuals who survived the Flood—providing a logical rationale as to why more than two hundred different Flood traditions exist on every continent of the planet. Clairvoyant insights also suggest that humankind had become so evil and degenerate during Noah's time that misshapen mixtures and half-human beasts had begun to populate the earth, and would eventually become the basis for the legendary creatures of Greek and Roman mythology.

Various legends also provide interesting insights into Noah's story. For example, in addition to the difficulty of scaling Mount Ararat, according to Armenian legend the Ark is guarded by angels who protect the craft. Some researchers suggest that rather than being literally upon the mountain called Ararat, the biblical account describing the Ark as coming to rest "upon the mountains of Ararat" (Genesis 8:4) could suggest the entire range of mountains, causing some to believe that the Ark may be upon Cudi Dagh (Mt. Judi) approximately 200 miles to the south. Regardless of its exact location, the Armenian legend contends that when the time is right the Ark will be revealed as a means of validating Noah's story and enabling individuals to reawaken their faith in God.

In addition to being a symbol of spiritual faith, for some the Ark is also considered to be a psychological symbol—an archetype of human experience. The Flood story is an archetype because it is a part of the human experience all over the world. Over and above its literal truth, in Jungian psychology the Ark can be seen as a symbolic representation of transformation and change because the ship's occupants underwent a journey over which they had no control and yet somehow ended up at a higher level of awareness because of their catastrophic experience. In most of these diluvial accounts, legend describes how a family survives a deluge of enormous proportions. Prior to the disaster, the family generally pulls together everything that is part of their world (such as the animals in the story of Noah described in Genesis) and finds refuge in a craft or a ship in which they can ride out the storm. Oftentimes, the family has no control over their journey for the ship is inundated from above and below and they are forced to simply ride out the storm. At the end of the flood, the craft generally finds higher and stable ground and the occupants can disembark and begin their lives anew. Everything that was a part of their old world is now a part of their new (e.g. the animals get off the Ark as well). The difference is that now all of the ship's occupants find themselves upon higher ground.

Jungian psychologist Eleanor Bertine (ca 1944) found much archetypal significance in the Flood story and suggested that the Flood epic itself was far older than either the biblical or Gilgamesh accounts. Like many researchers, she pointed to a Sumerian version and its Ziusudra Noah that is traceable to at least the third millennium B.C.E. The biblical and Gilgamesh tales agree with all essential details of the Sumerian version. Bertine was convinced that both the Gilgamesh and the biblical accounts were traceable to the Sumerian version; however, she was also certain that the Sumerian version had been based on something even earlier: "dating back so far that the bottom falls out of time . . . " (Rohrbach, Pg. 197)

As an archetype, the Great Flood Myth symbolizes the pattern of being overwhelmed by personal transformation and change and yet somehow becoming a more enlightened individual because of the experience. What is fascinating about the archetypal significance of the tale is that in the last decade of the twentieth century the story of Noah experienced a tremendous rise in popularity. Almost overnight the market seemed flooded with numerous children's toys, night lights, magnets, collector's plates, ornaments, clothing, figurines and even several movies about Noah's Ark. The archetypal reason was not because for some inexplicable reason this man and his family suddenly fascinated society. Instead, it was because so many individuals apparently felt in the midst of personal transformation and change themselves that the psychological archetype resurfaced. People felt motivated to put a Noah's magnet on their fridge because subconsciously it resonated to something they were experiencing deep within themselves.

For me, perhaps the most important result of examining all of the various perspectives on Noah's story is that some unanswered questions finally begin to make sense. Questions like "Are life spans approaching 1,000 years even possible?" "Is there enough moisture in the earth's atmosphere to initiate a world-wide deluge?" and "How could a family of eight feed over 2,000 creatures every single day for a year?" became answerable. In the process other questions had rationale explanations as well. Until that time, questions like "Why did Noah become drunk?" (Genesis 9:21) and "What reason did Noah possibly have to make his grandson Canaan a slave?" (Genesis 9:25) defied explanation. It is not an exaggeration to state that for nearly thirty years this story has preoccupied many of my thoughts and much of my time and energy.

In my opinion, all of this information simply enriches one of the most profound biblical stories of all time. For myself, what began as a simple excursion into the material gave way to a fascination with the tale—a fascination that eventually resulted in this novel in an attempt to bring together all of the various details of the story. Rather than simply creating a compilation of facts, however, what I experienced was an epic that has truly became a part of my life's journey. In the end, I came to love Noah and Methuselah and the rest, for they became very real to me. Although at first I watched the story as an observer, I eventually became very much a participant—frequently knowing just moments before the characters what was to transpire or not seeing it until they had lived it out for me. I began to realize that something beyond anything I had ever dreamed was taking form and I was simply there to relate my experience on paper.

The experience started with a very old man, Methuselah, the oldest man in the Bible, and an attempt to explain the historic or symbolic significance of his death at the age of 969 during the year of the Flood. He became as loved by me as any friend who has crossed my life's path. In the beginning, I felt his joy as he related all that he had come to know to Traibus, a giant who roamed the earth in those days. I laughed at his humor and listened to his every word as he explained to me (and the others) some great philosophical truth. I met his grandson, Noah, and felt the younger's hope that there might still be time to save the peoples of the earth from themselves. Yet, I knew what Noah could not know just then: that the world would not change, and many of Noah's efforts would become for naught. Near the end, I felt Methuselah's sadness when the time came for him to say goodbye.

I have come to believe that the Ark does indeed remain hidden upon the slopes of Ararat, for in my mind's eye, I was there when the waters began to subside and an enormous vessel became lodged upon the highest of two mountain peaks. I saw the window coverings of the gopher-wood ship removed and the excitement of the patriarch and his sons as they looked upon a sky that had been hidden from their view. I watched Noah disembark with his wife, and his sons, and his son's wives, and nearly 2,000 creatures that had been saved from the Deluge and a metaphysical cleansing of the earth. Truly, this story has been one of the most memorable experiences of my life. Taken together, much of it appears quite amazing; a great deal of it seems to be true.

For those who are challenged by the ideas of Atlantis, pre-deluge creatures called "Mixtures," various unbelievable possibilities, or the very idea of correlating such a vast array of seemingly unrelated information, I would remind them that this is simply a story of fiction. To those who are open to the unknown and the possibility that there might be much more to this tale than we have yet dared to imagine, I would invite them to consider these things as I did from the very first moment when I asked myself, "What if?"

This is the Noah I have come to know . . .

Beginnings
(125 years before the Flood)

Her name was Lapeth and never before had she been so very much afraid. She lay silent amid the cover of the forest with her belly pressed so firmly against the soft underbrush that her robe had grown wet from the moistness of the morning's dew. Her skin was damp from the stifling humidity of the early morning air. The thin cloth of her robe stuck stubbornly to her back and slender legs. Yet she did nothing to correct her discomfort—above all else, silence was their one chance of escape.

All around her, the lush fronds of flowering ferns kept Lapeth and her daughter from being seen. The tiny child, Rezepatha, was less than two and much too young to understand what was happening. Lapeth watched the sleeping girl with uneasiness, fearing they would never escape. The denseness of the oak forest was their only camouflage. For a short while, at least, the thick vines of underbrush and the denseness of tree trunks kept them from being seen but they couldn't remain. The overseer's men were looking for them, and Lapeth had to find a way to safety.

The thought of capture terrified her. The overseer's men were "Mixtures," brutal creatures more beast than human, who banded together in patrols and followed any order from their taskmaster. Her own skin was fair and her features gentle, and she knew what sport the foul-smelling creatures would pursue before returning her to the overseer. For three days she and Rezepatha had managed to avoid the patrol, and still she sensed they were not safe.

Lapeth was conscious of her own hunger and realized how long it had been since she had last picked one of the red melons which grew within the forest clearings. There was plenty to eat, from soft-shelled nuts and tiny purple berries to the small seeds of yellow flowers and vines thick with fruit but their eating had been sparse, as she had been careful not to leave behind a trail to follow.

In the last few days everything about their lives had changed. She was certain they had been followed, at least as far as the edge of the forest. Somewhere on Shinar's plains was her husband, Basil, and somewhere ahead lay sanctuary. The choice of abandoning him to the patrol had not been easy but Rezepatha had to be taken to safety.

The three had never planned on venturing to Shinar. Stories of the city's disintegration had spread as far as their home in Dodanim, on the edge of the Black Sea. They had left in search of a better way of life, for Basil had often spoken of the fair city of Sheba, whose shores touched the warm waters of a clear ocean brimming with fish. There men remained free and children could grow without threat of the overseer.

Lapeth turned toward her daughter and sighed. The child's eyes remained closed, and her breath was slow and regular. Short wisps of black hair accentuated the beauty of the little girl's forehead. Her skin was fair, like her mother's, yet she possessed her father's noble chin and the gentleness of his smile. Perfect in every detail, Lapeth and Basil had long been certain that their daughter was destined for greatness.

Suddenly, she heard a sound.

Softly, at first, and then louder, came the noise of a branch being stepped upon, and then another. Lapeth strained to listen, and the sound came again: unmistakably, the rustle of leaves being pushed aside as though someone approached. Fearfully, she closed her eyes and pulled Rezepatha close to her body. Silently, she pressed her own head deep into the underbrush and remained completely still.

The noise moved closer, until she could hear the rattling of branches and the crushing of vines being broken underfoot. For the first time, she gave up all hope of ever getting away—though she mouthed one final prayer for deliverance. As the footsteps moved closer, the forest scents gave way to sour smells and the odor of filthy bodies. Lapeth was certain that the patrol stood within a few cubits. Only seconds of freedom remained. Something bent down and touched her face, and she shivered, but the moist texture against her skin was only a massive leaf being pushed aside. She imagined what the creatures looked like, with their great hairy chests and limbs, and rotting animal skins carelessly girded about their loins. Suddenly, the harsh voices of Mixtures rose above the sounds of branches and leaves.

"How far are we supposed to go?" one of them demanded as the air from his throat caused a whistling sound to move between broken teeth. "I say we do it here."

"You'll do exactly what he said—just like the rest of us," one of them snarled in reply.

"There's no telling what lurks among these trees," the whistler commented more to himself than to the others.

"I still say we'd have been better off to do it by the compound—at least the slaves would have seen it."

"There is nothing more worthless than a slave scared to the breaking point."

"We could be attacked out here!"

"By what?" a soft voice asked, with disgust. "You can still see the plains through the trees. Look behind you."

"Umhh," the whistler grunted, after pausing for only a moment, "but we won't if we keep walking."

"Kana wants it done in the first clearing—the one used by all who stay off the main roads—not before."

"We ought to burn these trees down . . . ," the whistling voice said, fading as it moved out of range.

Lapeth listened for the sounds of other voices but heard none—only the dwindling noise of rustling leaves and underbrush fading off into the distance. For a long while, she shook with fear and confusion. The patrol had passed right next to them and still they had gone undetected. Cautiously, she opened her eyes and attempted to peek through the wide fern that lay across her forehead. At the same time, Rezepatha began to stir and then struggled to break free of her mother's embrace. Lapeth retained her hold, pondering their next move.

"Stop!" the child said irritably, as she managed to pry herself loose.

"Shhh," Lapeth said softly, moving a finger to her daughter's lips and touching them gently. The little girl watched her curiously and remained quiet.

Ever so slowly, Lapeth rose to her feet, watching for signs of the overseer's men. Cautiously, she turned to take in their complete surroundings in the light of day. Although countless trees blocked much of her vision, she looked in every direction. A moment later, the realization of their location caused her to catch her breath in horror.

They had traveled in a circle!

Off to the left, through a grove of trees, lay the plains of Shinar. The overseer's fields lay just beyond. Somehow, in the darkness of the forest, she had gotten turned around. Their passage all through the night had been for naught. The patrol that had passed had not even been looking for them. Realizing the danger of their surroundings, Lapeth lowered her gaze to Rezepatha and responded to the child's wondering blue eyes. "It is time for us to move on."

She headed in a direction away from both Shinar and the overseer's patrol. Her steps were slow and hindered by thick grasses and wild ferns that grabbed onto leather sandals. The ground was damp and dotted with small pools of standing water. Even if a path had been cut through the greenery, it would grow over again in just a few days.

She walked for more than an hour, cautiously looking at every shadow and in between the trunks of towering pine. Her only thought was of escape, though every so often, Basil's face came to mind, and she grew sad. She said a prayer of thanksgiving for their safety and asked the One, again, for assistance. She tried as best she could to calm Rezepatha when it became clear that the child had grown much too hungry. It was while she pondered their next course of action that she heard a sound, a sound so shrill and eerie that her feet froze to the ground. In horror, she stood completely still.

Lapeth turned her head in the direction from which the sound came and wondered what creature could make such a frightening noise. The cry was long and fearful, as if some great bird was calling from the highest treetop. But after a moment, her mind realized it wasn't a bird at all. The call was too deep, and the cry was one of intense pain. Still, the screams continued without softening, until even Rezepatha's eyes opened wide with alarm. The sound was of a creature in death.

The noise from the screams grew louder, until Lapeth began to shake and her face grew white with fear. Still the high-pitched eeriness of the cries continued until Lapeth fell to her knees, feeling sick, and huddled close to her child. Together, they lay in the soft grasses and waited. Finally, when it seemed as though she could take it no longer, the cry ended just as a loud 'pop' rose above even the trees—and the two listened in horror to the ripping sounds of human flesh being torn apart.

He had been captured, beaten and dragged to the holding pen like a wild beast instead of the man he was with the capacity of speech. He had been hauled to the center of the slave encampment with a rope about his neck. His hands had been cut by the gnarled rope, for he had desperately clung fast to prevent his neck from being broken. Rocks and stones had cut his knees and thighs, as he had been carelessly dragged over the ground by two ape-like creatures toward the central pen. The gown he had worn from Dodanim was in shreds. His name was Basil, and he was very much afraid.

His cries had gone unnoticed in the noise and confusion of these new surroundings. The ape-men had hauled him to the doorway of an enormous cage where he was forced to stand on weakened legs as they stripped what remained of his garments, peeling away blood and clothing. Basil cried out and fell to his knees, and a patrol of eight of the overseer's men gathered around the naked human and pointed with interest at his appearance.

The man was perfect in form! The realization caused the patrol to nod and mumble amongst their group with renewed excitement. One of the eight reached down and fingered the man's flesh. The human's skin was soft and pliable, lacking the appearance of fur and hide that covered much of their own flesh. The others reached down to touch the man, as well, for much of his skin was bare like that of a child. There was no question, Malock, the overseer, would be pleased with the find.

When his captors had grown tired of fondling him, his naked form was thrown into the center of the large wooden cage, where he landed in a pile of rotting field crops. Basil pulled his knees to his chest, keeping away from the bars so that none of his captures could reach through and touch him.

Although some of the creatures about the cage seemed more human than ape, most had protruding foreheads or seemed to hunch forward as they walked. A few appeared half ape and half human, with hands dragging upon the ground and matted fur covering most of their bodies. Though Basil had seen Mixtures previously, never before had he seen such numbers. There were dozens, and though they spoke in the language of humans their throats often emitted grunts and rasping sounds, as though it was difficult to speak. Many were outfitted in the manner of the patrols, sweating profusely beneath leather uniforms.

Still crouching amid the spoil of discarded vegetables, Basil remained perfectly still and waited. He had done nothing wrong. There had been no signs of trouble, no forewarning. Near an old canal artery, two creatures had appeared out of nowhere and had taken them. It had all happened so fast. Lapeth had screamed; Basil had attempted to fight them off. Somehow, his wife had escaped with their daughter into the cornstalks and had remained hidden. Both Mixtures had been outraged that a female (carrying a child!) had managed to outwit them. Thankfully, the creatures' lengthy search had turned up nothing.

Suddenly, the Mixtures began to stir—the noise bringing Basil back to his imprisonment. He heard the name "Malock" being spoken in hushed whispers. Creatures in front of the barred door quickly moved aside, and Basil turned his head to see the face of the overseer.

Malock was a giant—a huge giant, taller and more fearsome than any creature Basil had ever seen before. Appearing nearly six cubits in height, Malock was more than half again the size of a normal man. The giant's face was pulled tight by cracked lines of browned flesh, baked into permanence by the hot, humid air of the open fields. Thin, black whiskers created an uneven mustache just below his upturned nostrils. He gave the human prolonged observation, gazing upon every inch of the man's body.

The crowd was silent, for never before had so perfect a specimen been taken. Malock's personal guard—four of the largest creatures—gave the others threatening glances with their hands held fast to leather whips. All waited for the giant to speak. Malock glared at the human, taking note of the man's appearance and condition. He could not help but notice the man's beauty, as well as of the scabs on his knees and arms. He looked at the rope that dangled loosely about the prisoner's neck and eyed the pile of filth upon which he had been discarded.

"Who brought this one in?" the overseer finally asked, just as two creatures moved forward in the hopes of receiving their reward.

One managed to speak, "It was us, Lord Malock," while the other simply smiled in anticipation.

The giant nodded and turned to his personal entourage, while pointing to the two. "Were these two alone in bringing the hairless one to camp?" Malock asked, as Kana, the lead guard, nodded back to him.

"Fine," the giant replied calmly, "for what they have done—hang them!"

The two fell to their knees simultaneously. At the same time, the crowd roared with excitement, for what they were about to witness was even better than had been anticipated. Kana nodded in agreement.

"But how have we offended you?" a voice cried from below. "We captured the human in order to please you." The other Mixture shook with terror, unable to speak.

"Did you hope to please me by choking him to death, or did you believe I would be more amused by your dragging him through the fields in order to break his limbs?" The giant's voice was harsh. "Perhaps you wished to please me by the sight of his blood? Which of these did you think would amuse me most of all?"

The crying voice pleaded aloud, "We believed it better to bring back one such as this bruised, than not at all. He fought hard to escape!"

Malock's glaring expression turned to disgust. "You would have me believe that the human put up a worthy fight against the two of you?"

"Even a mere man may pose a threat when he aims to protect his female."

Whispers broke through the crowd, for the woman who had outwitted them had not been mentioned previously.

"Where is she?" the overseer asked lustfully.

"She escaped into the fields and lies hidden within your domain." The shaking guard thought it unwise to tell of the child who had hampered the woman's movements for that would make their offense appear all the larger.

"Very well," Malock said, nodding approvingly. "To whomever

finds this woman, I will pay twenty pieces—twenty pieces of *gold*!"

Astonishment filled the air, for such was a prize indeed. A few Mixtures on the outskirts of the crowd broke loose and gained a head start into the fields. Others followed as they realized what was happening. Very shortly, only Malock, his personal guards, the two on their knees, the prisoner, and a dozen spectators remained at the pen.

"So that we might look for this female as well," the captain spoke eagerly, "shall we not carry out the hanging immediately?"

"Please have mercy on us!" one of the kneelers begged.

The giant was quiet for a time, and looked from Basil to the two creatures. Though he was a giant, his mind was quick and he had great plans for the human.

Malock rubbed his giant palms together, speaking softly to Kana, "No, have the human cleaned and dressed and brought to my chamber."

"As for the two?"

"Strip them of their garments and throw them in the pen. In two days time, they may return to their rank."

"You are most kind," the shaking voice beneath him cried joyfully, as he and his companion bowed submissively to the moist ground.

Basil could have never imagined the existence of such wealth amid the fields of Shinar's plains. He stood in an enormous room that appeared to be part of a palace. Long, hand-dyed fabrics and silks from the East hung from each of the chamber's walls. The richness of woven rugs felt plush against the bottoms of bare feet. Tables laden with goblets and serving trays of silver and gold were ornately displayed between himself and the giant's throne. Each platter brimmed with roasted vegetables and plump cobs of basted sweet corn. Pitchers of freshly squeezed fruit juices and a flask of gourd liquor stood surrounded by porcelain goblets.

Basil had been dressed in a long, flowing robe of purple cloth and golden thread—clothing worthy of a king. The scent of sandalwood incense filled the massive chamber, putting the giant at ease. A dark-skinned woman outfitted as a Persian beauty (though she was not) ran to Basil's side, holding a pair of silk slippers. She fell to her knees and gently placed the man's feet into the shoes. When her task was complete, she scurried from the room.

The giant leaned forward in his massive chair and waited. His large hands were folded, and for a moment he rejoiced inwardly at the splendor of his newest guest. "If you feel hunger, you may taste of anything laid before you. I assure you, the food is delicious," Malock added, when the prisoner made no move toward the tables.

Basil's body had been washed and his wounds cleansed with scented herbs and aloe. The purple robe fell about him gracefully, and Malock eyed the man's beauty with envy. His brown hair had been combed back with a carved shell by one of the house servants. In the presence of such perfection, the giant felt his own enormous dimensions suddenly become all the more obvious.

"Why do you not eat?"

"My mind is filled with many questions." Basil's voice gave the giant a start, for he had never heard the man speak, and the human's voice was very beautiful.

"Then ask what you would wish to know."

"Why was I brought here?"

"You are to be my guest. I apologize for your earlier treatment. My men are not accustomed to finery. If you have any desire, I shall grant it to you."

"I wish to leave this place . . . "

"Any desire but that one," the giant interrupted.

"What do you mean to do to me? I have done no wrong."

"Some might say that to appear as you do is crime enough. You were lucky my guards found you before one of the bandits who scour the plains; they would not have been so kind." The giant appeared quite at ease. "Here, you are to be my guest. You shall live as a prince. Any woman within my domain shall be yours for the asking. Though they may not be as you are used to, they still provide pleasure."

"What of my wife?"

Malock hesitated for only a moment. "If she is found alive, I will return her to you. But, I fear there is little hope. Few people of the plains are as gentle as your own race."

Basil's eyes dropped to the floor.

"You should take nourishment, for there is nothing you can do," the giant told him.

"How long must I stay?"

"For as long as you live this is to be your home. Together, we will be of great service to one another."

"What do you mean?" Basil looked up to the giant.

Cautiously, the giant looked around the chamber, making certain it was free of servant ears. When he was satisfied, he spoke with his voice lowered: "With my wealth, and power," he said, rubbing his massive chin in contemplation, "and the seed of your loins, we shall build a great race. The plains, the forest, one day even Shinar, shall be mine. In exchange, all that I have is yours. From this day forth, I will call you son."

Malock's fiery eyes looked at the human for any sign of reaction, but found none. He reached for the goblet in front of him and drained its contents in great, gulping swallows. When he had finished, he wiped his mouth with a silken cloth. "Have you not found words for my offer?" he asked somewhat irritated.

"Although the offer is most generous," Basil said cautiously, "you would propose to give me all that was mine before my capture. Before your men brought me to this place, I possessed all that I could ask for."

"But here," the giant said, motioning to the beauty of his own chambers, "we shall both possess what we desire together."

"If I remain, it is because you hold me. I would never choose to remain."

"We shall see, hairless one. We shall see." Malock pondered the situation. He wished to have the human won over without serious harm; after all, the man was to be a breeder.

"Your captors were given two days to contemplate their actions," the giant said, finally. "You shall have two days in which to see the generosity of my offer." Malock turned in the direction of the doorway and bellowed a familiar call: "Kana!"

Immediately, the captain appeared in the curved portal, hurrying toward the giant, his prized whip dangling at his side. To Basil, at least, it was obvious that Kana had been listening all along.

"How can I serve you, my Lord?"

"For two days, he is to work the fields, though no harm is to come to him." The overseer words caused Kana's mouth to fall open in astonishment. "Still, he is to remain at his post and do his labors, without threat of whip or blade. Do you understand this, Kana?" the giant asked, watching the captain closely.

"But Great One," Kana asked in surprise, "without threat, how will he work?"

"He will work. He will discover what the fields are like and make a choice between the crops or these lodgings. There will be no other option."

"Yes, Lord Malock," Kana agreed. "But without our standard procedures how would you have me prevent his escape?" The captain shrugged helplessly.

"Rope him securely to his post." With that, Malock signaled that the discussion was over.

In response, Kana gripped Basil's arm and began to lead him away. After a moment, the giant's voice trailed behind them, "Remember, human, it is entirely up to you to decide."

Basil was red from the sun, covered with sweat, and his breathing was hard. The royal robes had been removed and replaced with a spoiled piece of mildewed hide, tied carelessly about his waist. His task was to dig the troughs for planting. He was on his freshly scabbed knees and his hands were bleeding—though no one had harmed him by force. The tool he used to till the soil was made of white oak, and splinters frequently lodged in his hands. At first, he had been given a wooden shovel, petrified with age, but the hardness of the instrument had cut deep into the soft soles of bare feet as he pushed the shovel's blade into the earth. His flesh was not tough and callused like that of the others.

Hot air from the brightness of the vapored sky beat down upon tired backs. The slaves he had been assigned with worked a large expanse of fields newly acquired by the giant. Nearly seventy of them toiled endlessly, for fear of being beaten by the guards. Meanwhile, the guards had become bored with yet another day that lacked any sign of rebellion. A patrol of nine watched the field, each eyeing the perfect human specimen with disgust.

Basil's parched throat longed for liquid, but a slave wasn't entitled to water until he had completed fifty cubits' length of labor.

To accomplish such a task using only a coarse hand implement seemed impossible. Few workers among Malock's fields possessed stone tools; the instruments were far too expensive and seemed wasted on easily replaced laborers who didn't last long in the fields anyway. Stone appeared reserved for the knives of the patrols.

It was the morning of Basil's second day in the fields, and his thighs and legs were caked with soil. The rope around his neck rubbed continuously, cutting flesh with thin, scratchy threads of woven twine. It was anchored to the ground with a huge stake that had been driven deep into the earth. The rope was thirty cubits long, giving him plenty of room in which to move around, but the cord had grown heavy, and his back ached, his knees were bleeding, and he grieved for Lapeth and Rezepatha whom he feared dead.

All over the field, men broken by slavery worked mechanically at their tasks. The slaves included creatures and men from all parts of the world, all beaten to a point where they no longer retained the hope of escape. Those who died in the midst of such labor were simply tilled beneath soil already rich with minerals. Carcasses of plainsmen and merchants, farmers and craftsmen, even other Mixtures, fed the current crops of what promised to be the overseer's best vegetable season.

An ominous wooden guard tower had been erected in the center of the open acreage. Two guards sat comfortably on the ledge of the open windows, sipping from a flask. They stared out over the backs of workers in the beet fields, as well as the bean, potato and corn fields which lay just beyond. Both had grown bored with the idle days of late and hoped the captain soon would permit them to make sport of an elder slave. One of them whisked a huge fly away from his hairy face, swishing until the insect found lodging in the tough hide of his exposed belly, where it didn't seem to bother him.

There had been a great deal of talk in the guardhouse the last two nights about the perfect man. None of the patrols wanted to believe the story, yet Kana had confirmed it: Malock planned to make the human master of them all. They were to become subservient to a slave! For that reason, each of the guards had found cause to stare in anger at the man. The human was nothing! Only the fear of Malock had kept Basil alive.

Stories of how the human had stood before the giant in royal robes and had been offered the bounty of the giant's tables were everywhere. Even the household servants hated the man, for they had spent years vying for their own place of honor. Throughout Malock's kingdom it had been whispered that something had to be done.

For that reason, the giant's own guards made certain the overseer heard the news from the fields: The man was weak in mind and body; he tired easily and pined away in sickness for a mere woman; he was unable to labor as well as even the dullest of slaves; the human bled when he hadn't even been touched; his flesh was soft and useless like that of a child's—surely there existed far better specimens. The litany of weaknesses continued without abatement until the magnificent vision of the man in purple robes had faded from the giant's mind. Finally, in an effort to see the human's worth for himself, the overseer made a visit to the fields.

Basil had grown weary with the passage of hours. The second day's labor was even harder than the first. His muscles had grown swollen and tired, so that all movement was painful. Blood from his fingers had begun to stain the wooden tool he used to scrape the soil. The only thing he had discovered since his capture (for no other slave had been anxious to speak with him) was that few of the crops they tended even went to Shinar. Higher prices were obtained elsewhere, and the city was fast becoming one of great poverty.

The man heard the commotion of Malock's entourage and turned to see the overseer surrounded by a great following of personal guards and house servants.

"I'm sure you've had time enough to think," Malock said, more angrily than he felt. His eyes quickly scanned the extent of the man's injuries and regretted that it had been necessary. "My guards tell me you are not made for this work." His words were spoken harshly for the benefit of those around him. "I too have doubts as to whether you could last a year among the crops. Many do not."

Basil's head turned up to the giant, but he did not speak. He saw the hatred of those around him and knew that it was far better for his family to die than to be in a place such as this.

"Have you nothing to say?" the giant asked angrily. "Speak for yourself while the choice is still yours to make."

"I know not what to say," Basil said hoarsely, barely managing a whisper as the rope cut into his throat.

"Would you prefer to work in the fields or in my household?" Malock thought it best to keep the full details of his offer between them.

"Answer your master!" Kana pushed him forcefully.

"Well?" the giant asked again. "Decide!"

"You would have me choose between imprisonments when my desire is freedom?" Basil wiped his dirt-caked palm across his forehead and pulled back his wet hair. "Neither offering is to my liking—but the thought of serving in your household to be part of this abomination sickens my soul. I would choose to be free. Yet, if I must choose—then let it be the fields." The human managed a tone so defiant that the Mixtures closest to him grew silent. Even Kana opened his eyes with amazement at the man's stupidity.

"You have blasphemed our lord!" the captain finally shouted. The crowd murmured with anticipation over what was to come.

It wasn't until the noise died down that Basil finally spoke, looking upward directly into the giant's eyes. "He is not *my* lord."

Commotion spread through the beet field like a wild fire. Slaves stopped their labors, while additional guards ran to see what was happening. Some climbed the ladder to the tower in order to look over the crowd. The captain's face flushed with embarrassment.

Malock's mouth fell open, stupidly, as if he had been knocked unconscious. He began to realize that his conversation with the human should have taken place privately. The giant knew very clearly that everyone was watching so he spoke with much anger: "Do you realize what you've said?" he roared, his voice coming from a tremendous height. "These fields, these crops, these people are mine!"

"The land may be yours, the fields and these crops—but the people belong to no one."

Finally, one of the servants found the nerve to ask, "Did you hear his defiance?"

"He dares speak back to Malock!" another replied.

A few of the other field slaves saw the opportunity for reward and began to chant, "He deserves death. He deserves death!" Malock's personal guards and many among the patrols joined in with the call.

The Persian-looking female moved through the crowd, holding tightly to her small son and joined in with the cries of those around her. The child turned his protruding forehead from side to side and listened intently to all that was being said. Some chanted the death call while others recalled how Basil had been defiant with, “The people belong to no one,” and “He is not my lord.” His mother moved to Kana’s side. Though she could never be certain the captain had fathered the child—it could have been any from the personal guard—she had told the captain what was best for her son’s benefit.

The young boy looked inquisitively between the kneeling slave and Malock, who towered over them all. The furor of the Mixtures’ voices continued until Kana voiced the words: “You must kill him.”

“I cannot,” the giant whispered to himself. “Another few days in the fields will change his mind.”

“If you do not kill him,” Kana did not hide his anger; “you shall make yourself the fool!”

“Forget not to whom you are speaking,” Malock roared back. “This one can serve my purposes.”

“A master no longer feared is without respect,” the captain said bravely.

“Enough! I shall have your tongue removed if it wags against me further!” the giant said with finality. He held up an enormous palm to silence the crowd; the time had come to speak. Much more slowly than usual, the people grew quiet, while Basil looked at the young boy held by its mother and smiled.

The child smiled back at him and decided to join in the game the others were playing. All at once, the child released his grip around his mother’s neck and pointed up at Malock. Before the giant could begin to speak, the boy spoke the words he had heard: “He is not my lord.”

There was only quiet.

The giant face became hot with anger, for the decision had just been made for him: "Kill the hairless one," he managed to say, though the words nearly stuck in his throat, "and do it far from my fields." He pressed through the crowd quickly, trying to control his own shaking frame.

Kana called after him: "How shall it be done?"

"The choice is yours," the giant said hurriedly before speeding away, lest any of his people should see his face.

Kana watched as the giant nearly disappeared among stalks of corn—though Malock's head still towered above the crops—before signaling a patrol to his side. Basil knew his time had come, although he was not afraid.

"This one needs to be an example to others of his race," the captain said hatefully. "Take him to the forest clearing where those of his kind have been seen before. There, carry out Malock's orders."

"And the method of death?" one of the guards, who had longed for sport, asked excitedly.

"It matters not," Kana said, looking over the squatting man's body one final time. "Simply make certain his flesh loses its perfection."

Immediately, the patrol took the prisoner, dragging him into the oaks. The man's body was pulled over the soft underbrush. In the time that remained, Basil closed his eyes and began to pray for his wife, his daughter, himself, and even for Malock and the slaves of the fields.

It was a long while before Lapeth dared move. The screams still echoed in her ears. She and Rezepatha remained covered by the protection of the flowering ferns and the lush plants that stood thick, moist, and green beneath the towering heights of white oak and scattered pine. She pressed the small child tightly to her breast and waited. They must be quiet a while longer.

Rezepatha no longer shivered, nor did she even think about the sounds they had heard. The fear had passed, and she grew irritated at having to restrain any movement. Her short hair had grown wet with sweat, and the damp clothes from both their bodies were beginning to stick stubbornly to her soft skin. The child watched the woman closely and wondered what it was that her mother was doing. Finally, she had had enough. Rezepatha made tiny fists and tried, unsuccessfully, to push her mother away. "Stop it," she said loudly as her hands continued to push. "Let go!"

Her daughter's frustration caused the woman to rise, finally, and she released Rezepatha on her own wobbly feet. The scent of wild grasses and pine rose to Lapeth's nostrils as she looked about their surroundings, grateful they could no longer see the plains. When certain of the proper direction to take, she bent down, lifted her daughter, and said, "Let's be quiet, just until we can get something to eat."

They headed in the most promising direction, watching closely for any signs of movement among the tree trunks. Her sandaled feet made crunching noises muffled only by the underbrush around them. The sound made her a little apprehensive, but they had to get far from this place and away from the circle in which they had traveled.

When she finally saw a clearing up ahead, her heart filled with joy and her steps quickened. There they would find something to eat. For the first time since the start of their ordeal, her heart became glad and there was hope. Even the underbrush grew less encumbering as she moved closer, and the scent of lavender flowers replaced that of pine.

And then she stopped, picking Rezepatha up and pulling the child's head tightly to her own chest. She stood on the edge of the clearing, growing weak. Her empty stomach had nothing to give, so she merely choked. Her eyes refused to believe the sight, though her face grew white as she gasped for air. Her knees buckled, and she stumbled to the earth.

He hung from a tree, impaled on one of its branches, with his limbs dangling in inhuman directions. Blood still glistened from his wounds. Although the face was mangled, she knew the man. Her eyes turned to the ground as she strangled upon her own saliva. She wasn't even aware of Rezepatha's cries, though she held the child tightly. Her own breathing was hard; she felt faint and sickened, and then she heard a sound.

A noise approached that hushed even the child. There was nothing else to do but cry—softly at first and then from the depths of her soul. The sound was of footsteps moving toward them and she gave up all hope of escape. It was over. As her fear mounted, even the sight of the dangling man was pushed from her mind. She cried for the three of them. Still, the sounds of vines being crushed moved closer until, finally, the noise stopped just behind her.

She felt the warm touch of a hand upon her shoulder, and she wanted to scream, but could not. She turned quickly, clutching Rezepatha in her arms, and stared up at her captor.

"Fear not, my child," said an old, bearded man. "We have been sent to help you."

Lapeth laid her head in his arms and sobbed.

It was a long while, indeed, before she was able to speak, or to do anything other than follow the old man and his companion even deeper into the forest. She was oblivious to their appearance, save that they wore long, simple robes of gray. Her only thought was of clutching Rezepatha and of their walking—their continuous walking. She almost remembered eating something, for her hunger had subsided, but she could not be certain.

In reality, they walked for half a day, pausing only long enough to take nourishment or to let the old man rest, for he claimed his feet became sore. In time, the forest grew dark and her own feet began to throb. Finally, amid the cover of the trees, when they were reasonably safe from being spotted, they lit a fire. Shadows of light danced about them, illuminating ferns and creeping vine, lavender buds and underbrush.

When they had seated themselves around the fire, and the old man had found comfort by gathering a soft pile of grass beneath his feet, Lapeth suddenly realized just how distracted she had been. Not in all their walking had she noticed that the old man's companion was a giant!

Both men sat across from her, framed from behind by the darkness of evening. The giant was the largest man she had ever seen, with enormous features accentuating a surprisingly kind face. He remained quiet, simply nodding in agreement as the old man chuckled or whispered in hushed tones. He wore the same garment as the old man—a gray, flowing robe—though one much larger in size.

The old man saw Lapeth staring at the giant and winked at her. "My friend's appearance takes some getting used to," he said with a grin, "though I assure you, he is quite harmless. His name is Traibus."

The giant nodded in acknowledgment, and Lapeth moved to speak. "I am called . . . "

"You are Lapeth," the old man interrupted, waving his hand, "and your daughter is Rezepatha."

"How did you know?" she asked with alarm.

"Quite simple, my child. If we were meant to help you, then we would need to know who we were helping. It is as easy as that."

"But how?"

"There will be plenty of time for questions," he said reassuringly, as he waved his hand, "and there is much we must discuss—tomorrow. However, the evening calls for a tale. A long tale, I believe, for you have been through a great deal."

Lapeth's eyes grew moist, and a sob leaped from her chest, yet the old man continued speaking as though oblivious to her state.

"I am Methuselah," he stated matter-of-factly and began passing out honeyed wheat cakes from his robe. He broke a piece off for Rezepatha as well. The giant pulled a flask from his own clothing and set it before them.

"You shall eat, and listen, for this story is long; it is interesting, and it is ours," he said, nodding to himself.

Though Lapeth attempted to speak, the old man wouldn't hear of it. He began to narrate a lengthy account, emphasizing parts of it with his hands as he spoke. The tale lasted long into the night and although Methuselah was the central storyteller, the giant commented at frequent intervals along the way, for there were times when Traibus believed the old man's version of the facts were somewhat different than his own.

Lapeth had no choice but to listen. It was a story of great mystery and adventure. Even in the midst of her sadness, Lapeth felt wonder and surprise and came to believe every word. The story they related was of the things that had transpired between them, of their meeting, of their work, and of the old man's family and things that had happened when the world was young, a very, very long time ago.

In the end, the two related everything about themselves—save for a secret they had shared for many, many decades, though its exclusion did not ruin the overall tale since Lapeth had no knowledge of it. Yet, when the time finally came, and the woman and child had both fallen fast asleep, the robed figures took time to reminisce the matter between them, assuring one another, yet again, that the hour had not yet arrived to tell anyone else of the gold.

When the World Was Young
(600 years before the Flood)

Ever so gently, as he came out of the deep meditation, Methuselah began to hear the tinkling sounds of pushcart bells and the clash of human voices outside in the market square. Even with the first light of day, the city of Shinar and its frenzied people were bustling. The Tigris River met the Euphrates near the edge of the city's borders, making the city a center for all kinds of commerce, and seldom were the citizens or the visiting merchants or the wandering beggars at rest. Sometimes the commotion was continuous. Even the clang of tradesmen and their wares, however, could do nothing to upset Methuselah's peace of mind. The day was to bring a wonderful blessing, for he knew before the last glimmer of light had disappeared from the overhead clouds he was to become a grandfather.

He sat cross-legged on the cobblestone floor of his small room, palms placed firmly upon his knees. Here in the midst of all the noise and confusion of the market—and the vile things that could be had for a price—was his place of solitude. With eyes still closed, he said a prayer of thanksgiving to the Lord of his ancestors, and ended with the psalmist's song—his lips moving softly as he said the prayer handed down by his father, Enoch. The day brought with it a journey, for he desired to be at his son's cottage before midday. By then, his grandchild would be delivered of Ashmua. He rose to be on his way.

His room was sparsely furnished; the old man's only possessions a thin mat upon the floor where he slept and spent time in the silence, a three-legged stool, and a wobbly desk on the verge of collapse. Just above the desk was one small window. He had spent many evenings at the desk by candlelight, studying the ancient parchments of a manuscript. The text, hundreds of aged sheaves, had passed through his family for generations. Enoch had received it from his father and had, in turn, passed it to Methuselah.

His sandaled feet took him to his desk where he carefully stacked the pieces of parchment from which he had found inspiration the night before. Its story told the answers to questions that the children of the earth no longer remembered to ask. Though it was hard to fathom the possibility, the document also told of Creation in Adam's own script! Methuselah had often imagined how Adam had shown his own son, Seth, the pages he himself had scripted with reed in hand. In turn, Seth, and all who had come after had added their own words to the text, just as Methuselah had done in the present.

Gently, Methuselah grasped the stack of parchments in one hand, returned to the thin mat of bedding on the floor, and lifted one corner out of the way. Beneath the tile was his place of safety and it lifted easily with the proper touch. Here he kept the manuscript, as well as a small supply of his gold coins.

When Methuselah had concealed the document under the floor, gathered up a few glistening coins, and moved the tile back in place, he rose, carefully checked the placement of his belongings, dropped the gold pieces into the tiny cloth bag concealed up his sleeve, and walked toward the door. He threw open the hard-oak latch and stepped out onto the landing of the second floor. Immediately, the air felt warm and moist against his neck and bearded face.

The landing led toward other tenement rooms on the second floor, though none of his neighbors had ever ventured a visit. He locked his room's entrance with a stone key and turned to go down the stairway which led to the market. The noise of voices and of bickering merchants grew louder with every step, and his nostrils quivered at the drifting scent of poppies. He heard the ghastly roar of a giant (though not the voice of Traibus, whom he knew best) as his final step took him from the cover of the stairway into the main street. Once again, he took a deep breath to brace himself for the sights of what the children of the earth had done to themselves.

Tradesmen were everywhere. The people and the Mixtures of the city filled every available space on the streets. People pressed closely together, wearing the signs of ancient homelands: Long robes of Persians brushed against Syrian stripes, the garments of merchants, or the ragged cloth of a peasant. Small youths and disheveled children scurried among haggling adults caught up in the intensity of the marketplace, and the clamor of so many voices calling out for attention or arguing over a price was deafening.

Many strained eyes and limbs to see the veiled dancers who were just beginning their show at the far end of the marketplace. Others leaned over pushcarts or makeshift tables, hoping to purchase a vial of opium or a flask of gourd liquor. Overly ripe vegetables and fruits of every description were picked over, as shoppers quickly purchased what was necessary before moving on to more enticing diversions. People pushed up against one another in an effort to get by or to be the first to reach a vendor's table.

Methuselah watched one tiny girl with long, tangled hair wander aimlessly through the crowd in a great deal of confusion. Her gnarled hands gave away the fact that she was a Mixture. Though the rest of her limbs were frail, their proportions appeared normal. Running a few cubits behind was the girl's mother, whose own arms and legs were covered with whiskers. She grunted in irritation as she hurried after the child, one leg dragging badly behind the other.

Elsewhere, a haggard woman sat against the tenement wall with a small object cupped in her hands. Her face and hands were human, for the most part, but the woman's skin had grown deathly white. A sore had formed at one corner of her mouth, and it was obvious from the woman's sounds that she heard neither the rabble of merchants nor the clang of music drifting from the opposite end of the plaza. The crone opened her mouth, exposing a row of broken teeth. She raised her cupped hands to sniff the remains of a bird. Slowly, she began to devour the creature, feathers and all.

Methuselah turned his eyes in another direction and scanned the row of handcarts, pondering which way he was supposed to go. Just as he had decided to proceed in the direction of the music, he spotted Traibus, the largest man in the city, moving toward him, head and torso above the crowd. The man was a giant, nearly six cubits in height, but possessed very human features. Traibus was an imposing figure. A trapper by trade, he wore a deer-hide jacket girded about his enormous chest. As he moved through the marketplace others parted to make clear his path, for none wished to anger a giant.

Methuselah folded his hands and waited for Traibus to approach. The two were well acquainted, and both seemed to relish their game of riddles and words.

"Good morning, little man," Traibus bellowed from his tremendous height. His breath was so warm and forceful that the old man felt it upon his forehead. "It has been many days since our last meeting. Perhaps you've grown tired of looking for any within Shinar to heed your words?"

"No, Traibus," Methuselah responded quickly, "I've busied myself even when there are none who will listen. Your work is to clothe bodies, while I tend to souls."

"You waste your time," the giant smiled, exposing an enormous set of white teeth. He motioned a large hand in the direction of the marketplace. "Not one among them has any soul that I've seen!"

"Time is not wasted on the eternal." The old man's eyes sparkled. "I tell you, these souls only think they are bodies. They've become trapped in an illusion and no longer remember how to perceive beyond it."

"How can this be?" Traibus asked cautiously, not wanting to be tricked yet again. "How can that seen by the eyes be only an illusion of the mind?"

"In the same manner one's dream appears real to the dreamer."

"Must you ever speak in riddles?"

"I speak the truth, Traibus." Methuselah paused momentarily as a marvelous idea came into his head. He scratched his chin to appear in thought and realized that the giant might be led. The old man smiled, staring up at Traibus who was silhouetted against the overhead clouds. "Think of it in this manner," the mystic said, choosing his words carefully. "Often at night, do you not close your eyes and see pictures as you sleep?"

The giant hesitated before responding, "At times."

"And these pictures, do they not appear real?"

"Yes—while my body sleeps."

"Then I ask you," Methuselah went on matter-of-factly, "how can that which exists only in the mind appear real to eyes closed in sleep?"

The giant was very intelligent and quick to respond. "Because the mind does not know that the body sleeps and it regards the images as real. But you know as well as I, when the body awakens, the mind realizes what it saw was only a dream."

"Correct," Methuselah watched him closely, "and the same is true for the soul. In one respect, each soul is asleep. You might say that everyone here in the marketplace is simply dreaming. To be sure," the old man added with a hearty chuckle, "many of us appear to be having the very same dream, making it appear all the more real. But I assure you, it is only a dream. The mind sees images of space and time—when one wakes in eternity these things cease to exist."

"Would you play me the fool?" Traibus eyed him cautiously. "The argument you pose proves nothing. You claim the soul sleeps while it is in flesh—just as our bodies do in rest—and that just as the mind knows the images of sight were untrue upon awakening, the soul shall come to know what it thought real has only been a dream."

"That's it, exactly!"

"But even if true," Traibus reasoned aloud, "the argument could only prove itself. To move beyond words and prove the existence of that which is unreal is beyond anything you are capable of, little man."

"Ah ha," Methuselah clapped his hands with excitement, "that is something I can do."

"None of your tricks," the giant ordered, for he had no desire to be outwitted.

The marketplace remained ignorant of the two and their game of words. The tradesmen and the city's inhabitants pushed their way through the streets carrying parcels or straining to see the plaza's enticements. One harried merchant robed in pale yellow pushed his cart past them both, appearing ignorant of their presence. His cart was much like the others, constructed of pine from Shinar's forest, for white oak was harder to work with. Two large wheels, sixteen spokes each, were anchored toward the front, while two short legs kept the cart level whenever the merchant's wares were on display. He was a potter, as his father before him. Ceramics and baked wares tottered dangerously close to the edge, as the man was in a tremendous hurry to see the writhing young bodies of the dancers before the show was over.

Traibus turned from the merchant and looked back toward the old man. "I will strike a bargain with you. If you can prove the existence of this soul you speak of, then I might learn much from you. If you can do this, then your ways must be true and I will be yours to command. For the rest of my days, I will follow you . . . "

Methuselah interrupted, "I don't seek your praise, nor will I have you subservient to myself. If you say, instead, that you will come to learn all that I might share with you of the One, then I will agree. This will be our bargain."

"Do not agree so quickly until you have heard *my* terms." The giant flashed an enormous smile. He placed his hand upon Methuselah's shoulder and continued. "If the proof of your claim is sufficient, I will learn of this One. However, if you are unable to win the wager, then you must agree to answer one question for me."

"Certainly I will agree!" the old man replied excitedly. "Your terms are quite agreeable."

"The question," the giant said, his voice softening, "may cause you to change your mind." He lowered his head and whispered into Methuselah's ear so that only the old man could hear him. "If the wager is mine, I wish a confession. Where is this place that you keep the gold?"

The words were so startling that Methuselah caught his breath. He had never expected such a question, for he always passed alms with the greatest of care.

After much silence, he was finally able to ask: "How have you come to know of the gold?"

"Have we not tested wits enough for you to know that I am not simply an oaf who wanders these streets? There are rumors of gold coins appearing out of nowhere in every poor street of this city. At first, I thought it idle fancy, but the rumors persist. Now, you know as well as I do, a fifty shekel gold piece just doesn't appear from nowhere, so I began to ask myself 'Who in this city, if they possessed the means, would simply hand out in secrecy gold coins to the needy?' And you know what, little man? Yours was the only name that came to my mind."

Methuselah was silent. If the giant had figured it out somehow, might not another? It just wouldn't do to have every thief in the city stalking him as he moved about.

"How many others think they know of this gold?"

"Do not worry," the giant said joyfully, for his hunch had been correct, "there is only I. The city is filled with fools who spend their lives in superstition and magic. Some claim the coins themselves are enchanted; others have yet to believe the tales. Your name does not arise." Traibus reached to caress the gray sleeve of the old man's robe between his thumb and forefinger. "Though you are seen as mysterious, you wear the garments of a beggar. It would be unthinkable to dress as you do and possess a fortune."

"I ask you with all my heart," Methuselah pleaded, "to keep these suspicions to yourself. There is much to be done in Shinar—the coins are only a small part of that. There are many who need help. I beg you to remain silent."

"You will have my silence," Traibus said honestly, "for you see, in all of Shinar it is you alone I can trust. If you agree to my terms, I will believe you."

For an instant, Methuselah saw a potential for the future begin to form within his mind's eye but just as quickly it drifted beyond his sight. Although he couldn't quite grasp its significance, it had something to do with the giant. Methuselah smiled and extended his hand. "I agree to your terms, but I think you may be in for a surprise."

"You needn't worry." Traibus appeared quite confident. "Surely there is enough gold for us both, and I will not be greedy."

"And I shall not lose so easily."

"When do we begin?"

"We will begin tomorrow as the first glow of light illuminates the clouds. I'm going to teach you to see, Traibus, and the results will amaze you. Come to the cottage of Lamech, the woodcutter, on the edge of the forest. He is my son; I will be staying with him this night. Be early, for we have much to accomplish."

The giant nodded in agreement before turning away. He towered above the rest of the crowd as he walked in a direction opposite from the many pushcarts. Traibus only took one final glance at the old man before disappearing down a side street.

When the giant was out of sight, Methuselah headed east, remaining on the main road leading out of Shinar. He was able to walk quickly, for most of the people were busy with purchases and enticements and moving toward the other end of the marketplace. His robe flowed effortlessly over the beaten path. As he moved further from the market, the number of shadowy side streets and alleys began to diminish and the road of inlaid bricks began to narrow. The buildings on either side of the street appeared hastily constructed. They were tall and somber, with little attention to carpentry. Each possessed small, squared windows and narrow doors and stairways. Moisture from the heat of day constantly ran down the sides of the structures, creating permanent stains. He caught the glance of a few people as he scurried along, though none moved to nod or to exchange a wave as he passed. Those who recognized him simply moved out of the way or whispered to companions in hushed tones. For a time, he pondered his conversation with Traibus and wondered what adventure would unfold for the two of them.

Suddenly, the cobblestone street came to an end at the city's borders, and Methuselah proceeded by way of a trampled dirt road which led through the huge expanse of plains between Shinar and the edge of the forest. The trail was dotted with enormous ferns on the one side and vast trenches for crops on the other.

Field workers had already planted their corn, for the old man could see tiny sprouts peaking through cracks in the soil. Methuselah rested only once on the journey—at the canal artery to quench his thirst. When he was refreshed, he continued on his way. When almost two hours had passed since leaving Traibus in the plaza, the old man spotted the familiar log cottage set back approximately thirty cubits in the trees.

The house was one story high, with large, open windows decorated on either side by dye-printed curtains. Long flower boxes filled with lavender buds hung beneath each window. He was halfway to the door (and quite thankful the journey was over, for his feet were tired) when Lamech ran out to fetch him. Methuselah was startled, for his son was in a panic.

"What's wrong?" he asked urgently. He grabbed his son's arm as they headed toward the cottage. "Is Ashmua all right?"

"Yes, father," Lamech stammered, appearing quite frightened. His skin and hair were dark and rough—witness to the long hours he had spent out-of-doors—though his features were without blemish. "It is not Ashmua, but the child," he finally managed to say.

Methuselah was greatly alarmed. "What is it?" He shook his son's arm for an answer. "Did the baby not survive?"

"The baby is alive—a son just as you said—but there is something quite strange." Lamech looked pale as he spoke. "I could not father such a child, for it resembles less Ashmua and myself than it does an . . . an . . . an angel."

"What?"

"See for yourself, father," Lamech said, as the old man nearly pushed him aside to enter the bedchamber.

Ashmua lay on their massive, stuffed mattress holding their infant son. She had covered herself with a thin, patchwork quilt, and her dark brown hair was pulled back behind her ears. She never looked up at the men, for her eyes remained focused only upon the child.

The baby was perfect. His small, five-fingered hands grasped the edge of his mother's blanket as his legs kicked in joyous rhythm. Methuselah was filled with a sense of wonder, for Lamech had not exaggerated. Although both parents were dark, the child's skin was the color of cotton. His head was covered with white, tiny wisps of silken hair, as well. The child turned to face Methuselah. The old man was startled as he felt his own heart leap in his chest. The child's eyes were the deepest blue he had ever seen, and his countenance caused Methuselah to feel awed. But the most startling thing of all was the light, a pure glow of radiance that seemed to engulf the child and everything around him. Truly, the babe appeared as an angel.

"Do not fear, my son," Methuselah finally managed to say. A surge of joy rose from the depths of his soul and his eyes became moist. "This child has been sent by the One—he is the answer to our prayers. In humility, we should give thanks for this blessing. What have you decided to name him?"

"He appears as one destined to bring comfort to many," Lamech said proudly as he noted Methuselah's reaction to the baby, "so we shall call him 'Menahem.'"

Methuselah nodded, whispering the child's name as he knelt to the floor in thanksgiving. Lamech, too, descended to his knees, while Ashmua gently stroked the baby's arm and closed her eyes. Together, they prayed as of old, in the way that had been passed down to them.

It was to be a blessed day. In fact, it would begin the most wondrous year of the old man's life—the year his grandson was born, the year Methuselah himself would become 369.

The young man sat by himself on the old wooden stump about twenty cubits from the doorway of his parent's cottage. The stump had become his place of refuge—though the house was in plain view and he could still hear much of what went on inside. Still, this was his place when he wished to be alone with his thoughts.

His hands were clenched in fists and he could feel the tightness inside his stomach. His eyes were damp but he refused to give in to the tears. He was seventeen years old and much too old to cry. And so he sat, completely still, beneath the enormous white oaks that surrounded their clearing and stared at the cottage in disgust. His name was Tubal-cain and sometimes he couldn't help but hate his father.

He was far enough from the house to feel like he wasn't in the middle of the adult argument but he was close enough to hear the angry bickering of voices. He couldn't understand how they were able to scream at each other at the top of their lungs, saying all kinds of horrible things they didn't really mean and then watch each other in embarrassed silence after the fight was over. He had seen the arguments many, many times before and they always ended the same way. His parents would look at one another and be afraid to say anything for a long while, hoping the things said in anger would be forgotten. And when the intensity of the fight had passed, things would be back to normal; quiet would return to the cottage—at least until the next outburst—and everyone would pretend to forget what had happened.

But Tubal-cain could not so easily forget. At times, he felt seventeen years of bickering pent-up inside of him. His father was fighting again with his two wives, and to Tubal-cain it was simply about jealousy. His birthmother, Zillah, the senior of the two, was not about to let the younger wife, Adah (who was the most pleasing to look upon), forget her subordinate position. After all, Zillah had been Lemech's first wife. Tubal-cain's jaw tightened when he heard another shout coming from the house and the sound of something heavy being thrown, and he wished—more than anything—that there was somewhere else he could go.

At times, he hated Zillah for the way she treated Adah, but the older woman was his mother. The idea of hating Adah had never even entered his mind, for she was extremely loving. It was his father he blamed for the situation. After all, it was his father's fault for marrying two women to begin with. How could his father have been so stupid? The act was unheard of among the faithful.

As time passed, the warm, humid air that surrounded him caused his thick brown hair to fall down over his eyes. Tubal-cain simply moved his thoughts from the cottage and daydreamed to get away. He thought of Methuselah and longed for the old man's next visit. Although he had no way of knowing, at that very moment, Methuselah was leading Ashmua and Lamech in prayer.

All around, the beauty of nature remained untouched as it had for thousands of years. Trees with heavy limbs of rich, green leaves towered far above the moist soil. Grasses grew in dense tufts in the clearings among the trees where even tropical yellow flowers with blooms nearly a cubit wide grew in splattered groves. Tiny, purple buds sprouted as far as his eyes could see—from the base of the oak trunks to the crevices of the large boulders just behind the cottage. The gentle buds numbered in the tens of thousands; their scent was of lavender and it was everywhere. The beauty of Creation made him think of the One—the One of whom Methuselah spoke; the One his own father no longer believed in.

Suddenly, he heard the shrill voice of Zillah scream at the others as she stormed out of the cottage. When his mother had reached his place of solitude he asked: "What is it now, mother? Are you all right?"

"No I am not," her bright red lips said angrily. "I fear things will never be the same again!" She was a plump woman and always wore enormous flower-patterned dresses. After the argument, she appeared quite disheveled.

"Tell me what happened—what were you fighting about this time?"

"Sometimes I get so angry, I could kill that woman!" she replied, without answering his question. The lines around her mouth and eyes had grown tight, puckering with rage. "I could kill her in an instant—and your father too for that matter. Lord, how I hate her!"

"Please don't do this," he said, placing his hand gently on her shoulder. "You should both try to get along a little better. I don't understand why you can't be friends, mother. I really don't. The two of you have so many things in common."

"How dare you say that," Zillah answered, her eyes glaring hatefully. "We are nothing alike. A sly little witch is all she is, and the sight of her makes me sick. I have longed for the day when she would leave our home, but it seems now as though she never will. I can't stand that woman!"

"Don't say that mother! This is her home, too. Don't you understand? Father loves her, and I love her. She's been his wife for more than twenty years."

"And I've been married to him for forty!" she said quickly. "Forty years with your father and half of them have been with that sneaky little witch. She stole my husband from me, Tubal-cain, and I hate her for it!"

"Mother, she didn't steal him. Father loves both of you."

"Listen to me," she said hotly. "Your father does not now nor has he ever loved that woman! He loves me. I am his wife and the mother of his only child. Adah means nothing to him—absolutely nothing!"

"Then why did he marry her?" Tubal-cain asked, as the tightness returned to his chest.

"Because he is a man. Do you understand yet what that means? He is a man, and sometimes he can't help himself."

"I don't understand what you're saying."

"Twenty years ago, your father and I lived alone in a tiny home on the outskirts of Shinar; you know, right where the largest canal artery is located?"

"I know, mother. You've told me before."

"Let me finish." Her thin, red lips pursed in thought. "Anyway, we were very happy, just the two of us. It was before the city had changed—quite a number of the faithful remained. Sure there were the Mixtures; there have always been Mixtures. But I think, even then, the faithful outnumbered the rest. For a very long while, things were perfect between your father and me, and then he started spending a great deal of time in the marketplace. At first, I thought he was talking to his friends: Methuselah, old Cainan, and, let's see—that joker Henoch. But I was wrong. Lemech was visiting one of the vendors in the market square."

"Well, not really one of the vendors," she added for clarification. "Specifically, he wanted to see the man's daughter because she was so beautiful. Actually, there were those who said she was beautiful, but *I* never thought Adah was much to look at. You know, her eyes are so close together, and her hair is so yellowed and stringy. Lord if I had hair like that, I don't know what I would do!"

"But your father thought she was beautiful, and he wanted her—he wanted her badly. You know, how a real man wants a woman? And so he worked out this arrangement with Adah's father. I have never cared to hear the details myself. The point is, Tubal-cain, he never loved her. He only wanted her, and there's an enormous difference."

"I don't understand," Tubal-cain replied in confusion. "Why would father want Adah if he didn't love her? Why would her beauty have anything to do with it?"

"Are you still so young my son that you don't know the ways of the world?"

"Yes, mother!" Tubal-cain said with disgust. "I know what you're trying to say, but I can't understand why father would be interested in Adah because others said she was pretty. It doesn't make any sense."

"Oh, not just others; a lot of people thought she was pretty. But like I told you, I never felt she was much to look at. Your father, however, thought she was a real beauty . . . ."

"But how could father . . . ?"

Zillah interrupted his angry tone: "You can't understand that your father thought Adah was pretty? There's nothing wrong with that. There are a lot of men who might be bewitched by a sneaky little . . . "

"But my god, mother!" Tubal-cain replied in complete frustration. *"Father is blind!"*

She paused for only an instant before nodding her head in agreement. "Sure he's blind now, but he hasn't always been so. Surely, someone's told you this before?"

"Who would have told me? Everyone's afraid to discuss father's sight." Tubal-cain was dumbfounded. "I would have remembered! Father tries to ignore it; he doesn't even like help when we're trapping. I thought he was born blind."

"Well, he wasn't, but there have been times when I know our life together would have been much happier if he had been. His eyes tricked him into bringing that woman home and things have never been the same between us. You know, someday I may just take that woman's throat between my hands and . . . "

"Mother! You were going to tell me about father."

"You know how sensitive he is about it. Lemech believes his blindness is a curse. And if you ask me, it's all Adah's fault. That's why she's never mentioned it to you. Adah's the reason your father lost his sight, as well as his friends among the faithful. After the marriage, everyone avoided us. I can't say that I blame them, really. And when your father's eyes began to fade, there was no point in staying where we were not welcome. That's why we moved here."

"Anyway," she continued, rather enthralled with her narrative, "many of the faithful said your father would be punished for what he had done. They said, and rightly so if you ask me, that your father's action was an abomination."

"Even Methuselah?"

"Oh, not him," Zillah said assuredly. "Methuselah has never been one to judge. In fact, that old man treated Adah with the greatest of respect, right from the start, which was rather considerate of him when you think about it. Methuselah's the only relation your father will speak to. Even Methuselah's own son, Lamech, the woodcutter, won't have anything to do with us. Well, he likes you," she added quickly, "but he won't speak to your father."

"And that's because of Adah?"

"Partly so, but I think he resents the fact that your father is a direct descendant of the Cursed One, you know, Cain. But that wouldn't explain why he likes you so well. Maybe it's because your father is the seventh generation, and you're the eighth, and somehow you're no longer responsible. I just don't know." She shook her head in confusion. "It never made much sense to me."

"I think the woodcutter has always been jealous of your father because he's such a big, burly man. You know, your father's name means 'vigorous youth,' and that's just exactly what he's been, very strong and energetic. I think the woodcutter knows he'll never be the man your father is. I don't really know why your father has never cared for Lamech."

Zillah's shrill voice continued as though she was delighted with her tale. "Methuselah did his own son a great disservice by naming him after your father. Well their names aren't identical, exactly—Lemech, your father, and the woodcutter, Lamech—but they're close enough. I think Methuselah intended it as an honor, but it never worked out that way.

"You know," Zillah said, lowering her voice so no one else could hear, remaining completely unaware that she had lost her son's attention, "I think your father is jealous of Lamech. Of course, he'll never admit to it, and don't you tell him I discussed this with you but I think your father is jealous. You see, the blood of Seth flows through the woodcutter's veins, while Cain's blood flows through his own. Now, have you ever heard of anything so ridiculous? Personally, I don't see how it can make a bit of difference, but your father doesn't see it like I do. I mean, the curse was on Cain, not his descendants. I've tried to tell him but he won't listen."

"Did I ever tell you this story?" Zillah asked excitedly. "When we lived in the city, rumors still surfaced from time to time that someone had seen the Cursed One prowling through the forest. I mean, my god, that would make him more than 900 years old!"

"You've told me, mother." Tubal-cain looked at the ground and toyed with the moist soil at his feet with the toe of his moccasin. He thought he'd give it just one more try. "You've told me about Cain, but you haven't said what you were fighting about this morning."

"I wasn't doing anything!" Zillah denied emphatically, with her hands planted firmly on her enormous hips. "That woman started it. I had nothing to do with it. And don't you let that little witch tell you differently!"

"Then tell me what's going on. What has Adah done now?"

"I can't, I really can't." Her eyes began to moisten. "You'll find out soon enough. This has changed everything, and I don't know what we're going to do. Tubal-cain, if I started talking about it, I'd just cry." She wiped the tears from her eyes while Tubal-cain tried to decide whether or not they were genuine. Zillah was so prone to exaggeration. He moved to put his hand on her shoulder, but she backed away and shook her head in refusal.

"I've got to be alone for a little while," she repeated. She turned away from her son and walked toward the path that lay between the largest boulders. Her long dress nearly reached the soil as she moved. It had been dyed with lavender and yellow-seed flowers, making her the brightest object in the clearing. Her ever-present apron had been tied haphazardly about her waist. As he watched her through the rocks, Tubal-cain wondered if she had simply given up trying to appear beautiful next to Adah.

He had almost decided to follow after her when Adah came out of the cottage and moved toward him. She was smiling and appeared even more radiant than the last time he had seen her. Her hair was blonde, falling gently over her shoulders, and her robe was the color of pale cream. She wore sandals made from a hide that Tubal-cain had brought back to her.

"Have we upset you, again?" she asked him.

"I'm fine." Tubal-cain glanced back at the cottage and wondered what his father was doing.

"Lemech's getting his crossbow together. He's going out again, and he says he's going alone. But Tubal-cain, if you don't mind, I'd really feel better if you went with him. I hate it when he hunts by himself. His ears may be keen enough to track the movement of a bear or even an elk but I still don't like it. He claims he can hear the breath of a lion blowing against the grass, but I'm not too sure. Do you mind?"

"No, I'll go." He was silent for a moment and then asked, "Is everything all right?"

"With me it is," she replied softly, "but I know Zillah feels threatened. I'm afraid your mother thinks she's about to lose the one thing that she's always been able to hold over me."

"What's that?"

"It's you, Tubal-cain. You're the only reason her position has been stronger than my own."

"But why does she think she's losing me?"

"Not losing you so much as losing her position. You see, Tubal-cain, I'm going to have a baby."

He was silent, feeling a twinge of jealousy, for he had no wish to share her. "But how? You said you couldn't have children."

She reached for his arm as if reading his thoughts. "You have nothing to worry about. I'll always love you as my own. Ever since the day you were born, I have loved you; it took me a long while before I got over the pain of having you call Zillah 'mama.' I had to learn something very quickly when you were born or I'd have died of jealousy."

"What was that?"

"I learned that sharing someone in love can be more special than loving them all alone. Zillah and I may not have much in common but what we do have is you. We both love you and your father very much. And now, I'm going to have a child of my own." Adah added after a moment, "In spite of our argument, I think this baby will finally heal my relationship with Zillah. You see, she's always had to share with me—first your father and then you. At long last, I'll have something to share with her. After the baby is born and she falls in love with the child, she may find that she loves me as well. Then, at last, after twenty long years we shall become friends."

"When did you find out you could have a baby?"

"I never thought I could, but Methuselah said differently the last time he visited. He said *the time had come*." She smiled as she remembered the occasion. "We went for a long walk in the forest, and he showed me what herbs to take, what bark to peel and stew over an open fire, and the roots I needed to eat. Some of it tasted awful. But it worked. I have conceived a child!"

Tubal-cain was happy for Adah but he couldn't help but wonder about his own mother. "What do you think Zillah is going to do?"

"I'm sure it will be a long while before she gets used to the idea of my having a child, but do you know what I honestly think? You know your mother as well as I. She's probably decided there is only one thing left for her to do. Zillah will try to get pregnant."

"But mother is too old!"

"Don't be too sure, Tubal-cain. Stranger things have happened." She looked back at the cottage and shook her head in frustration. "I hope Lemech isn't planning to sneak out the back so he can get his way. I'd better check on him. I'll ask him to come get you." She winked and headed back to the cottage, "Remember, you have nothing to worry about. Only good shall come of this baby."

Tubal-cain remained on the stump, with many thoughts going through his mind as he waited. He thought of Methuselah and wished that he could spend more time with the old man. There was so much the mystic could teach and even more that Tubal-cain wanted to learn. He thought about Zillah and wondered if things would improve when another baby arrived. He thought of the woodcutter, Lamech, on the edge of the forest and wondered why the man and his father didn't get along. He thought of the faithful and wondered why their numbers seemed to be so few.

All of these things were on his mind as Lemech, his father, appeared in the doorway of the cottage. With the sight of his father, Tubal-cain had one final thought: He wondered if Cain, the Cursed One, the legendary tiller of the soil, could still be alive.

As they walked beneath the mighty limbs of the trees, Tubal-cain watched his father cock an ear to the side in an effort to listen. He wondered if Lemech's hearing was unlike his own; perhaps voices sounded different to him, somehow. It might be that the sound Tubal-cain heard when Zillah's sharp words were spoken was not the same as that heard by Lemech. Of course, Tubal-cain knew better than to ask about his father's senses, so he remained quiet and his thoughts remained his own.

They were in one of the densest parts of the forest, where trees were dark and thick and not as straight as those that grew near the cottage. The trunks and limbs had become covered with aged bark, cracked, loose, and crawling with insects. Whatever illumination was able to peak through the overhead entanglement of limbs was dim and cast shadows in every direction. Small mounds of earth were struck by the light in such a manner that huge pits seemed to hide behind every weed. No trail or even a hint of a path was near, and Tubal-cain couldn't help but wonder how Lemech was able to venture through these parts alone, with only a crossbow and a long rope about his waist.

Their feet sank deep into soil topped by rotting leaves. The air was musty and reeked of mildew and spoiled vegetables; the scent of lavender was missing and had been replaced by the humid stench of mold. Beneath their feet, the underbrush was gnarled, irregular, and composed of darkened leaves and blackened vines that curled about dead branches of fallen trees. Tubal-cain kept his eyes open for insect webs and poisonous snakes. He couldn't understand why his father had chosen this place. Surely, neither deer nor rabbit could be lurking about this place. He hated to think what kind of creatures were hiding in the darkness or in the shadows of the trees. He wanted to take his father's arm because Tubal-cain felt there was reason to be afraid. But his father was not one to calm fears. Instead, he looked up at Lemech and wondered what he could say to break the darkness.

His father was a big man, with a massive chest and huge veins that rose above his muscular arms. He was tall as well, and appeared to have descended from giants though not a giant himself. His hair was dark but had begun to thin a few months back. He walked with long strides and seemed to move every muscle of his body in rhythm with the steps. And by his father's movement, Tubal-cain could see that Lemech was quite sure of himself and of where they were going and so the young man said nothing.

It had grown darker and the trees had become denser. Moving was much more difficult as vines of weeds entangled themselves around Tubal-cain's moccasins. He brushed up against his father's side occasionally, hoping Lemech wouldn't notice. The forest was eerie and Tubal-cain couldn't help but feel that they needed to be afraid. He also didn't know how much longer they could continue. The underbrush was becoming thicker and damper and the ground made sucking sounds as they lifted their feet from the rotting soil. It was the only sound they heard as they walked along and still the forest became darker. Long, black vines hung down from the crooked boughs of trees, blocking out the light. His breathing became hard, for every step was a struggle. He knew that Lemech was having a difficult time, as well, for his father's breath was louder. And although Tubal-cain was seventeen, he was becoming afraid; yet, he remained more fearful of his father's anger than of the darkness that closed in around them. So he said nothing and continued moving at his father's side, hoping the trees might begin to spread out again or that the light from the clouds might somehow filter through the snarled branches. And as he walked—sucking noises of the wet earth rising from the ground—he waved his hands and arms in front of his eyes to keep away from slimy vines that clung to hair and skin. He noticed that Lemech was waving the crossbow in front of him and had readied an arrow in its place, just in case, causing Tubal-cain to wonder if his father was becoming alarmed and that thought terrified him.

But they continued moving, each worried what the other might say should they admit to fear, and each hoping that the other might say something. Eventually, all Tubal-cain could see were the shadows, and he wondered if that was what Lemech saw in his blindness: shadows, or nothing at all. He wanted to ask his father; he wanted to ask him more than anything, but Tubal-cain knew he should not. Still, he had to say something in order to break the sounds of their labored breath and the sucking noise of the earth. The feeling of fear growing: He had to speak while he still could; if he waited much longer, it would be too late. He was surprised at how his voice cracked through the silence.

"Where are we going, father?"

The older man paused for an instant, as if the answer to his son's question was completely obvious, but when Tubal-cain made no other sound, Lemech answered: "We're going north, toward the lake."

Immediately, Tubal-cain knew what had happened, though he did not know how and his answer was quick, without thought of his father's feelings, since Lemech had never done anything like this before. "But we're going southwest!"

As soon as the words were spoken, Tubal-cain saw it. He saw it out of the corner of his eye, lurking in the shadows of the trees. And it moved. The shape turned, slightly, and stared back at them with yellow glaring eyes. As it moved, Tubal-cain grabbed his father's arm and screamed. The sound was so alarming that even

Lemech's legs froze in place. Neither of them could move.

Tubal-cain saw the outline of grayish skin and deep, dead eyes. Loose flesh clung in long stretches from brittle bones—bones that had long since been bent with age so that the creature was hunched. The gray flesh dripped with moisture, the droplets falling onto decayed leaves where tiny, black spiders ran for their lives.

The darkened form turned its face so that Tubal-cain could see the horn: a thick growth of withered bone protruding from the creature's forehead. Tubal-cain screamed again and wondered if they could run. He tightened his grip on his father's arm—the arm with the crossbow.

Lemech's heart beat faster, and he heard the sound. He couldn't see the dying creature in the shadows, but he felt it, and he could smell it. The odor was nauseating, for it made him think of the carcasses of a thousand rotting maggots and his stomach turned.

They remained frozen in silence and fear. Not one of the three shifted positions, for each waited for the other to make the first move. Tubal-cain glanced first at his father and then at the disfigured creature, which made rasping sounds as it struggled for every breath. He didn't know what to do. The idea to run entered his mind once again, but as the creature glared directly at him, yellow eyes staring at every part of his body, fear overtook him, and he began to shake, tightening the grip on his father's arm.

Lemech felt his muscles grow tense, and he tried to deduce the creature's exact size and location. Suddenly, without warning, the older man felt a strange tingling at the base of his spine. Somehow, it was familiar, though a little different than he remembered. The sensation caused Lemech's attention to be drawn, momentarily, from his fear to the tingling that raced up his back. Slowly, his senses became even more alert and though he was quite blind, shadows began to form before his eyes. His blindness briefly parted until, suddenly, he could see a faint outline of the shadowy figure standing before them.

And somehow, Lemech knew the creature had a knife and meant to kill them. With that thought, the tingling subsided and he was left unaided as before: totally blind, very much afraid, frozen in place in the darkness of the forest. He heard the withered creature take a step forward, as his son's nails dug even deeper into the flesh of his arm. The older man tried to shake off Tubal-cain's grip but to no avail. The boy held on too tightly. And when Lemech moved, the creature took another step forward, until the irregular light passing through the trees fell down upon the beast's head, illuminating its horn. Lemech tried to pry the boy's hands loose with his free hand but the creature waved its knife in full view, and Tubal-cain clenched his fingers in place.

"Let go!" Lemech screamed. The creature, dripping with sweat, took another step toward them; Tubal-cain held fast.

Finally, Lemech swung his left arm around to the boy's face, and with one swift blow knocked his son to the ground. Tubal-cain passed out atop a heap of blackened vines and mildewed leaves, and the blind man was left alone with the creature with yellow eyes.

Without pausing for even an instant, Lemech lowered his crossbow in the direction from which he heard the slimy creature, slid the arrow into place, and fired. A quick "whoosh" sounded through the air as the shaft flew the short distance to its target. Mercifully, the sharp point lodged swiftly and deeply into the creature's heart, and the figure fell to its bony knees with a single, muffled cry. A moment later, the shadowy form was dead, and Lemech couldn't even imagine what he had just killed, nor did he possess any desire to run his hands over the creature's face and find out what it looked like.

He stood in place, trying to figure out just how they had gotten lost and how he had been able to see the outline of the creature, even if for only an instant. And though neither made any sense, his confusion over what had occurred was quickly replaced by the realization that his son was lying silent somewhere upon the ground.

He slipped the crossbow through a knot in his roped belt and listened before lowering himself to the entanglement of vines and wet leaves. With his head cocked to one side, he located the boy's position by the sound of his breathing, and Lemech's hands went out to him. He gently felt Tubal-cain's chest, arms, and legs for any signs of an injury, all the while calling out his name. There was no answer. Repeatedly, the older man called but there was no response. Tubal-cain did not appear hurt, only unconscious, so Lemech slid his arms under his son and lifted. He would carry the boy back the way they had come, for by now Lemech was quite certain he had regained his bearings.

His steps away from the dead beast were slow and unsteady at first. Tubal-cain was heavy and the ground was not stable. Lemech's feet sunk even deeper into the mucky soil than they had earlier. After a distance, he felt the sweat of strain dripping down his back, but there was no time to rest. He wanted nothing more than to get away from this part of the forest. Besides, Adah and Zillah would be waiting, and it wasn't wise to leave the two alone.

As time passed and the ground beneath his feet grew firmer, Lemech's steps became more certain. No longer did the hanging vines brush up against his face and the air was much easier to breathe. He could also feel that the surroundings had opened up into a wider expanse. They approached Lemech's own clearing, free from the binding growth of trees, and he knew that, above the clearing, could be seen the water vapor canopy (though he hadn't gazed upon it himself in nearly twenty years).

His walk was steady, only jostling Tubal-cain when it was necessary to adjust his son's weight in his arms. He didn't want to set the boy down and delay their arrival, for he still wasn't sure whether or not his son needed any looking after. So he continued, ignoring the strain in his biceps and upper back and trying not to think about how tired he was becoming. It was getting late; Adah would be worried; Zillah would be angry.

Occasionally, Lemech repeated his son's name to see if he was coming around. He knew the boy had been hit solidly, though he hoped desperately that Tubal-cain wasn't seriously hurt. Lemech felt horrible, but there had been nothing else for him to do. Never before had he even raised a hand against his son. After a long while, Lemech began to hear the sounds of the night birds that surrounded his own clearing. His feet brushed up against familiar grasses lining the well-trodden path and his nostrils filled with the scent of lavender. He was home.

All around were the things to which he had grown accustomed during their years in isolation. Fifteen cubits ahead, where the worn path took a sharp turn to the right, a knobby stump of an ancient, felled oak was still in place. On either side of the trail, scattered amid the massive oaks and the tropical flowers, a few clusters of birch put off a scent that sometimes overpowered even the smell of purple buds.

He shifted the weight of his son one final time before approaching the cottage. Lemech's steps were sure, yet he braced himself for the sharp sound of Zillah's voice. As he followed the memorized steps in his head, the smells of roasted corn and vegetable pie rose to his nostrils. He realized how hungry he had become, and he hoped that Tubal-cain would be strong enough to eat. Suddenly, Lemech's thoughts were jarred by the abrupt sound of his elder wife.

"My god, Lemech! What happened to him?" Zillah ran from the cottage door, holding a long wooden spoon that she had been tapping at her side in irritation over their delay. Her eyes glared with fear. "Oh, Lemech," she pleaded, wiping her son's forehead, "what happened to him? Is he all right? Answer me, Lemech!" she demanded, without giving him a chance to speak.

Adah's gentle form appeared in the doorway, though she stopped herself from running to his aid.

"There was a Mixture," Lemech said gruffly, "a hideous creature that crept out of the shadows toward us."

"My god!" Zillah screamed again, and felt to see whether Tubal-cain's heart was beating. "What did it do to my son?"

"It didn't do anything to him, Zillah. The creature meant to kill us—I had no choice. I had to knock Tubal-cain out of the way."

Zillah felt her rage build until her hands clenched into fists. She almost lashed out at him but her husband had such a look of deep sadness upon his brow and closed eyes that now was not the time.

Adah could stand it no longer. She spoke in the only manner that Zillah acknowledged. "Zillah, maybe you'll want to tell Lemech to bring Tubal-cain inside to his bed. If you don't mind, I'll get a compress."

"Yes, that will be fine," Zillah agreed as she whirled around, shaking the wooden spoon she carried at the younger woman. "You get a cool cloth for his forehead." She turned and put a firm hand on her husband's shoulder, pushing him in the direction of the cottage.

"Hurry up! Take Tubal-cain to his room so I can attend to him." Zillah ushered him into the house and beneath the low doorway that led to her son's room.

Already, Adah stood by the side of the bed, with a moist cloth ready to pass to her sister-wife. Lemech leaned forward and gently laid the boy on the thick, stuffed mattress that was covered with one thinly stitched quilt. When he stood, his arms and upper back felt immense pain—the strain had been great. He started rubbing his own sore muscles for relief, as Zillah took the cloth and began wiping Tubal-cain's forehead.

"Is he going to be all right?" Adah asked nervously.

Tubal-cain's breathing became stronger, and Zillah responded with a soft voice in a manner totally unlike her usual self, "He'll be just fine."

Adah looked up at her husband. "What happened?"

Tears came to Lemech's eyes as he remembered the feel of Tubal-cain's soft chin against the palm of his hand. "Adah and Zillah," he said sadly, "I have slain a creature that meant to kill me and I have injured my own son."

"He's coming around now," Zillah replied, as Tubal-cain's eyes fluttered open. She brushed his hair aside and smiled. "How are you feeling?"

"I'm fine," Tubal-cain tried to sit up on the mattress, but his mother pushed him back.

"Don't try to move. We've got to make certain everything is all right."

"There's nothing to worry about, mother." He glanced at the three faces leaning over him. When his eyes fell upon Lemech, he was quite embarrassed by the panic he had felt. "I'm sorry, father. I don't know what happened."

"You have nothing to be sorry about." Lemech patted the boy's arm. "I was lucky. I didn't have to see what the creature looked like."

Lemech's words brought complete silence, for he had never

before referred to his blindness. Zillah watched their son, closely checking him over for signs of broken skin or swelling. When she was convinced there was no serious injury, she demanded to hear the entire story, making him start at the beginning.

Tubal-cain lay with his back against the overstuffed mattress, describing exactly what had happened. He told everything, from the time they left the cottage clearing, leaving out only his hunch, early on, that they had gotten lost. He spoke of the darkness, the deformed trees, and of the foul-smelling air. Finally, he described the monster in every detail. The whole while Zillah merely shook her head in agreement.

"That's him! That's got to be the one," she kept saying as Tubal-cain spoke of his fear and of the panic he had felt when the creature raised a stone knife.

"That was him. I just know it!" Zillah said positively, gesturing with her hands for emphasis. Adah shook her head in amazement, while Lemech's mouth fell open in horror.

"I tell you," she stated vehemently, "that was him—the curse and everything: a horn through his forehead." Lemech wanted to disagree but Zillah wouldn't allow it. "I'm telling you for a fact!" she said loudly. When she finally realized the significance of what she had said, her face became pale, and her voice turned to a whisper. "My god, Lemech, after seven generations, you've killed Cain, the wanderer!"

"No!" Lemech denied immediately. "It cannot be true! If I have killed another man, then surely I am guilty of the most grievous sin of all!" Lemech lost all reason. He forgot the fact that the creature had a knife; he forgot that the deed had been done in defense; he forgot both these things. Instead, he saw his crime as yet another sin for which he would be punished and his crying continued.

He fell to his knees and began to sob. "Yet," he continued as a new thought had struck him, "if Cain was felled by my bow, will I not be pitied? If the Cursed One purposefully murdered Abel, who was not avenged for seven generations, surely I, who killed a man in ignorance, will be treated with justice? If Cain wasn't avenged for sevenfold, surely I won't be punished for at least seventy and sevenfold!" He hung his head in his hands and wept.

"We can only hope, my husband," Zillah replied gravely. "We can only hope."

New Directions
(600 years before the Flood)

The days of the giant's training passed slowly at first, so slowly that Traibus wished he had placed a time limit on their wager. The hours spent with the old man were long and confusing, often leading to discussions that the giant neither fully understood nor could possibly believe. Yet, he was constantly under the mystic's watchful eye, as if Methuselah were afraid to let the giant out of his sight. Traibus wondered, time and again, how much longer it would be before the old man gave up, but the longer he waited, the more clear it became: Methuselah had no intention of losing. They stayed together from the earliest hours of morning until the last threads of light had dwindled from the overhead clouds. They took walks through the streets of the marketplace, around the rich fields bordering the city, and to and from the forest that began where the Shinar plains came to an end. Methuselah claimed he had to teach the giant how to look at the world around him. Without true perception, knowledge was impossible.

The whole while they walked, the mystic asked Traibus what he saw and the giant answered. Each time, after Traibus had finished his response, Methuselah pointed out what the giant had missed: how one petal upon a flower appeared a lighter shade of violet than the rest, the way a blade of plains grass grew at a different angle than those which surrounded it, or how an all but hidden insect clung to a tall stalk of corn. Methuselah often placed his finger on the object and explained its significance: By itself, it might appear to be nothing, but in reality it was an integral piece of the whole. Again and again, the giant became irritated for having missed something so completely obvious.

As the days turned slowly into weeks, Traibus grew accustomed to spotting the finest detail with just a momentary glance. He could see a tiny crack—no more than a sliver—in the whitewashed brick buildings lining the streets. He noticed pebbles lying upon the cobblestones without even thinking about it. The ability caused Traibus to wonder if his eyes were getting better but Methuselah claimed the giant's eyes were the same, only his perception was changing.

By the time the weeks finally turned to several months, Traibus had become nearly as proficient as his teacher at examining their surroundings. However, when the giant reached this stage, Methuselah changed the way their game was being played. No longer was seeing the obvious sufficient. Methuselah wanted him to see things that couldn't possibly exist. The old man talked of a light, a light that surrounded everything. Methuselah insisted it was there, though it was a light the giant could not see. Day after day, the two stared for hours as Methuselah described what Traibus couldn't even imagine. They watched the motionless wings of a butterfly as it tottered atop the blade of a pine, until the giant thought his eyes would bulge from the strain. The old man patiently tried again.

"It is a light," Methuselah said for the hundredth time, "a light so fine and delicate that your eyes couldn't possibly see it, so stop squinting. You'll never see it with your eyes, but only with your mind."

"How can I see it with my mind?" Traibus asked, continuing to stare at the black-and-yellow wings, still squinting in spite of the fact that he had been told not to do so.

"Have you forgotten what we've discussed of dreams? You see in sleep, yet your eyes are closed. This is what I want you to do while awake."

"But if the light is really there, why can I not see it?"

"The reason you do not see it is because you do not believe it's there. Part of your mind tells you that the light cannot be, so your eyes look upon what your brain has already decided. Why don't you just look at the creature without holding any notion of what you think you should see?"

"I don't understand." Traibus looked at the old man.

Methuselah used his hands to show Traibus what he wanted him to do. "Place your hands over your eyes and close them tightly. Keep your palm against your face so that no light whatsoever creeps into your vision." He waited until the giant followed his instructions before continuing. "Now, what do you see?"

"Only darkness."

"Good, now I want you to imagine a butterfly. A large orange butterfly with gentle wings and a beautiful pattern designing its soft limbs of flight. The creature is as light as a feather, and its wings flutter with precise rhythm. Can you see it?"

"Yes, I see it."

"Fine, now tell me how you did it."

Traibus's eyes remained closed, his palms still pressed against his face. "I imagined a butterfly, and in the next instant, it was in my mind."

"But," the old man said slowly, "how were you able to imagine what it looked like?"

"Because I have seen butterflies before. I know how they appear and can therefore picture one in my mind's eye." Finally, Traibus opened his eyes.

"That's correct. You have an idea in your head of how the creature will look and that is what you see. Do you realize, my friend, every time you look at a butterfly you take this same preconceived notion from your mind? You place that notion over the creature's true appearance, so that what you see is a cross between what is actually there and what you think you should see. You are letting your eyes fool you."

Methuselah continued, "When you look through a window, do you ask the window what is on the other side or do you simply look out at what is beyond? What I'm trying to tell you is never look at an object with your eyes. Instead, look through your eyes. Try not to decide what it is you're going to see before you even look upon it. Do you understand?"

"I still don't understand what this light consists of."

The old man nodded his head and began walking away from the pine, Traibus following at his side. They had crossed the canal bridge and were heading back toward the marketplace. The bright light of the clouds warmed the air, making it humid all across the plains. Already, the giant's tight, leather breeches and loose-fitting tunic had grown damp from the sweat on his back and underarms. Methuselah appeared completely comfortable as his long robe brushed effortlessly over the dirt clods. He moved quickly in order to keep up with the giant's strides.

"The light I have spoken of is a force. You could say it's a force of holiness, surrounding all living things, from the tiniest of insects to the largest of oaks. It is a creative force abiding in all things. More simply—though I know you can't yet believe this, Traibus—the force is of the One, the God of the faithful. It is His force that is in all things, and when you've seen this light you will have seen a fraction of His Spirit. And when you've beheld His Spirit, you will have glimpsed the substance of the soul."

For a while, Traibus walked in silence, simply trying to decide what Methuselah had just said. He rolled the words over and over again in his mind to see if he really understood, but after a while, he became disgusted with himself. None of it made any sense. Part of his mind wanted to see what the mystic talked about, and, yet, another part was annoyed for falling for the absurdity of it all. Ultimately, he couldn't believe Methuselah, for that was the point of their bargain. Why should he be upset with himself for not seeing what wasn't there to begin with? A smile passed over his lips. Methuselah was trying to outwit him again.

Traibus walked the rest of the way in silence, only half hearing Methuselah's praise of the plains and the beauty of the forest. He missed out entirely on all that the old man said of Malock, another giant, and of Methuselah's own fears that the evil was growing.

The two stood in a crowded alleyway, not far from the central marketplace. The middle of the afternoon had arrived, and most people were returning home after visiting the pushcart vendors or wandering to a tavern in search of gourd liquor and amusement (dogfights had gained in popularity for there were shekels to be won). The giant and the old man concealed themselves in the shadows of a building, backs pressed firmly against cool brick, while Methuselah asked Traibus to describe all that he could see.

The giant was surprised to find his perception so keen, even within the shadows.

The street was narrow, lined on either side by the tall facing of a tenement structure. No light from the clouds had fallen upon portions of the cobblestone pavement in nearly a hundred years. The coolness of the walls allowed a thin growth of moss to cover much of the once pale bricks. Tiny rodents made their homes within the walls, scurrying over the inlaid street whenever anyone approached; some Mixtures found them quite palatable.

All this Traibus had seen before, from the darkened doorways to the weary Mixtures crouching in the darkness, awaiting the passage of time. He saw an old hag, her arms wrapped tightly about her knees as she rocked herself back and forth. Her hunger had subsided, and she was content: A vendor had discarded soft vegetables into the gutter. Other Mixtures passed by without a glance.

Although Traibus had seen her on countless occasions, this time he noticed something quite different. It wasn't merely that her eyes seemed more withdrawn or that the scab at the side of her mouth was larger—though these things he saw more clearly. What he saw for the first time, however, was something he could only describe as sadness—sadness so deep and touching that he was moved to pity. He felt sorry for her, and he was certain what he saw was not the way it was supposed to be. The thought was completely foreign to him, and it made him uneasy. If what he saw hadn't been intended, then there had to be a plan, a plan forgotten somewhere along the way. He looked down at Methuselah to see if the old man had sensed his discomfort. He found his companion with his eyes closed in prayer.

The sight of the old man praying restored the giant's senses. Methuselah's hands were clasped, while his lips moved together in silence, causing the giant to see the mysterious man he had known from the marketplace rather than the companion of late. When Traibus finally looked back at the haggard woman, all he saw was an old woman crouched in the alley—his mind had been playing tricks on him.

When Methuselah finished his prayer, he opened his eyes and looked up at the giant.

"Your gold will be wasted on that one," Traibus said callously. His words were spoken softly so that Mixtures in the alley wouldn't hear. Five of them, sitting side by side, spoke lustfully of the sights they had seen that very day in the marketplace. Four were men, but the fifth appeared to be female, and her elongated fingers tapped continuously against the grime of the street. Repeatedly, her mouth opened as if to speak, but one of the four males always interrupted.

"First of all, my friend," Methuselah replied seriously, "the gold is not mine. It belongs to the One, and you can be certain He guides the distribution of every single coin . . . "

The five who continued their discussion hadn't spotted the shadowed figures; neither had any who passed through the alleyway. The giant was becoming impatient, for their wait had been long; Methuselah had told him that, this day, he would see how the gold was dispensed, and that's what he had been waiting for.

" . . . and gold will not cure what ails her," the old man finished. The woman continued to rock herself, arms wrapped tightly about her knees. "It is not a bad thing to feel for this poor woman. We are no better than she."

"At least we're aware of what's going on around us," Traibus replied gruffly. "Look at her; she's totally ignorant of her surroundings."

"Don't be so positive of your awareness. Though it is better, in a sense, you are still no more certain of your reality than she. There is much more to life than you've allowed yourself to believe. Right now, you couldn't possibly imagine its scope."

The giant shook his head in disgust, thinking his companion a fool.

"Don't overlook what I'm saying," Methuselah replied, then added, "Let me ask you this question, my friend: Who has the greatest handicap? That poor woman," he stretched out a robed arm and gestured toward her, "who is incapable of seeing her surroundings, or you who refuses to look at them? I promise you, that woman has made far greater progress on her journey than either of us could possibly imagine for, you see, the lesson she sought was humility."

"You forget, little one," Traibus interrupted, "I have no faith in these 'lessons' you speak of."

"Give it time." Methuselah managed a grin. "You're getting much closer to the end of our wager than you think."

"The end cannot come soon enough for me, for I wish to see the gold."

"If it's only gold you wish to see, then turn your eyes here." Methuselah raised a clenched fist far above his head, toward the giant's face. His hand opened to show Traibus two shiny, golden coins lying in the center of his palm—a small fortune in the mind of the giant. Traibus lifted one of the coins out of its resting place with his own enormous hand, dwarfing Methuselah's in comparison. The giant massaged the coin between his thumb and forefinger, glancing from the old man to the gold piece that glistened even in the shadows. It was a long while before he spoke.

"How many of these do you have, little one?" the giant asked finally.

Methuselah smiled as he answered, "You have seen all that remain in my possession. All I have left, tucked inside the cloth bag of my sleeve, are a handful of shekels—and these we will need on our journey."

"What journey?" Traibus handed the gold back.

"This very day, before light disappears from the clouds, we leave for the coast."

"You forget, Methuselah," the giant said, shaking his head in disagreement, "I have already spent far too much time away from my work. To travel such a distance and return would take a fortnight. I must trap hides if I wish to keep my belly full. I do not have the benefit of a gold supply, like yourself, to purchase all my needs."

"Once again, I remind you, the gold is not mine. We journey to Persia for more of these coins you find so precious; there is work that needs to be done."

"Then you have decided to show me the gold!" Traibus exclaimed excitedly, though he was careful not to speak loud enough to be heard. He patted the old man on the shoulder, "Then you are going to forfeit our wager?"

"Do not be so quick to declare yourself the victor, for you have yet to win."

"But if you're taking me to your hiding place, does that not mean you're showing me the gold? How can you be so certain that I won't decide to take it nonetheless?"

"Let me put it this way," Methuselah said mysteriously, scratching his bearded chin, "you won't even be able to see the gold unless I win, and if I do win, you will no longer want it."

"Have you not tired of speaking in riddles?"

"It's no riddle, Traibus, I assure you. If you're not able to see the light I've spoken of, then you won't see the coins; both exist in the same realm."

"I do not understand!"

"You will, my friend," Methuselah said softly, "you will. Let us learn to be patient."

In order to halt any further discussion, the old man waved his hand from side to side, "Time is short. We must dispense with one coin before we leave; the other we will deliver on our journey."

"Is this what you've been doing ever since the rumors started?" Traibus chuckled, "Standing in the shadows and throwing your wealth to any who pass by?"

"I do not give it out as casually as you would suppose, nor do I simply spend my time passing out gold. Many days go by where I haven't removed a solitary piece from my tiny bag. If it were otherwise, I can assure you I'd be making far more trips to the coast than I'd ever care to. There are days when I roam these streets looking for those who are sick or those who have been injured by the evil in this place. I give them what they need, be it a poultice of herbs or the setting of a bone. If there is one in need of counsel, I present myself. If one needs a hearty meal, I'll make it. Whatever is asked of me by the One, I attempt with all my might."

"Do you really expect me to believe that this One tells you what to do each day?" the giant asked disgustedly.

"Believe it or not, but it is so."

"Fine, so who shall receive the gold today?" Traibus couldn't help but be amused by Methuselah's convictions.

"The first will go to a younger man; I saw him only once in my mind's eye." The giant just stared in disbelief as Methuselah continued, "He is very poor, yet he still must support a wife and three small children. By trade, he is a carver from Elam. He came to Shinar in search of work, but sadly for a woodworker, there is none to be found. He wishes to go to Nineveh, for it is his last hope to find a job. And you know what?" Methuselah's eyes twinkled. "There he will find what he is looking for."

"You can't be serious!"

"Very serious, indeed." The old man nodded. "This man from Elam used all that he had to come to Shinar. He has but a half-shekel left, and with it, he intends to buy one final meal for his family—or so he thinks."

Methuselah continued, looking from time to time at Traibus while he spoke, "He does not know what else to do. Last night, in desperation, he and his wife fell to their knees in prayer. They prayed aloud to a God they only vaguely remembered from their childhood."

"So this One you'd have me believe in," Traibus was quick to retort, "will help only those who ask."

"No, my friend. The One will help any who allow. Many I aid have never heard of Him."

"Well, then, let's find this carver," Traibus said irritably, "if there is such a man, so we can be on our way."

"You needn't worry, Traibus, the man I speak of exists. However, there is no need to move from this spot for he will pass down this very street on his way to the marketplace."

"Let me know when you see him," the giant appeared disgusted.

"Oh, at your height, you will see the man long before I do. His skin is the color of ripening olives, and his hair is dark, tied beneath a wide cloth turban. He wears the flowing robe of a Persian, although it is tattered from his travels. Just keep your eyes open."

Traibus turned in the direction Methuselah was pointing—down the alley past the sleeping woman. At a distance, the street angled off to the left and joined another. All he could see was the end of the alley bounded by the rising walls on either side.

"How long will I have to wait?"

"Not long."

The giant kept looking and then asked, "So who gets the other coin?"

"The other one goes to Menahem, in the cottage of Lamech."

"Your new grandson?" Traibus forgot what he was supposed to be doing and whirled around to look at the old man. He was very much appalled. "The child is only an infant!"

"I know," Methuselah said matter-of-factly, "but this is my guidance."

"So you think this One wants you to give your grandson a fortune—when there are so many in this city who starve?" The giant laughed aloud, "Now I know you are crazy."

"It is important to remember to never ask for guidance unless you intend to follow what is given. I do merely what I have been told."

"This is the greatest foolishness I've ever . . . "

"Quiet, Traibus," Methuselah interrupted, before the giant could finish. "Tell me who you see approaching." He gestured down the alley and was silent.

Traibus turned his head, and his mouth fell open in amazement. His breath caught in his throat, while his hands began to shake slightly. It appeared for a moment that he would be sick, for his face turned quite pale. When he was able to speak, his voice was unsteady: "It is the one you spoke of."

"Excellent," the old man said casually. "My eyes have never grown accustomed to these shadows. Now, I want you to be silent and watch. You may learn something of use to you."

The giant could barely hear Methuselah's words. Instead, his gaze remained fixed upon the man who approached them—the very individual Methuselah had described. Traibus couldn't believe what he was seeing.

The traveler walked slowly, as if his thoughts were of greater consequence than the steps he took toward the central market. He was deeply troubled and unaware of his surroundings. He saw neither the woman lying in the street, with her head pressed against the ground, nor the group of Mixtures, nor the two figures in the shadows. None of these things were of concern to him. His thoughts were with his family, for he had no idea what they were going to do.

Although his steps were slow, they were steady. He was still proud, for his trade was honest and good, and his desire to work was real. If only someone would give him a chance, he might show his skill as a craftsman. If he could only get to Nineveh, things might be different. Yet, there was no way of getting there and no jobs to be had in Shinar. He was worried; that was a certainty.

His head was held high, his dusty turban wound precisely in place. His nose was long and noble and his skin the color of the plains' people. A thick, black mustache brushed the bottom of his nostrils, and his features were highlighted with dark eyebrows, almost joined at the center of his forehead. The long, flowing stripes of his Persian robe fluttered behind him as he walked. Inside the left arm of his sleeve was his small woolen sack, tied securely in place. It contained one meager coin—all they had left. He would buy his family one final meal; beyond that, he had no idea what they would do.

Just before the man reached their place in the shadows, Methuselah whispered up to his companion. "Watch."

As the Persian went past, Methuselah followed close behind. Traibus remained still, with his back against the wall, and kept his eyes focused as the old man crept closer and closer to the traveler.

Throughout it all, Methuselah didn't make a sound. In fact, it even appeared as though the old man's robes began to flow with the same motion as the garments of the Persian. When the two moved completely as one, Traibus was able to see Methuselah's hand reach around by the sleeve of the stranger and quickly dart inside. It was over in an instant, so swiftly that Traibus doubted he could have seen it without his previous training in the game.

Casually (though his grin was enormous), Methuselah returned to their place against the wall and looked up at his companion. "Did you see it?"

"You amaze me. I would wager you've become the finest pick-pocket in the entire marketplace."

"Not really." The old man shrugged his shoulders, "I broke the young man's string which held his purse fastened. However, he will lose neither his coin nor the gold. But he'll be quite surprised when he goes to pay for their meal."

Methuselah motioned for him to come out of the shadows. "Come, my friend. We have a very long journey which awaits us, and I have much to show you."

It was the morning of their third day after leaving the bustling crowds of Shinar behind. Traibus sat on the ground, his back against one of the largest trees in the clearing of Lemech's cottage. At his right was Tubal-cain, and together, they watched Methuselah.

The old mystic sat upon the ancient stump, his gray robes flowing down around him. The air was filled with the morning's dew and the sweet scent of lavender. Methuselah spoke to the three while, not too far away, Adah watched with reverence.

Zillah was inside the cottage, preparing a hearty breakfast for Traibus and Methuselah before they continued on their way. She slammed drawers shut and complained of the inefficiency of her adobe oven that vented through the back wall. Though Adah had offered to help, Zillah wouldn't hear of it. Everything had to be just right, and a great deal needed to be prepared—the giant ate enough for three men. A few times, Zillah had called Lemech's name for assistance in lifting something, but her husband had disappeared since the first break of light.

Flowers in full bloom filled the clearing and dotted the landscape. Even the giant couldn't help but be moved by the sight of large, yellow petals that shot from thick, green stalks and leaves that appeared soft and moist from the morning's dew. He couldn't ever remember feeling so peaceful before. And he was becoming more impressed by the scope of the mystic's knowledge and the air of reverence that even Adah and Tubal-cain seemed to hold for him.

A beaming grandfather, Methuselah finished speaking of his tiny grandson and waited for Tubal-cain to ask another question. "Why is it," Tubal-cain asked, pulling his hair back in place out of his eyes, "that there are many times when I feel lonely, even though I'm around other people? It's like I'm missing something but I don't know what it is. It can happen at any time."

"It is one of our greatest blessings," Methuselah said reassuringly, "and it has been as such since our beginning . . . "

"How can any lack be considered a blessing?" Traibus interrupted.

"Although the statement appears to contradict itself, it does not. Consider this for a moment." The old man waved his hand in the direction of each of them. "If you were always happy and completely at peace with yourself, then you might naturally become quite satisfied with who you are. And if you were completely satisfied with yourself, that would be the end of your growth. Yet, as long as a soul finds itself in this sphere, further growth is possible. Until all remember the separation and move to correct it, the work of the faithful will not be finished in the earth. This is the reason that loneliness often exists. At times, it is but a gentle reminder that there is much more to our being than we could possibly imagine. So when you feel alone, as if something is missing, turn within yourself to the silence. In this place you will often find the very thing you are looking for."

Traibus moved uneasily, for the few times he had attempted the practice of meditation he had not been successful.

" . . . and when you find it," Methuselah added positively, "do not forget, your growth is not yet complete. For a time, you may be content, but at some moment in the future, your heart will find an emptiness once again."

As he finished speaking, Lemech walked out from behind the trees lining the pathway to the clearing. His eyes were closed and his brow drawn together as if uneasy thoughts had been passing through his head. He looked troubled, and his steps were less certain than his normal, confident pace. Everyone was silent as the muscular man approached. Adah wondered whether she should run to her husband's side but Methuselah shook his head and placed a finger to his lips as if to tell them all to be silent. Except for the sounds of the birds, Lemech heard nothing but quiet as he approached.

"Has the sight of my presence struck you all dumb?" Lemech asked as he came to a stop. His chest was held high in order to emphasize his girth.

"No, my cousin," the old man said calmly. "We were but waiting for you to join us. Come and rest awhile."

"There can be no rest for myself," Lemech replied sadly.

"Please, sit and relax."

"This I cannot do," Lemech said gruffly, "for my mind moves as swiftly as a river."

"Have you forgotten how to quiet your thoughts?" Methuselah asked innocently. "You were once among the faithful."

"That was a very long time ago." The blind man's muscles tensed.

The giant watched Lemech with renewed interest, for it was quite intriguing to think that such a man once believed all that Methuselah taught.

"There is rest in the silence."

"There can be no rest for a man like myself!"

"Then what is it that troubles you?" Methuselah folded his hands in his lap and waited.

"You have been here two nights thus far. Surely someone has told you of my sin."

"I know of no such sin."

"I have erred, even as Cain," Lemech replied. "No greater sin could there be." The blind man bowed his head sorrowfully and looked to the ground, awaiting Methuselah's judgment.

"My cousin," the old man began tenderly, "though it may be true that you have erred as Cain, it is not a murder I speak of."

"What are you saying?"

"Neither you nor Cain ever found a way to forgive yourself. God has not judged you, you simply judge yourself and find reason to condemn."

"Explain yourself," Lemech replied gloomily.

"Have you become as blind in thought as you are in sight?" Adah and Tubal-cain caught their breaths; Methuselah continued. "Ever since your second marriage, you've condemned yourself, and in your blindness you've believed that the One was punishing you. You see, my cousin, when others condemned you for your marriage to Adah, you began to condemn yourself. Part of your mind wished to be punished for what you had done, and it became so. You became blind. But Lemech, the punishment was self-inflicted; God had nothing to do with it. And now, you seek to be punished for this latest deed. Believe me, my cousin, if you wish for it hard enough, it will become so, but the punishment will be of your own making."

"Are you saying I killed not a man, but a beast? Was it not Cain in the forest?" Lemech asked hopefully.

"To say it was Cain or a beast matters not. The creature meant to harm you and your son. You acted in the only manner you could. Do no continue in this foolishness, my cousin. You know what I say to be true."

"Was not the curse prescribed for Cain a horn through the forehead?" Lemech was persistent.

"You are determined to find fault with yourself, aren't you?"

Lemech was silent.

"Very well, I will tell you this. When Cain slew his brother, he wished more than anything to hide from the One. It is written, 'Man was not always so ignorant of the Divine.' So Cain attempted to hide from a God he knew to be very real. But he hid, not out of fear, for even Cain knew the One was not to be feared but because he was ashamed—ashamed of what he had done. Now, in his shame," Methuselah directed his comments to each of them, "he wanted to be free from the reminder of what he had done, and that reminder was God. You see, Lemech, it was Cain's wish to be blinded as well, but his blindness was of the soul. No longer did he believe himself worthy to feel the presence of the Divine, and from this, he extracted his own punishment. The 'curse,' my cousin, was of Cain's own making: To be in the earth but to never again sense the presence of the One."

"And so, as the years passed, Cain the wanderer became less and less aware of the Divinity around him." Methuselah continued, "The gland through which spiritual sight is possible became stiff and hard. It turned to bone and covered itself in stubbornness. It began to take on the appearance of a horn, and Cain got his wish. No longer could his body feel that from which he had hidden. But if you were to ask me," Methuselah said quickly, before Lemech could respond, "whether the beast you slew in darkness was the wanderer, I would respond no. The soul of the wanderer took on a deep sleep, never to be conscious again until his body had perished. Now as to whether or not the body you slew once belonged to Cain, how could I possibly know?"

Before anyone could utter another word, the weary form of Zillah appeared in the cottage doorway. She held her hands tightly against her broad hips and looked with irritation at the gathering. Her lips puckered, and her words were spoken with much annoyance:

"Just what is everyone doing? I've been working all morning, cooking sweet pies and creamed oats, and if you think I'm going to let them get cold while they wait for you to decide to eat—well, you'd better think again. I've got better things to do than attend to folks who haven't got the sense to come in and eat when a decent meal's been prepared for them."

Methuselah concealed his smile as he rose from the stump. "We're coming, Zillah."

"Well, it's about time! I've got Traibus's plate sitting at the back window again. He can look in as we gather around the table; the house wasn't built for giants."

Zillah turned from the doorway as the five moved toward the

cottage. Traibus walked around to the back of the house and saw, once again, how his place had been prepared with the greatest of care.

Their entire journey was without incident. Not a single plainsman dared to confront the old man and the giant. The two journeyed without interruption, taking a great deal of time for themselves to simply talk or to point out the beauty of their surroundings to one another: rich grasslands whose blades were long and soft and sweet to the taste. They drank freely from clear springs and ate of the land, and Zillah had packed food as well. They tried to cover as much distance as possible each day, before the light disappeared from the vapors overhead.

It took several days before they had left the enormous forest behind them and the last gigantic oak had faded into the distance. The lavender and yellow-seed flowers were replaced by flowering shrubs which grew no taller than Traibus's knees. And as the days passed, their friendship deepened. They spoke of days gone by, as if each wished to share a part of himself that was unknown to the other. Traibus told of his years of loneliness and the isolation he had often felt due to his stature. Methuselah spoke in reverence of his father, Enoch, and of the unusual circumstances surrounding the man's disappearance. Once, the old man even mentioned his wife, Anna, who had died while birthing a daughter—the baby had died as well. The tale brought tears to Methuselah's eyes, so that the giant chose not to pursue it.

Traibus couldn't help but be awed by the gentle old man, who wore a simple robe, yet possessed the wisdom of countless rulers. He treated Methuselah with admiration and respect. And

Methuselah, in his turn, was astonished by Traibus's knowledge of the plains. The giant had traversed most of Assyria and a great deal of western Persia; he knew of trails and roads that led to the gulf in a shorter manner than the way the old man generally traveled. They journeyed together as long-lost brothers who were overjoyed at finding one another after so many years.

Methuselah showed the giant how to make a poultice of herbs that could heal a small cut or an upset stomach equally well. While they rested at evening, sitting upon the lush grass, he gestured toward the sky and pointed out the dim light that often filtered through the clouds and he told the giant of his belief: The light was of a different source than the brightness they saw at day. He didn't accept the notion (which was a common belief) that the vapors themselves came alive with illumination, causing the difference between night and day.

Traibus carved the old man a staff of birch, for they had passed by many clusters of the trees as they journeyed alongside the river. Whenever possible, they traveled along the path of the Tigris, for it emptied into a tributary of the gulf. During the day, Traibus often pointed out birds and other creatures that the old man had never even seen and told all that he knew of the animals. Traibus's knowledge was immense; he could speak of tiny birds that fit into the palm of a hand or the enormous elephants to the south with equal authority. Not only did he seem to know what these creatures ate but he was well acquainted with their habits as well. With a single glance, he could distinguish between a rabbit hole and that of a prairie dog.

Methuselah made it a habit to spend time in the silence once in the morning and again just before retiring. And as each day passed, Traibus grew more accustomed to the practice, even deriving pleasure from it. When it came time to say a song of thanksgiving at the end, the giant joined in as well. He even began to sense that there might be something to the practice, after all. However, it wasn't until the fifth morning after leaving Lemech's cottage, when they arrived at the gulf, that the giant realized something even more amazing: Not once, since leaving Shinar's forest had he even given thought to the gold.

The light of day had been in the sky about three hours when Methuselah finally dropped his walking staff to the ground and sat down upon the bank at the river's edge. The earth around them was fine and sandy and much of it sparkled brilliantly due to the shape of the grains. Methuselah removed his sandals and plunged bare feet into the smooth blue waters of the small tributary. He wished to rest for a while.

Traibus removed his leather jacket and lowered himself to the sand, lying flat on his belly. He leaned over the edge of the elevated bank and dropped his hands and arms into the sparkling waters. Though the water was only slightly cooler than the air around them, the moisture was still soothing to tired limbs. He was impressed with the beauty that surrounded them—this was one spot to which his own travels had never taken him.

Methuselah sat with eyes closed, letting tired feet soak. With its slow-moving water and a forty-cubit distance between either shore, the area looked more like a huge pond than it did a river. Thick, tropical vines and enormous leaves and flowers thrived along both banks as far as the giant could see. The large, yellow flowers Traibus had seen back in the forest were scattered in an array of brilliant colors. In addition to the yellow, blossoms of pink, orange, and fiery red dotted each bank. The minerals in the water caused the plants to bloom in a myriad of colors.

He heard the bubbling sounds of water as it crashed down the gentle rocks of a waterfall—out of sight and farther down the river. The air contained the rich smells of soil and grasses, so that Traibus found it hard to recall the smells of Shinar's marketplace. He lowered his cupped hand to the water and let the smooth, clear liquid fall from his palm back to its source. He heard the call of a wild parrot and looked up at the trees to find it. The limbs of the trees were everywhere, bearing tiny almond-shaped leaves that caught the light at countless angles, so that it appeared to the giant as if he and his companion had been engulfed by greenery.

With the thought of Methuselah, Traibus turned to the mystic and spoke the words he had long been pondering. "I've been thinking," he said slowly. "I wish to release you from our bargain."

The old man's eyes fluttered open, and he smiled. He pulled his legs out of the water, backed away from the embankment with the palms of his hand, and brushed the soil from his hands. "Why would you wish to do that?"

Though there was a pause, Traibus finally managed a response. "Because I have found something more precious than all the gold in the world—and that is a companion and a friend." The giant gazed at the thick grass along the bank, for he was not able to look at the old man directly. "I do not wish to lose what I have found between us."

Methuselah reached out and grasped Traibus's enormous fingers for a moment. "You needn't worry, my friend. I have no intention of losing you—from now on we will work together."

"I feel so badly." Traibus was finally able to look at him. "It was wrong of me to make such a wager."

"Don't feel badly, for without the wager we would not have come to this point. Besides," Methuselah said with a wry grin, "the odds have always been very much weighted in my favor."

"What do you mean?"

"Remember when I told you that the light of Creation and the gold existed in a similar realm?"

"Yes, and that is one of the many things I still do not understand."

Methuselah waved his arms about them. "Everywhere about us is the light of Creation. It surrounds all living things, from the flowers and the vines along the embankment, to the grass beneath us. It is all around us, and I can see it . . . "

"But I can't!" the giant interrupted.

"Perhaps not yet, but trust me, it is there, nonetheless. You might say that I have trained myself to see this next realm consciously. Call it an invisible world if you like."

Methuselah continued, confident that the giant was following him. "Now, only a fraction of this world is visible to me at present. There is a great deal more that might be seen from an altered state—let us say, during a period of the silence."

"But what does this have to with the coins?"

"My friend," Methuselah said, smiling and pointing along the shoreline, "I have brought you to the very hiding place. The gold lies in great, heaping stacks along the very banks of this river."

"Surely this is a riddle?"

"No, it is true. The gold surrounds us even now."

"So you're saying there are golden coins, thousands of them, right here," Traibus pointed to several places along the bank, "hidden just beyond sight?"

"That's it, exactly! You see, Enoch hid the gold while in an altered state, and it is only in that same state that the coins can be found. To retrieve the gold, I must enter the silence."

The giant frowned. Deep wrinkles formed at his eyes, and he shook his head in discouragement. He opened his mouth as if to speak, but then closed it quickly.

"If you have a question, then speak it."

"I have many."

"Then let me see if I can help you." Methuselah crossed his legs beneath him and folded his hands in his robed lap.

"To begin with," Traibus asked, logically, "while you gathered the gold, what would happen to you? I mean, I cannot see the light, so would I not see you either?"

"Excellent question!" Methuselah appeared quite proud of his student. "The answer is yes and no. You would see this body, with my eyes closed and my hands sitting upon my knees. My legs would be resting under me as they are now, and you might see my chest rising and falling in slow, steady breaths. All this you could see."

"However, what you would not see would be a nearly transparent figure, with the appearance of myself, moving over the grass and along the bank, picking up coins that appeared just as transparent as the figure. When he had finished, you also would not see this figure walk over to the old man seated in silence and sit down until the two became again as one." Methuselah then added, "As the old man came out of the silence, however, you would most certainly see the golden coins begin to gradually appear in his lap—my lap."

"Are you trying to say that you can leave your body in the silence?"

"Exactly! Though I want to emphasize that this is not the reason for the silence, only a possibility because of it. One should seek the silence simply for the presence of the Divine."

"Why is it," the giant asked skeptically, "that every time I start to believe everything you say, you tell me something so unbelievable that I can't possibly accept it?"

"You would not have asked unless you were ready to hear," the old man said matter-of-factly. "Still, as I always say: Believe it or not, but it is true."

"Then answer me this question," Traibus said quickly. "If the gold can be hidden in another dimension, why not take it to Shinar and hide it there instead of having to travel for days each time you need to replenish the supply?"

"Wonderful, my friend!" Methuselah was very excited. "You are making amazing progress. I assure you, there is a reason."

"Then tell me."

"Anything that occurs in one realm," Methuselah answered, scratching his chin in thought, "affects what is happening in another. The invisible dimension within this place is just as peaceful and vibrant and beautiful as we see now—more so really. Whatever occurs in the third dimension, one should expect to find in the fourth."

"You mean to tell me that the invisible realm surrounding Shinar's marketplace would be evil?" Traibus was horrified.

"In a sense," the old man replied. "You see, the marketplace is filled with sadness and crime, lusts and filth. These same things would be present as vibrations." Methuselah saw the look of confusion on the giant's face. "A vibration is really nothing more than energy, like the light, but this energy is made by thoughts."

"If I were to hide the gold in Shinar," Methuselah continued, "instead of being surrounded by peace and beauty, as it is now, it would be engulfed with thoughts of crimes and evil that the people have contemplated for centuries. Even if the deeds were never actually committed, the thoughts would still be there. And in my mind, Traibus, such a place is not worthy to contain the One's wealth, so it remains here, right where Enoch placed it."

"I am confused by much of what you say," the giant confessed. "I want to believe."

"Do not become disillusioned, my friend. You will have the proof you desire, but it will probably come only after you no longer require it."

"You mean, after I already believe."

"Exactly! Now, I believe the time has come for us to gather what we came for. Do not appear so gloomy. Even if you cannot look upon the coins now, I'll show them to you when the silence is over." He nodded reassuringly before closing his eyes, and breathing deeply in an effort to relax.

Methuselah heard the sounds of the wild parrot calling to its mate, as well as the slow, steady movement of the river. He could also hear the sharp, heavy sounds of Traibus's breath as the giant also prepared to enter the silence.

But as Methuselah relaxed, the sound of the giant's breathing faded away. The noise of the parrot ceased for him, and the old man felt his body become completely at peace. He inhaled the moist air with hearty, deep breaths and began to clear his mind of all distractions. He gradually lost consciousness, unaware of the sensations in his body. No longer did he feel the touch of the garment against his skin, or the hardness of the ground beneath him. He thought only of the One.

With eyes closed, he began to see a tiny ball of light. It was bright and demanded his attention. At first, it appeared as a tiny speck of fire surrounded by a vast darkness, but as he watched, it moved closer until it filled his entire range of vision, even as his mind sought no other thought than the One. Almost immediately, a pleasant shiver shot up his spine with a single wave of energy. Though he was not conscious of the sensation or of the fact that his forehead had begun to grow warm, his hands began to pulsate, gently, and for a few fleeting moments every cell in his body seemed to glow.

Gradually, Methuselah saw, with his mind, a brilliant light surround him; with it came the realization that he had crossed over. The color increased in intensity, just as his vision began to focus, and—through closed eyes—he began to see the incandescent glow of the river's edge. The beautiful hues of soft pink and glimmering violet engulfed the petals of flowers along the bank. He was overcome with emotion by the sight of light blue vapors that swam just above the river in gentle whirlpools of motion. He could see and feel the sparkling, white light that surrounded everything. Thick stalks of grass seemed alive with a steady flow of green that he saw through fibrous veins. The upper branches of knotted trees were afire with the luminous glow of the vibrant light. Even the clouds appeared bright, with yellows and reds intertwining and dancing along the vapors' edge. Methuselah was so overtaken by the beauty of nature that a long period passed before his gaze came to rest upon the gold: three enormous stacks of coins, nearly as tall as Methuselah.

The gold was stacked along the embankment, towering over the river, just as his father had hidden it. Three mounds had been heaped next to each other, so that the coins of one pile mixed with those from the next. In addition, a thousand coins lay scattered over the ground, as if Enoch had not had time to place them in one of the piles. The gold was emblazoned with color due to the pureness of light that fell from the clouds. At certain angles the coins appeared transparent, though the old man knew transparency would disappear once he retrieved the gold back into consciousness. As much as he wanted to remain and observe all that surrounded him, it was time to begin.

With one thought, he felt himself stand (though his physical body remained behind). The feeling never ceased to amaze him, and he turned to look at his seated self: Upon the moist earth was the body of an old man deep in silence. The man wore his garments and had the same gray hair. The figure's eyes were lined with tiny wrinkles, just as his own. Methuselah looked down at his own transparent self and then turned to see the giant. Traibus was still except for the huge expansion of his chest as he breathed in deeply. The giant was in the quiet of the silence.

The old man turned his gaze and began roaming along the colorful embankment. One at a time, he bent over and picked up coins and placed them into the cupped palm of his left hand. He wondered how many coins to take to Shinar; generally he took twenty, enough for a month. But with Traibus working with him, he might need more. Besides, in the company of a giant, he needn't fear the bandits or scavengers who roamed the plains.

He began to pick up the coins lying on the farthest edge, where knotted trees towered upward to the vapor. The flashing light of almond-shaped leaves filled the sky, as did the song of the birds that flocked to the branches above him. He went on about his chore, smiling at the sound of the bird's music, and picked up a coin or two scattered in the grass before moving to the next spot.

Suddenly, the sound of something other than the birds came to his ears. He stood completely still and listened. The sound grew stronger and louder, though Methuselah had no idea what it was. Out of the corner of his eyes, he looked at Traibus but the giant remained in silence. In stillness, he listened and then realized he heard the sound of splashing water; something was swimming toward the shore.

He was so completely startled that he forgot his own transparency. With extreme care he tiptoed toward the heaping piles of gold and squatted down so that he would be concealed. He turned to see if Traibus remained immobile and saw his own form sitting next to the giant. The sight caused him to shake his head in disgust at his own foolishness. After all, no one could see him.

Methuselah set the coins down, walked around the great piles of gold, and stood on the river's edge. When the sound began again, he turned in the direction of the splashing. To his right, coming up the river, he saw an enormous fish swimming swiftly toward him. Although he couldn't determine what type of creature it was, its large tail broke the surface of the water and glistened with sparkling beads of moisture. When the tail submerged, another splash echoed to the old man's place on the bank. He stared down into the depths of the river and waited. He could barely see the brilliant flash of scales as light touched the creature's shimmering form. The tail crashed to the surface once more before the fish swam alongside where the old man stood.

Methuselah dropped to his knees and peered into the river for a better look. He began to wonder if a small whale had somehow made its way up the tributary, for he had never seen such a tail. The underwater figure flickered past once more. He had almost decided it was a whale when the creature—with one quick movement—rose to the surface and shot its head out of the water. Methuselah gasped and almost fell backward. The face he looked upon was that of a golden-haired woman.

He couldn't believe it. His eyes opened with astonishment at the figure of a woman who seemed to stare back at him. Only her head and neck, and the top of her shoulders were out of the water and instead of the scales he had expected, he saw only the whiteness of soft flesh. Her long, glistening hair was matted down against the sides of her face, though the tips of her curls floated carelessly upon the surface of the water. Her eyes were green, while her moist lips were the lightest shade of pink. Her eyebrows were thin and the same yellow-gold as her hair. She was beautiful.

Methuselah was speechless. He found himself staring into the depths of the river, watching the flashing scales of the woman's tail beneath the water. The woman brought her arms to the surface; they were the same softness as her face and neck. He thought it extremely strange that the woman seemed to be looking right upon him as if she could see his transparent form. He leaned forward just as the woman smiled back at him.

"Are you a sage?" she asked, in a tone which was smooth and clear. The purity of her voice surprised him.

"How is it that you can see me?" Methuselah asked in astonishment. "I mean, how is it that you can speak?"

"I would imagine in the same manner as you," the woman said gently, "and I can see you as clearly as I see the gold upon the shoreline." She lifted a soft hand from the water and pointed. Great beads of water fell from her flesh, dropping back into the river as she moved her arm. "So, are you a sage?"

He continued to look into the water at the movement of the woman's tail. Though he had heard fables of such creatures in his boyhood, he had never actually seen one.

"Well, are you?" She became a little impatient.

"Though some have said so," he answered finally, "I make no claims. Why is it you ask?"

"Because you seem to possess two forms: one that is misty and speaks to me and the other sitting by that giant. You are either a wizard or a sage." She paused for another moment. "Why do you stare at me so?"

"Please forgive me." The old man waved his hand for emphasis and chuckled. "It is just that I have heard stories of gentle beings like yourself, though I believed them to be fables."

"A wise one such as yourself should know that many a fable has sprung from truth."

"It would appear so." He finally regained his composure. "What is it that you call yourself?"

"If you're asking my name, it is Sarafeee." Her lips moved carefully, as if it took a great deal of thought to speak. "But if you're asking what creatures like myself call our race, we are sirens."

"Yes, I have heard the name—siren, not Sarafeee," he added quickly.

"What are you doing in this place, sage?"

"I am Methuselah. I have traveled to this spot, with my friend, to gather coins. There are people who find themselves in great need."

"There are things worth far more than gold," she said gently. "It will pass away, but the eternal endures forever. Have your people not heard of the One?"

Methuselah was astonished. "You know of the One?" The woman nodded, as he continued. "This is wonderful, indeed! I only wish those I tend to had your faith."

"Why do they not?"

"Where I come from, many need food and drink merely to survive. They have no longing for an eternity that can do little to clothe aching bodies. Besides," the old man added, "the voice of the One has not been heard in a very, very long time."

Her eyes took on a fearful expression. "Have things changed so greatly since I walked upon the earth?"

He looked at her inquisitively. "Who are you really? You speak of rebirth and the One as though you are part of the faithful."

"I am as I appear, a simple siren." She became sad. "I believe your people would call me a Mixture."

"How do you know of the One?"

"Very well," she glanced at the water's surface before looking into the old man's eyes, "though you see me as a siren, it wasn't always so. Before this, I once lived upon the very continent of the faithful—as a priestess in the temple, though I traded it all for these shimmering scales." She looked sorrowfully at her own tail keeping her afloat.

"You remember your past?" Methuselah was fascinated.

"Not all of them but I do remember the last with much clarity." She seemed surprised. "Do you not remember yours?"

"Rarely," he said, smiling so she would know it didn't matter, "and never with completeness. To me, this has been a blessing, for I tend to live in the past. Were I to remember my soul's journey, I would spend little time in the here and now."

"You have yet to answer my question." Her eyes remained sad.

"What question is that?"

"Have things changed so much since I was upon the earth? There was never a lack in Poseidia."

Methuselah remained quiet. For a time, he looked upon the peaceful surroundings of the river and its banks. He heard the song of tiny birds and spotted the beautiful colors of the leaves. The rich smells of minerals rose from the water and soil. Beneath the purity of vapors, amid all these things, it seemed difficult to explain a place where there was lack.

"Even to myself," he finally began, "to think of a place where there is want seems only as a dream in the presence of such magnificence. Yet, I assure you, this place of neglect exists and I have heard that many throughout the earth now cry out in need. Even since the days of my own youth, things have changed greatly." He added with a softer voice, "And I do not know how to stop the transformation."

"If things are as you say, it would appear that the faithful have become idle in their work."

"This is my greatest fear," he replied, more to himself than the siren. He looked into the woman's eyes and couldn't help but sigh at her beauty; her hair was just beginning to dry in the morning's radiance. "You are so wise, Sarafeee. How did you come to be in this place?"

"If I were as wise as you imagine, Methuselah, I would never have taken on this form. I am as I appear because of my own desires. They alone caused my downfall."

"I do not understand." Methuselah was amused to find himself giving the same reply that Traibus had uttered more than a hundred times.

"My story is not difficult," she stated softly. "As I said, before this, I was a priestess in Poseidia. Often, when time allowed, I wandered from my duties, venturing among the alabaster columns, down marble steps to the gardens. Only there, near the peaceful serenity of flowering shrubs and the sweet smell of incense bulbs, could I find a moment to myself. It was of much concern to me that so many searched for something all of their lives and never actually found what they sought. Even among the faithful, there were many who lacked guidance and I often doubted my ability to assist them."

"Frequently, I strolled to the gardens and sat upon the edge of the inlaid tiles which surrounded the ponds. For hours, I observed the clear pools and the bright water lilies that floated on the water's surface. Then, I'd cup my palm and dip my hand into the cool brilliance of the water, finding the serenity I had lost in the temple. I watched the brightly colored fish of orange and glimmering gold as they swam beneath the pond's surface, and more than anything I longed to feel as peaceful as they appeared."

"Much of my life was spent in this fantasy. I reveled in watching their gleaming bodies dart gracefully about the pools, swimming easily beneath the lilies, as if they could experience a total engulfment that the flowers only dreamed of. To be in the water was to be completely at peace—and this I began to believe without reservation." She stopped speaking and appeared as though she would cry."

"I misunderstood what was happening in the garden" Sarafeee continued. "While I was feeling at peace and serene, it was due to the presence of the One, not because of the gracefulness of the underwater creatures. Though I possess their beauty, the presence of the One can be but a memory in this form."

Methuselah waved his hand aside for her to know she needn't continue. "Then you have learned a valuable lesson," he said with encouragement.

"It is not one I will easily forget," she said wistfully. "But I have learned something else as well. A time must come when the children of the One are no longer able to fulfill their every desire. Unless something is done to prevent us from incarnating in various forms, it is my fear that we shall never escape from the earth. In human vessels, we have a chance, but without them we are lost."

"I have come to believe," Methuselah said softly, as he reached out and touched her chin, "it is our destiny to succeed."

She nodded before glancing toward the great stacks of coins, and then she smiled. The sadness left her eyes, and she looked toward the old man with the same joyfulness he had first seen.

"There is another lesson I have learned from this," she said playfully. "All that glitters is not gold."

And, at that very moment, Traibus opened his eyes to the world of transparency. He had made the crossing, and his transparent jaw fell open in amazement. Not only could he see the rich clear colors around them and the enormous heaps of gold, but he saw the invisible form of Methuselah sitting on the edge of the river's bank—and a siren surrounded by a vivid, white light.

It was the first time Traibus saw the pure light of Creation, and it was something that he would never ever forget.

475 Years Later
(125 years before the Flood)

Menahem walked peacefully in the solitude of the early morning hours, contemplating the beauty of his surroundings and relaxing in the tranquility of his own thoughts. The pale white weave of his robe floated effortlessly over the mineral-rich soil that pressed easily beneath his sandals. The moistness of daybreak felt damp and cool as he journeyed along the trail leading even further into the heart of the familiar forest. Only the sounds of treetop birds and the occasional swish of his garments against the greenery broke the stillness of morning. Everywhere, tall trunks of white oak towered upward so that the overhead entanglement of branches and leaves blocked the sight of most of the vapor-laden sky. Creeping vines, rich with wild berries, covered the lower girths of many of the oaks. Tiny, hair-like limbs of creeping vine encircled even the stalks of the scattered yellow-seed flowers.

The smells of moist plants and wet earth bombarded him and his nostrils quivered at the fertile scents rising from the earth. Up ahead, a movement through the brush revealed a large brown buck, crowned with five-pronged antlers on either side as it jumped gracefully across the trail before running in the direction of the freshwater lake. He briefly pondered the possibility of spending some time at the lake himself but he was on the verge of a discovery with Tubal-cain, and his cousin was not known for patience.

The men had become more like brothers than distant cousins whose two families continued to feel uncomfortable around each other. Even all of Methuselah's wisdom could do little to remove the barrier which Lemech and Menahem's own father, Lamech, had built between themselves. As it stood, Menahem was completely accepted on Tubal-cain's side of the family and the reverse was certainly true.

He continued moving eastward, taking time to watch the splendor of lush greenery. His large, blue eyes looked out at the world with compassion. It was rare for him to find fault with anyone. He seemed to possess a serenity that caused even the most arrogant to be humbled by his presence. To be sure, there were times when Menahem wondered how long it would be before Shinar (already swelling at its borders) would begin to take part of the forest as its own. Thousands of trees had been felled with stone axes and charcoal fires to meet an ever-growing population. The magnitude of the masses had caused even Methuselah and Traibus to move back to the safety of the forest—spending their days wandering the city streets, but the city could no longer guarantee safety at nightfall.

With the thought of his grandfather, Menahem became conscious of the cool object dangling from the chain about his neck. To this day, he possessed the golden coin, wearing it always for it reminded him of his grandfather. And Menahem's assumption that the gold piece was one of a kind made it all the more meaningful.

When he approached the clearing and the trees on either side of the trail began to thin, he breathed in the sweet scent of lavender and spotted the cottage. The home of Lemech, the hunter, remained standing as it had for centuries, but the clearing had been greatly expanded to make room for another cottage, a barn, a few stretches of fence posts, and two clay ovens in the shape of large mounds. A dozen trees had been cut down in order to make room for their increasing numbers. Tubal-cain was married, though his wife, Mariah, remained barren, and Lemech, himself, had fathered three additional children. Yet, somehow, the beauty of the soft grass, purple buds, and flowering shrubs had yet to be affected. The ancient stump, Tubal-cain's youthful place of quiet contemplation, had never decayed; instead, it had grown hard as stone and marked the exact center of the clearing in front of the cottages.

Menahem walked past the stump and looked about for signs of Tubal-cain or any member of the family. The immense doors of the barn stood wide open. Three milk cows busily crunched morning blades of grass, indifferent to his presence. Only the sounds of forest creatures and the noise of chewed cud broke the silence.

He swung around to look at the cottages: Tubal-cain's on the left, Lemech's expanded home on the right. Lemech's was larger, with stone walls supporting chimneys on the north and smooth-planed logs for siding surrounding some of the stone. The most striking difference between the two, however, was the clinging vines that virtually covered Lemech's place—save for the doorway and spaces between the windows. As he stood admiring the beauty of the leafy vines, a sharp female voice broke the morning's stillness.

"Well, it's nice to see someone decided to get up when they

were supposed to!" Zillah said irritably. She scurried between the cottages, coming from the well, carrying a large pottery bucket in front of her. She used both hands, for the bucket was heavy. Tiny spurts of water splashed over either side of the rim as she waddled slowly toward him.

He walked to her, reaching down to take the container from her hands, "Let me help you, Zillah," he said gently.

"Absolutely not," she insisted. "Why, the day I can't fetch water from the well will be my last! I may look like an old woman to you but in this clearing I still do the work of ten!" The lines around her thin red lips deepened as she spoke, and she appeared completely unaware that a good deal of water had splashed out onto her apron. Her long dress fell down about the enormous curves of her frame. "I suppose you need something to eat?"

"No thank you, Zillah. Mother had quite a meal prepared this morning; she invited me to their table. I think she worries I don't get enough on my own." Menahem was smiling.

"Sure she does," the old woman said, finally lowering the bucket to the ground. "You spend so much time with that old giant and your grandfather, how could you? I'd worry about you, too, if you were my son."

"There's no need to worry," he said, reaching out and touched her on the shoulder. "I'm a grown man now."

"That's right, you are," the old woman said, interrupting him, "and it just doesn't make sense why you haven't found a wife by this time, Menahem. You're getting to be an old man, and you'd better find a woman while one will still have you." She paused and then continued, "You've always been something to look at. Lord knows your mother and I've discussed it often enough but your looks won't last forever."

Menahem smiled, squeezing her shoulder with his smooth

palm. "It seems to me we've talked about this often enough. You know how I feel."

"I'm telling you, it just won't do." She shook her head back and forth. "You were meant to have children."

"Zillah, I just don't think a woman would want to adjust to the way I live." His face was radiant with the light as he spoke. "Besides, even if a woman would have me, she would have to come second to my love for the One. It wouldn't be fair to ask anyone to live like that."

"You're right. It wouldn't be fair," Zillah said quickly, "but it happens all the time. You know how I suffered for years, being second in my own husband's eyes and Menahem, I was second to a woman, not a god. It was not easy living like that, but you know how I struggled to make it work. For years, I tried to befriend Adah and you know how well the two of us get along now! We're the best of friends. Adah is like a sister to me, and between us, we've birthed four children for Lemech: I have Tubal-cain and my darling Naamah, and Adah has two fine sons, Jabal and Jubal, but in our hearts we love each of Lemech's children as our own."

"So you see, Menahem," Zillah added, "although I was second in my own home, I overcame the position thrust upon me, not by pity, but by hard work. In my opinion, if you took a wife, she could do the same."

"This I cannot believe," Menahem said softly as he finally lowered his hand to his side, "for the Law is quite clear: Thou shalt love the Lord God with all thine heart."

"I know what the Law states," Zillah said quickly, "but can't you find love for your God and another as well? How can someone so wise in some things be so foolish in others? If you love only the One and cannot find love enough in your heart to share with another, your love must be small indeed."

"Zillah, I don't think you understand what I'm trying to say."

"I know what you're saying. My ears still hear as well as any but you don't appreciate what I'm telling you. Even Methuselah, with his knowledge of the ways of the Law, found love for another. He wed Anna, your grandmother, and without their union you wouldn't be here."

Menahem was silent. His bushy, white eyebrows moved closer together as he watched the woman intensely. For a moment, he wondered if she even understood the full magnitude of her statement. For the first time, he suddenly realized that by not becoming a father he might affect generations yet unborn. The thought made him want to seek guidance: He had to be certain his decision to remain alone was correct.

"Who would have me, anyway, at this age in my life?" Menahem asked aloud and then wished he had remained silent.

Zillah, believing she had won, clasped her hands together in joy. "There are two I know of," she said softly, looking around to make certain no one else was listening. "Your mother has told me of a girl who seeks your company. I, myself, have seen her on two occasions and thought her quite plain, but she has shown an interest in you and is, therefore, suitable."

"Who do you speak of?" He couldn't help but be amused by their conversation. "I know of no such woman."

"You wouldn't know a woman was after you unless she came right out and said it," Zillah said disgustedly. "Sometimes your lack of knowledge amazes me! I'm talking about Waila, daughter of Raki'el."

Menahem smiled and shook his head in disagreement. "We are but friends and have been for many years. Her father is a clothier, and I see him when there's the need. Besides, she is not so plain as you would have me believe." His eyes opened wide to peer at her.

"I can see beauty, even if it's not my desire to possess it."

"Well, I know some might find her attractive," she said, trying to dismiss him, "but I don't see it. Her nose is so tiny and she appears too frail, I don't know what a man would see in her. Let's just say she has a desire for you."

"And the other who has this desire for me?" he asked, containing his amusement.

"She is a beauty," Zillah said wistfully, "and why she hasn't been betrothed before this time—well, I just can't imagine. She is gorgeous, with hair that sparkles beneath the illuminated sky. She is small in stature but mighty in worth. Her skin is soft and supple and her voice that of an angel. I just can't believe she is still without a husband."

"Who is this beauty you speak of? I have never seen her."

"Don't be a fool, Menahem. Who else could it be? I'm talking about Naamah."

There was a noticeable length of silence as he stared in disbelief. "Sister of Tubal-cain? Your daughter?"

"Certainly my daughter," she said, as her fists clamped down hard on her waist. "There is none other as worthy as she seeking your attention. Though I don't mind saying, I've often wondered why she's drawn to you. You barely pay her any attention at all."

Menahem shook his head slowly. "Although she is the sister of my best friend, I don't even know her."

"It's no wonder," Zillah said, just as she spotted Tubal-cain coming out of his cottage toward them. "You haven't given her the encouragement to become acquainted."

Both stopped speaking and waited for the robust figure of Tubal-cain to arrive. Zillah bent over to grasp the pail, deciding it was best to remain cautious with her words in front of her son.

"So what are you two arguing about this time?" His hand habitually pulled the thick, brown hair back behind his ears. "Let me guess, Mother. You wanted to know why he isn't married?"

"Just never mind!" she said sharply. "Had you risen with the light of day you could have been present for the conversation. I've got work to do." She turned with her bucket and headed in the direction of the larger cottage. Neither of the two men spoke until after she had entered the house.

"I'm sorry I'm late," Tubal-cain apologized. "Had I been here, Mother might have left you alone."

"Do not worry, my friend, she merely tries to help. I think she is concerned for my future."

"And I think her concern is that she may not get her way with you." Tubal-cain placed his hand on Menahem's shoulder and led him toward the kilns.

The earthen structures rose nearly four cubits above the moist soil of the clearing. Both were constructed of large bricks and covered with clay. Each mound had three openings on the side, from top to bottom, the largest being in the center. Fires were lit in the uppermost and ground-level chambers. The pottery was placed in the center to be fired. Thick plates of squared crockery covered the oven doors whenever the kilns were ignited.

Between the kilns, a long oak table standing two cubits high was covered with various shapes and sizes of pottery bowls, wooden spoons, stirring rods, and glazed ceramics. The work-table was a mess. Fine grains of sand and different mixtures of soil and minerals had been collected in clay bowls and cups, and each had been scattered all over the top. However, the bowls were marked with symbols designating soil type and its location in the forest.

With an open palm, Menahem brushed some of the loose sand off the tabletop, letting it sprinkle to the ground. Many, many times he had mentioned the importance of keeping the area clean but apparently Tubal-cain thought it unimportant. Besides, his cousin knew the contents and whereabouts of every container (or so he said) and was always careful when mixing ingredients or while working at the kilns.

Beneath the table was stacked chopped wood that had been cut with one of their stone axes. Large blocks of coal had been gathered as well and placed next to the logs, as the two had discovered that coal burned a hotter fire than wood. Though they weren't yet certain what temperature the kilns needed to be, they hoped to find a molten material that cooled to a substance tougher than stone, fired clay, or even the hard wood of the forest. Results that hadn't quite worked were simply thrown in a heap behind one of the kilns.

Tubal-cain was first to reach the ovens. The air around the base of the structure remained quite warm. He knew from past experience that embers would still be burning amid the ashes. He turned to Menahem, appearing hopeful. "Do you think we should look?"

"Well, if it hasn't happened by now, we've got the wrong substance. Go ahead and open it."

Tubal-cain nodded and turned to the oven. He reached to the table and lifted a long pair of wooden forceps. The instrument had been constructed of white oak, which became sturdy, compact, and waterproof as the sap dried away. He leaned over the oven and peered inside as hot wisps of air rose past his face. With the tool, he carefully lifted a large ceramic bowl and in one swift movement withdrew the container and set it on the table.

"Well?" Menahem asked excitedly as he hurried to the table to glance between the bowl and Tubal-cain's eyes. He didn't require a response, however, for as the forceps were removed from the container, the liquid's surface rippled like water. "No, it's not hardening."

"Perhaps it needs a chance to cool?"

"It's cool enough for solidification," Menahem said with disappointment. "Look at it." He shook the rim of the bowl, causing another slight wave. "It has the appearance of black mud."

Tubal-cain's eyes scanned the table as if looking for something they had inadvertently omitted. His glance rested momentarily on a few of the soil samples before shaking his head in disgust. "I just don't know," he said finally. "Do you have any suggestions?"

"We seem to be going backward instead of forward; a few of the others have been better."

"But nothing has been as hard as wood, or even close to it. The few successes we've had were as brittle as porcelain."

"I'm positive we will find it."

"I'm not so sure anymore. Maybe my brothers are right."

Menahem was startled and jerked his eyes from the table. "What have they said?"

"Only that we should stick to carpentry. As least we can build something of value; there's no market in Shinar for a bowl of black tar. If someone's looking for pitch or tar, they can find plenty in Baghdad or Id."

"We're not in the tar business!" Menahem said reassuringly. "We're into something much more important, no matter what Jabal and Jubal have come to believe."

"You're right." Tubal-cain contemplated his brothers for a moment. "Besides, what can a tentmaker and a musician know about soil and minerals anyway?"

Menahem simply shook his head and watched Tubal-cain sort through the numerous containers in order to formulate their next attempt. Tubal-cain reached out for a bowl on his left and then another stacked beneath a pile of containers. He looked at a grainy ore for a moment, as if to decide whether or not to use it, and then moved on to the next container of red clay. He appeared so immersed in what he was doing that Menahem was surprised to hear him speak.

"So what was mother trying to convince you of this morning?" Tubal-cain asked, without lifting his eyes from the table.

"Still the same, only now she claims to have found two women who seek my attention."

"Oh really," Tubal-cain said, with enough amusement to bring his eyes up from his work. "Who are they?"

"You've met Waila, from the settlement?" Menahem replied, as Tubal-cain nodded in agreement. "The other is your sister."

Tubal-cain dropped his container, causing great quantities of the minerals to scatter as the bowl hit the tabletop. His grin turned to a chuckle and then to a laugh from the depths of his belly. His palm slapped the wood workstation as tears formed in his eyes; he couldn't seem to help himself. The harder he laughed, the more confused Menahem became.

"Just what is it that humors you?" Menahem asked finally. "Is it the thought that Naamah could find love for me or that I might find love for her?"

For a moment, Tubal-cain was able to stop, though his cheeks streaked with moisture. He opened his mouth to speak, but his smile returned, followed by more snickering. When Menahem could stand it no longer, he reached out and touched his cousin's muscular arm. Immediately the laughter ceased, though the foolish grin remained in place.

"Now can you speak?"

"I just tried to picture in my mind you and my sister as husband and wife."

"And?"

"My dear cousin," Tubal-cain spoke softly lest anyone should hear, "have you not noticed something similar between Zillah and Naamah? They speak the same; they think the same; their actions are alike. Sometimes they even walk in the same manner. Beloved Menahem, it is as though my mother raised a daughter to be exactly like herself. This is the reason Naamah has yet to find a husband."

Menahem grew silent.

Nine days later they found it, although little did they realize the impact their discovery would have upon the rest of the world. As the days followed their first successes, the bowls of clay and soil samples that had proven useless were discarded. Large barrels were constructed to provide storage for the ores that Tubal-cain had collected on the eastern edge of the forest. In time, the two found that by increasing the circulation of air within the kilns and raising the temperature and adding mineral grains, the substance's strength and hardness could be varied. They called the discovery "iron" because it could be hammered into various shapes and forms.

Only gradually did they see the diverse uses to which the new material of fused ore could be put. From the first, they had wanted to find something to create more durable tools. Iron picks and hammers of the metal substance replaced those which had been made of stone; trowels and other hand tools were fashioned from the metal instead of from hard oak. To their delight, they then found that metal hammers could drive a wooden peg with greater accuracy than their stone counterparts. Iron seldom splintered like oak, nor was it prone to cracks and fissures like rock.

Tubal-cain worked with pouring molten iron into molds in order to create implements of similar size and shape. They tried molds of polished wood and stone before finally settling upon molds of hard iron. The molten ore could be cooled sufficiently before pouring so that the molds were not damaged. After further cooling, the implements were hammered into the desired final form. For weeks, Tubal-cain tried to make a set of forks, spoons, and knives which could replace the wooden utensils Zillah had used all her life; more than once, he had tasted oak splinters mixed with his meal and he believed iron would remedy the situation.

Because their burns were numerous, in the beginning Menahem collected a great deal of aloe. Over time, however, they became used to working with the liquid ore, the molds, and the new iron forceps, which conducted heat throughout their length. Mariah made them mittens and thick woolen pads to protect their hands.

Finally, Lemech's other sons began to take an interest in their work. Jabal asked Tubal-cain if it might be possible to make an iron needle—the thick leathers he worked with often caused oak implements to split when he threaded two pieces of hide together. Several days later, Tubal-cain formed one to Jabal's liking by hammering a tiny shaft of cooling iron into the proper shape and while the thin sliver of iron was still malleable, Menahem struck a tiny hole in its head for the twine. Carefully, the hole was lengthened in order to accommodate the heavy thread Jabal would be using. When completed, Tubal-cain held the long pin before his brother's eyes while Menahem watched proudly. Jabal took the needle and fingered it for a long while before passing it on to Jubal for his own approval.

"It is remarkable," Jabal said excitedly. "How many days would it take to fashion a dozen such as these?"

"Once we have done it successfully, it requires little time at all." Tubal-cain looked from his partner to his brothers. "The question is how much would you be willing to pay for twelve more?"

"I see two carpenters have become businessmen," Jubal joked aloud.

Jabal thought for a moment and then answered: "We will dig you twelve barrels of ore, one for each of the tools. Together my younger brother and I may sew many tents with the speed it once took to do one. These we will sell in Shinar to the plains people. The next time we do business, however," he added slyly, "we will pay with shekels and you will dig your own ore."

Menahem placed his palms on the worktable and leaned forward to speak. "And with your payment of shekels, we shall hire a boy to dig."

The four shook hands, each pleased with the terms that had been transacted. Jubal and Jabal imagined the many seamstresses they could hire and the many tents they could make, while Menahem and Tubal-cain rejoiced in their first sale: twelve needles for barter payment. Later that same day while Menahem and Tubal-cain were still working at the kilns, the two saw Traibus, the giant, and Methuselah approaching. Between the robed figures walked a beautiful woman carrying a small, dark-haired child. The sadness of loss remained on the woman's face, for it had been but three days since she had been found in the most evil part of the forest.

"Welcome!" Tubal-cain extended his hand upwards to shake Traibus's and then turned to welcome Methuselah. "It's been a while since you've been here."

"Too long, Tubal-cain." Traibus was the first to speak. "It's here I can rest."

Methuselah was pleased to see Lapeth eyeing the appearance of his grown grandson. She looked Menahem over carefully (for she had never seen hair so white or eyes as blue as his). Menahem merely watched her and smiled in return. Her gaze turned to Tubal-cain, whose strong build and olive complexion reminded her of Basil and she turned away lest her tears return.

"I have found a daughter and a grandchild," Methuselah said proudly, touching Lapeth on the arm, "and I have brought them to meet the rest of my children."

The tiny Rezepatha watched, wide-eyed, as the adults met each other. The infant felt especially drawn to Menahem. Only when the cows began to grow restless and bellow for fresh hay did her attention move elsewhere.

Shortly, the remainder of Lemech's family ventured from their cottages to see the visitors. Lapeth's beauty and perfection awed both Jabal and Jubal. The soft-spoken Mariah embraced the woman and was joyful at the thought of having a sister. Finally, Adah appeared in the doorway of the cottage, while old Lemech clung tightly to her arm. The two moved slowly toward the others. Adah was much older than Lapeth but remained regal. Her hair no longer hung loose but had been fastened at the back of her head.

Lemech did not look well. Though the man was younger than Methuselah, his appearance caused him to look wary and much older than the mystic. No longer did he walk in the long strides of his youth; his back seemed weighed down with age, and the muscles and veins of his arms had long begun to sag. Even his eyelids were dark and recessed, accentuating his blindness.

"Welcome my friends," the old hunter said softly, for even the gruffness of his youth was gone.

Methuselah placed the gentle hand of his new daughter into that of Lemech's just as Zillah glared through the doorway of the cottage. The brightly-dressed woman turned and hollered back into the house, loud enough for all to hear: "My god, Naamah, you're never going to believe this," she said excitedly, "come here!"

A few moments later, her daughter stuck her head through the open door and peered at the large gathering in their clearing. For the first time, Menahem noticed that, although Naamah was attractive, it did appear possible that her features might one day grow into those of her mother's. Already she possessed the same reddened lips. Zillah whispered a few instructions into her daughter's ear and approached the assembly just as Naamah disappeared back into the cottage.

"A fine thing it is, Methuselah, to arrive without notice," she said loudly. "I suppose you're all hungry." Her gaze landed upon Lapeth and Zillah appeared relieved to see that the woman had a child.

"We would be pleased to eat from your table," Methuselah replied, as he moved forward to take the woman's hands.

"I thought so." She paused long enough to acknowledge Traibus and to meet the dark-haired woman and baby. "Well, it appears as though I've got a great deal to do if I'm expected to feed everyone."

Both Adah and Lapeth offered their services, but Zillah wouldn't hear of it. She told Lapeth her stay in the clearing would be as a guest, and to Adah she said pleasantly, "My sister, would you entertain our friends while Naamah and I make preparations?"

Adah nodded and Zillah turned toward the cottage, "I can't

promise much," the older woman said with her back to them, "but I'll try to make do with boiled potatoes and whatever else I can throw together."

Tubal-cain waited until Zillah had entered the cottage before turning to Lapeth. "Mother is really very pleased to meet you."

As the days turned into weeks and the weeks gave way to each other, their discovery of iron spread throughout the plains. Merchants came to the clearing to buy products: tools, harnesses, pins, utensils, hoes, spikes, forceps, and molds. Often the tradesmen went away with more than iron implements; they had watched Tubal-cain and Menahem at work. Others began to melt their own ore (though much of it lacked the quality of that from Lemech's clearing, but still it was iron and it had countless uses).

Candlemakers in Shinar began using iron molds, for their wares could be made faster than by dipping. Molds of iron were more versatile and of better quality than those of wood, ceramic, or stone; craftsmen and artisans began using the products immediately. Those who dealt in woodwork began using metal nails in addition to their wooden pegs. Those who dealt in livestock trade made harnesses, and tools of every possible description were fashioned to speed up the work of the fields.

It was a long while, however, before Menahem or Tubal-cain realized the negative consequences of their discovery. Swords and lances could be made of higher quality for even greater marksmanship, and sharper knives were fashioned so that hidesmen could skin wild animals faster and in greater numbers, causing carcasses to lie all too numerous in parts of the forest for only leather and bone were of any use. Vegetables, vines, grains, and fruit were so bountiful that only the sick in mind would even consider eating animal flesh. As a result, it was not long before the stench of rotting meat filled the air in the vilest parts of the forest, as well as in the darkest alleyways of Shinar.

Since tools had been improved for the fields, Malock raised the quotas expected of each slave. Soon the fieldworkers were held captive by metal chains instead of the ropes that had been used for centuries—and iron was heavier than rope.

New weapons and tools were fashioned faster than most could keep track. For this reason, Menahem and Tubal-cain long remained ignorant of the abuses Mixtures were finding for iron. Two tools did come to their immediate attention, however, for the discovery had ramifications throughout the entire forest. The ax was improved and the saw was invented; trees which had grown for ages were felled with little time or labor. Malock expanded his domain throughout much of the area and Shinar began to claim additional land as its own.

As time passed, the clearings of Lamech, the carpenter, and Lemech, the hunter, grew more threatened. Yet, for many months, the two partners remained oblivious to all the dangers that had come as a result of their discovery. In fact, they started working with other materials and ores so that Tubal-cain and Menahem soon became known for quality workmanship in both iron and brass.

Menahem was alone, sitting cross-legged on the moist earth next to the freshwater lake. His eyes were closed in silence, and his spine remained straight and firm. His palms were placed downward on his knees, while his legs were folded in the same position he had been shown by Methuselah. He was by himself, next to the edge of the water in tranquil contemplation. Many weeks had passed since his vow to follow the five-pointed buck to this place of natural beauty but only recently had he found the time. Their work at the kilns had detracted a great deal from the quiet life he was used to but today he needed more than anything a time for solitude. So he remained still, alone with the quiet, oblivious to his surroundings and for the first time in a long while at complete peace.

All around, the splendor of creation remained unspoiled; the frenzied growth of Shinar and the fields had yet to impact anything near the large, sparkling lake. The dark blue waters were surrounded on three sides by mighty oak and pine and lay hidden from all but the most experienced backwoods traveler and the countless creatures of the forest—all gentle and trusting of the white-haired man.

Huge butterflies with silken wingspans almost a cubit in width and colored orange and red and gold, fluttered carelessly above the yellow flowers. Large petaled plants grew abundantly along the shoreline with thick stalks that shot up from the wet earth and roots that dug down deep for grounding. Small mice ran through the wild grass not bothered by the wide-eyed frogs which stared upward at the yellow petals and at the butterflies and the tiny insects they feasted upon.

The lake itself was filled with healthy fish whose speckled bodies often became food for the large brown bears of the denser forest. They waded skillfully through shallower parts of the clear water, standing on hind legs as if it were as natural for them as for the humans and some of the Mixtures. Several families of ducks, many of cream yellow and some of darker brown, floated effortlessly on the lake's surface. They swam together in small groups, and in harmony, regardless of their feathered appearance.

In the tallest branches of the oaks soaring above the lake's edge settled the swallows that, like the doves on lower branches, left the nest only in search of food. The forest provided its bounty abundantly, with nuts and berries and vines and melons, and gnats and worms, which feasted continuously upon the fallen plenty of overripe fruit and untouched seeds from the flowers and pines.

Herds of elk and deer lived in close proximity to each other and to the water's shore, for neither species had learned to be sickened by the smell of the other. Often, small numbers of both would graze side by side upon wild grasses or the lower branches and bark of the trees. Squirrels chattered back and forth above their claimed territories of twigs and nuts.

For centuries the lake had been the meeting place of mid-sized and smaller creatures. It was a few days' journey to the southeast, in the most tropical part of the forest, that the scattered watering holes of the larger animals lay hidden amid jungle vines and deep pits of mud. Menahem had heard stories from Traibus and his grandfather of large elephants and rhinos that peacefully ate plants and enormous leaves, while warthogs scurried angrily about and hippos lay immersed beneath dark waters. Giraffes and monkeys stuck their curious heads into the most unusual heights, while disturbed birds squawked angrily at the intrusion. There, large cats stalked the gazelle, much as the smaller cats of Shinar crept upon unknowing rodents. Although Menahem had never seen some of these animals, they had been so carefully described to him by Traibus that he was certain he could recognize even the most wild simply by sight.

Menahem's eyelids flickered as the rate of his breathing increased and the sounds of the lake creatures flooded his ears. In his final moments of quiet, he sent out prayers for those in the city and in the fields who were without hope. The frantic splashes of a flock of geese taking flight from the water's surface finally caused his eyes to open in complete consciousness. Quietly, he spoke the last few lines of the psalmist's song and rose to his feet, brushing off a few grains of the moist soil from his dangling robe. He wanted a little more time to himself, taking a peaceful walk around the lake before returning to the kilns.

He walked as best he could through the tall grasses that often rose to his knees. A few female deer watched him cautiously as he neared their young but they returned to foraging after recognizing his twinkling blue eyes and the bouncing white tufts of his hair. Menahem merely nodded to the herd as he passed, glancing at the fragile legs and twitching ears of the young. He wondered if any of the creatures of the forest sensed how much he loved being near. His eyes turned to the lake and the smoothness of the water. Suddenly, he stopped in place amid the close-cropped blades of greenery, munched low by the herds, and savored the shimmering reflection dancing atop the water's flat surface. The dense clouds of the heavens shone back at themselves from the clear water. No ducks swam nearby, so the reflection lacked any disturbance or tiny wave, and the reflection of the clouds thrown back by the water was perfect even to the smallest wisp of detail.

Menahem looked first to the sky and the denseness of the vapors and then lowered his gaze to the same scene reflected by the light of the clouds. He became engulfed by the serene picture and wondered how he had missed seeing it before: this sparkling spectacle of the sky's beauty. So moved was he that the sight began a stirring at the base of his spine and Menahem felt a gentle tingle of energy rise through his body. His eyes remained fixed on the water's surface, as if he were unable to look upon anything else. Still the energy rose and in the next instant he saw a flash of light and then darkness. The lake disappeared from his sight, though his eyes had not closed, and in its place was a vision so terrifying that Menahem's mouth fell open and his eyes stared in horror upon the scene:

There was an earthquake, though the ground upon which he stood did not move and the earth split open in a hundred crevasses spewing forth hundreds of millions of rivers of water and darkened mud that had been contained and pressurized for countless eons. In every land, splendid trees of centuries began to break apart like twigs, as the earth moaned in sharp pangs and the most solid foundations of stone trembled. Mountains crumbled and toppled down upon the seas, covering marble palaces and wooden hovels alike. The oceans roared and churned from themselves pillars of water that crashed into the gentle shorelines of every continent. The clouds of light became darkened with ash and red cinder, as towering peaks blew off mountainous ridges all along the lands of the East and molten lava and liquid pools of fire shot forth. Dew sizzled and burned into hot air moments before flames engulfed acres of tropical vines and rich vegetation. Animals ran for their lives, only to be swallowed up by fissures in the earth or to be buried beneath tumbling rocks. Birds in flight became vaporized in a single flash of flame from the heat of the sky, while lakes of cool waters began to boil, cooking huge fish into lifelessness.

And Menahem stared in horror as his eyes began to see that which no eyes had looked upon before: drops of water cascading from darkened heavens, falling upon ruptured hills and scorched plains. For the first time, the sky loosed its tears. Saturated soil, split open from the falling liquid, began to release pent-up rivers from underground caverns and water from every sea and ocean and lake and inlet began to rise and flood the already saturated earth.

But the worst part for Menahem was the shrieks: human cries rising above the noises of the earth; and even mouths which had known silence were able to scream. He saw sheets of water, a hundred cubits in height, crash down upon seaside ports, while Mixtures and people of every age tumbled into fluid graves. Small islands and whole peninsulas sank beneath rising tides and the sounds of death were choked beneath the twisting white caps and rolling breakers. Scenic valleys of lush vegetation turned to rivers and lakes before finally becoming one with the surging oceans.

Something was to befall the peoples of the earth; he knew it with certainty and he fell to his knees and sobbed, trembling with fear as the vision faded from his sight.

"This cannot be!" Menahem screamed. So loud was his cry that even the birds nesting above were disturbed into flight. His face became muddy with dirt mixed with tears, and his sorrow was anchored in the depths of his being. "Be merciful, oh One," he sobbed shakily. "It cannot be true!" And the moisture ran from his eyes until his tears were spent. He clenched his fists and shook his head in refusal until the muscles of his neck ached. Slowly, he rose to his knees and looked out over the calmness of the lake: His peaceful surroundings were in sight, yet the beauty of the forest moved him not.

Menahem clasped his hands together, wringing them toward the vapor-laden sky. "Where is Thy mercy, oh Lord above? Why must Thy children perish? Hear me! Hear me! Hear me!" he called out to the sounds of silence.

Suddenly, he felt a tingle race up his back and he shuddered for fear that the vision of death was about to return. Instead, a smoky haze began to form on the surface of the freshwater lake and rise, twirling and spinning, into a single glow of immense light. The circle grew in intensity and glimmered with yellow fire so bright that it outshone the illumination of the clouds. However, the blaze put off by the ball of fire remained cool and the brightness gradually condensed into the solitary form of a man standing two cubits above the waters of the lake.

The robed figure of white emitted from itself rays of golden light that shot out for a distance then vanished. Its visage was so bright that Menahem was forced to squint his eyes. The sight alarmed him and his head bowed in submission.

"My son," the glowing figure said. Though the figure did not speak, Menahem heard the voice register inside his head. "You have been heard."

"Who am I," Menahem's voice trembled, "that I should behold an angel of the Lord?"

"Fear not." Again, the words formed inside Menahem's mind, though his eyes remained focused on the moist earth. "You are blessed among all your generation. Fear not, and look upon me."

Slowly, Menahem raised his head to the glimmering light and saw the golden face of a man looking back at him from above the water. The purest light of yellow rays shone forth from the figure and illuminated the water's surface and much of the shoreline. A sense of calm began to replace the uneasiness and he watched in wonder as the sparkling figure lifted a shimmering arm and pointed down at the lake. "This that you saw need not be," the golden figure said without words. "There is still time and you are among the few remaining hopes."

"I don't understand," Menahem said humbly. "Will the One not show mercy upon His children?"

"It is not the One that His children should fear," the being said softly. "It is by their own desires that they bring these things about; their thoughts of contempt and hate and malice and greed do murder the very ground upon which they stand. It is they who attempt to kill the earth and not the Blessed One."

"Yet will even He, the Lord above, not intercede?" Menahem pleaded hopefully. "The power of Creation flows from His Being."

"It is written in the Laws of Old, those which came from your forefathers, that the One has given His children the mightiest gift of all. To each, He has given free will and He will not take away that which was bestowed in complete love. Even if the people of earth choose against Him, He will not come unwelcome into their hearts."

"Shall we be lost?" Menahem asked sadly.

"There yet remains hope," the shimmering figure answered reassuringly. "It is through you that the One shall share His love. You shall be the intercession of this darkness. You must go to your people and tell them to repent of their wickedness. The retribution you saw shall indeed come to pass—unless they quicken the Light of the One within their own beings. If the danger comes, it is of their own doing and not from the One who is naught but Love."

"These people, will they listen to the voice of a single man?"

"Your grandfather and others have not forgotten the Light," the voice said quickly. "With them, you shall find help. Go to Methuselah and tell him what you have seen. He will aid you."

"By what name shall I call the one who says these things? They will ask it of me."

"Tell all that inquire, I am but a child of the One. No more worthy am I than those who are in need. Upon this planet, I walked in flesh. I am he who was of the Law. I am he who was taken up by the One. I am he they called Enoch. I AM." The voice reverberated between Menahem's ears, and he was moved to bow low.

"You have done much to be of service, my son," the voice of Enoch continued. "You and another have given His children metal to ease the toil of their hands. You have walked with grace and have been humble. You shall deliver these people from their bondage. From this day forth, you shall be called 'Noah'—one who would save these people from themselves."

The voice stopped and Enoch and the light vanished. Noah was left alone on the shore of the freshwater lake.

Transitions
(125 years before the Flood)

Lemech was dying and even the healing arts of Methuselah could do little but ease his pain. He lay prostrate on the stuffed mattress with a thin blanket pulled up to his chest. The once-mighty trapper trembled uncontrollably, as breathing grew more difficult and the rasping sounds of his throat began to fill every corner of the dimly lit room.

The loose drapes of the solitary window were drawn together to keep out the light of day, for he claimed the brightness hurt eyes that could not see. His head was propped upon the feathered pillow so that Methuselah could administer a draft of boiled herbs; it seemed to relax the strained muscles of his throat and brought warmth to the aching numbness in his joints. Methuselah sat upon the corner of the bed and lowered the goblet to Lemech's parched lips. As the liquid was poured, the weakened hunter tried desperately to swallow. When the cup was pulled away, a few drops of the brew remained on Lemech's lips; Methuselah wiped them away gently with the thumb of his free hand.

Adah stood silently at the foot of the bed with her two sons at her side, and the three watched in inconsolable grief. All feared the time was near. Each had much they wanted to say, yet not one proved able to speak. To do so would only bring tears and voices would turn to sobs. No one cried for fear of alarming Lemech; instead, they remained still and waited.

Mariah and Lapeth had proven to be of the greatest service to Methuselah. Lapeth brought damp cloths to cool the rising temperature of Lemech's forehead. Mariah put together a meal of greens and berries, so that the others could stand at Lemech's bed side. All knew what they waited for, though none dared to speak of it. Even Rezepatha—following her mother's every movement—kept silent much of the day.

Zillah stood directly behind Methuselah, her hands clinging tightly to his shoulders. It was she who appeared most affected by all that was happening. Her sharp voice made no attempt to break the silence. Instead, she listened to the uneasy breathing of her husband and knew helplessly there was nothing more she could do. Both her children stood nearby, looking continuously from Zillah to their father. The last two weeks had been harder than any she could remember. She wished it was all over so that the waiting could pass, and the thought brought her much guilt. But even grief seemed easier to bear than the unspoken pain of watching him fade, knowing there was nothing to do.

Jabal and Jubal were going to leave, planning to move eastward beyond the Persian gulf. They claimed the time had come to seek their fortunes. Zillah called it foolishness but the two called it destiny. The forest was changing—no one could deny that—and they had no desire to remain in the land of their forefathers. They would journey to the east, with their knowledge of iron and tents and farming and make new lives for themselves. When the time was right, they would send for their family—this they had promised both Adah and Zillah. Then, once more together, they could grow prosperous in a new land of hope.

Jabal had heard stories of beautiful women in the east, learned in the art of weaving and stitchery; he would find a seamstress (and a wife). Jubal was excited over the thought of adventure and seeing for himself the mysteries of the east. He had often heard foreign merchants sing songs of their homeland and had a tremendous desire to see such beauty firsthand. The two would be leaving after the death of their father; they had given no further details. Adah had refused to discuss it while Lemech lay dying. She couldn't stand the thought of losing all that was hers.

So much had happened of late. As if Lemech's death and the departure of two of his sons weren't enough, they had Menahem's story to contend with. Zillah refused to believe it; the whole idea was preposterous. Though she loved him as a son, she feared he had lost his mind. It mattered little that Methuselah and Traibus seemed to believe. Who could even imagine water falling from the clouds of light? It didn't make sense. One thing she knew for certain, however: She wasn't going to call him "Noah," for he already possessed a fine name.

Lemech's harsh breath continued without much change. Mariah asked Methuselah if she should prepare another draft but he merely shook his head; there wasn't time. Gently, he stroked the trapper's unshaven whiskers and wondered if Traibus and Noah would return from the forest before it was too late. Twice, he turned toward the open door and was disappointed to see that it stood empty.

"My friend," Methuselah said softly, "if you would speak, we will hear you." There was a long pause before the mystic finally added, "Are you asleep?"

"No," came the raspy, hoarse reply from the weakened hunter. Everyone in the room moved closer to hear his words. "I do not know what to say." Lemech's voice was strained. "The time has come so quickly."

"It comes quickly for us all." Methuselah took his hand for encouragement. "Though it is not a time to fear."

"I'm not afraid—really," came the hushed words from parched lips. "There's so much I might have done differently. I have many regrets."

"You have many things to be proud of, Father," Tubal-cain said, holding back his tears. "We all love you."

"You've made me proud to be your wife." Adah clutched a hand from each of her sons. "You have set an example of much good."

"Maybe not always," the blind man said quietly. "I have erred."

"So have we all, my husband," Zillah said in speech as normal as she could muster, "but you don't hear us talking about it. We do the best we know at the time. Only later can we see how things might have been different. I love you, Lemech, and the family you've given me." She started crying and hurried to Adah's side for comfort. Jabal and Jubal moved aside while their mothers embraced.

Lemech's four children took turns kissing the old man's whiskered cheek and softly touching his brow. Even Lemech's eyes filled with moisture. "I was blessed," he said softly, "though for too long I remained unaware of my blessings." When the words had been spoken, Methuselah turned to the doorway and finally found what he had been waiting for. Noah had returned. The white-haired man nodded to his grandfather before approaching the bed. When he reached the dying man's side, he bent low and kissed Lemech on the forehead.

"Who is there?" Lemech asked softly.

"It is I, Menahem," he said, using his old name for the very last time. "You have been my second father, and I will always remember you."

"I thought you might not return in time," Lemech said hoarsely. "The thought frightened me."

"I would not leave you now," Noah said. He added quickly, "Traibus offers a blessing and his love." Lemech slowly turned his ear to the side as if to listen for the giant. "He stands outside the window."

Naamah hurried to the drapes and opened them so that the giant could peer inside; in all his years of traveling to the clearing, he had yet to go inside the house, for his height prevented it. Traibus' large brown nose and friendly face stuck into the room and though his speech was low all could hear his words: "The forest and I will miss you greatly."

"I will miss you too, my largest friend," Lemech said, so softly that Naamah had to repeat the words in Traibus' ear; they caused his eyes to grow as moist as the rest.

"Two more have come to see you, Lemech." Methuselah rose from the bed and moved out of the way. Everyone turned to the doorway, but it was Zillah who gasped at the sight.

"Who is it?" Lemech asked, straining to hear.

"You would never believe it, my husband!" Zillah exclaimed. "Ashmua and Lamech, your cousins, have come to see you."

The two figures walked toward the bed. Lamech's green eyes sparkled as he nodded to the others. Ashmua was the first to bend down toward Lemech. "May the One be with you," she said, kissing him gently, "until we meet again."

"Thank you, Ashmua," Lemech said weakly. "Your visit means much to me."

"I only wish we had come sooner," she said honestly. She moved from the bedside toward Zillah and Adah so her husband could approach.

Lamech dropped slowly to his knees at his cousin's bedside. He found the courage to take Lemech's hand and placed it within his own. "My cousin, all I can say is, I'm sorry—yet, that does not seem to be enough."

"I, too, have sorrow," Lemech said, a tear rolling down his cheek. "Do you know how often I have wanted to speak with you, to make amends, though my stubbornness prevented it?"

"And mine," Lamech added quietly.

"And yet," Lemech began, with as much strength as he could summon, "I always felt you would come if I needed. I only hope you sensed the same."

No longer could Zillah and Adah hold their tears. Their sobs rose above even Lemech's harsh breath and Naamah and Ashmua joined them in grief. Jubal and Jabal appeared wounded to the depths of their souls and Noah wrapped his arm around Tubal-cain's shoulders. Then they all waited.

Lemech began to feel a tingle at the base of his spine. It reminded him of the time in the darkest regions of the forest when he had been with Tubal-cain. A spark rose along his back until even his forehead began to grow warm. For a brief instant, the dying man thought he could dimly see the faces of those around him and then they were gone, replaced by shadows. Lamech squeezed his cousin's hand one last time before placing it back upon the man's chest. "We now part as friends."

Methuselah sat down on the bedside as before and stroked the side of Lemech's cheek. His eyes remained closed while his lips whispered a prayer to the One. When he had finished and the time was right, he leaned over and kissed the center of Lemech's forehead. He moved his lips down toward the trapper's ear, and in Lemech's last conscious moments of life, the mystic whispered: "Seek the Light, my friend, just seek the Light."

A few moments later, Lemech passed on. Three weeks earlier

he had celebrated a birthday, so when he passed on he was 777.

There was so very much to be done and the four people couldn't help but feel weighed down by the magnitude of the task. Methuselah and Noah led the way, while Lapeth and Traibus followed closely behind. They journeyed in silence, each contemplating how best to proceed. Only the cry of birds sitting high above the ground broke the stillness of the dense forest.

The four headed toward the outermost border of the city, each believing in the work that they had set out to do. At first, Traibus and Noah had been concerned about letting Lapeth come with them but Methuselah had insisted, for they would need all the help they could get. No one really knew where to start, so at Noah's suggestion they would begin within the closest sector of the city. It was but a few hours from Lamech and Ashmua's home, where they had spent the night, and not yet as vile as the central marketplace where Methuselah had once lived.

Tubal-cain had been forced to remain in Lemech's clearing; otherwise, he would have joined the travelers. The forty days of mourning had yet to pass, so he and Mariah were pretty much alone in tending the fields and looking after the cows. Jubal and Jabal were preparing to leave as soon as their mothers' days of solitude were over. Naamah, though stricken with her grief, kept watch over Rezepatha. She clung to the tiny hand of the child continuously, never letting the little girl out of her reach. Adah made certain all else was tended to. As was customary among the faithful, Lemech had been buried beneath an unmarked grave not too far from his cottage—the body was merely a vessel of the soul, so there was no reason to mark the spot where empty flesh was interred.

As the four moved ever closer to the city, Lapeth found herself walking quickly just to keep pace with the giant. Noah and Methuselah had grown used to his enormous gait. Lapeth's last journey through the forest seemed ages ago, yet, in truth, Basil had been dead for less than five months. At times, her sorrow still surfaced (as when the others had mourned Lemech) but she had found a new home with Methuselah and his family. There were days when she felt as though she had been a part of them forever. At night, however, she couldn't help but dream of Basil and of the way they had lain together and of the home they had left behind. Traibus never gave thought to his old way of life. On a few occasions, he remembered the wager once made with Methuselah, but its memory only brought a smile to his enormous lips. Few still remembered him as the trapper who had once frequented the marketplace. He was simply a robed figure every bit as eccentric as his companion.

The sounds of treetop birds became less common as they journeyed closer to the outskirts of the city. On either side of the trail, tree trunks and vines began to grow less dense and the path grew wider. The scent of pine and moist plant life diminished with the thinning trees and instead the smells of dirt mingled with the odors that drifted from the city. Suddenly, Methuselah's nostrils began to quiver due to the scents made by humans. He found the rich fragrance of the forest much more to his liking. He walked quickly, using his staff for knocking dirt clods away from his feet, and he appeared confident in the success of their mission. After all, the One had sent them. As always, a few coins were tied within the sleeve of his robe and Traibus had money as well. (Noah and the others knew Methuselah's father had left money behind, but no one had the slightest idea of its magnitude.)

When they reached the city's edge, the growths of vines and

trees and occasional yellow flowers suddenly stopped and the four stepped out from the cover of the forest. The dry dust of the bare ground replaced the splendor of the mighty trees. The forest appeared to end in a straight line running parallel to the closest shops. Far to their left, the smells of stables and horses that had journeyed from Arabia came to their attention. Few were able to afford stallions (the animals were of little use in the forest anyway), but there remained a steady demand for the creatures as beasts of burden. Storefronts, featuring wax and cloth, and an inn for weary travelers stood off to the right. The city's citizens were everywhere, and the people robed themselves in garments from throughout the continent.

Those from Shinar wore the hides of trappers or the robes of merchants or the tattered and mixed raiment of peasants; women dressed in dull blouses and long skirts hanging to the tops of leathery moccasins. Men from the north wore open-necked shirts and hand-sewn breeches. Immigrants from Arabia dressed in linens banded by black stripes: The men wrapped turbans proudly around their foreheads, while the women remained hidden behind cloth scarves. Few clothed themselves in the long flowing robes of Noah and his family. A few mongrel dogs and pet goats ran along the buildings, chased by children, or among children being chased by one another.

Lapeth was the first to speak. "Do the overseer's patrols come to this part of the city?" she wondered aloud, for the people appeared relatively harmless.

"Rarely, my daughter." Methuselah leaned on his birch staff and spoke wisely. "Although his spies are everywhere. There is little for his guards to do amid the calmness of this sector, and some of these people refuse to trade with them. Malock is known for unfair prices and his choicest crops are traded to the east.

These people," he waved a hand in the direction of the first row of shops, "have opened up their own routes to the south."

"Remember, Lapeth," the giant spoke from two cubits above, "there are places in the city you cannot venture. Even if I were with you, you would not be safe. Men would commit murder in order to possess your beauty. You must offer the people of this sector only the Law that you've found to be true. Our hope is that they, in turn, will take what they've learned to places we dare not go."

"How will we get them to listen?" she asked.

A few women watched them curiously before disappearing inside merchants' shops or journeying down side routes. Some of the braver pushcart vendors bid for their attention with beckoning calls and hand gestures. Children playing stickball noticed the strangers for a few moments before screaming for the ball to be knocked toward them or racing away with waving arms.

"We will be shown," Methuselah said positively. "But it is a certainty we will accomplish nothing by standing here. Follow me." He walked toward the central street that cut a path through the busiest part of the sector. On either side, shops and offices rose as high as three stories above the ground. Cobblers, merchants, storekeepers of pottery and backers of trade expeditions found themselves amid pushcart vendors, beggars and produce sellers. The four journeyed up the street, one of the few cobblestone roads in the entire sector, looking for a place to begin. The farther they walked, the more people crowded around and the more the shopkeepers came to the doors of establishments and beckoned for the visitors to come see for themselves "the finest wares in Shinar."

Even in the open-air market, Mixtures and merchants from lands far away appeared as interested in talking among themselves as they did in transacting business. For nearly an hour, the four did little more than brush up against garments. As a group, they were eyed with caution. Some of the shopkeepers even appeared hesitant to converse with such an unusual foursome. Finally, Methuselah spoke his mind: "We're going to have to split up; otherwise, we will never find anyone to talk openly with us."

"What are we looking for?" Traibus asked, curious. "You'll not find a member of the Law in these parts."

"Perhaps not." Methuselah looked up to his partner. "But we'll most certainly find someone who has heard of it, or of the One. It is with that individual, someone familiar with this city and its people, that we need to begin." He continued, "Let us go two by two and seek out someone with whom all are familiar. It may be someone from the inn or one of the more prominent merchants, someone who is known to everyone. From this person, we might learn a great deal, for he who listens to the voices of many could carry the very wisdom we seek."

"Perhaps it is best not to mention the One—at first," Traibus said cautiously. "Instead, we should say that we look for a traveler of many lands, an explorer of sorts, one who is familiar with routes to the east."

"Agreed," Noah and Methuselah said simultaneously.

Methuselah and his grandson turned down a side street toward the inn, while Traibus and Lapeth remained in the market sector; all had agreed that Lapeth would be safer in the company of a giant. They were to meet at the edge of the forest at least one hour before the light disappeared from the vapors. That would give them enough time to return at least a portion of the distance home before dark.

As soon as the four split up, shopkeepers and vendors watched the beautiful woman and the old giant more openly. The two drew looks of curiosity instead of distrust. Most wondered what the relationship might be between the two. Merchants approached to converse or to draw them into a shop. The pair spoke to those with pushcarts, as well as to the wealthier merchants with elaborate storefronts and paid labor. Though descendants of giants were not uncommon in the city, Traibus was still forced to bend low in order to pass beneath most of the doorways.

Lapeth waved to barefoot children running alongside and encouraged them to come closer, telling them the giant was not to be feared. A few dogs barked excitedly at the giant's heels, but Traibus merely nodded to those around him or spoke cheerfully to peasant women who crowded around the stone wells that appeared in the center of every third or fourth block.

One solitary old cobbler, with thinning hair and a number of cracked teeth peeking between rough lips, watched from the doorway of his shop. He studied them closely, squinting at the giant as if to see better, and wondered why the huge man looked vaguely familiar. However, try as he might, it was impossible to remember where he had seen the giant before. Traibus spotted the cobbler immediately because of the game Methuselah had taught him. He recognized the old man as one who had once lived in the central portion of Shinar's marketplace. The giant turned to the cobbler and motioned a greeting. Traibus even spoke a few words, asking about any who might be familiar with journeys to the east, but the old man never recognized him.

Lapeth found it easy to speak with the women and children who gathered around rock wells, ran errands for merchants, or stitched fabrics in the shade of storefronts. Most were awed by her beauty and a few were too bashful to exchange a greeting. Some merchants watched the slender woman lustfully, but the presence of Traibus diverted their eyes. One of the braver women approached Lapeth and asked if the robed giant were her husband. Lapeth merely smiled and spoke truthfully:

"He is a friend of my father's, and my dear friend as well."

Without incident, the two explored countless dirt roads and many side streets of the sector. When they had grown tired from walking and wanted something to eat, Traibus pulled a few shekels from his sleeve and paid for their lunch. They sat on a stone bench near one of the wells and ate wheaten cakes from a bakery and a small sweet melon from a pushcart. They drank the juice of crushed pomegranates, and continued on their way only when they were completely rested. Much of their time was spent speaking casually with whomever approached. After several hours, they had covered a great deal of the sector. Everywhere they went, their story was the same: they looked for someone knowledgeable in trade routes to the far east. The question did not seem strange; everyone simply assumed that Traibus was partner to a merchant who wished to finance an expedition.

Many of the women and most of the children had no answer to their query. Some recommended one merchant and then another; some advised them to seek out the moneylenders; others offered their own advice on a particular route; some gave the names of relatives. But through it all, one name continued to be mentioned more often than any other. It arose in nearly every street in which they stopped to converse. At first, the individual didn't seem to be quite what Traibus thought they were looking for but after several hours it became clear they needed to seek the man out. For that reason, almost an hour later, they approached the stables of Gravas, the horse-trader, who seemed more publicly known than any other man in the city.

It surprised neither Lapeth nor Traibus that Noah and Methuselah had found Gravas first; Traibus had even jested that they would probably arrive at the massive barn and stables after the two had already found it. Methuselah smiled at his old companion and couldn't help but ask: "What took you so long, my friend?" although, in truth, the two had just barely arrived themselves.

Noah and his grandfather sat at a long plank table across from a short, round fellow with close-cropped red hair. The man was Gravas.

The fat horse-trader quickly invited Lapeth to sit next to him. Traibus simply sat cross-legged on the ground at one end of the table so he remained at eye-level with the others. Gravas called out to one of the stable hands beyond the oak fence and, momentarily, the newcomers were brought polished wooden mugs filled with light ale.

"For much of this day, I have received rumors of two travelers coming my way; at times they were described as sages, and in the very next instant I would hear of a beautiful woman and a giant. I began to wonder," the man said smiling, "what men possessed the power of chameleons and whether shape shifters had entered Shinar's borders." He took a stiff gulp from his own mug and waved for the young boy to bring a pitcher. His fat, stubby fingers wrapped around the container of ale as he drained the last drop. After setting the cup back on the tabletop, he looked at the four faces seated around him and began to chuckle. "I heard that the travelers who sought my presence were interested in backing a merchant caravan to the east. My eyes, however, don't believe the story. It appears as though you may have other business with Gravas of Persia?"

"You are correct, my friend," Methuselah said without hesitation. "We've no intention of going to the east—at least not before the hour is right. Yet, the help we seek will be worth far more than a hundred speculative journeys."

Gravas chuckled to himself and poured another draft of ale. He passed the fresh pitcher to Traibus, the only one who could match his pace. All around their gathering, through the expanses of fenced acreage, stable hands walked large stallions in exercise or fed nursing mares freshly cut grass. Gravas's men were used to many visitors, so that even a giant as formidable as Traibus caused little commotion. The horse-trader nodded at the mystery of his guests' visit and took another gulp of ale. "Why, then, was your story that you sought a route to the east?"

"Our words claimed that we wanted a merchant who knew of such passage. Never was it actually our desire to take it," Methuselah said matter-of-factly.

"Ah ha!" the portly man exclaimed and slapped the table with the palm of his hand. "Now I know who you are!" He looked at Lapeth, seated next to him, and laughed. "You know, beautiful child, were it not for your presence, I would have known these three immediately." He waved his palm in their direction while they watched with a great deal of interest. "What might your name be," Gravas asked amiably, "so that I will know the four of you?"

"I am Lapeth," she said softly. "But how is it you know my companions when it is we who had to seek you out?"

"It is really quite simple," he laughed. His breath was heavy with the scent of expensive ale. "Only one man in these parts speaks in riddles and travels in the company of a robed giant. I have heard much about you, Methuselah, and you, Traibus, who has become as wise as your teacher." Gravas looked across the table, staring at Noah for a few moments. "In all my travels," he finally managed to say, "I have never seen one with hair so white or eyes so powerful to gaze upon. I warn you, do not travel alone near the borders of the overseer's fields, for in Malock's domain, you would not be safe." Gravas raised a toast. "I have heard of your recent discovery of iron, Menahem. You have made a find indeed."

"My friends now call me Noah," he said, just as the thought of saw blades and lances entered into his mind, "and I've often wondered, of late, if that which is used for evil outweighs the good for which it was originally intended."

"There is a continent to the west," Gravas said, after swallowing another draft, "where I've journeyed twice. On one occasion, wise sages sat in debate over this very issue."

"You've been to Poseidia?" Traibus was amazed. He leaned over the table to capture every word.

"Some name it so," the jovial man stated quite simply.

"What was the outcome of these debates?" Methuselah was curious.

For a time, Gravas closed his eyes and pictured what he had witnessed so many decades before. Tiny lines formed at the corners of his eyes as he squinted in thought, recalling beautiful gardens, fountains, and temples of white marble. The continent had been one of vast wonders and mysteries.

"I remember the land possessed more beauty than I had seen before—or have since." His eyes opened, looking intently at each one of them. "I felt the possibility for goodness in everything, whether it was the peaceful shorelines or in the gentle calm about the cities. There was much in the way of beauty to be found."

"Yet," his voice softened, "there was also a darkness which lurked just beyond sight. I sensed a very powerful force below the surface of the good. My mind reasoned that the purpose behind these debates was that the people themselves were growing uneasy. Surely, the continent's inhabitants were not strangers to what I could feel as a mere traveler. Poseidia was the only place I've journeyed where I wept when it came time to leave. I cried, not only because I wanted to stay, but also because I knew that if I ever returned the darkness would have grown stronger. Years later, my second voyage to the land of marble temples was much shorter; I had been correct."

"The debate?" Noah reminded him.

"I rarely become so engrossed in one of my own tales," Gravas chuckled and gulped from the mug in order to moisten his throat. His fat hands rubbed together while finishing the story. "It was agreed, and wisely so, that something created for good would remain essentially the same, regardless of the use it was put to. Even if an evil aim might be attained, the good would prove the stronger."

"Yet the debate did not end there," Gravas added cautiously, "for it was decided, as well, that anything fashioned for the purpose of evil would remain so. Even if goodness could be conceived from its creation, the darkness of evil would overshadow the virtue. It was as if the sages of Poseidia had found the motives behind the island's two peoples."

"What two peoples?" Lapeth asked.

Gravas looked at her, somewhat surprised that she had posed such a question. "Has not Methuselah told you? The people have divided themselves into two nations: They have become the Sons of Belial, as well as the Children of the Law of One. No longer is the land of your forefathers as it was in the past." Gravas looked directly at Methuselah.

"Without knowing this for certain," the old sage replied sadly,

"I have long feared as much."

"You have more knowledge than we dared wish for," Traibus said in an attempt to dispel Methuselah's gloomy countenance.

"So it is my knowledge of people and not trade which brought you to the stables." Gravas shook his head as if the thought amused him. "How is it that you four—educated in the ways of old—have come to me for answers?"

"For what we are in need," Noah said somberly, "there is none other. May I ask a question?"

"It would appear as though you have asked many," Gravas said, noting with pleasure that Traibus took another mug of ale. "What would you know?"

"Why do the people know you so well and do you know as much about them?"

The giant added, "You possess a popularity and means greater than even the wealthiest merchants I have known. Nowhere else have I seen such bounty." He turned his head to look again at the many fields, the busied laborers, the enormous barn, and the livestock.

"We had best become fast friends, if I am to speak so freely."

"We were friends long before our appearance at your stables," Methuselah said mysteriously. "You may speak without fear."

Gravas watched the old sage curiously before continuing. "There are those who claim my wealth is second only to Malock's; this I know not for certain. I do know, however, that I would not be safe near the borders of his fields; the overseer would have me taken in an instant, but he would not have me for my appearance," he added, glancing at Noah, "as he would have you." Gravas clasped his hands at the base of his belly, chuckling as he spoke, "I do not believe Malock has need of any perfection I possess; rather, he sees me as a threat to his plans."

"This belief," he continued, a little more softly, "is folly. The city has grown so diverse and is filled with people from so many nations, even Malock couldn't hope to hold dominion over every sector. Yet, at times, I believe that is exactly what he has in mind: to control all of Shinar, and even the forest beyond."

"How does a horse-trader pose a threat to the overseer?" Lapeth asked, curious. "You do not have the appearance of an enemy."

"I do not understand," Gravas began, "how a beauty such as you ever wound up with the likes of these? I swear to you, Lapeth, were it not for the fact that I possess two wives already, I would begin a courtship immediately." He laughed even jollier when her eyes opened wide in amazement. "Worry not," he added. "They reside in Persia."

"Malock does not fear the might of a horse-trader," he went on, responding to Lapeth's question. "My other dealings are those which offend him. You see, I do not trade only in livestock. I've continued my speculation on merchant vessels and trade caravans from the Great Sea to the east. My gains have purchased shops and trade mills, single dwellings and tenements. Much income now comes from these rents. I own a majority of this very sector; perhaps that is why I am known so well."

"But why would the overseer feel threatened by your rents?" Lapeth wondered aloud.

"Because, my daughter," Methuselah interrupted, before Gravas could speak, "a merchant who rents from Gravas becomes yet another tenant not subject to Malock's demands."

"Exactly!" the fat man said excitedly, "and if you had a choice, with whom would you rather bargain? Although I am a business-man, I believe myself quite reasonable. I know of the hardships experienced by some of these merchants and tradesmen. Many,

many decades ago I was no better off. I have not forgotten what it was like. If rent is late, or even forgotten, something can be worked out. Believe me, much have I given away but it has been returned a hundredfold." He looked eagerly at his mug and swallowed anew.

Traibus spoke sadly. "Horrible tales of Malock's deeds to his own tenants are whispered in the streets and alleyways. Some have been made homeless or imprisoned in the fields with their entire families. Others have been given the choice of turning daughters and wives over to Malock and his guards for a few days. Even sons have been taken at times."

"Of late," Gravas said, without boasting, "I have loaned shekels to some of Malock's tenants faced with eviction. I do not think that giant has any love for me."

Lapeth's eyes became horrorstruck with the discussion of the overseer. Gravas wanted to comfort her but felt it unwise. Instead, he looked to the old sage, for Methuselah hadn't yet spoken of the reason for their visit.

"You said you needed assistance."

"And your advice," Noah added quickly.

"Gravas," Methuselah began slowly, "you possess a wisdom deep within your soul. For this reason, we have been sent to you. We have brought with us a story, and I can only hope it will ring as true for you as it did for the rest of us."

Methuselah's tone was serious, so Gravas poured a final mug of ale and took one sip before Noah told his story.

"It may be difficult, at first," Noah said calmly, "to believe. Yet I swear to you, every word is true. It is the very tale that brought us to Shinar. It is this very tale which brings us to you."

Gravas nodded his head and motioned for Noah to begin. He watched the man intensely, looking around the table at the others only when the story was well underway. And as Gravas watched their faces, first Noah's, then Lapeth's, then Methuselah's, and, finally, the giant's, he realized how completely the four believed—though three had not even seen what was being related as fact.

Noah told everything. He spoke of seeking quiet near the freshwater lake, of wanting to be away from the business of iron for a few hours. He told of the peace of the silence, a peace that Gravas had never actually experienced but had heard of in his travels. He told of the two apparitions, visions he called them: one of the quakes, with waters pouring from the sky, and the other of a man surrounded by light. He spoke for a long while, not pausing until the story was complete. Throughout the telling, it was Traibus who moved Gravas the most, for never before had he met a giant with such an unshakable faith in the One.

"So it is our mission," Methuselah interjected when his grandson had finished, "our calling, to be of service while there is yet time. For I say to you, Gravas, even without these apparitions, I have known that the day draws near. The people of this city and upon every continent of the earth have forgotten their purpose and the purpose that they have adopted is killing them. We must find a way to spread this warning, else much that was begun in ages past will be lost."

Gravas did not speak immediately. Instead, he waited and contemplated all that had been said. He had always prided himself on logic and rationality, though the story was far from rational—water had never fallen from the vapors, and he had never seen an apparition for himself. Still, he kept an open mind. He glanced one final time at the belief on the giant's face before speaking. "How would you have me believe," Gravas asked seriously, "in a warning from your One of whom I know so very little? He may exist, as you say, but I know not for certain. Neither do I doubt

He may not exist. What would you have me believe?"

"We ask not for your faith," Traibus replied, "only for advice. Should you work with us, however, there is little doubt you would come to believe."

"You've had an excellent teacher in riddles," Gravas chuckled, looking at the old sage and then back at Traibus. "Advice I offer—freely—but as for belief, that you must earn."

"Agreed," Methuselah said happily, extending his hand across the table to grasp the horse-trader's. "What we seek is this: For too long, we of the One have been perceived as mysterious. These people of your city think our teachings strange. They see us as a remnant of the past. We must earn the trust of your people and show ourselves friends. As friends, we might reach out with the Truth."

"You know as well as I, Methuselah," Gravas replied honestly, "there are those in this city who don't desire even a single friend; some, diseased in mind, know scarcely of their own existence, let alone the presence of another; others have been so abused that they are no longer capable of trust. And some would win your trust only to betray you."

"Then how can we find those who would listen?" Lapeth asked hopefully. "Even a few could do much to help."

"There is a way," Gravas said positively. "Become part of this city. Come here with a trade, an enterprise, as merchants. Then, begin to mix with the people—and as you do so, you may spread your truth."

"But what do we have to sell?" Lapeth asked.

"Iron!" came the simultaneous reply from both Noah and his grandfather.

"Exactly," Gravas said, "and I happen to know of a landlord from whom you could lease." He pointed in the direction of the main street. “I have a vacant shop not too far distant. You’ll find my terms quite reasonable.”

“Wonderful,” Traibus said happily. “We can begin.”

“Shall we drink on it first?” Gravas lifted his mug to the giant’s and began a hearty laugh.

Twenty-Three Years Later
(102 years before the Flood)

Naamah leaned against the fence post near the abandoned kilns and wistfully thought of Noah and the others. She couldn't help but wonder when one of them might decide to visit Lemech's ancient clearing again. As she turned from the barn and the solitary cow and looked toward the cottages, the radiance from the vapor sparkled atop her brown hair. Her eyes fell upon the clinging vines that had spread from the larger house until most of the smaller cottage was covered as well. During moments like these, when it was quiet and she surveyed what remained in the clearing, she felt so very much alone. There remained only herself and her mother, living all alone where her entire family had once been. And every time she realized how totally isolated they were, she believed, more than anything, that Zillah had been wrong. They should have moved with the others.

After Lemech's death, their numbers had dwindled. First, her brothers had gone and neither had been heard from in more than a decade. The last word had come by way of a traveling merchant in Shinar: Both men had found wives; Jubal had his music and Jabal had his tents. The merchant carried a promise from the two that they would return one day and visit the family they had left behind; apparently that day had yet to arrive.

Tubal-cain and Mariah had been next, moving to be closer to their work, and with their departure Naamah had lost her best friend. Even Adah had left, shortly thereafter, at Ashmua and Lamech's invitation. Adah's move, Naamah was certain, had affected Zillah most of all. Her mother was more cantankerous than ever, constantly bickering and complaining about the smallest things: The cow was old and not giving enough milk; the vines on the house were too thick; there was far too much work for them to do alone; even the light from the vapor sky was often too bright. Her chatter was endless, and Naamah had listened and listened and listened, until she thought she would go crazy.

And with each passing day, Naamah grew more disgusted with their life. No longer did she desire the clearing's solitude; she wanted her friends. If it were necessary to go to Shinar to be with them, then she would go. She was angry and depressed. Although the city continued to expand and grow toward them, it wasn't close enough. She missed the laughter of Rezepatha, who had become more beautiful with each passing day and she missed the giant. She had grown weary of her mother's constant bickering and, more than anything, she had become lonely for a man who didn't even know she was alive.

Noah had grown older and still he was unaware of her desire for him. Zillah had embarrassed her often enough by trying to put the two of them together, but he didn't seem to understand. Finally, Zillah had given up trying to talk to Menahem (for she refused to call him Noah) about marriage. Perhaps he would never have a wife. Naamah only hoped that he hadn't fallen in love with Waila, for she was very beautiful and lived near him. But Zillah assured her that he was as blind to Waila's advances as her own. The One and the work seemed to be Noah's only inclinations, and Naamah knew little of the One and even less of the work. Zillah claimed that all of the rest of them, Gravas included, had become deluded. Water could not fall in rivers from the clouds, regardless of how many people believed it.

Naamah walked from the crumbling fence and the two kilns that had long ceased to give off the odor of melted ore. She headed toward the edge of the clearing and glanced at the oaks and the thick, broad-leafed plants that engulfed the outermost edges of their land, but she failed to notice their beauty. Her mind was elsewhere.

She often ached inside, and the feeling was growing more insistent. It wasn't her anger or disgust with Zillah that twisted her stomach until she thought she might scream. Instead, Naamah didn't know how much longer she could live without him. She had often thought about moving to Shinar, regardless of whether her mother went, if only to be close to Noah. She thought of his beauty, his white hair, and the sparkling blue of his eyes. She had difficulty remembering if he had ever even spoken more than a few words to her, but she imagined he had done so. She knew her mother would think she was wasting her time, but she found herself imagining the children they might have together: two girls, both with light hair and eyes as beautiful as their father's. She didn't want sons, for her brothers had shown how indifferent men could be to their families. She would have daughters, for daughters were much more loving than sons.

"You would think you could fix your mother some breakfast once in a while," a voice bellowed from the cottage. "Lord knows I've fixed yours often enough."

Suddenly, she knew the day was destined to become much like the rest (though she reminded herself that Zillah never actually meant the harshness with which she spoke). She turned to her mother, who appeared more wrinkled than ever.

"Just tell me what you'd like," Naamah said quickly, "and I'll fix it for you."

"No need for that!" Zillah's thin lips mouthed positively. "I'm up now. A day hasn't gone by that I've sat idly by and watched others work in my place. You know that."

"Yes, Mother."

"Well, you come along. I'll fix you something."

"I can't eat now; I'm not hungry."

"I don't care if you're hungry or not," Zillah said angrily. "You've got to eat something unless you want to be sick. It's a wonder you're not sick already the way you've been acting lately."

"Good lord, Mother," Naamah said, using the woman's own tone, "I'm old enough to take care of myself."

Zillah was stunned for a moment and then shook her head in sadness. "So you've become too old to listen to someone who loves you. I just don't understand what's happening to you."

"Nothing is happening; I just haven't felt like myself."

"Well, for god's sake, get inside and have something to eat!" Zillah planted her hands firmly on her hips. "I don't want you taking sick."

Naamah entered the cottage door behind her mother and realized what had to be done. She wasn't going to live like this any longer. She had to get away from the clearing and from having only Zillah to talk to. In a few days, she'd leave for Shinar, even if her mother refused to go.

Once and for all, she had to discover how Noah really felt about her.

Gravas chuckled to himself as he walked down the main road in the direction of the shop. Red curls bounced up and down as his fat frame eagerly took each step. He glanced upward at Traibus and smiled. The giant's stride was much slower than usual because it was difficult for Gravas's short, plump legs to keep up. Gravas waved to the cobbler and the candlemaker, both friends and tenants and then, for no apparent reason, chuckled again. He had promised Noah they would arrive at the shop before midday and they were just going to make it.

Traibus finally asked, "Gravas, why is it that you find reason to laugh? There's still much to be done this day."

"Exactly!" Gravas said excitedly, "but it's the thought of the evening that makes me joyous."

"The gathering?"

"You may call it such, if you wish," he chuckled, "but I shall think of it as a party. A party with great heapings of vegetable pie and sweet corn, freshly cut melons and seed cakes, and red berries and cream. And then, there shall be ale—great quantities to drink. These are not the makings of a mere gathering but of a cause for real celebration!"

Traibus laughed aloud. "I only hope your men can transport enough ale to the party to quench your thirst as well as our own."

"You needn't concern yourself, for if the occasion demands, I shall hire more men. Two decades in iron have made for a very fat profit indeed. In another century," he said, "I shall buy out Malock."

"You jest too loudly for the open streets," Traibus cautioned. "I'm not the only giant in these parts."

"Then let us complete the day's business, so we might retire to a more hospitable location and the celebration which awaits us."

They hurried the remaining distance past the moneylenders, pausing only long enough to wave at merchants or to exchange a greeting with pushcart vendors. Over the years, business had been exceedingly good, causing Traibus, Noah, Tubal-cain, and Methuselah to become almost as well known as the horse-trader.

Their shop was located on the end at the left side of the main street. The remaining steps were taken in silence while Traibus wondered how much business they might transact that day and Gravas toyed with the idea of crossing the street and purchasing plump sweet melons from the Persian vendor.

"Later," the giant said, as if reading Gravas's mind. He placed his palm on the horse-trader's shoulder and guided the shorter man through the entrance of the iron shop.

The store was one of the largest on the block, with a double-doored entrance that led into the front display room. A thin, woven cloth hung over the entrance, from the door post to the ground. The fabric was a purchase from the weaver next to them, partly to foster a good relationship but mostly to keep out the large flies that darted through open streets in search of produce. The wooden doors were bolted only at night when the shop was empty. Traibus bent down and parted the hanging cloth in order to walk beneath the wooden beam over the entrance. Gravas stole one final look at the fruit vendor before following his friend into the shop.

Once inside, the giant was able to stand upright, for the ceiling had been erected nearly seven cubits above the smooth, planked floors. Due to the double row of windows that lined the store on the front and on the side facing the end of the block, the massive room was filled with light. The windows were criss-crossed with sturdy, tubular bars, anchored firmly within solid, white bricks.

Overlaying the bars was a fine-mesh screen designed to keep out the insects and small rodents.

On the other side of the room, Methuselah stood near the counter leaning on his staff. He spoke eagerly to three dark-skinned men. They appeared to be traveling merchants who had entered the shop to place an order; each seemed enthralled by Methuselah's tales of the Shinar of his youth. The gestures of the old man's hands alerted Gravas, who had heard the stories many times before, that Methuselah was just beginning to speak of the beliefs of the faithful who had once dominated the area. No doubt the merchants had heard of the Law, in their travels but the old man had a way of describing the people and their lives in such a manner that the stories came alive and filled most travelers with questions.

Display cases between the entrance and the counter exhibited brass and iron wares. Countless designs of cooking and eating utensils were set out on long oak tables, for viewing and handling, all neatly arranged at Noah's insistence. Crates filled with long picks and shovels and boxes of durable hammers with oak shafts and iron mallets were stacked along the floor. At either end of the tables, large barrels were filled with countless nails, some no bigger than a child's finger, others with large spikes for splitting rock. Any tool imaginable was for sale, from v-shaped plows to iron forceps, hand trowels, and buckets of every description. Circular rims used to reinforce pushcart wheels hung from the walls, along with some metal objects for which Gravas couldn't even fathom a use. However, amid the countless iron and a few brass objects, no saws were displayed. They were made by special order for any who had a valid use, such as a carpenter, as Methuselah insisted they had no reason to aid in the destruction of the forest.

The rear of the shop housed kilns and airshafts that vented

through the roof. Most of the work was completed within the store, and each of the partners had become adept at many of the tasks. Even Gravas spent much time in the shop and had arranged for a banker to collect his rents and for his stable hands to care for the livestock. On occasion, he speculated on traveling caravans, but iron ore had become his past time and Methuselah's family had become his own.

Tubal-cain came through the back doorway and walked toward the front of the store. Iron ores stained his flesh and clothing, causing his olive skin to appear darker. Even his brown hair was dusted with a fine layer of soot. Ashes from the kilns fell from his leather apron and breeches as he approached.

"I see you've been working again," Gravas said, chuckling at the sight of him. "I could venture to guess the appearance of the workroom."

"You needn't bother," Tubal-cain answered disgustedly, "I knocked over one of the barrels. Both Mariah and Lapeth have vanished on the one day I need them most."

"Ashmua's need was greater than your own," Traibus replied quickly. "Gravas tells me they prepare quite a feast. It's been a long while since we've all sat at the same meal. Besides, surely Gravas ought to be handy with a broom?"

"Indeed, I am, after working around the both of you," the portly man chuckled. "We promised Noah we would arrive by midday. Where is he?"

"He spoke with a group of women by the well earlier this morning. After that, he said a few words to Methuselah and disappeared. By the look on his face, he did not appear happy."

"The work goes slowly," Traibus replied. "Few listen, and even fewer understand."

They nodded, and Tubal-cain led them toward the counter,

just as Methuselah shook hands with the merchants and bid them good day. They would return for their wagon rims as well as for more words from the old man in a few days' time. When the merchants left, Tubal-cain asked the mystic, "Are you ready to depart?"

The old sage eyed Tubal-cain's appearance carefully, for his own gray robes offered quite a contrast to the soiled leather garments he saw before him. "I am ready, my son, but you require some attention before presenting yourself at Ashmua's. I suggest we head for the stables first and then continue only after you change. I believe Mariah would have much to say if you appeared before her as you do now."

"I believe you are right," Gravas agreed and swatted Tubal-cain on his back (giving flight to red dust and soot). "Go see Raphael at the barn. He's loading up the ale, though he'll have time to assemble some clothes for you."

Methuselah led the way to the front door, with Tubal-cain following closely behind, brushing himself off.

"What happened to Noah?" the giant asked, just as the mystic parted the fabric to leave. "Does our progress concern him?"

"He has more on his mind than the work of late," Methuselah said, pausing, "but I assure you, he'll be at the gathering."

"Is there something we can do?"

"I believe the entire shop is in need of a good sweeping." Methuselah pointed at the trail of dust that Tubal-cain left behind him.

"He meant for Noah," Gravas said.

"Worry not." Methuselah waved his hand from side to side for emphasis. "He needs to be alone with his thoughts for a time but the floor appears to be in real need of your attention."

Methuselah parted the curtained doorway and started to go

but turned once again. "A few hours hence," he said seriously, "a tall Syrian with a thin, black mustache and a white turban will come to the shop. He looks for an axle. I have already placed what he needs on the floor behind the counter."

"A special order?" Gravas asked eagerly, imagining the shekels they might charge.

Methuselah simply shook his head, "How could it be? The Syrian of whom I speak has never even ventured into the shop. I merely relate the story so you'll both know. You see, this man will be your final customer of the day. When he leaves, you can return to the forest."

With that, the old man departed through the drapery.

Noah walked alone a few feet from his parents' cottage but the density of the forest left him in complete solitude. More than anything else, he was confused. He couldn't explain how he felt to anyone, for he hadn't been able to understand it himself. He walked beneath the overhanging branches of white oak and towering pine and for the first time in his life he did not know what he was supposed to do. His feet stepped heavily upon the layered mulch of centuries as he made his own path through thick vines and massive ferns that covered the ground in every direction. Only one hour remained before the gathering, and he had hoped the decision would come to him before the meal. Already, smells of roasted vegetables filled his nostrils but the emptiness in his stomach was not due to hunger.

At times, he convinced himself that the confusion was due to his schedule. Their work in Shinar in the shop and in the city streets left him with few occasions to be alone. He even wondered if the slow progress of their task was causing his sadness. For twenty years, they had been in the city, and in all that time, the only person won over had been Gravas. They had gained acceptance, to be sure, but few really listened to what the Law was all about, and none had committed to belief. And now, he was beginning to sense that something was missing in his life and it was something he had never wanted before. Methuselah's only advice had been for him to look within his own soul, but the answer he received was not the one he had expected and he felt lost. For weeks he had engrossed himself with small tasks that needed to be done. When he wasn't in Shinar with the work, he found projects. He had mended fences for Gravas, tended to the garden in his mother's clearing and even offered his father, Lamech, his services as a carpenter—anything to keep his mind occupied and away from the problem. But no matter what he did, his confusion remained.

Often he visited Raki'el, his father's neighbor, and Waila as well, hoping their company would end his melancholy. Raki'el often questioned whether or not the entire remnant of the faithful should return to Poseidia. For her part, Waila made no secret of the fact that she wanted a husband and her attentions remained fixed on Noah. (If the white haired man remained uninterested, however, she was ready to move to Poseidia, as well.)

All his life, Noah had believed he would never marry for his devotion was to the One. But someone had changed the plans of a lifetime, causing great confusion. Somehow, he had fallen in love with Naamah, and Noah had no idea what he was supposed to do about it. He would spend hours thinking about her, though he tried not to. He had spent much time in the silence asking if it was right, and though the answer was clear, he didn't know how it could be. He had never desired a wife. Perhaps Zillah had been right all along: His love was small indeed if it could not be shared with another.

When his thoughts had exhausted themselves, he found himself returning to his parents' cottage. He tried to find cheer in the thought of their gathering, for it had been a long while since they had been together and he didn't want to spoil the occasion. Besides, there would be time later to think about Naamah. After a few more steps, he could see the outline of his father's house, and the surrounding cottages gradually came into view. He brushed a few moist leaves from his robe as he stepped from the underbrush and onto the trodden ground of the circular clearing. He passed his father's house on the left and Raki'el's on the right, before proceeding to the enormous open space where they would come together.

Much had been accomplished since his walk. Three tables had been laid end-to-end (it had taken four stretches of cloth to cover the distance). Lapeth, Waila, Adah, and Rezepatha had assisted with the cooking and stacked the tables with wooden bowls and platters. Rows of utensils, fashioned by Tubal-cain, and huge mugs able to hold drink enough even for Gravas were in place.

Noah's look of sadness was replaced with amazement as he spotted the great quantities of food. There were plates of roasted nuts and yellow flower seeds that had been toasted over a flame. Wheaten cakes and bowls of fresh fruit had already been set out. Anything that didn't need to be served fresh from the ovens was neatly arranged on the tables. He looked from peaches and red melons to plump grapes, tomatoes, and cucumber wedges. Apples and moist figs were arranged inside deep bowls. At one end of the table, eight pies (browned to perfection and sprinkled with beet sugar) were cooling.

Gravas's men, dressed only in breeches, unloaded a wooden

cart at the far end of the clearing. Massive oxen waited patiently as the wagon was emptied of its cargo. Gravas had outdone himself. Six enormous barrels of ale were lowered to the ground by three stable hands as old Lamech directed their placement. Barechested men, sweating from their labors, also lowered two barrels of a darker wood from the wagon. These contained cider for those whose thirst was different from Gravas's and the giant's.

No one was certain how many would be coming but there was plenty of room on the ground as well as on the dozen scattered tree stumps. Rezepatha waved to Noah from the steps of Methuselah's cabin. She was only twenty-five but already possessed the dark beauty of her mother. Noah waved back to her and turned to face his own mother, who approached.

"How are you feeling, my son?" Ashmua looked into his eyes and gently held his arm.

"Overwhelmed by all you've done," he said, ignoring the intent of her question.

"The others have done as much as I," she said, pointing to the long table with approval. "I'm glad Methuselah decided to bring us together. We still can't be certain how many will be coming. Gravas invited everyone at the stable and I know Methuselah invited a few from the city."

"We'll have a wonderful time. Do you need me to do anything?"

"Well, we've made so many vegetable pies. When the time comes I'm certain Lapeth and Adah will need help bringing them to the tables." She patted him on the arm before returning to her labors. "If you need to talk later, just let me know."

It wasn't long before the clearing began to fill with those eager for celebration. Raki'el stepped from his cottage and helped himself to the first mug of ale. When Methuselah and Tubal-cain arrived, both looked suitably attired for the occasion. Gravas's stable hands ushered the wagon from the clearing, planning to return with a group of friends. While Raki'el stood next to the supply of ale and discussed with whomever might listen a possible excursion to Poseidia, vegetable pies were removed with Noah's assistance; thick crusts promised to keep saucy vegetables warm until everyone arrived. By the time Traibus and Gravas appeared and told of their Syrian customer, the clearing was filled with people. Twelve men from the stables had returned to the gathering as well.

"Do not worry yourself," Methuselah said to Noah when they were finally alone. "In a very short time your path will be made clear."

"How can you be certain when the decision has not even become clear in my mind?"

"How about some ale?" The old sage put his arm around Noah's back and led him in the direction of Raki'el and Gravas (who had no desire to leave the vicinity of the barrels). "In your uneasiness you've blocked out the answer, which your mind has already come to know. Just relax." Methuselah winked and then added, "I promise, everything will correct itself."

"What are you seeing?" Noah asked impatiently.

"Not now." Methuselah waved his hand for silence. "We need to celebrate."

"Has either of you tasted the ale?" Gravas asked, lifting his mug in toast. "I do believe Raki'el has gotten a head start on us all." He swallowed a draft, laughed, and wiped his face with the end of his sleeve.

"Someone has to watch out for the drink," Raki'el jested as well, pouring a tall mug for Methuselah and Noah.

Rezepatha was suddenly surrounded by eight stable hands, each running to her side with a glass of cider. Lapeth watched her daughter for only a moment before continuing to lay out the meal; Rezepatha could care for herself. With Mariah's assistance, the two began slicing vegetable pies into large servings.

Nine of their friends came from the city, and the area in front of the cottages began to fill to capacity. Wooden stumps were the first seats taken as some of the guests gathered together in groups of three or four. People dressed in robes, breeches, or even the tattered garb of the city sat side by side upon the ground, tasting delicacies that had taken three days to prepare. When everyone had gotten something to eat and had found a seat upon the ground, a stump, or a bench, Tubal-cain looked up from his plate, stared at the trees beyond the edge of the clearing, and swore he had just seen something moving between the oaks. A moment later, his eyes opened in amazement and he cried out in such surprise that Gravas was startled and spilled a good portion of ale from his mug.

"Mother!" Tubal-cain shouted, jumping up from the bench and running toward the oaks to Zillah and Naamah. They walked from out of the forest, and Tubal-cain embraced them both.

"Careful," Zillah said in her usual irritation. "We've come a long way and my back is already bothering me."

Naamah kissed her brother on the cheek. "We've missed you terribly."

"I've missed you too!" He motioned for Mariah to come and greet them.

"Well, you'd never know it," Zillah's thin lips retorted quickly. She straightened her floral-print dress with her hands before looking her son straight in the eye. "You haven't been to see us in nearly two fortnights."

"He's been busy," Methuselah said, stepping forward and kissing her. "We've all been busy."

Noah turned around, cautiously looking toward the commotion. Adah and Lapeth stood in the way of Naamah, so he couldn't see her, but he saw Zillah, and she was looking right at him.

"Well, good lord," she said disgustedly, "are you going to kiss me or not?"

Though somewhat nervous over what was to come, Noah rose to his feet. He walked to Zillah, kissed her on the cheek, and embraced her so tightly that she had to catch her breath. Then he turned to Naamah, who had finished greeting Traibus, and embraced her.

"I've got to speak with you," she whispered in his ear.

"And I you."

Naamah and Noah waited until everyone had welcomed one another before disappearing into the shadows of the forest. They walked together in silence until the clearing had disappeared from sight. Only the occasional sound of laughter rose to their ears, but they were alone.

"I have been thinking about you everyday." Noah gazed into her eyes. "I was ready to head to Lemech's old clearing by morning."

She smiled. "Do you know how long I've wanted to be alone with you?"

"Had I not been so foolish," he said taking her hands into his own, "you wouldn't have waited so long. I love you, Naamah. Maybe I always have. I know now how much I need to be with you."

"I came tonight," she said softly, "so you would learn how I feel. I've loved you for so long, Noah, that I just had to tell you."

He bent forward and kissed her lips. She wrapped her arms around him for a long while as they embraced. Noah felt the warmth of her body against his own; the feeling was exhilarating.

Naamah couldn't believe what was happening.

"I will ask Methuselah to marry us within the week?" he said, asking for her approval. She nodded.

When they returned to the clearing, Methuselah was the first to notice. He pointed them out to Zillah and said so that all could hear, "I believe my grandson has an announcement to make."

"My friends," Noah said as soon as there was quiet, "this day Naamah has consented to be my wife."

Gravas started chuckling and poured himself another draft. Ashmua and Lamech ran toward the couple to congratulate them. Tubal-cain and his mother stared at one another in complete surprise; for once, even Zillah was unable to hide her amazement. Soon, voices of laughter rose anew, and everyone filled their mugs to toast the couple. Adah was brought to tears by the good news and even guests from Shinar and the stables were delighted.

Waila, however, was not thrilled by the announcement. She ran to her father's cottage to be alone and spent the greater part of an hour in tears. It was only after she was able to regain her composure and make herself presentable that she spoke to Raki'el about leaving as soon as possible for Poseidia; for too long she had waited for a man who didn't want her.

In time, plates were cleared away, and one of Gravas's stable hands began to fiddle. At first, only Naamah and Noah danced, but others soon joined in with the rhythm of the music. Rezepatha was kept dancing continuously by an endless line of suitors, and even Lamech and Tubal-cain became brave enough to dance with their wives. Lapeth took Methuselah by the hand and led him out before he could give it a thought. Gravas grabbed onto Zillah and led her out to a flat piece of earth. And even Traibus, towering over any partner he might choose, moved gracefully through the crowd with Adah.

The music lasted long into the night, and the food and the nuts and the pies were eaten until almost nothing remained, for the guests kept coming back for more. The betrothal seemed to be the most exciting thing that had happened in years. Methuselah had known it would all work out, and Gravas, as anticipated, had come to a mere gathering and found a real celebration instead—a celebration to acclaim Noah's engagement at the age of 498.

She had been blessed with motherhood since the second year of their marriage some five years earlier, but still there were days when Naamah found it hard to believe that she and Noah had three sons of their own. She clutched the youngest in her arms, against her firm breast, while the infant suckled. Like his brothers, he was perfect in body, with tiny limbs destined for the same magnificence as his father's. His hair was the lightest of the three, with scattered curls of blonde just beginning to cover his month-old head. His birth had been the hardest for her (more than a day in labor), and for that reason, Noah had decided the baby, Ham, would be their last.

She was propped against the bedroom wall of their cottage, sitting atop the thinly-stuffed divan that Zillah and Adah had stitched as a wedding gift. Her bare back leaned against the soft draperies which fell down in smooth ripples of pale silk; the cloth was from Gravas, who had been gone for seven weeks on a journey to the East. Tubal-cain had traveled with him in order to fetch, at last, the horse-trader's wives from Persia. Naamah and some of the others wondered if the women would even return with the jolly fat man after so many years. Zillah, on the other hand, remained positive that Gravas had returned to his homeland for yet another bride, and she made quite certain that everyone heard her opinion.

Already, Naamah missed her husband. He had risen, as always, with the first break of light and headed for Shinar. He was away from their cottage frequently, but she had always known the work would come first. For that reason, she tried to cope with his absences. It wasn't easy, especially with three small children, but she did the best that she could. She never complained about the loneliness she felt.

Her hair had been braided and pulled up in a bun to keep it off the soft skin of her neck and shoulders, but the air was so moist that she frequently perspired, regardless of how her hair was kept. Her mother often complained that the humidity was much greater than it had been back in Lemech's old clearing, but in reality, even Zillah had grown used to life in their new home. Methuselah's family had become content with their lives near Shinar but still Naamah dreamed of a day when she and Noah might be alone with their sons.

For now, she was grateful to have Rezepatha's help. The young woman often looked after the two older boys while Naamah was occupied with the baby. Japheth was eldest, a full two years older than Shem and the only one of the three to possess his father's gentle disposition. Shem was barely fourteen months old, but already he showed signs of becoming as secretive and mysterious as Methuselah, his great-grandfather. Without Rezepatha's help, Naamah didn't know what she would have done. With Noah's absences, the young woman had become her favorite companion.

Although Zillah was constantly around, she remained as negative as ever, spending much of her time with the older members of the family: Adah, Ashmua, and Lamech. Though the four had ventured to Shinar on occasion, the city lacked the peacefulness of the forest and Malock's men were being spotted more frequently throughout the entire city. Gravas joked that the overseer was infiltrating his holdings, but no one found the jest amusing. As a result, Zillah watched after the grandchildren, reminisced about her blind husband, mended clothes for the work being done in the city, or simply complained about everything.

Adah's youthful hair had turned to silver, though she remained as soft-spoken as ever and provided the balance that Zillah so desperately needed. She often reminisced with Zillah about their husband or wondered aloud what might have become of her sons. She was one of the few who didn't mind Zillah's constant bickering, although the work in Shinar was never discussed between them. Adah believed Noah completely and was confident that Methuselah and the rest could bring about the necessary changes; her sister-wife had other ideas.

Zillah was sick of hearing stories about Mixtures and the troubled souls of the city. She found it totally unbelievable that everyone still held fast to Noah's story. There wasn't any doubt that Noah believed what he was saying, but the others had no reason. She spent many long hours sitting in the clearing, staring upwards at the misty, vapored sky. The clouds appeared soft and stable, just as they had for centuries. She couldn't understand how anyone, especially one as wise as Methuselah, believed water could fall from the vapors. Just how could it be possible for the mists of the air to hold something as substantial as water from the lake? It didn't make any sense, and the thought that so many members of her own family believed the impossible disturbed her greatly.

She had tried, repeatedly, to argue with any who would listen, but always without success. She continued to call Noah "Menahem," at least when she remembered; after so many years, it was becoming easier to forget. Although Noah was certainly a loving husband and father when he happened to be around, he had become a little bit crazy—and everyone else in the clearing was a fool.

Ashmua and Lamech certainly believed their son, but belief no longer seemed as important as in days gone by. They spent much of each day tending large plots of crops which fed the clearing: sweet corn, potatoes, string beans, melons, tomatoes, squash, and fruit trees. Ashmua was content staying amid the rows of vegetation, plucking ears of corn or bending low to pick an intruding weed. She helped Lamech construct trellises for tomatoes to cling to and wandered between fruit trees, gathering the ripest peaches and apricots to steam into juice.

Lamech simply enjoyed being near his wife, spending time with her in the gardens. He had retired from carpentry, though he'd often mend a bench or table or make suggestions to one of Gravas's apprenticed woodworkers. He frequently envied Methuselah, for it seemed strange that his own father possessed more energy than he did himself. While Lamech was becoming plagued by tiny aches and tired bones that needed time to rest, Methuselah never seemed to change.

Naamah didn't understand it either. Somehow Methuselah, Noah, and even Traibus managed to stay the same, yet after birthing three children, she had begun to gain weight, and tiny lines had begun to form at the corner of her eyes. Though Noah was a great deal older, she was beginning to fear that, before too long, she'd appear his senior. She was worrying about the prospect just as Mariah, Rezepatha, and her two sons burst into the room.

"Are you back so soon, Mariah? You've only been gone a few hours." Naamah lowered Ham to her lap, closed her robe, and made room for Japheth and Shem to jump up on the mattress.

Both gave her a wet kiss, while she reminded them to be careful of little Ham.

"I came to get you!" Mariah said excitedly. "Methuselah sent me; he wants us both at the shop, within the hour."

"Do you know why?"

She shrugged her shoulders, "I never thought to ask him. You know how convincing he can be. Traibus is outside waiting. One of Malock's guards was spotted near the inn and Methuselah didn't want us to be alone."

Naamah nodded, lifted Ham from her lap, kissed him on the cheek, and passed him to Rezepatha. The young woman smiled and cheerfully took the infant. She was becoming more and more beautiful, with her mother's piercing eyes and angular cheekbones. Naamah rose from the mattress to fetch her sandals.

"You don't mind watching all three of them, do you?" She asked Rezepatha, though Naamah knew beforehand what the answer would be.

"Not at all! I'll take them outside to see their grandmothers, or maybe Lamech can tell one of his stories. Would you like that?" she asked the baby. Ham cooed in her arms while Japheth jumped up and down at her feet. Shem jumped as well, simply because he did everything that Japheth did.

Mariah giggled at her nephews before turning to Naamah. "Are you ready?"

"Almost." Naamah bent to give each of her sons a kiss, and then Rezepatha led the way out into the yard, carrying Ham.

Japheth ran past them all and headed toward Zillah. The old woman sat next to Adah, in a lounging chair in the middle of the clearing, pointing out how light and air-like the clouds appeared just over their heads; she spoke loud enough so that the giant could hear. Traibus managed to refrain from smiling but sometimes Zillah's obstinance amused him. The old woman stopped speaking just long enough to let Japheth and Shem into her lap.

Traibus bid goodbye to all, save Mariah and Naamah, who followed him out of the clearing. Both women had to walk quickly in order to keep up. Naamah sensed, somehow, that Traibus knew why they'd been summoned, and his hurried pace was to keep them from asking. She clung to the sides of her robe, lifting the cloth from the damp soil and scurrying as fast as her feet would carry her without running. Occasionally, the women looked at each other due to the pace, not knowing whether to cry or to burst out laughing. The giant did not slow his steps until the trees began to thin, and the rich smells of fertile earth were replaced with the scent of trampled dirt, dried cobblestone streets, and the occasional fragrance of burning incense. Much time had passed, and they were exhausted.

"Stop!" Naamah cried when she could walk no farther. Her heart beat quickly, and the back of her head and neck had grown moist with sweat. Her breathing was fast, and she turned to Mariah, who appeared just as worn out.

"We made it!" Naamah said breathlessly. She pointed toward the shops and dwellings that faced the forest's edge before turning to the giant. "You could have killed us."

"I assure you," Traibus spoke, using the tone he had learned from Methuselah, "you would have fainted first. Catch your breath so we can continue."

They were allowed only a few minutes before Traibus began heading toward the main throughway. Their pace along the cobblestone street was as swift as their journey through the forest; both women were grateful when they finally reached Methuselah, standing in the doorway of the shop. The old man raised a finger to his lips as a sign for their silence. Naamah noticed the crowd that had gathered at the end of the block.

About thirty people assembled near the corner of the iron store were listening to the voice of a man standing in the exact center of the cross streets. Naamah recognized the voice immediately as Noah's, so she left Mariah and Traibus standing next to Methuselah and pressed her way into the crowd. The people were peddlers, merchants, Mixtures with enormous features and hairy limbs, and peasant women who had stopped on their way to the well. In order to see Noah, Naamah pushed her way through, but she was stopped from reaching the front by a couple of women who jealously guarded their view.

Naamah was forced to peer between heads just to catch an occasional glimpse of her husband. He spoke to the gathering in complete sincerity, gesturing with long sweeping motions when emphasizing a particular point.

" . . . so you see, my friends, there is much we should be doing. It is not enough merely to be alive, or to try to fill our bellies. Instead, we need to be good for something, something which may lend a service to another, something which may be of aid to someone less fortunate."

"And I give you this promise: As you begin to be gentle, as you begin to show kindness to those around you, as you begin to show forth the very best you have within you, then you become the recipient of the very good you have offered to another. This is the Law, a promise, as true today as it was in the beginning. The seeds you sow become your harvest. There is no escape in this, merely a choice as to how you bring it into your own experience. Shall we become gatherers of the fruits of our love, or shall our decisions reap the thistles of selfishness? There is good and evil set before you this day. Choose thou."

Noah paused, turning in the direction of his wife, although

Naamah wasn't certain he could see her. His blue eyes were afire with the same sparkling intensity that was in them after a period of the silence. Standing before the people in his long white robe, looking from face to face, he appeared radiant. In some, he saw only confusion, in others doubt. A few watched him with blank stares, and some whispered among themselves to avoid his direct gaze. Finally, one of the peasant women on his right found courage to speak, yet her eyes remained transfixed on the cobblestones. She rubbed her hands nervously together.

"Sir, you may speak the truth, though what would I, who has naught, give to another?"

"Daughter," Noah spoke softly, "let not a day pass that you do not speak a cheery and encouraging word to someone else. Then, you will find your own heart uplifted, your love appreciated, your life opened, and your purpose will be understood."

"Thank you, sage," she said quickly, after stealing one further glimpse of him.

"Who gives the sage knowledge, but He who is Maker of all?"

"I'd believe anything he wanted," one of the women in front of Naamah whispered, loud enough for her to hear, "for a single evening against his firm flesh." The other woman giggled without removing her eyes from him. Naamah began to turn red.

"He's nice enough, really," a young merchant commented behind Naamah's head, "and as fair a man you'd ever meet in these parts. But at times," he chuckled and drew a circular motion against his head, "he's as crazy as they come."

"Unless each soul," Noah began again, turning in the direction of the merchant, "makes the world a little better, a little more hopeful, a little more patient, and shows a little more kindness, then that life is a failure. Though you gain the entire world, how little must you think of yourself to lose the very purpose for which you entered into the earth. Would all but learn: Know ye people, the Lord, thy God, is One! And each stands equal in stature before Him."

He finished speaking and walked to the peasant woman to offer a few words of encouragement. As the crowd dissipated, many wondering what the man had been saying, Naamah returned to the storefront and stood next to Methuselah.

"I have never heard him speak before a crowd." she said. Naamah wondered how many people thought him crazy (as well as how many women had been lusting after him). "I appreciate being sent for."

"How can you show gratitude," Methuselah asked curiously, "when you don't yet know why you've been summoned? It was not to hear your husband that I requested your presence."

"What then?" Naamah looked first toward the dwindling crowd and then at Noah, who continued speaking with the woman.

"Look not there." Methuselah grasped her shoulder and turned her around facing the main street. "It is this I called you for."

Naamah focused on a single caravan coming in their direction. Two strong horses pulled the elevated wagon gracefully over worn cobblestone; four immense wheels clicked rhythmically with every turn of the axle. Suddenly, she recognized the red curls of Gravas's forehead, and Tubal-cain sitting next to him. The horse-trader waved proudly to friends who ran alongside the carriage while Tubal-cain drove the team.

The wagon made a wonderful spectacle, its dark wood finish and painted gold trim accentuating oil lanterns that hung from four corners. A few merchants shouted greetings from their storefronts; the pushcart vendors waved to the two they had come to know so well. The commotion of the approaching carriage caused

Lapeth to come through the veiled door of their iron shop; however, it was Methuselah who stepped forward and offered his hand to Tubal-cain first.

"Welcome home, my son."

"It is good to be back!" Tubal-cain was smiling from ear to ear. He clasped Methuselah's hand firmly, then looked toward Naamah. He saw Mariah standing behind her and jumped from the driver's platform, running first to embrace his wife, then Lapeth, and then his sister.

"What a pleasant sight you all are!" Gravas called happily. Methuselah helped him place his feet in the wagon's fittings in order to climb down. "The roads have improved greatly since my last journey." He dropped to the ground, grasped Methuselah's hand and held it between his own. "We've been there and back much sooner than I had hoped."

"My friend," Methuselah replied, with a twinkle in his eye, "you've arrived just as I anticipated. Where is this family you've brought to join us?" He gestured toward the carriage doors.

"Will I ever be able to catch you by surprise?" Gravas laughed joyfully, slapping a fat hand against the knee of his breeches.

"For both our sakes, let us hope not."

Traibus came forward and placed his enormous palm on the fat man's shoulder. "I hope your jokes have not grown more stale in your absence."

Finally, Noah joined the group and greeted them with such fervor that Gravas had to laugh. "You act as though we've been gone several years instead of a few weeks!"

"I am relieved by your safe return."

"Never had I hopes for such a reception!" Gravas said and turned to his audience. He winked at Methuselah's family as well as at the people along the storefronts, who he knew best. "And this is well, for I have brought home my own family—which should come as a surprise to all but this one." Methuselah offered no comment as Gravas pointed to him; instead he gestured for the horse-trader to continue.

"As you may know, I returned for my wives, yet only one found it in her heart to come with me." The look in his eyes suggested that he had not found the loss disagreeable. "But in addition to one," he went on, a look of amusement forming upon his face, "I was able to bring two more females who now possess my affections."

Naamah turned bright red and wondered what her mother would think; Mariah stared toward the carriage in horror, and Lapeth simply shook her head in amazement. Their reactions brought additional delight to the horse-trader:

"Fear not," he said, chuckling, "these females are mere babes. It would appear that the death of my brother-in-law, six months past, has made nieces I never knew into daughters of my own." He walked to the carriage, swung open the door, and reached in to take a woman's hand. (Naamah hadn't been certain what to expect, but the small woman stepping from the carriage wasn't it.) Gravas's wife's features were quite feminine, and she possessed a gentle appearance that proved quite a contrast to her husband's endless chuckle. In age, she was the maturity of Adah.

"May I present Tamari of Persia," the horse-trader said dramatically, for the benefit of the crowd.

"Welcome to your new home," Lapeth said pleasantly, for she remembered her own uneasiness when first meeting the family. "I am Lapeth, daughter of Methuselah."

"I have heard much about all of you, especially your father."

Lapeth introduced her to the crowd—family and merchants alike—while Gravas returned to the carriage.

He reached in and lifted two small girls, one at a time, to the ground. Many of the women marveled at the appearance of Gravas's adopted daughters, the elder no more than three, her sister nearly two. Both wore beautiful lace dresses, purchased from the finest bazaar in Persia, and both had hair braided back behind the ears. The elder girl squeezed her sister's hand tightly when the giant turned toward them, but neither child uttered a sound.

"Why, they are perfect!" one of the women in the crowd exclaimed.

"The eldest is Shelobothe," Gravas said, patting each on the head in turn, "and this is little Maran."

Methuselah finished greeting Tamari before looking in the direction of the girls. At their sight, a tingling sensation began to race up his spine. For an instant, he lost his look of composure and stared in complete astonishment. He had known they were coming, for he had seen it in the silence. He had even sent for Naamah because of their arrival, for she had always dreamed of daughters. Yet, as he looked upon the children now, he saw what had not been revealed in the silence.

He wiped his gray forehead with the sleeve of his robe and gazed at the two children. For a long while, he couldn't help but stare in amazement: While he watched Shelobothe, Shem's face appeared in his mind's eye; when he turned to Maran, he suddenly saw Ham. Something was happening, he knew with a certainty, but its significance lay beyond his grasp. Just when it seemed that the meaning might come within reach—for his grandson's faces became clearer and the young girls seemed to mature before his very eyes—it was gone. The vision disappeared from his mind, and all Methuselah could see was the innocence of the two children before him.

But the beauty of the children did nothing to alleviate the sadness he suddenly felt inside. Methuselah's eyes became moist, and he began to tremble like a very old man, and he suddenly realized beyond any shadow of a doubt that they were all running out of time.

With the Passage of Time
(5 years before the Flood)

No matter how elementary the problem appeared to others, Japheth thought it through with the same seriousness he gave the most difficult of decisions. He analyzed everything, for that was his nature. Sometimes his cautiousness made him appear slow to Shem and Ham but in reality the eldest son of Noah was the wisest. He stood against the outside wall of the massive barn and surveyed the long rows of crops he had sown. Only a few weeks had passed since the planting and already stalks of corn shot up straight and tall, covered with elongated shoots that would become the sweet yellow meat his family found so appealing. On either side of the central rows of corn, evenly spaced mounds of soil had been piled high and encircled with ankle-deep trenches to catch the dew that fell from towering green stalks. So soon after planting, tiny melons the size of fists lay hidden beneath the mingled shade of vines and upturned leaves.

He had transplanted small seedlings of raspberry from the freshwater lake less than one month earlier. Now, tiny buds sprang from the prickly vines of a dozen waist high bushes. Cucumbers were on smaller mounds and climbing plants of tomato and string bean clung to wire trellises only a few cubits in height. Growths of squash and lettuce and peppers and long rows of thin-leafed vines, whose underground roots would swell in size to become two varieties of potatoes, all waited expectantly for the harvest.

Japheth loved the soil, the earth, and the beauty of nature. These were his concerns from the first break of light until darkness began to fill the white vapors. He loved being near the creatures of the earth, spending long hours near the freshwater lake, watching animals live together in harmony. He was truly happy only with the surroundings of nature, so Noah allowed him to stay and tend the crops, work the fields, milk the cows, and watch over Naamah, Mariah, and Rezepatha, whom he had married.

With the passage of time, things had gotten worse in Shinar instead of better. The city grew larger and poorer and Malock continued to claim more land as his own. The city's dangers had caused the family to abandon the home of Ashmua and Lamech, returning instead to Lemech's ancient clearing. Japheth thought the move was the thing that had finally brought about the change in his mother, Naamah, for she now complained about everything: There was too much work to be done; the cottages needed a thorough cleaning, there were too many to cook for, and the clearing had become overgrown with the spreading vines of forest greenery. Something had happened which only Tubal-cain had foreseen: Naamah had become as critical, harsh, and demanding as her own mother before her. At the same time, however, Zillah surprised everyone by never uttering a word of protest; even at her advanced age, she worked harder than ever during the move. When the return to Lemech's clearing had been completed, the old woman had died unexpectedly and peacefully and was buried in an unmarked grave.

Adah had hoped that Naamah would eventually return to herself but the years passed and the change did not come. Naamah had become jealous of the work and of Noah's long absences, so that by the time Adah lay on her own deathbed (without having heard from her own sons in more than a century), the Naamah of younger years was all but forgotten.

Japheth spent long hours in the fields, away from the cottages. His mother's constant bickering drove even the beauty of the forest far from his mind. Often, in late afternoon, Rezepatha joined him amid the crops, where they could hold hands and gaze at the sky or talk peacefully, hidden behind the forest trees. They took long walks together so he could absorb the beauty of nature and breathe in the pleasant aroma of moist soil and wild ferns and the sweet scent of lavender.

His love for nature had been passed down from Lamech and Ashmua, and he couldn't help but wonder, as he stood near the barn, what they would have thought of the long rows of greenery he surveyed. The two had taught him all they had cherished about the earth; when it came time for the harvest, he would miss them even more. Ashmua had been dead for nearly five years and the forty days of grieving for Lamech had ended but a few weeks earlier. With the passage of Adah, Zillah, Ashmua, and Lamech, their numbers had become smaller but their work was no less demanding.

Japheth raised his eyes from the crops toward the forest trees growing beyond the cleared fields. The huge trees of white oak that surrounded the clearing and the fields had been on his mind for months, as many towering trunks of the century-old oaks were becoming uprooted. It had started a few weeks before Lamech had taken ill and had continued unabatedly. It appeared that the ground was saturated with more moisture than it could absorb, and the heaviness of limbs, branches, and leaves was simply pulling the roots out of the soil.

Although Japheth had thought long about the problem, he didn't have any ideas about what he could do. On a number of occasions he had been standing amid the crops and watched with horror as one falling trunk crashed mightily into another, causing a neighboring oak to become uprooted as well. Twice he hadn't even seen the fall but had heard the sounds of crashing limbs being muffled by forest mulch. At the base of some of the uprooted trunks Japheth had found underground burrows dug by the forest's moles and gophers. Sometimes he saw tiny beds of grass, chewed twigs, and underground dens burrowed deep inside the earth. Gophers, especially, loved to dig beneath the tall oaks and make homes inside tangled roots and natural cavities. For this reason, Lamech and some of the others often referred to the mighty white oaks as "gopher-wood." Between the saturated ground and burrowing animals, Japheth didn't think the trees had much of a chance.

"It saddens me also, my husband," Rezepatha said as she walked toward him, "but I don't believe there's anything we can do to stop it." She slipped her hand around his firm waist and kissed him on the side of the mouth.

"There's so much we're unable to do anything about," he said gloomily.

"Things will get better; your father is still quite certain. That is why he spends so much time in the city?"

"I thought it was to keep away from mother," he said, half seriously.

"You know that's not true. Noah's the only one who appears oblivious to what Naamah has become."

"What's mother doing now?"

"She's showing Mariah that the floors have yet to be cleaned to her satisfaction. I swear to you Japheth, Naamah is no longer who she once was. Sometimes I can scarcely believe the transformation."

"Mother has forgotten the Law and the One, even as those in Shinar," he said, more to himself than to Rezepatha. "Until she remembers, there can be no change for the better. I just wish father could help her become happy once again."

"Noah has too much on his mind to attend to this; he fears for the city."

"No," he said, taking her hand in his own and squeezing it softly, "he fears for the world."

Tubal-cain stood quietly against the counter, his once-white apron covered with soot. He watched the six youths carefully and although they were no more than boys, the fierce glare in their eyes and the gruff sounds of their voices as they whispered among themselves were enough to convince him that they had long passed innocence. Each wore torn breeches and a hanging shirt and their nervous steps caused Tubal-cain to think they were planning to take something.

The store had been robbed so often of small hand tools, iron goblets, brass silverware, and even plain metal bars that he had lost count. To make matters worse, the number of iron merchants competing with their business continued to grow. Much to Gravas's dismay, costs far exceeded income, and the horse-trader had been forced to subsidize their work in Shinar with his own rents. Although Noah wanted to retain the store as their one hold within the city, Tubal-cain wasn't certain the iron shop was such a good idea anymore. He wouldn't have thought it possible, but there appeared to be even less interest in the One than there had been before they had started.

A dozen taverns now spread throughout the sector, and Tubal-cain could remember a time when there had been but one. It wasn't the fact that the inns served gourd liquor or that gambling took place that bothered him; instead, it was that the people spent what little they had on the games and drink instead of on proper food. Disease was spreading, and infections were common on exposed faces and limbs. And the moneys the Mixtures wasted went to Malock, who owned the taverns.

"Would you like me to help you or not?" Tubal-cain finally asked, still leaning against the counter.

Four of the youths were startled as the man's voice broke the heavy silence but two of them (brothers it appeared) moved closer. "Sure you can help us," the eldest replied as the shorter youth snickered. "We need something from your store."

"What is it?" Tubal-cain asked suspiciously, finding it hard to believe they meant to buy anything.

"What do you think?" the darkest said, stepping right up to Tubal-cain. "We want money!" The youth watched the older man's eyes, expecting to see fear.

"I see," Tubal-cain said calmly, "and just what do you want money for?"

"We need it!"

"Umhh." The sound rose from his throat as he looked around the room. It didn't appear they were starving. "What would you buy if I gave it to you?"

"It's not your worry," the eldest said with a wry grin. His snickering companion moved closer.

"If you are in need of a meal, I will gladly buy it for you—

for you and your friends."

The snickering youth stood next to his brother and looked Tubal-cain over carefully; the man didn't appear to be much of a threat at all. He was dressed in a plain, simple robe, the type rarely seen in the sector anymore, with a long, discolored apron tied haphazardly about his waist.

Tubal-cain remained calm, although he wondered why the one boy looked him over so critically. After a while, he grew disgusted with the youths' silence; if they wanted something to eat, all they had to do was ask. "What have you decided?" He gazed first at the elder boy and then at his brother.

Tubal-cain's gentle appearance, apparent age, and calm attitude were taken by the snickerer as a sign of weakness. The youth pushed his older brother aside and stared hatefully into the eyes of the bronze man.

"I see you've become the spokesman," Tubal-cain said calmly. "Very well. I'll ask you one more time, and then you'll have to leave. Do you want some food?"

"We don't want food!" the youth said fiercely, at the same time ramming his clenched fist as hard and fast as he could into Tubal-cain's stomach.

In spite of his strength, Tubal-cain was so unprepared for the blow that he doubled forward and gasped for air. Before he had a chance to regain his breath, however, one of the other boys ran forward, lifted a metal bar from the table, and slammed it down hard on the back of his head. Tubal-cain let out one muffled cry and fell to his knees, wavering, before finally hitting the floor. In his last conscious instant, he thought of Methuselah, and then he saw only darkness.

The youths needed only a minute to find the small cash-box behind the counter. There wasn't much money to be had but they split equally what had been found. Each took three shekels, except for the snickerer, who took four. A moment later, they were gone.

Gravas leaned closer and kissed Tamari firmly on the forehead (while Shem and Ham looked on). Although Gravas had been back from his most recent journey for more than a fortnight, he continued to treat his tiny wife as though he had just returned. While the horse-trader wooed his wife, Shelobothe and Maran stood behind their aunt, carefully stealing glances at Noah's sons.

Shelobothe was most interested in Shem, with his smooth angular features and the thick waves of his brown hair pulled back behind his ears. Maran wanted to be with Ham, whose hair was lighter and whose features were darker. Yet, the sisters would have settled for the attentions of either. However, Noah's younger sons were cautious of displaying feelings to any woman. They wanted wives, to be sure, but they had heard such stories of their own mother's transformation that they weren't anxious to make the same mistake. Methuselah had assured them both that they would know when the time was right.

"We shall be back soon, my darling," Gravas said, kissing Tamari once again. "I've had Raphael assemble a few maps in the back room of the stable for us. After I've decided our route to Mizraim and discussed the plans with Noah, I shall return." He began to chuckle, and he winked at her. "Then we shall be alone, again, for a time."

"I am an old woman," she said, her eyes pleading, "and selfishly, I must ask you not to leave so soon. You just returned from Arabia and now you expect me to grant another leave?"

"It is a must," he said, shaking his head so red curls bounced from side to side. "Regrettably, there is no other choice."

"Father had great hopes for Mizraim," Shem volunteered, "yet on our last journey, very little occurred. Perhaps the time is right for the people, and they will listen."

"It is so far!" Shelobothe exclaimed, without considering what Noah's sons might think.

"If five years have made a difference in Mizraim's people," Tamari said, her eyes somber, "then the change is not likely to be to your advantage."

"We have to try," Ham insisted.

"Yes," Gravas nodded in agreement, "for without trying, we shall never know for certain. The work is too important; they must have a second chance."

"The peasants and merchants in Shinar no longer hear you," Maran said huskily, peering around her aunt at Ham. "What makes you think Mizraim will bend an ear? I sense your efforts will be wasted."

"Nonetheless," Gravas insisted, "with Methuselah's blessing we depart; without it we shall stay. Besides," he said, chuckling in an effort to break the seriousness of the moment, "we'll be gone two months at best, not a long absence when compared with some of our other journeys. There are many who need help; if we can't find them in Shinar, then we must look elsewhere."

"As you wish, husband," Tamari relented. "May the three of you seek out and find those who are ready." The men nodded in agreement and left for the stables, leaving Tamari and her nieces alone in the cottage.

The house was relatively small, considering the horse-trader's income at one time, yet it was comfortable and filled with dark wood furnishings and striped-cloth patterns that had cluttered

Tamari's home as a youth. When the cottage was built, it had been constructed far enough from the stables and with an acre of hay in between to avoid the pungent aroma of manure that constantly rose from the earth. The entrance had once faced Lamech and Ashmua's circular clearing, but since their deaths, a million trees had been felled, and the home now stood against Shinar's outermost border. Only a few scattered oaks remained outside the door of the cottage; ramshackle merchant dwellings and some of the smaller shops now stood just beyond.

"I continue to feel uneasy," Maran said suddenly. She rubbed her hands together, trying to concentrate. "There *is* danger."

"On the journey to Mizraim?" Tamari trusted Maran's senses, for her niece's gift of the Sight had been praised even by Methuselah. The woman appeared greatly concerned. "Should they not go?"

"I know not," Maran said with frustration, dropping her hands to her sides. "It is gone."

"What was it like?" Shelobothe asked, grabbing her sister's arm. She feared for Shem.

"There was a presence I do not know and danger, but mostly I felt the movement of evil."

After Gravas, Shem, and Ham left for the iron shop in search of Methuselah and while the light of the vapors was just beginning to fade from the sky, a solitary figure lay crouched in dark vines and scattered ferns that lay just below the few oaks outside the cottage door. He wore tight breeches and a deerskin vest open down the front. A thin black whip tied firmly about his waist dangled at his side. In the darkness, he sucked continuously on a burning length of tobacco leaves rolled between cornhusks.

For three days, he had watched the cottage, and he had become certain that the horse-trader prepared for a journey. He had seen stable hands load the small caravan with great quantities of traveling foods and he had heard Gravas himself utter "Mizraim" to the other two as they had left the cottage.

His cold eyes peered over the long blades of greenery and he watched the single curtained window excitedly. If only he might see the shadowed form of one of the young women again, he would be satisfied. He licked his curled lips, imagining how they looked beneath their long dresses. He had heard they were perfect but wasn't quite certain what that entailed. If they possessed smooth flesh and breasts soft to the touch, then that would be sufficient. He would have them first, and then the others back at the fields could do as they wished. He watched the cottage carefully and saw only two obstacles to overcome: There were stable hands on the property and an old woman in the house. The stable hands tended to remain near the barn and the livestock, so if he entered the cottage at night, he could probably steal away in darkness with the two women bound and gagged. The older woman could be silenced quickly before the two were taken.

His plan would have to be swift, that was certain. A cry of alarm would alert the stables. Although one of the stable hands was always awake and patrolling the grounds, the crouching figure knew the route by this time, and there would be no problem avoiding the guard. He realized he could have gotten help from the fields; many might have volunteered for such an assignment. Yet, he wished to receive solely the praises that would come his way, and he was bound to be promoted in rank and receive tribute as well. Besides, he lusted after the women exceedingly and had no desire to share their flesh just yet.

The thought caused him to inhale another long draw from the smoldering, dark tobacco.

Traibus was weary and frustrated to the depths of his being. Why didn't the people harken to what was said? Even Truth didn't seem to move them. He stood silent, towering over Lapeth, listening to her speak to those who had gathered outside the inn. She was still very beautiful, and the giant knew that a few of the wanderers and shopkeepers only gave them notice in order to look upon the woman. She remained as dedicated to their work as ever but the crowd's disinterest caused him to feel like the tired old giant he had become.

While Lapeth was speaking, a huge, bald man came out of the inn and began walking toward her as soon as he heard the sound of her voice. He moved closer in an attempt to see the gentle outline of her figure beneath her silken robe. The potent odor of gourd liquor rose from his pores and it was obvious that the man was drunk. Traibus concentrated on the man, watching him closely in an effort to determine if there was danger.

Lapeth turned to the newcomer and continued, " . . . so you spend your days complaining, wondering why there isn't enough to feed you until your stomachs are full, or why you have so little with which to clothe yourself. But I tell you, there shall never be surplus in your lives as long as you continue to waste what little you have." A few men whispered angrily among themselves, but the drunkard silently watched the woman's movements beneath her gown. Lapeth continued speaking:

"It is a waste to throw that which you need for food upon the gaming tables, or to slide it across the bar. It is a crime to spend in this way what should have gone to your families."

A man wearing a coarse apron, one of Malock's innkeepers, yelled out angrily, "You would call what little enjoyment these men are able to receive a crime? Their days of labor are not easy, yet you would keep them from their friends and the games?" A few voices of agreement joined in after the man's words were spoken.

"Is it no less a crime that your children must scour darkened streets in search of scraps to eat, while fathers drink up a full day's wage in an hour? Is it not wrong that these neglected youths turn to thievery themselves as the most natural way?"

The innkeeper laughed aloud and slapped the fellow next to him on the back earnestly. "She would blame all the crimes of Shinar on mere games of skill and chance? Can dice be evil, can the cards possess it, or perhaps it's the chips on the tables?" His laughter caused others to join in.

"The games themselves are not evil," Lapeth said. "What is wrong is the importance they now play. There are some in this sector who live and work and breathe only for the pastime." She looked among the crowd for a sympathetic woman and continued. "Have you not watched those around you grow old and die in poverty and sickness before their time? All over the city, those who die of sickness, starvation, or open wounds were once like you. Would you not have this come to an end? Have you no cares for the reason you were granted life?"

"This I already know," laughed a Mixture with hair covering his face and palms. "It was because my father, in spite of his drunkenness, found his way to where my mother slept." The laughter rose around him with renewed force.

Lapeth closed her eyes and shook her head in disagreement. "Each of you," she said softly, her long, dark hair trailing down her back, "has the same purpose, and it is this: that you might know yourself to be yourself and yet one with the Creator, the One."

"Show me this One you speak of," the large drunken man said, reaching forward to finger the woman's clothing. Lapeth backed just out of his reach. Traibus's arms tightened angrily, but he remained still and waited.

"Is this giant the Creator you speak of?" the drunk jested. "Why, he wears the dress of a woman, like yourself!"

"I wear a robe of the Law," Traibus said without emotion.

"The giant can talk!" the drunk exclaimed, and the others began laughing. "What is this Law he speaks of?" he asked Lapeth directly.

"It is simply this: The Lord thy God is One Lord. And thou shalt love the Lord thy God with all thy heart, thy soul, and thy mind; and thou shalt love thy neighbor as thyself."

"If you are my neighbor," the drunk said lustfully, "then I would choose you to love!" He reached forward, taking Lapeth by each of her shoulders and pulled her toward him. Traibus jumped swiftly, reaching for the man's arm, but the drunk swung powerfully into the giant's belly. The blow caused much pain, but Traibus remained unmoved as he tried to grab hold of the man's fists.

"Cease this!" a voice rang out loudly in the ears of all near the inn. "Crantal, I command you to stop!"

The man heard his name, released the woman, and turned fearfully to see who had called him.

Lapeth cried out, "Methuselah!" as he approached.

The gray haired mystic walked slowly forward with the aid of his tall staff. Those around the inn laughed heartily at the sight of such an old man who had caused Crantal to jump with such a scare, though a few knew the sage and whispered, "Methuselah," and backed away. Traibus took Lapeth by the hand and moved her toward Methuselah.

"Who are you, old one, to issue a command!" Crantal bellowed with anger. "I should teach you to whom you speak." He spat a mouthful of saliva onto the ground.

"I know to whom I speak," Methuselah replied. "Did I not call you Crantal, your name since birth?"

Many in the crowd began to laugh at the riddle. Crantal rubbed his massive hands together and moved toward Methuselah, breathing harsh-smelling breath onto him.

"You shall be taught a lesson this day!"

"I wish you had even one lesson to teach," Methuselah said calmly, "but, alas, you have none." Traibus and Lapeth moved behind him, wondering what he was doing. The crowd laughed at the old man's words.

Crantal bellowed, "But you don't know enough to fear your own words, for with them you have made a most grievous mistake."

"I wish the mistake had been yours," Methuselah said quickly. "If you had lived a life of mistakes, there might have been growth, for he who chooses, even wrongly, may learn a lesson. Yet you, Crantal, have been idle in drunkenness and have done nothing and have therefore learned nothing. And for this reason, you have no lessons to teach."

"You shall die, old fool," Crantal said when the laughter grew too much for him. His face turned red, and his bald head began to sweat profusely. He clenched his fists, and Lapeth immediately grabbed onto Traibus's arm as she saw the drunk's muscles flex and swell with rage.

"The first lesson you should attempt to learn," Methuselah said seriously, "is that the spoken word is much more powerful than it might seem. For this reason, it would be senseless for me to even raise one hand against you."

"Enough!" shouted Crantal as he prepared to swing.

"Besides, your hands are broken," Methuselah replied just as the sounds of cracking bone and splitting fibers came from Crantal's enormous fists.

The man's screams brought terror to the faces of everyone in the crowd. He began jumping and crying out for someone to help but the crowd began to disperse immediately, some even running in fear of the old man. "Did you see that?" the innkeeper shouted, as he ran for safety. One by one, merchants and peasants fled, until the tear-streaked man was left alone with the three robed figures.

When the crowd was gone, Methuselah lowered his staff toward Crantal. "Let thine hands be whole," he said.

Immediately, Crantal stopped screaming. He looked at the old sage for an instant, but when he realized that he alone stood with the three, he turned pale and ran toward an alleyway.

"I have never seen you do that!" Traibus said in amazement when Crantal was gone.

Lapeth looked between the two and was hopeful. "Crantal may learn and change because of this day," she said.

"No," Methuselah offered dismally, leading his friends away from the inn. "Even now, he seeks a place to quench his thirst. He has become far too sober for his own liking."

The giant eyed his old companion with suspicion. "Were Crantal's hands broken or did he only think that they were?"

"Have you not learned by this time, Traibus, to merely think something in the earth makes it so. But come, we have other matters to attend to. Tubal-cain has been injured."

With each passing hour the watcher became angrier. Darkness had overtaken the clouds long ago, and still he remained crouched low behind thick fronds of wild ferns and the loose blades of hay scattering the area. He could not force himself to leave, just yet. A return to the fields would be met with appropriate discipline (the praise he had hoped to receive from the overseer no longer filled his imagination). He had stayed way too long, beyond his leave. He would be punished, and the longer he delayed the more severe his discipline. Yet, he continued to be torn between heading toward Malock's fields or inflicting his anger upon the fat horse-trader.

He was two days late returning to his post. Patrols would be hunting for him but he had remained near the cottage, hoping one of the women would come near enough for capture. His need to possess them could not be shaken, although his fear of the overseer grew stronger with each moment of delay. The crouching figure grew tense with hatred of the horse-trader for ruining his plans. Behind the cover of leaves, the smoldering ash burned close to his lips.

The journey to Mizraim had been canceled. He had known for almost a day and a half, ever since the small caravan had been unloaded. At first he hadn't known why, so he crept around the fields of hay to the back of the barn and overheard the stable hands. Twice, he had been brave enough to crouch beneath the window of the cottage, listening to the faint voices of those within. The journey had been postponed on the advice of the one they called Methuselah. Still, Gravas had made the final decision. Besides, it was the horse-trader that Malock's guard had always been trained to despise, for Gravas was hated, while the wizard was feared.

He had heard rumors of Methuselah's tricks. Many in the overseer's fields knew of the magician. A few braver guards had sometimes debated (in whispers) Malock's own fears of Methuselah, which certainly explained why Malock hadn't destroyed the fat man's properties.

The skin on the guard's lips began to singe as the tobacco burned almost to its base. He angrily spit the butt out in the grass and listened to the faint sizzling sound of his own saliva quenching hot ash. Habitually, he reached within his vest for another rolled husk, but then decided against it. It was almost time for the stable hand to make his rounds, and the lone figure didn't want the smell of tobacco betraying his place of hiding.

Suddenly, he heard the sounds of footsteps. He huddled low, beneath the fronds, remaining completely quiet. His presence had gone undetected for five days, crouching amid grass or scurrying among buildings. Nearly a half-hour passed before he felt it safe to move. The sound of footsteps had stopped, and he was again confident that he was alone. He reached inside his vest for the tobacco and placed it eagerly between his lips. From the other side, he pulled a jagged pebble and a piece of flint. When it was lit, he sucked in a deep draw, relaxing as the dark smoke filled his lungs. At that moment, a wet, clammy hand wrapped itself firmly around his bare arm. He was so startled that a piece of smoldering ash dislodged to the ground, igniting a single blade of hay. Another hand reached down and quickly pressed out the tiny flame.

The man looked up at his captives and saw two huge baboon faced guards—Malock's men glaring back at him.

"You shall wish we had not found you, Sterba," the one with the cold hand growled. "Malock has plans for you."

Sterba continued to hold his tobacco between his lips and freed himself from the clammy palm. "Where's the rest of the patrol?"

he managed to ask, sounding a great deal calmer than he felt.

"Is that all you've got to say to us?" the guard growled. "You've abandoned your post. Why even now a group gathers near the holding pen in anticipation of your sentence. Only Baird and myself have come this far."

"What about the stable hand?" Sterba asked, rising to his feet before inhaling another puff.

"You needn't worry about him," Baird lisped. "He has been dealt with." The hairy ape toyed with the black whip he held extended between his hands. He pulled the cord taut to emphasize that Gravas's man had been strangled.

"There are more in the stables, you know," Sterba said knowledgeably, motioning in the direction of the large structure.

"They sleep quietly with the smell of strong ale on their lips," the one growled. "We will not be bothered." He clapped his hand tightly around Sterba's arm and shook him until more ashes became dislodged. "Come, you've wasted enough time."

Sterba lowered his eyes to the ground. The spark of his ash ignited a tiny piece of loose hay that sizzled before finally going out. As the flame disappeared, Sterba had an idea. He might yet avoid discipline and still not speak of the females. In the future, he could return for them both.

"We have orders to take you," Baird said, tightening the whip between his hands. "You are to be spared until your sentence, though we are certainly allowed to bring you back unconscious if it proves necessary."

Sterba shook free a second time. "There will be no sentence," he said confidently, "and if you return me just now, it is you who will be disciplined."

The growling man looked at Sterba with blank eyes and confusion.

"Do you not know whose cottage this is?" Sterba gestured at

the small house. "The owner and his wife sleep, but surely you know the man's name?"

"It is Gravas, most hated of all Malock's enemies. But how can that excuse your delay?"

"I have been waiting," Sterba lied quietly. The two bent closer to hear. "Waiting for the right moment. I'm going to set fire to the stables!" He plucked the burning husk from his mouth and threw it carelessly to the ground.

Both guards opened their eyes in amazement. "Do you not fear what the magician will do to you?" Baird asked nervously.

"I fear nothing!"

"There are those who say," the other man growled in whisper, "that even Malock does not harm the fat man for fear of Methuselah."

"Have you asked this of Malock, yourself?" Sterba inquired. "I have seen waggling tongues removed for less. "Now, are you with me?"

After a momentary pause Baird offered: "Perhaps we have nothing to fear if we only watch what Sterba has planned," to which the other one only shrugged.

A short time later the three walked cautiously through the hayfield with eerie shadows of light falling down from the evening clouds. Sterba did fear Methuselah but his fear of Malock was greater. In his mind he quickly created a plan which would enable him to return to his rank among the guards. Although he was concerned for Gravas's nieces, there was a chance that someone would awaken before the flames spread through the hay and devoured the cottage. If they survived, perhaps some day he could return for them.

As the three made their way to the stables, the rich odors of manure became more powerful, and the few horses near the wooden fence grew restless. The animals watched the men suspiciously, their massive brown eyes pulled back at the corners in distrust. The largest was a beautiful gray stallion with a shimmering coat. It made short, grunting sounds as it walked uneasily along the fence, whisking its well-groomed tail in annoyance at the men's approach.

Sterba watched the gray creature for a moment in complete fascination. Although the light was dim, the animal appeared without blemish. The man moved closer to the fence, his bare arm extending toward the stallion; the horse simply raised its head, snorting angrily at the intruder. For a moment, Sterba wished he could capture the animal, along with a couple of brown colts, but he couldn't take a chance of awakening the stable hands. Instead, he untied the whip from around his waist and held it as a threat toward the creature.

. The animal's hooves began to prance nervously, its long, gray ears perked back in revulsion. After clicking its long legs against the ground, it began nipping at the other horses, forcing them to back away from the fence. Sterba shook the whip once more before the animal and its companions galloped off toward the far end of the fenced property. The distance was so great that the shimmering creature disappeared in the darkness with the others.

"Why did you do that?" Baird asked ignorantly.

"When the fire starts, we don't want the sounds of panicked stallions and mares waking the entire stable," Sterba said disgustedly. "The horses are far enough away that the flames won't bother them until it's too late." He smiled, for the deed was sure to illuminate the sky, possibly even as far away as Malock's own fields.

He bent over and began ripping great handfuls of hay from the soil. He looked at the other two, shaking the first bit of soil from the roots, and motioned for them to do the same. Both shook their heads in refusal.

"You alone shall face the old wizard," the one growled.

Sterba piled great heaps of hay against one wall of the stables. He had picked the site because it lay opposite the living quarters of the stable hands, giving the men more time to awaken and rescue the women before the cottage was in flames.

When Sterba was thoroughly covered with sweat and dust, and his nostrils had grown accustomed to the pungent smells around him, he took one cornhusk from his vest and lit it. As he inhaled the dark smoke, he fantasized yet again of smooth-skinned females who were but a hundred cubits away. Finally, he lowered the red, burning ash to the hay, ignited the heap in several places, and nodded approvingly.

Immediately, tiny sparks shot into flames that licked against the wood planks of the building. Sterba's companions seemed pleased at they watched the fire catch hold of the stable wall. The wood smelled of pine; it would burn much more quickly than the oak fencing.

"Let's go," Sterba said finally, when the heat from the flames had grown too intense.

As they left, Baird looked over his shoulder again and again, expecting to see Methuselah; each time, however, he was disappointed. He had been hoping to see exactly what the old magician could do.

Tubal-cain hung his head in sadness and tightened a sympathetic arm around Gravas, whose eyes were quite moist. The stables, the fields of hay, even the cottage, were completely gone; all that remained was blackened earth, still smoldering warm as a reminder of the nighttime blaze. Thin wisps of smoke continued to rise in scattered areas around the property, its smell swallowing up even the odor of horses.

"My friend," Tubal-cain said sadly, "all I can say is I'm sorry." He wiped his dirt-stained forehead with a grungy arm and watched as stable hands walked through rubble and overturned smoking soil with the same shovels they had used all through the night. The men were tired, yet despite their exhaustion and their sadness, they continued working through what was left of the buildings.

Thirty merchants, those nearest Gravas's property lines, had awakened to fight the blaze as well, shoveling moist soil between the horse-trader's property and their own. Most had combated the flames in order to prevent their own places from burning. As soon as their own danger had passed, the merchants deserted their labors. Gravas's frequent absences and journeys away from the sector had done much to lessen his popularity among his neighbors. The greatest shock that had greeted them after the fire's damage had been surveyed was that Raphael had been murdered.

Raphael's body had been found, burned beyond recognition, pressed low amid the place where there had once been a field of hay. They knew it was Raphael because he alone had been missing. The angle of his head made it apparent that his neck had been broken. Apparently, Raphael had been murdered during his rounds. Everyone else had survived the fire.

Tamari stood between Maran and Shelobothe, staring in defeat at scorched ground and rubble—all that remained of her cottage and Persian furnishings. Her robe was torn and mud-streaked, like those of her nieces. Throughout the night, the three women had run water from the stone well to the surrounding buildings in a frenzied attempt to keep the blaze from spreading to the larger field; the horses had survived without injury. The only loss had been Raphael, but it was a loss that occupied Tamari's mind heavily.

"What are we to do?" Shelobothe asked aloud to herself. Her tangled hair fell in knots to her shoulders. "Poor Raphael. He was so full of goodness."

"It is a waste, indeed," Tamari said wistfully, wringing her hands together. "Though, I must be grateful that both of you, and Gravas, survived the night. I will say many prayers of thanksgiving throughout the day." She glanced at Tubal-cain, who supported the weight of her husband, and softly whispered a prayer in appreciation for the man's presence. He had awakened during the night to alert the rest of them; if not for Tubal-cain, the tragedy would have been far worse.

"I should have sensed the danger," Maran's husky voice said angrily. "I should have known!"

"My child," Methuselah's familiar voice assured her as he approached, "even I didn't know until it was too late." She swung around and saw him walking toward them, somber faced. His gray beard swung back and forth slightly as he hurried along, clutching his staff. "We came as soon as I realized what had happened," he added. Behind him walked Shem, Ham, Lapeth, and Traibus bringing up the rear.

"But one of us should have known!" She clenched her fist and flung it against her side. "Raphael has died when he might have lived!"

Methuselah took her face between his hands and stared deep into her eyes. "Listen to me," he said gently. "Even Light cannot shine through darkness for a time when evil acts on impulse. There is nothing we could have done."

Gravas walked to Methuselah, his curls held in place by dried sweat and earth. "What would you have me do now, friend?"

"We shall return to the forest. The time has come for us to live as one." His eyes sparkled as he spoke, though Gravas sensed sorrow on his countenance. "Even now, Japheth readies the foundation of a new cottage."

"What of Naamah?" Tamari asked quickly.

"She has no choice in this," Methuselah said firmly. "It will be best for us all. Rezepatha will speak to her."

"And Noah?"

"He knows what has happened and has gone to pray."

Gravas nodded. "Before we leave," he said sadly, bending with some difficulty to pick up the shovel at Tubal-cain's feet, "we must bury Raphael."

"No, my friend," Methuselah said compassionately. He put one hand on Gravas's shoulder and, with the other, took the shovel. "We bury a body. Raphael has gone to the One."

"I will not have it!" Naamah uttered defiantly. "There is not enough room for them here, and I can't feed that many people every day!" She wrestled her arm away from Rezepatha, who was trying to comfort her.

"Japheth has begun another cottage," Rezepatha's beautiful voice said happily. Her high cheekbones became even more striking as she spoke. "It will be wonderful to have everyone together."

"It will be nothing but work." Naamah waddled to the front door and peered out. Already she was a large as Zillah had ever been and had taken to wearing clothing like her mother before her.

"We will all work together."

Naamah shook her head in disgust and watched Maran and her eldest son walk around the dimensions of a new foundation not too far from the petrified stump. "I suppose they'll want something to eat as soon as they get here."

"Yes, Naamah, they will be hungry, and tired and filled with sadness."

The hefty woman turned around, her long apron trailing behind her, looking as though she was appalled. "Because an old barn burned to the ground?"

"No, because a man has died."

"You didn't tell me that," Naamah said fearfully. "Who was it?" For an instant, irritation faded from her face, and Rezepatha thought she could see a glimmer of the old Naamah.

"Raphael."

Naamah shook her head in genuine sadness and turned into the kitchen. It would be a while before her look of defiance was displayed again.

Japheth watched his mother turn into the cottage and waved to his wife, trailing after her. He wondered what Naamah was really thinking, for she usually hid her true feelings. He looked down at the ground and the outline of the foundation they had traipsed through the soil, trying to imagine what the cottage would look like when it was complete. The doorway would have to be at least six cubits in height and the ceiling seven. It would be easier to build the structure to accommodate Traibus, rather than having to rebuild it later. He knew from experience, for it had taken nearly a month to rebuild the proportions of Tubal-cain's home after Traibus and Methuselah had moved to the clearing. The old dwelling of Lemech, the hunter, was dwarfed in appearance by the house standing next to it.

"What can I do now?" Mariah asked eagerly. She remained as pleasant as ever, in spite of Naamah's constant bickering.

"Help me find a log," Japheth said sarcastically but grinning. He smiled, in spite of his true feelings, so she smiled back at him. All around the borders of their clearing, oaks of centuries had released roots from the wet earth. Many leaned in cross-angles against upper limbs of more solid trees; others had managed to fall completely to the ground.

The two walked around long rows of vegetables in the direction of the smaller trees. Japheth reached for the ax that lay against the abandoned kilns and waited for Tubal-cain's wife to catch up with him. He still hadn't discovered how to stop the mighty oaks from just slipping out of the soil. The loose dirt on top of the ground was usually dry, but beneath it, the water table appeared to be rising, saturating the clay and minerals below. He was positive there had to be something he could do, at least to make root systems stronger, but he wasn't sure what it might be. When his father returned from the lake, he would ask for further suggestions. Surely, amid all of Noah's wisdom, there was a remedy that had been overlooked. If his father didn't have any ideas, he would have to ask Methuselah.

Japheth was quite certain that someone had to have a plan for the gopher-wood trees of the forest.

Noah remained in the silence with his legs crossed, sitting upon the shoreline of the lake. He had been praying with all his might for an answer. His eyes were closed, his mind was directed within, and his white hair had been pulled back behind the smooth flesh of his ears. For hours, he had remained completely still, listening and waiting for the answer. More than ever before, he needed to know what he and the rest of the Law should do? What should they be about? Where should they go? The guidance had not come. So he remained perfectly still, listening for an answer to rise within his own heart.

Twice that morning, he had fondled the golden coin and chain about his neck and thought of Methuselah. Even his grandfather didn't know what came next, and that was frightening. There had once been a time when the One's presence had been felt continuously, but the world had changed.

In his contemplation, Noah made quite a spectacle for some of the forest creatures that watched him curiously. A spotted doe cocked her head and elongated ears and wondered if she could hear what the familiar man seemed to be listening to. A few tiny field mice sniffed at the grasses and soil near where he sat, looking up at his enormous size with glossy black eyes, holding him in awe. Finally, one of the white doves soared down from the limb of an oak, circling within a cubit of the man's head, in order to see what he was doing. None of the creatures feared the robed figure, yet all were curious as to why he hadn't moved in such a long while. The smallest rodent wavered uneasily on hind legs, sniffing at the air, whiskers outstretched for clarity, trying to sense whether the man was injured.

When the light from the vapored clouds reached its pinnacle in the afternoon, Noah remained still. So deep was his meditation that it was a very long while before he heard his name being called by a voice that seemed to rise from the surface of the lake.

"NOAH!" the voice called aloud again, and Noah finally heard. He opened his eyes and was awestruck by the brilliant form of

Enoch standing with arms outstretched above the lake.

The body appeared human, though it shimmered with yellow rays of light that flew from its form in glimmering shafts. Thousands of individual sparks circled around the golden figure in continuous whirls of motion, soaring through the air with the hum of countless bees as the being stayed aloft. The illumination grew so intense that Noah found it difficult to keep his eyes open.

"The time has come." The words sounded in his ears, though Enoch had not moved to speak.

"Then it is true," Noah merely thought, yet the sound registered in his own head. "We have failed the One." He bowed as though broken in sorrow.

"Much has been accomplished," the voice boomed so powerfully that Noah raised his head. The golden figure nodded and pointed a glowing arm at him. "Your work and the labors of thy family have been the intercession, as was foretold; even now, thousands all over the world prepare and harken to the One. And your faith has done much to make this so."

"I know not of these thousands."

"They roam every continent of this planet, though you know them not. Your work, and the deeds of those with you—in Dodanim, in Mizraim, in Sheba, in Cush, in Arabia, near the Great Sea, in Persia, even in Shinar—have helped to awaken humankind throughout the earth."

"But I never met them. The work was spent on those who would not hear."

"A prayer, a good deed, a kind thought are never lost." Enoch glimmered with an array of gold and yellow light pouring from his form. The words rang in Noah's ears. "Your family did much to bring the Light. Many now prepare for that which must come. Many will be saved; many will find peace because of your faith."

The figure of Enoch began to fade, gradually, as the golden form lowered his arms to his side.

"But there are millions!" Noah spoke aloud, not wanting him to disappear. "What are a thousand in the face of these?"

"They are the hope that remains."

"Shall all not be saved?" Noah asked fearfully, as Enoch's form dimmed further.

"Fear not. You remain the intercession of this darkness." Enoch's voice grew softer. "You shall indeed save these people from their bondage. Thou art perfect among thy generation, Noah, and have found your peace with God. This peace I leave with you." The words stopped, and Enoch was gone.

Noah moved to get to his feet when it happened. He felt it along his back—a burst of power more forceful than he had ever sensed in the silence. His neck and forehead began to throb with a fire he had never known, and he fell forward to his knees as a sound exploded in his ears. It was mighty and overpowering, yet possessed a purity that moved him to tears. And it was followed by a voice more beautiful than even Enoch's:

The end of all that is of the flesh has come before me!

Noah bowed low, closed his eyes and cried. His whole body shook as the tears swelled, for Noah knew to Whom he was listening:

For the earth is filled with violence through those who would destroy it, and behold they would destroy themselves with the earth.

Noah continued to shake, wondering if the Voice had ceased.

Finally, he heard the guidance he had sought:

> **Make thee an Ark of gopher-wood. Rooms shalt thou make in the Ark, and shalt pitch it within and without with pitch. And this is the fashion which thou shalt make it of: The length of the Ark shall be three hundred cubits, the breadth of it fifty cubits, and the height of it thirty cubits. A window shalt thou make to the Ark, and in a cubit shalt thou finish it above; and the door of the Ark thou shalt set in the side thereof; with lower, second and third stories shalt thou make it.**
>
> **Everything that is of the earth shall die.**

The warmth continued rising up Noah's back; he heard every word between the sobs that overcame him.

> **But with thee, I have established this covenant, and thou shalt come into the Ark, thou, and thy sons, and thy wife, and thy sons' wives, and they whom harken unto thee. And of every living creature, at least two of every sort shalt thou bring into the Ark, to keep them alive with thee; they shall be male and female. Of every clean beast thou shalt take to thee by sevens, the male and his female. And of beasts that are not clean, by two, the male and his female. Of fowls of the air by sevens, the male and his female to keep seed alive upon the face of the earth. And of every creeping thing of the earth after his kind, two of every sort shall come unto thee, to keep them alive.**
>
> **And take thou unto thee of all food that is eaten, and thou shalt gather it to thee; and it shall be for food for thee, and for them thou doest bring into the Ark. These**

things thou shalt keep mindful, for upon thine own heart they have been written.

And so may it be, Noah! My son, who harkened after the way.

Immediately, the voice stopped ringing in his ears, and Noah fell unconscious to the ground, alone on the shore of the freshwater lake.

It was early evening, when all but the dimmest light had disappeared from the vapors. Noah was awakened by the gentle touch of an aged hand upon his shoulder. Slowly, he turned his head and looked upon the face of his grandfather.

"What has happened?" Methuselah was visibly shaken by Noah's appearance and tear-streaked eyes.

"Know you not?" the grandson asked weakly. He tried to rise to his knees, but was strained by the effort. "Has your Sight abandoned you?"

"Tell me," Methuselah said, shaking, "I know nothing."

"Then know this. The vision which we feared will come to pass. By the very words of the One, I have heard it spoken."

Methuselah's eyes opened wide in wonderment. He fell suddenly to his knees and dropped his staff to the earth. "My humble son," he managed to say, through tears of his own, "His voice has not been heard for a very long time. What would He have us do?"

Beneath the cover of solid oaks and towering pine, Noah spoke of all that had transpired upon the shore of the lake. He told of Enoch and the One and of the Ark they were to build. For a long while they spoke, until well into the evening, and the message of what was to be done became engraved on the heart of the grandfather, as well.

Much later, when Methuselah returned to the clearing, he recorded it all on parchment and hid it along with the rest of his manuscript.

Six Months Later
(Four-and-one-half years before the Flood)

The strain in Maran's neck had become excruciating, but she refused to give thought to rest. She leaned over the uppermost limbs of the fallen oak and took aim with her hand ax, pushing all thought of painful shoulders from her mind. As the blade struck its mark, breaking the green branch from the main trunk, she tried to focus only upon what she was doing, though her concentration deserted her. Too many things were running through her head at the same time; some thoughts she barely sensed and couldn't grasp for certain, but she was positive of one thing: Ham's stubbornness was beginning to anger her more than she would have ever thought possible.

She glanced quickly, lest he was looking, toward the other end of the fallen oak where he stood, almost twenty cubits away. Even at this distance, she immediately saw the glistening film of sweat running down his bare back. The muscles of his tan flesh tightened into corded fibers as he raised his ax handle, longer than her own, over his head and brought it down mightily with a crash, dislodging chips of bark and thin layers of wood from the large branch. Each time the tool struck the limb's base, thick slivers of oak shot through the air and landed on either side of him.

Ham continued stripping the lower branches from the main trunk as she chopped away at smaller boughs. Maran knew his gruff features would be pinched together in concentration, and the corners of his mouth would be turned down in annoyance but he would never mention his need for rest. She watched him pause and shake beads of moisture from his sopped hair by spinning his head back and forth, then running a callused palm through his scalp. She sighed once to herself before looking down at the countless twigs, leaves, branches, and limbs which awaited her; if she had to, she could be just as stubborn as Ham. But she couldn't help but be sick of his superior attitude.

Too often, she had seen Ham's weariness and commented on her own exhaustion just to force him to take a break, and each time he had made some comment about her being a woman. No longer, however, she assured herself as she brought the ax down on a lengthy bough; Ham could drop to the ground in unconsciousness before she'd worry about him. If he passed out due to senseless pride, it would be his own fault.

Her eyes scanned the smooth bark of the white gopher-wood and the pile of branches she had discarded next to the enormous trunk. The ground beneath her feet was covered with damp mulch and scattered vines as well as the broken twigs and fallen leaves from the tree itself. Clusters of wild fronds grew heartily a few cubits from where she stood. The smell of oak mingled with cut pine and the soft scent of crushed lavender rose above the dampness of soil. After the oak had been stripped of its branches, Gravas's horses would drag it to one of the woodpiles that continued to rise on the edge of their ever-expanding clearing. The clearing grew a little larger each day but only a fraction of their work had been completed.

Months of strenuous labor had passed but even their combined numbers had scarcely managed to clear the acreage necessary for the construction of the craft. Most of the outlined area was finally free of uprooted oaks. In addition, a hundred other trees, oaks and pine, had been felled in order to accommodate the dimensions of the Ark. The length of the structure alone would be 300 cubits and the ground they required for its construction was almost twice that.

The massive cleared space was surrounded on two sides by alternate piles of stacked logs and scattered heaps of broken branches. The clearing began at the three cottages. The only things familiar about Lemech's ancient clearing were the huge boulders and jagged stones that remained embedded in the earth at the back of the cottages, just as they had for centuries. Lining the outer edges of one side of the immense clearing was Japheth's bountiful fields. The rows of produce had been lengthened, and newly planted fruit trees grew alongside evenly spaced trenches of corn, beans, tomatoes, and wheat. An acre of hay had been planted for the horses. Rezepatha and her husband spent a good deal of each day tending the expanded crops, which were larger than Lamech could have ever dreamed possible. Gravas often chuckled over there being such an excess that even he couldn't begin to devour it. And Naamah simply complained to her husband that the food would be wasted; there were only so many vegetable pies she and Mariah could bake, or that everyone could eat. But Noah approved of the extent of the crops; the poor in Shinar could be provided for, even if most of their own time was devoted to the clearing. Six months had passed, and although the Ark demanded his attention, Noah's compassion remained with the city. He dreamed of building the craft, then of returning to Shinar—there might yet be time to help the people.

Time, too, was on Maran's mind as she broke away smaller twigs with her bare, scratched hands. Even with their combined efforts, she felt that their work was moving too slowly. Though they arose to begin at the first break of light and often didn't finish until only the filtered glow of evening lit their way back to the cottages, it didn't seem to be enough. Rarely did they even take meals together anymore, eating rather in groups of two or three during short periods of rest. Sometimes, Maran and Ham walked wearily toward Naamah's kitchen, but often Tamari brought their meals to the far edge of the field. Progress was slow, and Maran began to wonder how long it would be before even a handful of felled timbers had been cut into planking. She couldn't fathom how many years it would be before they needed pitch to paint the joints and the seams. They could get great quantities of it only three days' journey from Baghdad, in Hit or Id, though as her uncle had joked there was no sense packing for the trip just yet. They had plenty of time.

Or did they? She wondered to herself, as she glanced with irritation at Ham's sweating back. Even if they continued working at the same pace, it would take decades to finish; of this, she was certain. She couldn't understand why Methuselah or even Noah didn't know how much time they had left. After all, Noah had seen the vision. He should have some idea how much time remained; he just had to. So, for that reason alone, Maran assured herself, there was no cause to worry.

Once every few weeks, Methuselah gathered them together at the end of the day by the petrified stump. There they sat for hours just talking around a small fire or listening to Methuselah as he related a story. He never told the same tale twice (or he changed it with so many variations that it never appeared to be the same). Japheth brought fresh melons or large bowls of fruit to pass around to their numbers: fourteen when Naamah did not see fit to join them, though generally, all fifteen were present. Sometimes they sang the songs of old until late into the evening or played games among themselves in an attempt to relieve the burden of their enormous task.

Gravas saw to it that there was plenty of ale, and both he and Traibus made certain none of it went to waste. Tamari taught them the games she had learned as a child: making up riddles to describe simple objects or the things which grew around the lake and clearing, or guessing games that stumped even Methuselah. Often, Shelobothe thought up her own versions until they had such a number of diversions that everyone found a favorite.

They sported with round pieces of quartz, ground into perfect spheres by Ham and Shem, and wagered (on occasions when Lapeth would allow) with nimble sticks broken from the pine and gopher-wood. Gravas kept a set of horseshoes in the barn to toss toward iron stakes, requiring a great deal of skill for the throw and near perfect sight. Tubal-cain taught games of skill with the bow and sling, using a mat of woven hay against the side of the barn as a mark. Shelobothe excelled at the pastime, as did Ham and Shem, but she could get the others to play only when enough light filtered through the evening vapors, about once a month.

Noah seemed delighted with whatever they played, as long as they did it together. And if Naamah had a favorite, no one knew what it was, for the look of disgust remained on her lips regardless of what they were doing. There were a few things she absolutely refused to participate in, such as when Tamari and Mariah could be coaxed into a duet, and everyone else simply sat in quiet, listening to the blend of their beautiful voices.

Maran found all these things enjoyable, but what she liked most of all was listening to Methuselah. She loved to hear him talk, especially of the faithful, and could have spent days hearing of Mahalaleel, Enos, Jared, and Seth, and everyone else who had been a part of the past. She would often stare at him in complete fascination as he sat on the stump with the others gathered around him, the flames of the fire casting steady shadows on the trees, cottages, and barn.

Their gatherings near the stump did much to rejuvenate them, at least until the next time when the weight of their work bore down heavily. Methuselah retained control of these times, but the work of the Ark was Noah's, for the gentle, white haired man had become their undisputed leader, and it was Noah that Maran suddenly saw fast approaching.

She pulled the loose strands of hair back behind her shoulders and looked at him with a smile as genuine as the one he returned. Noah walked toward the felled oak without speaking, looking back and forth between his youngest son and Maran. His blue eyes began to sparkle brilliantly in the light of day, and the woman quickly sensed that he knew what was going on.

"Ham!" he said, in a voice that rose above even the crash of the ax.

Ham stopped the swing in midair and lowered his blade to the ground, though keeping hold of the wooden handle. He turned and looked directly at Noah while moisture ran down from his hair, flowing into his eyes. "Yes, father," he said hoarsely.

"Have you not sense enough to rest?" Noah asked calmly, tucking his thumbs inside his roped belt for emphasis. "You will be of little use if you push yourself much farther."

Ham stared blankly for a moment and then looked at Maran, who had returned to her labors.

"Well?" Noah said softly. "I want you to see your mother and get something to eat. Don't return for at least an hour."

"What of Maran?"

"Can you not see that she has work to do? Now go." Ham simply nodded, dropped his ax completely, and turned toward the cottages. He took one final glance at Maran before heading for the kitchen.

When he was finally out of earshot, Noah continued, "In a short while, you may wish to join my hardheaded son."

"Not too quickly." She stood upright and looked at the robed figure before her, finding it very difficult to conceal her grin.

Before he could speak again, Maran spotted a single flash of yellow light jump from between the fingers of Noah's closed fist. She moved to speak, to discover what was in his hand, but he spoke first.

"I have come to you," Noah said softly, "seeking counsel."

Her mouth fell open in amazement, and her husky words asked, "What of Methuselah?"

"You needn't worry," Noah began to laugh. "My grandfather will have his say—whether I ask him for it or not."

"What would you ask of me?"

"Just tell me," he said, raising an arm and pointing toward the massive clearing. "What do you see?"

Maran noticed that his left fist remained clenched but she diverted her eyes and complied with his request. She was surprised that the words came so easily: "I see that we have done much, yet there remains a great deal more we have yet to accomplish. I see our families have become as one, unified for a single purpose, though even as one our task is staggering."

"The oaks must be cut into smoothed timbers and planks, though a few of our number haven't the strength to handle a saw. As you've stated, all outer beams need to be at least a cubit thick and fastened end-to-end with cross-boards, iron pegs, and bitumen pitch. Yet, when these beams are joined together, do we have numbers enough to raise even one section and attach it to the ribs of the hull? Can even a dozen of our strongest handle the task, or do they lack the strength to raise one single rib of the Ark into an upright position?"

Maran looked somberly into Noah's eyes and continued. "I look at the clearing and am grateful for the moist earth which aided us in the removal of the trees, but now the soil will work against us. As soon as the first plank is laid, the lumber shall begin to settle into the ground but the Ark itself must be level, so how can we rectify this? A platform must be built the length and width of the ship and needs to be completed before the first rib can be joined, and upon this platform three stories will be raised."

"For all these things, we will need the horses." Maran wondered aloud, "Yet how many of those we now have penned will still be alive when the day comes to construct the uppermost floor? By the time we've cut timbers for the posts, planks, and beams, and finished the entire platform, my guess is an entire decade will have passed. We can buy a few horses with what remains of Gravas's resources; the rest we could capture in the wild. As Traibus has suggested, we might travel deep into the jungle for a pair of elephants but we haven't the time for an afternoon in Shinar let alone a journey my uncle claims would take two weeks."

"The Ark you've described, father Noah, will take many decades to complete. Even your children's children may have a hand in its construction. Were our numbers a hundred instead of fifteen, this need not be. Still, it is the work of the One, a work we've been asked to do, and for this reason we shall labor though it takes a century."

She finished speaking, amazed she had been able to voice what had been on her mind. However, there was one thing she decided not to say, and Noah saw it in her face immediately.

"What have you held back from me?"

"It is not mine to say." She lowered her eyes to the ground.

"If you feel it," he insisted, "then it becomes yours to counsel. I shall decide on the course of action but you and my grandfather have been chosen to advise. Say what you would keep to yourself."

Slowly she brought her eyes up to meet his. "Though we are unified in desire, at the pace we now move, the work may be for naught. I feel we are running out of time."

Noah nodded and turned his head, first to the empty clearing and then toward the stacked trees, thousands in number, lying untouched on the edge of the clearing. "I have sensed this myself," he assured her, "and I, too, wish our numbers were greater. Great enough, first of all, that there would be no need for the Ark; the people would have heard and believed and harkened after the Law. But this it seems cannot be, so there remains a need for more laborers. There is no other answer."

"How can you obtain the help we need?" Maran was confused. "They think our ways folly. Even Gravas's own stable hands would not follow us into the forest. Noah, imagine for a moment what these people will think. We are building a ship in the middle of the forest!"

"It matters not what they think or even what they believe. Perhaps Gravas's hands stayed in the city because we needed to become strong—unified for a purpose before help from the outside could assist us. And now, we are truly as one."

"But where can we get help?" Maran asked. "We have no money to hire these workers."

"I have meditated for an hour, my daughter," he said positively, "and the answer was quite clear. We shall indeed have the laborers we need."

She looked at him inquisitively. "What are you going to do?"

"I know not yet." Noah shrugged his shoulders. "Though the answer has something to do with this." He moved his left hand between them both and raised it up over her head. "And this has something to do with my grandfather."

He opened his clenched fist, dropping from his hand a single, golden coin dangling on a chain. It hung from his little finger, sparkling brilliantly with yellow gold as he twirled it in the rays of light that flooded from the clouds.

Noah found Methuselah along with Lapeth and Traibus, outside the window of Naamah's kitchen. The three had finally taken rest atop the rocks and were listening to Traibus discuss the numbers of snares required to capture the animals for the Ark. Methuselah listened in amusement to the oft-told tale, his staff lying on the stone beside him, while Lapeth watched the old giant's gestures in fascination. Her slender legs were crossed, dangling over the side of a boulder, while her black hair fell smoothly down her back. Her eyes focused on Traibus's description of the jungle, and she appeared as though she could almost see it.

"Don't you think it will be quite some time before the Ark is ready for even a single creature?" her beautiful voice rang out. (Naamah, peering through the kitchen window, simply shook her head in disgust.) "We have a score of years ahead of us."

"Not if we have help." Noah looked up at them from his place on the trail.

Naamah, hearing her husband's voice outside, pressed her lips together and leaned closer to be certain of hearing every word—though she pretended not to take notice by continuing to wash the same dish repeatedly.

"How would you get us help?" Traibus asked. He continued leaning upon the rock. Although his feet were on the ground, his eyes were level with Lapeth's; Methuselah sat a little lower on the first carved landing of stone.

"I have come to ask my grandfather that very question," Noah said, while the coin remained clutched in his hand. The mystic looked down at his grandson and waited for him to continue. Noah complied. "How is it, Methuselah, that this gift you gave me so very long ago could provide the help of a hundred?"

He opened his hand and dropped the length of chain just as he had in front of Maran.

Lapeth gasped at the sight of such a tremendous sparkle dangling below her eyes. Immediately, Traibus remembered the day his companion had made the gift; he looked toward Methuselah, who simply grabbed his staff and nodded, showing no sign of surprise as he spoke: "Traibus, it would appear the time has come. At last, it has finally come."

"What do you speak of?" Noah voiced the question.

"I have waited for centuries," Methuselah said softly, his excitement remaining hidden from all but Traibus, who knew him best. "Long ago," he remembered aloud, "my father took me to the shores of a sparkling river near the mouth of the gulf. He showed me the splendor that belonged to the One and asked me to keep it safe. It was to be used for His work, when the time was right."

Slowly, Methuselah climbed down off the rocks. With his staff, he walked the few steps to Noah. "I have hoped for this moment, never knowing when it might come to pass. Tell him, Traibus." Methuselah gestured toward his old friend. "For the secret has been yours as well."

The giant appeared completely surprised by the honor. He stood tall next to Noah and Methuselah and thought for a moment in order to compose his words:

"A long time ago, when I knew not even myself and Shinar was still my home, I wagered with a sage." He started slowly and told the tale of the wager, the gold, the mermaid, and his first glimpse of the Light. He spoke for a long while, without hurry just as Methuselah would have done, until his story came to the present.

"There shall be a journey to the west." Traibus assured them. "Many of us will be required, as well as Gravas's horses and more than one wagon for the task at hand will be great indeed. Yet upon our return, finally, we shall have the means to purchase whatever is necessary. Noah will get his laborers. Upon this clearing," he said, waving his robed arm in its direction, "the time has come to build an Ark."

Noah smiled wider than he had for many months and lifted his arms to help Lapeth down from the rocks. When she was upon the ground, she took the single coin from him and looked at it for a very long while. She tried to imagine how much gold there might be on the shores of the river near the gulf. (But even her imagination could not prepare her for what she would see firsthand within the week.)

Methuselah remained behind as the three walked around the cottage to find the others. He mouthed a silent prayer of thanks and looked out over the clearing to see the immense space where they would build the craft. He shook his head in amazement and spoke aloud only to himself. "With His own gold does the One plan to raise this Ark."

It was only natural for Gravas to become foreman of the new laborers. He still had a few connections in Shinar and through them he let it be known they were hiring crews. The chuckling, red-haired man had to do a great deal of jesting while explaining the nature of their task: They were building a ship, a half-day's journey inside the forest. On all sides, it would be surrounded by thick growths of ancient oak and pine but that wouldn't cause them concern, for the vessel's enormity would make transportation impossible. They had no desire to see it launched in the gulf, the Great Sea, or anywhere else that could handle the Ark's displacement. It would be constructed of gopher-wood for the most part; the wood was harder to work with but it split clean and dried sturdier. It was to be massive in design with a length-to-breadth ratio of six to one, yet there would be no need to construct it with the capability of being steered in any particular direction; there would be no tiller, rudder, or oars. What usually caught the agents' attention more than anything, however, was the fact Gravas promised payment in gold. It didn't matter where the portly man was getting his gold from, the claim was met with a great deal of enthusiasm.

Gravas journeyed to the offices of a dozen merchants, passing the word of what he was looking for. Without exception, everyone he visited was moved to laughter but whether the laughs were the result of the horse-trader's own joviality or the vessel's description itself, he was unable to discern. It didn't even matter, for the very first day (much to Naamah's irritation) the first group of five laborers showed up at the clearing. Two had worked for Gravas as stable hands before and all were eager to begin at once, despite the distance they had come.

Because of the long journey to Shinar, Noah had spent two days deep in thought wondering if it might be advantageous to make room for all they expected to employ near Japheth's trenches; they would need cots and portable shelters, enough for a hundred. Much more could be accomplished if the laborers were available from the first light of morning until nightfall. If they were forced to walk from the city and then return, he would lose three-quarters of each day in traveling time. He did worry that the evil in Shinar might become part of life in the clearing as well, yet this remained a possibility by hiring crews at all, whether or not they lived near the cottages. Noah counseled long with both Methuselah and Maran before making the only possible decision, and in the end Tubal-cain took charge to see that a tent city rose where there had been only a cleared field. It was the raising of the tents and not the construction of an Ark that the laborers found as the first job at hand.

They came in groups of three and four, friends and acquaintances from the shops and the tenements, the streets, and even the taverns of the city. Some sought out the clearing themselves; others were traveling craftsmen sent by agents to see Gravas. Fathers came with sons, and often brothers arrived together, until the once-peaceful site began to bustle with the excitement of men who had finally found employment. There were Persians and Syrians, people from the East, and a handful of merchants from abroad who just happened to be passing through Shinar when the announcement had been made. Men came from Gomer and Sarmatia, Libya and Mizraim, and four Black warriors arrived from Cush. They came from homes in Sheba and Dodanim, Macedonia and Tyre, and from places throughout the continent. Some came from the mountains of Aghri Dagh to the North, bringing milking goats, wives, and empty bellies that had known lack for much too long. There were Mixtures and men of every race and deformity; none accepting the call was turned away, regardless of age, skill, or knowledge of shipbuilding. A few had never even seen a boat before.

Then, too, some came as though destined to be a part of the work. One man, nearly perfect in appearance (though not of the Law) proudly displayed the bright red skin of his forefathers. He came from Poseidia and was called Anon and even knew of Raki'el and the elder's married daughter through his business with the temple priests. His training was that of an engineer, and Gravas persuaded him with a pitcher of ale and a great sack of coins to postpone his journey to the East; the land of Gangem could wait a few years for its mercenary builder. And wait it would, for Anon was one of the best and he was the first to admit it.

Tents rose alongside crops with the same speed that newcomers arrived in the clearing. Those with families received dwellings of their own, while individuals were bunked together: four to a tent, two on either side in upper and lower cots.

Tubal-cain had a few problems with assigning living arrangements. Some men refused to accept close quarters; others voiced an intense hatred of differing nations—for the gold they would work together but nothing could make them live together. Finally, Tubal-cain marked off a certain area for those who insisted on sleeping out-of-doors. Overall, however, he was delighted with the advantage that the raising of the tents turned out to be. In raising them, the workers became familiar with the tools they would use on the Ark. There were axes and saws, chisels and drills, hammers and wedges, blocks and tackle, shovels and chains of iron and rope. Slowly, the men grew used to the living arrangements and progress was made. Crews used the smaller boughs of trees for the posts and stakes needed for each tent. A number of men became quite skilled with the saws; some handled an ax without causing the wood to split and a few became adept at stitching great reams of cloth and pounding hides into canvas walls.

Under Noah's guidance, the barn was expanded, as well as the waist-high fence enclosures where Gravas's horses remained dutifully penned. New gates of pine were added, along with the increased footage to hold eight goats from Aghri Dagh and two mules which had made the journey through the forest with their owners, who hoped to be part of the clearing's excitement. Long, deep trench pits were dug amid the forest, several hundred cubits from the barn and the crops, for the placement of waste of every description.

Within several weeks, people of every color, race, and skill roamed the distances between tent dwellings and the piles of timber. They gathered water with the morning's dew or walked the short distance to the freshwater lake. They wore the garments of a dozen lands and whispered to one another in hushed tones or stifled laughter while Methuselah, Traibus, or one of the others of the Law happened to be near. Noah's family came to be called 'the fifteen' by newcomers, and rumors of the ship's proposed dimensions became as numerous and diverse as the workers' own backgrounds.

It was made clear that Noah would pay for an individual's labor, no matter what type of work he or she chose to perform. Farmers from the plains began working with Japheth and Rezepatha, for crops would be needed to feed six score and ten.

Naamah, Mariah, and Tamari moved the cooking fires to the old kilns and were grateful for the hired help of the wives and few children who had journeyed with their men-folk. Naamah had never had such an opportunity to complain and she took advantage of every occasion. Her words made it clear that there was too much to be done. She protested that the kilns had to remain fired all day long and that Tamari and Mariah seemed to expect her to do all of the supervision of the hirelings. Others heard her exclaim how no one was careful when they handled her ceramic pots, causing things to be chipped in the washtub barrels. There were also iron utensils missing from the kitchen. Anything Naamah could think of became the focus of her complaining.

But what Naamah found most irritating was the fact that one of the foreigners who had been hired to assist her took great pride in telling her how to cook! The woman, a dark haired Syrian named Nouhad, worked with Mariah and Tamari, and Naamah had repeatedly caught her sneaking additional spices and crushed mustard into a stew pot or a vegetable pie—activities, the Syrian claimed, which were simply to keep the food from tasting so bland.

Amid the smells of roasting vegetables, the new odors of human and Mixture alike, the noise of hammers and saws, the laughter of jokes, and the frequent gossip about the sanity of the project, there were growing rumors of the gold. All newcomers talked about it at one time or another, waiting with a great deal of anticipation for the day when they would caress the first coin of their labors. All had been contracted for six months at a time, room and board provided, and all would be paid at the end of that period. Anon had insisted on being the single exception, although the terms of his agreement were not generally made public.

Noah assumed, with prodding from some of his family, that there would be trouble with the same frequency he chose to pass out the wages: gambling, thievery, and jealousy. Uprisings of every imaginable nature were bound to ensue the moment each of the workers possessed a few shiny coins. For that reason, Shem (who had became quite fond of making rules) suggested certain guidelines. The crews were hired for six months only and would be hired for another six, and another, until they were finished. At Gravas's discretion, any unnecessary disturbance which became the cause of fighting or threats would result in immediate dismissal, although the discharged would receive fair payment for all work completed. The women, those of the Law and those who traveled with their husbands, were not to be harmed in any way, under threat of termination. Finally, a bonus would be paid to those laborers who remained honorable up until the end of six months' time.

Traibus began assisting Gravas with the supervision of the crews but wasn't certain the rules would eliminate disturbances. After all, some of the Mixtures had been hired for their strength and not their wits; some of the creatures couldn't even remember the task from one moment to the next, let alone try to keep track of the rules of employment. But to his great surprise, and in line with Noah's faith, there were no major problems to contend with. Instead of the growls and shouts of angry men, the ringing noise of tools filled the air. Some minor disagreements among newcomers took place, but for the most part, they were united for a common purpose: Everyone wanted the gold.

And, for a long while, as the hoes in Japheth's fields tilled rich soil and the enormous saws began the task of cutting gopherwood into planks and beams, there were whispers of golden coins and their possible hiding places. Some suggested one of the three cottages, but the buildings were clearly opened throughout the day and not a single dwelling was locked at night. There were rumors that the gold was buried, so many eagerly volunteered to dig the garbage pits, reluctantly giving up shovels when the task had been completed. The rumors regarding the gold's location were more numerous than those that discussed the Ark.

It was no secret to Noah, Methuselah, or Gravas, and especially not to Traibus, that the gold became the most important influence for keeping the workers on the job. Many laborers would steal all the wealth they could find given the first opportunity; they appeared loyal only to stay in the clearing. Their eyes were kept keen, however, watching the fifteen for possible clues.

Noah made a consistent effort to pray, hoping the motives of the crews would not have an adverse effect on the success of their project. Shem, too, frequently joined his father in prayer in the manner of old. Together, they constructed a small altar set off a little way from the lake. Usually, Shem brought offerings of vegetation from Japheth's fields to lay upon the altar—though his father explained that the One did not demand such a showing. Still, like his brother Ham, Shem was stubborn. He insisted that as their forefathers had done, they should give up a sacrifice. Reluctantly, Noah allowed him to use a few fruits and vegetables, since his son's prayers were sincere.

These trips of prayer gave rise to additional rumors: the newcomers suggested the gold was near the lake, or even at the site of the altar, and they watched for the return of Noah and his son for signs that it might be true. On occasion, a few followed the two men to their place of solitude, watching from behind the thick growths of trees and huge fronds of ferns which still flourished for a time in spite of the growing population in Lemech's ancient clearing.

The days of the crews' watch for gold turned to weeks, while crops grew abundant. The gopher-wood was cut, along with pine, into planks that dried slowly in stacks at the far edge of the clearing. Much of the ferns and the mulch and the vines died away, to be replaced by trails between the trees. Some of the animals left their homes at the lake in order to travel deeper into the forest—

a thousand birds fled to those places that remained thick with white oaks and towering pines. The scent of lavender soon disappeared from around cottages and the city of tents, for the tiny purple plant had been trampled to death.

And through it all, the gold remained undisturbed, just out of sight of the physical world, heaped in great invisible stacks upon the rocks behind Naamah's kitchen.

Eighteen Months Later
(Three years before the Flood)

Shem walked slowly over the trampled path leading to the city of tents. His sandaled feet dragged themselves through the pressed dirt trail which had become wide enough for the passage of two horses side by side. The appearance of the trail made him think of the countless thousands of footsteps that had been pressed upon the soil since the arrival of the first laborers. The walkway had permanently scarred the forest, so that not even a single blade of grass grew anywhere upon the trail between the lake and clearing. Even if the people and the Mixtures were to leave, the trail would remain pressed firmly among mighty oaks for decades to come.

The light of day had just begun to illuminate the delicate wisps of overhead clouds. He could barely see the misty vapors through the limbs and leaves of soaring trees that rose to tremendous heights on either side of the walkway. Set back from the trail, great tufts of green grass still covered portions of the rich soil and the yellow seed flowers found occasion to grow to maturity (but neither grew in the quantities of the past). Vines and ferns, too, had diminished in size and number, and the wild melons, sweet berries, and soft-shelled nuts had all but disappeared.

Shem had risen early, before any of the others, for some quiet time alone at the altar. With so many people it was hard to find the solitude he often craved. Sometimes he felt like the eyes of a dozen laborers watched him without apparent reason. Whether they envied his smooth features or stared in contempt, he was unable to discern. After eighteen months, he still didn't know the newcomers any better, and he doubted if the rest of the fifteen did either.

Many times, he had tried to find a friend among the hirelings, but to no avail. Sometimes, it appeared the workers themselves wouldn't allow it. On occasion, Shem had felt like an outsider among those he worked with, and it bothered him more than he had ever admitted to anyone except Shelobothe, with whom he had fallen in love. Unfortunately, her duties often kept the two apart. As a result, at times, the melancholy rose so powerfully in his chest that he felt like he was alone. Amid seven score people in the forest clearing, he had become lonely.

He had dreamed of ministering to people after the manner of Enoch ever since hearing Methuselah's tales of days gone by. But the people had no desire for his customs, his faith, or his knowledge of the Law. In the beginning, he had even shared his father's hope that the Ark might not be necessary. Yet, the newcomers had not changed, and beneath the cover of darkness, many still practiced vile things that were a part of the city. Even the examples in faith set by Noah, Lapeth, and Methuselah did nothing to shake them. Instead, many took Naamah as their model and sat around small fires, delighting in stories about her and her irritation with the huge vessel. They spoke of her criticism against Noah or how she lashed out at one of her sons for their stubbornness. And the reason behind Naamah's contempt became apparent to each laborer: She alone, among people of the Law, had not been told of the gold's whereabouts.

Shem dared not imagine what happened after the fifteen went to sleep. Things occurred in the night, he was certain, and they were things of unspeakable evil. Twice, he had heard screams coming from the depths of the forest while lying in the comfort of his own bed, in the enormous room he shared with Ham, Traibus, and Methuselah. On both occasions, he had bolted up on his mattress and stared toward the window to see something as alarming as the screams themselves: against the backdrop of an eerie light, Methuselah was huddled in prayer. Both times the mystic turned and told him to go back to sleep. Shem had obeyed immediately, as though there had been no other choice. And both mornings following the incidents, Methuselah's piercing eyes told his great-grandson that the matter was not to be discussed.

Shem knew for a fact that a few of the laborers, men he had known by name, had seemingly disappeared during the night. They had gone without warning and without collecting that which was due on their contracts. He couldn't help but wonder if they had been taken, but other laborers always had an explanation. He was certain that Naros, the last man to vanish had told of being a wanderer all his life, never finding the inclination or the woman with whom to settle down. Yet the man's companions said his disappearance was due to a sudden urge late one evening to rejoin his wife.

After the first few months, actual fighting among the laborers was rare, for Gravas had shown on each occasion that the rules of termination would be enforced. To be sure, minor scuffles occurred, sometimes daily, but that hadn't given rise to concern until Shem recalled that Naros had been involved in a minor argument the day before his disappearance. However, try as he might, Shem couldn't recall with whom the man had been quarreling.

And yet, all was not hopeless. Regardless of the alienation Shem felt as one of the fifteen, and in spite of the secrecy and evil he often sensed among the people and the Mixtures (and the laughter many enjoyed over the dimensions of the project), great progress was being made. Beneath the wide expanse of a vapor-laden sky, an Ark was indeed being raised within the huge clearing.

Shem walked the remainder of the well-trodden path burdened by thoughts that crept in to disturb his peace of mind. As he neared the clearing, the trees thinned and his feet slowed. The smells of people with their hair and their skin and their thick, withered flesh, grew overwhelming, and he knew he had arrived. To his left, great piles of lumber had been stacked: smoothed planks of timber, squared beams, and logs that hadn't even been touched. On his right, off in the distance, stood the cabins: Naamah's in front, dwarfed by the two behind it as well as by the immovable boulders which had remained steadfast for a thousand centuries. Directly in front of him, at a distance of six hundred cubits, was the city of tents; he could still catch the odors permeating its ground, even from where he stood. This day, however, his eyes weren't looking at the tents, the people, or the Mixtures (who were just beginning to rise and head toward the cooking fires). He saw only the makings of the Ark, and its majesty moved him.

Its huge platform had been constructed and covered a length of 300 cubits—just as Noah had been instructed. Thick, dried beams of gopher-wood, a single cubit in height and two cubits across, provided support beneath the massive base, which had become the pine flooring of the belly of the ship. The beams held the platform aloft, above the moist soil, and were spaced so that sinkage due to the weight of the vessel remained minimal. The planking was supported underneath with immense struts of white oak, nearly as large as the beams. The height of the platform from the bottommost struts, held aloft by the beams, to the planks of pine for the flooring, was a staggering four cubits. Already ladders, short scaffolds, and sloping walkways and ramps had been erected for climbing atop the huge floor and beginning work on the inner walls of the first story of the colossal structure. As the craft took form in the center of the clearing, many of the laborers had begun to ridicule the project as "Noah's Ark."

A great number of fallen trees had been used in the initial construction of the base, so Gravas issued a directive for the acquisition of additional timber by one of the working crews. Anon's engineering estimates had assured even Japheth that more trees were necessary before the Ark's completion. The Atlantean had scribbled out long rows of figures with his callused, red hand, after listening to Noah's repeated descriptions of the appearance of the craft. From these lengthy descriptions, Anon calculated the amount of lumber they needed: nearly 100,000 cubic cubits of timber, including 12,000 smoothed wooden planks, and nearly 1000 gopher-wood beams.

Gravas assigned specific crews to the many tasks. Some were to cut additional trees or to plane lumber into smooth planks. Others worked on the vessel itself, beginning the task of raising the first level of the side of the ship. Some began painting the seams of the planks and the joints of the beams with bitumen pitch. Others raised block and tackle or started building an intricate scaffolding system that would eventually encompass the entire ship. There were also those who worked long days in the fields with Japheth and Rezepatha, tending to the crops, while a few laborers chose to rotate their tasks in order to fulfill specific duties that Gravas or Traibus or one of the others had assigned.

Toolmakers, handpicked by Tubal-cain, learned the careful skills perfected by the aging bronze man. They made saws and shovels and picks for the Ark, and hoes and hand plows for the crops. In time, they became proficient at forming crosspieces for the beams and making wooden pegs and dowels for the smaller pieces of pine and oak. The entire craft was to be assembled using the skilled designs of mortise-and-tenon joints and dovetailing for the joining segments that would become part of a whole.

Although the master builder Anon had proven invaluable with his experience and insight, even he had no interest in Shem's knowledge of the ancient Law. For the Atlantean, the Ark was simply to be one more monumental engineering task. He gave no thought to Noah's vision or even the reason behind the vessel's construction. He showed no favoritism to either the laborers or to the fifteen, and he was not interested in the mysterious ways of the Law. Lapeth had spoken frequently to him of these things, and he certainly admired her for her ageless beauty but he was not interested in the faith, nor did he give thought to the whereabouts of the gold for he had already been paid in full. Anon's sole concern was the project, and he dedicated himself to it fully.

"Have you become lost in your thoughts again?" a chuckling voice asked. Gravas's fat hand slapped Shem firmly on the shoulder and woke him from his thoughts. "At times you appear as mysterious as old Methuselah."

Shem swung around to see the portly man and smiled back at him. "Perhaps mystery has become our only means of survival."

"So you've become versed in riddles as well!" Gravas laughed heartily. "Before long, we may have another prophet among us."

"There would be no need for prophecy would we all but listen to the ways of the One."

"How true," Gravas said, nodding and then wrapped his arm around Shem's back and led him toward the breakfast line. "But if we all listened, such majesty would not be before us." He motioned to the gigantic platform of oak and pine and the scaffolding rising along the beginnings of the first level of the craft. "And, then, you and I, my friend," the fat red-haired man said, winking, "would be out of a job."

For a moment, Shem's look of concern passed from his face, driven away by Gravas's joviality; he would have to repeat it to Shelobothe the next time they were together and alone.

Gravas's short, stubby legs moved quickly in order to reach his desired place in line. The hours between supper and breakfast were the longest his stomach went without food. Throughout the long day, the women made certain something was available to fill the bellies of the men—Gravas's own belly made the journey more often than most—but after supper, Naamah refused to fix another morsel. She made certain that Mariah, Tamari, and especially Nouhad, followed the rules as well.

The two walked toward the kilns near the small expanse of fence by the barn. They joined in behind a Persian man with sagging jowls and exposed lower teeth, who gave them only the most casual nods of recognition. No words were exchanged, for both Gravas and Shem had given up attempting conversation with most of the others before breakfast. Gravas had jested on more than one occasion that the crews were apparently unable to move their mouths without having first primed their jaws with food.

The food line at breakfast was longer than at any other time of day and it moved slowly. Always a haphazard attempt at single file, it was composed of people and Mixtures wearing the garments and colors of a dozen different lands. Most of the people of the Law still wore the robes of the ancient priesthood, but Ham and Shem had taken to the tight breeches worn by those from Mizraim, as they provided ease of movement. Shem wore a loose, open shirt, while Ham wore none at all. Anon clothed himself in the expensive, white gown of a master builder, trimmed in golden thread, yet, somehow Noah in his simple robe often appeared more majestic than any of the others.

The laborers' dress included striped garments from Syria, the woven fabrics of Persia, and the pounded hides of plains' people and the trappers. Some continued to wear turbans or the corded headbands that prevented sweat from running into their eyes. Many of the people had sandaled feet, while the soles of others were as thick as leather. A few children ran about in tattered garments, while the youngest toddler wore nothing to cover his nakedness.

The most colorful outfit, however, wrapped itself around Naamah. Her bright dress, with dyes from the yellow flower and crushed berries, was the easiest to spot in the crowd. Her shape and size rivaled that of Gravas's and the enormous flowers covering the many cubits of loose-flowing material became illuminated in the brightness of the morning clouds. Her dress restrained numerous rolls of flesh and dangled to the tops of fat feet swelling beyond the capacity of her sandals. Although her breath was constantly heavy with strain, her tongue remained as active as ever.

Traibus, whose chest and head towered above the others, reached the front of the line and was served a plate of softened corn meal and thick honey syrup. Naamah screamed in disgust at Nouhad who had spooned the mush onto Traibus' plate.

"Why is it that after all this time you still can't handle the simplest of tasks?" Naamah spoke loudly as though Nouhad stood at the end of the line instead of right next to her. Her lips pressed together in anger, ignoring Traibus who was trying to figure out what had set the woman off this time.

"What's the matter now?" Nouhad used a voice of authority that seemed beyond her small stature. She placed a dark hand against her hip, and with the other shook the serving spoon at the large woman in mock imitation.

"Can't you see that Traibus is a giant?" Naamah yelled. "And yet you give him the serving of a mere man. For years, he has supped at my table, and my mother's before me. He can eat far more than you've provided!"

"I've served him according to his request," Nouhad said flatly.

"Nonsense!"

"It is true, Naamah," Traibus volunteered quickly. The twinkling eyes below his aging forehead tried to calm the woman by thought, but her anger prevented it. "I require no more than this," he motioned to his plate and lowered it so that she could see he had a proper serving.

Naamah's eyes scanned his mush and she shook her head in disgust. She was very much aware of the fact that a hundred different eyes were watching her. "Then you no longer have enough sense to eat sufficient for your size!" She spoke angrily, her sagging breasts shaking with the force of her words. The giant moved to speak, but before he could say a word, Naamah heaped another portion of food onto his plate and waved him on.

"From now on, you will fill his plate as I have instructed," Naamah said, gripping the woman's arm for emphasis. "Traibus grows old and no longer has the sense to know what is best for him. Do you hear what I say?"

"Very well," the woman replied calmly. "From this day forth, I will heap such quantities together for his meals." Nouhad paused for a moment, making it quite evident she was looking at Naamah's frame, "as though I fed you instead of the giant." Nouhad swung around and served the next Mixture, ignoring Naamah's heavy breaths. Noah's wife began to shake so violently that Mariah had to lead her away; the two went inside the smallest cottage.

"Please excuse my mother," Shem finally said when he stepped to the front of the line. "She is not always like that."

"No, you're quite right," Nouhad said casually. "Most often she is much worse." She spooned a liberal amount from the metal pot and ladled some syrup unto his plate before moving on to Gravas, who was not afraid to request more, should his serving prove inadequate.

Gravas and Shem walked to the logs that lay on the ground as seats for those who wished to gather during the meals. Neither was invited to join any of the laborers. Instead, they found a place next to Traibus and sat beside him. While they ate, they discussed the prospects for the day. It was simply a part of the routine to discuss the schedule while surrounded on all sides by the forest trees.

A short while later, Anon gathered Gravas, Traibus, Methuselah, Noah, and Noah's two youngest sons around a wooden worktable next to the largest scaffolding. Anon's raised working surface was covered with parchments of hastily etched plans. One of his hands pressed against the drawings as he proceeded to indicate the next stages of the project with the other. The Atlantean preferred to call it "the project," rarely referring to it as the ship and almost never calling it the Ark. The whole while he spoke, small beads of moisture glistened evenly on the bald scalp of his forehead, and he gestured for emphasis toward one of the other sketches on the drawing board. Their early morning gatherings rarely lasted longer than a few minutes, and only Noah had earned the unspoken right to point out some discrepancy between Anon's plans and those he had envisioned in his mind's eye. The master builder took these clarifications without insult or injury, but his manner made it apparent that the allowance would be extended to no one else.

Although it was true that Gravas oversaw the workings of the hirelings, Noah retained complete control of the fifteen. Traibus and Methuselah had an impressive knowledge of the forest, its trees, and the area surrounding the enormous clearing. For this reason, Noah gave them the task of obtaining the choicest lumber, with crews assigned by Gravas. They sought out white oaks of the finest gopher-wood: wood that was difficult to work but always split clean. They directed crews to gather together huge stacks of timber, cut and dried to a planed finish. The heat of a fire was used to curve the wood required for use along the rounded edges of the craft.

Ham and Shem directed the labor of the crews on the Ark itself, working as hard as their hired hands. They cut pine flooring into precision pieces for days at a time, spacing occasional holes along the edges of the floored platform to be used as crawl spaces beneath the pine so that underside seams could be painted inside and out with the finest pitch. Already they had begun work on the lengthy ribs of the vessel. Although slightly curved at the underside, every piece would tower to a height of thirty cubits when raised in place. At even intervals all around the platform, holes had been cut to attach the end of each rib into the cross-joints beneath the sub-floor of the Ark. Every plank, beam, rib, stud, or post would be joined to several others and then painted with bitumen pitch for strength. Tubal-cain and his craftsmen made the tools and the joints, and began making cages of all sizes, at the instructions of Traibus, for holding the smaller creatures that would eventually make their homes within the vessel.

Japheth and Rezepatha had their gardens and a staff of field workers so skilled that the crops they reaped were more abundant than their need. The excess was put to use by Lapeth and Tamari, who taught both Maran and Shelobothe the skills of food preservation and storage. No one knew how long they would be aboard the craft or what would happen to the wild crops, the berries, and the fruits of the forest and open fields after the storm had passed. The women experimented with drying fruits and vegetables between thin layers of woven cloth in the open air. They dried beans and peas, apples and berries, and fresh apricots plucked from the very trees which had been taken, as seedlings, from around the lake. Some of the fruits, especially berries, did not dry well; Lapeth kept a list of all plants for which they would need to carry seedlings. A great deal of effort went into the planning of food storage—much to Naamah's disgust, for she couldn't believe a woman of Lapeth's intelligence had succumbed to such foolishness.

Once again, Tubal-cain and his craftsmen were called into service. They fashioned containers of iron and pottery, and wooden barrels with lids, as well as other necessities for the foods that Lapeth and Tamari thought important to store. The women tried wax as a sealant and kept dried produce in airtight containers in order to keep out excess moisture. They would need additional containers, some very large, for the seeds to be taken aboard in order to plant fresh crops. They planned to have enough food in storage to last through their time aboard the Ark, as well as plenty to last until the first harvest of freshly planted crops after the deluge had passed.

Anon thought their efforts appalling, for the women were wasting a great deal of time. As far as he was concerned, the project encompassed only the building of the structure and that was the extent of it. Certainly, the vessel wasn't going anywhere. But Noah sanctioned the tests: storing different foods for weeks at a time under several conditions, then checking each of the experiments for palatability. And because of Noah's approval, Anon's comments were generally kept to himself. However, more than a dozen of Ham's laborers believed the preservation of food served a definite purpose. It was becoming apparent that some of the faithful planned a journey. Although uncertain as to the destination, some hirelings became convinced that it had something to do with the gold.

The discussions of gold had turned to wondering how far away it had been hidden, for most had given up thoughts that it was contained in the clearing. Payment on their contracts was due again shortly, and a few grumbled that the fifteen might decide to leave the clearing with the stored food and no intention of returning or paying what was due. As Ham was away discussing the progress around Anon's worktable, some of his crew began to argue among themselves.

"Your fears are without reason," Fizel, a Black warrior from Cush, stated emphatically. "These people have been honest from the first and yet you continue to suspect them of treachery."

"I read only the signs," Dachnid replied, disgusted with the Black man's ignorance. His greasy hair had been pulled back and his nostrils flared as he watched the warrior direct the work of a dwarf down in the crawl space.

Fizel shook his head in disagreement, then leaned over to point out the wooden strut to which they would anchor the first rib to the starboard side. The smooth, dark skin of his muscular chest had yet to sweat and already Dachnid was up to his tricks.

The warrior stood near the edge of the Ark's platform, four cubits above the soil, and stared down into the opening of the crawl space at Boland, the tiny man of a mere two cubits in height. He couldn't help but wonder why Dachnid of Sheba was so intent on causing an uprising. He watched Dachnid's angry frown from out of the corners of his pearl-white eyes and thought it ironic that so many considered Sheba a city of reason. Dachnid, with his large blank pupils and thin mustache resembling Malock's, was anything but reasonable.

"It is ignorance not to suspect these people of something." The man scanned the faces of the rest of the crew and felt confident that he spoke for them all. "You can't believe their sole intention is to build this boat," he said, his chuckle beginning to imitate one he had heard used by Gravas on frequent occasion, "a ship that can never touch the sea."

"Noah's Ark!" one of the barechested Mixtures snickered from behind.

"I know not what to believe," Fizel said, lifting his eyes from the crawl space for a moment, "but I'm certain of one thing: these people have faith in what they are doing."

"You mean in what we're doing," one of the laborers growled angrily. "It is we who toil for days on end with little rest."

"And will get paid well for it," Fizel interjected. "They have yet to cheat any of us, nor is anyone in the clearing held against their will. Dachnid, you or those who find truth in your words are free to go as you please; I'm certain you will be paid your due."

"So, the Black man has switched allegiances!" Dachnid said, his nostrils flaring with disgust. "I remember a time, not long ago, when you too sought only their storehouse of wealth."

"My allegiance is to myself," Fizel said as he bent over into the hole and lifted Boland to the surface. The tiny man, with small pointed ears, was dressed in the breeches of a young boy, (though his age was decidedly past that of middle years). His leather sack of wooden pegs and the tiny hammer had been sized to fit him. The dwarf vigorously brushed his hands together and looked about for the bucket of pitch that had been reinforced with chopped straw. The dwarf offered no notice to either of them, for their arguments were becoming quite common of late.

" . . . and it is for myself," the warrior continued, "that I remain loyal to the task at hand. It is true, I came here looking for the same thing as you, but my belly was empty and my mind filled with dreams of what morsels might be purchased with a handful of golden coins. Now, I eat to my stomach's content and do honest labor for which I am paid. I fail to find deceit in any of this."

"Then you are a fool," Dachnid answered, clenching his fists together in hatred, "to settle for the few pieces of gold they have offered, when the hoard you once dreamed of might still be yours."

"How can you justify taking from these people when they have treated you so fairly?" The Black man, seeing his cue, grabbed Boland, who clenched his prize hammer, by the arms and lowered him back into the crawl space. Next, the warrior let down the bucket of pitch and the leather satchel. The dwarf shook his head in appreciation and handed up a piece of dried gopher-wood that had been left over after his careful placement of the cross-joint.

Fizel thanked the little man and set the oak strut beside him on the pine flooring. Through it all, Boland, who had been born without a voice, never made a sound, although a number among the crew was able to understand him by the gestures he made with his hands.

"Is it fair, or even just, that these people possess the wealth of a kingdom," Dachnid asked angrily, turning to the sympathetic eyes which surrounded him, "and throw it away on this idle pursuit? Can any of us even fathom the amount of money wasted thus far—and the hungry mouths that might have been fed among the broken tenements of Shinar or elsewhere?"

"Had the money been yours," Fizel said without looking up, "I'll wager the same mouths would have wanted, and another seven score without the means of their own sustenance. Those you call the fifteen have given us work when many among us had nowhere else to turn; it matters little that the task may be a waste of time."

"Would it matter if these people you place so much trust in meant to leave without fulfilling that which is rightfully ours? I tell you, they plan to depart without paying our due. They've grown tired of this game and have fashioned an escape so that not another coin is wasted. The costs have been enormous, yet only the platform is finished. The completion of the entire structure might well be beyond the means at their disposal."

Dachnid continued as the others showed their agreement. "Why else have they gone to such lengths to store food for a journey? Surely they know, as we do, that this craft will remain forever upon the soil, gradually sinking until it is gone. Why have they pampered the horses since our arrival, always making certain the creatures are well-fed beyond what is required, as if to keep them readied for some long journey. Anyone can see that the labor of stallions is not required on a task that employs more than a hundred men—men with strong backs and thinking minds. Yet, the giant directs the horses to be used on occasion, just often enough to keep their long limbs taut with muscle."

"I tell you the fifteen do not plan to remain in the clearing," Dachnid finished. "They have contemplated this departure since the first day of our hire."

Fizel stared at the man with complete contempt for what he was doing. The crew would be better off without his presence. Slowly, he opened his mouth, exposing teeth as white as his eyes, and said, "Gravas may find it worthwhile to hear the words you speak."

Dachnid clenched his hands tighter as if to strike, but quickly stopped himself. One of the fifteen could be watching, and he would be banished from the project for coming to blows (though he had to exercise a great deal of restraint to control himself).

"At least you have made it clear which side you are on." he said. The rest of the crew, with the exception of Boland, who stared out of the crawl space in an effort to see what was happening, began nodding in agreement while their voices rose in unison against the Black warrior.

"There is no need for the choosing of sides," Fizel said quickly, hoping to see some sign of rationality among them. "These people have made no plans to escape; you have yet to provide proof."

"Is it proof enough for you," Dachnid began slyly, "that even the master builder, with the same roots as their forefathers, has suspected them of treachery from the beginning?"

"You lie!"

"Then why did he insist on payment in full for his services, while the rest of us must wait six months for the sweat of our labors?"

"Where did you hear this?" the Black man asked immediately, still suspecting Dachnid of lies.

The possibility of Anon having suspicions caused the crew even greater uneasiness, and their voices clamored together in such anger that Dachnid had to wait to continue. "It is the truth," he finally said, "I heard it from one who would surely know: Naamah, wife of the Ark builder."

The mention of Naamah was enough to remove any doubt that remained. She, alone among the fifteen, thought the project foolhardy, and laborers from a dozen countries had come to trust her (and to relish the stories of her outbursts against her own family). Ham's crew began to yell among themselves with such hostility that the morning meeting around the worktable was brought to a halt. Gravas and Noah's sons ran to the starboard side of the craft to see what was happening.

With the approach of the faithful, the laborers calmed themselves and continued their work, since none wanted to be dismissed. However, Dachnid looked repeatedly at the Black man with contempt for much of the day. He would remember Fizel's threat to turn him over to Gravas, until late into the evening—and evening couldn't come soon enough.

When the last rays of filtered light had disappeared from the clouds, darkness had settled upon the clearing, and each of the fifteen, except Methuselah, lay huddled in sleep upon small cots and raised divans, Shem was suddenly awakened by faint screams breaking the stillness of midnight.

Afterwards, an old, gray man rose from his prayers against the window and crept out beneath the cover of a mighty oak forest, just as he had been instructed to do.

It had a great deal to do with luck—although Methuselah

wouldn't have admitted it to anyone. He had found the Black man's body hidden beneath a layer of pine mulch far from the central clearing. After the body had been freed from the loose, moist earth, even the mystic was startled to discover that the warrior's heart was faintly beating. Fizel had been left for dead, and should have been so from the look of the cuts that glistened in places where enough blood still remained beneath the surface of the man's flesh. The warrior was covered with cuts the length of his arms and legs.

He had been cut in the manner of torture which allowed a man to watch himself bleed to death: long rows of incisions skillfully slit below the knees, across upper thighs, over the stomach, and down the greater part of the length of his arms. Each wound had been skillfully cut so that he had been able to watch the life force flow from his muscular body for almost an hour, until consciousness mercifully deserted him.

Methuselah bent close to the man's naked form, inspecting with his fingertips the coagulation of blood that crusted the length of each slash. From the width of the drying scabs the mystic could plainly see that the incisions over the man's thighs and stomach had been the deepest and would take the longest to heal.

And the old mystic was confident they would heal, for being buried beneath the pine mulch and soil had saved the man's life. The minerals in the ground had slowed the bleeding, allowing the wounds to begin to repair themselves. If Fizel's attackers had not been so quick to dispose of their deed, the warrior would not have been so lucky.

The illumination of the overhead clouds was just beginning to light the uppermost treetops. Beneath them, the old man huddled with the injured laborer. Most of the tall blades of grass had been sprinkled with the dampness of early morning dew; it would remain visible for several hours. The rich smells of fern and dew and tree moss began to rise, overpowering the scent of blood that had filled the air just a short while earlier.

There was yet time for Methuselah to take the man to safety and begin dressing his wounds with cool ointment and sweet-smelling salve. By his own estimate, he would need three-quarters of an hour to get Fizel to a place of hiding where no one from the clearing could possibly see him. It was about the same length of time before the crews around the Ark would come to life and the shadows of the forest would fade because of the intensity of the overhead vapors.

Methuselah reached out with his long tapered fingers and grasped the walking stick he had carelessly flung to the ground next to Fizel's body. He brought the birch staff closer to the trunk of the gopher-wood towering over them; there, it would be safe from view, hidden from anyone who might pass. Many hours would elapse before he would have a chance to return, for the Black man needed close attention. He took several deep breaths and directed his attention inward. The large, muscular body of Fizel lay on the ground before him, measuring four and a half cubits in length, and the old man wished, for an instant, that he had brought Traibus along with him—at least to have the giant watch what he was about to do. The thought brought a smile to his face.

With trained eyes, Methuselah looked around their surroundings, scanning every trunk of the trees. When he was satisfied that no one was near, he slipped his thin arms under the man's head and legs and lifted the weight with his own small frame. Although he nearly stumbled once, he regained his footing and began to carry the warrior deep into the forest, where even the laborers did not venture. His walked carefully so that Fizel's limp body would be disturbed as little as possible.

The old mystic provided quite a sight as the smooth, silken fabric of his robe trailed over the mulch and the underbrush beneath him, turning over loose pieces of crumbled leaves and pine. Methuselah's long beard dangled atop the Black man's stomach as his head bobbed back and forth in rhythm to each step. The soft, withered flesh of his hands gripped the dark-skinned shoulders and thighs with a strength that surpassed the warrior's, yet his touch was gentle so as not to break the scabs. Despite the precision of his movement, and the apparent ease with which he handled the burden, he appeared as a little old man disappearing behind the cover of the forest with a tremendous weight draped between his hands. Suddenly, his mind became filled with the knowledge that Fizel's attack had something to do with the gold, and Methuselah realized that the problems with the coins had only just begun.

Three hours later, the old magician returned for his staff.

Eight days passed before Fizel could walk unaided, and during that time (and the weeks that followed), an uneasy friendship developed between himself and the man who had saved his life. Methuselah trusted the warrior completely and showed him how to dress his own wounds so they would heal. He even took to calling Fizel "friend." Fizel liked his benefactor as well and was astonished by the extent of the old man's knowledge, but there was something mysterious about Methuselah that the warrior couldn't understand, and its presence often made him feel uncomfortable.

While Fizel was first recovering, and was too weak to prepare his own meals, Methuselah always knew what the warrior felt like eating, as well as how much he would be able to keep down. When Fizel struggled to walk, his limbs feeling sore and limp, he leaned in pain upon the small frame of the old man. In his amazement, however, he felt not the weak bones of age holding him up, but the mighty shoulders of a fellow warrior. The awareness caused him to realize that he had been carried to the place of hiding by this old man, whose full stature rose only to Fizel's bare chest. During their time of walking and countless exercises designed to heal the warrior's muscles, Methuselah had never shown signs of tiring, though Fizel himself needed frequent rests from the strain of the exertion.

As time passed, Fizel began to believe the mystic was more than a mere man and possessed powers that Fizel couldn't even imagine. During his long hours of solitude, when Methuselah had journeyed back to the distant clearing and left him only in the company of his thoughts, the warrior began to wonder how many among the fifteen possessed the same magic. Certainly not Naamah, who didn't seem to know any of the mystic's ways, or Gravas, who seemed best known for his laughter. But Fizel began to believe that the gentle Noah might be as gifted as old Methuselah, and even Lapeth, with her deep, sparkling eyes, appeared to possess more than mere beauty. Traibus, too, might have some of the magician's powers.

Whenever Methuselah returned to his side, Fizel worried that the old man might be able to see his thoughts. Due to his nervousness, Fizel talked endlessly, telling more about himself and his life than he had ever told another person. He also told of his attackers, Dachnid and the other two, and of his own amazement that his body was healing without signs of a single scar. When the day came that his muscles had regained their strength, the soreness had left his body, and he had completely recovered, Fizel made the journey back to the clearing with Methuselah.

In the weeks that had passed since the midnight attack, every laborer had heard some version of Fizel's death and burial. Dachnid had repeated the tale with such pride and with so many variations that the story he proclaimed no longer resembled the simplicity of his initial vengeance. Dachnid even began to believe what his tongue recited in self-admiration.

Late one afternoon, as Dachnid stood speaking near the edge of the platform, silence suddenly and completely overtook every sound in the clearing. Unaware of the stillness of hammers and the fact that seven score laborers had grown quiet, Dachnid continued relating his method of revenge.

Whispers replaced the silence as Methuselah walked through the clearing with the tall Black warrior walking next to him. As all eyes turned to look, Fizel only smiled from ear to ear. All around him, however, men, women, and even a few children, stared fearfully at a man they believed scourged and dead. But Fizel moved about without limp or any signs of attack! One by one, whispers raced through the crowd: The old magician had raised a man from death!

As the two approached Ham's crew upon the platform of the Ark, Dachnid was persuaded, by the horror he saw in the faces of those nearest him, to turn. Slowly, he looked around and saw only Methuselah. For a moment he glared hatefully at the old mystic who had caused his story to be interrupted. At first, he did not recognize Fizel, for the warrior had been dead and removed from his consciousness for many weeks. Yet, as the realization came to him, Dachnid's legs grew weak. The hair on his head stood on end, and his nostrils flared, as a chill descended his spine. He made a sign against evil with his hands and then fell pitifully to his knees.

Given what had happened, it was actually a relief for Dachnid and the other two Mixtures to be dismissed from the clearing for their crime. Gravas paid them their due, placing gold coins in shaking palms, and instructed them never to return. With horrified looks in their eyes, none of the three could do more than nod in agreement. For several days afterward, they hid in the darker regions of the forest, crouching in terror at the sound of a breaking twig or the movement of a groundling. They convinced themselves that the old magician would eventually seek his own revenge. When they finally returned to civilization and places where other Mixtures roamed the city and the forest, the three whispered fearfully in hushed tones about the activities of the clearing—and about an old wizard who had powers even over death.

The rumor of Methuselah's deed followed the three to their eventual capture within Malock's domain. In time, they were questioned by an old, blind guard, whose eyes stared blankly beneath a sagging forehead, and even by Malock himself, who toyed with the edges of a dark mustache as Dachnid spoke. The overseer believed the tale, for he had never questioned the old magician's abilities. In fact, because of the story, Malock immediately changed his plans.

For more than a year after his arson on Gravas's stables, Sterba had convinced the overseer and his guards that Methuselah need not be feared. Sterba had reminded them all, between puffs on his cigarettes, that he had never suffered any retribution for his deed against the horse-trader. Not once had the magician confronted him and Sterba raised doubts about whether Methuselah possessed the power to do anything at all. However, each time the giant had nearly given in to the idea of an attack (mostly because he didn't want the patrols to think him fearful), something had happened—and Malock had delayed action with a sigh of relief.

First, the stories of the mystic's deeds of old had been repeated with such horror and detail by the female slave and others among the giant's household, that even Sterba was moved for a time to question the judgment of his plan. The eldest guards reminded those who thirsted for battle that Methuselah excelled in trickery—and a magic they did not understand. How else had he recruited Traibus into his tiny band of followers? That giant had once been a skilled trapper who roamed the marketplace. Now, he followed obediently after the old man. How had Methuselah been able to work his magic on Gravas, who now practiced all the old man's foolishness? The horse-trader had lost all of his great wealth in the process, the guards reminded the overseer (who relished this part of the story), and the conversion only heightened everyone's unspoken fear of Methuselah.

But after a few months of caution, Sterba's memory of Gravas's soft-skinned nieces overpowered his fear of the mystic. Rather than relating his plans for the women—for he still desired to keep their beauty to himself—he tried to convince Malock and the guards how much the patrols would be satisfied by such a diversion. Many among the fields—not counting chained slaves of course—had voiced boredom at the sameness of their work. An attack would provide a wonderful diversion.

However, when Malock had nearly reconsidered the assault, Kana, the captain of the guards, arranged for a drunken Crantal to be captured in Shinar and brought to the giant's household as witness to Methuselah's power. Although many had heard rumors of the incident, Crantal's recitation of the tale proved even more frightening. As sweat rolled down his frame, Crantal related with obvious terror how his fists had become broken and then renewed—simply with the magician's command.

At the time, even Sterba had been fearful. Yet, with each passing day, the threat of Methuselah seemed less real and the promises of what might be became more worthwhile. Finally, tales of the gold were added to Sterba's insistent list of reasons, and an assault began to seem reasonable after all. Rumors of the money held by the fifteen convinced Malock that an assault on the clearing could do much to increase his personal holdings.

However, Dachnid's story of what Methuselah had done to Fizel put any question of the old man's powers out of mind. Not a single guard thought an attack advisable in the face of such power; yet, none specifically stated their fear. It came as no surprise when the planned assault on the forest clearing was halted. Kana notified his patrols that the ambush had been canceled—indefinitely.

In the end, Malock expressed sorrow for having to "delay" the assault. It grieved him greatly, he told his personal guards, to have his men readied for diversion and then to have the sport canceled. For that reason, the patrols were given two Mixtures to do with as they saw fit. Sterba was handed over for trying to launch an attack in spite of the danger, and the old, blind guard was sentenced—at Kana's suggestion—because his age had outgrown his usefulness. Both men were stripped and allowed to run for the cover of the forest; a short while later, all of Malock's patrols hunted them down.

Afterward, guards went back to their usual pastime of drinking and sleeping and of occasionally being granted permission to single out one of the slaves for sport. But word continued to creep into the fields that seven score laborers were kept working deep in the forest clearing—and that payment was being granted in gold.

837 Days Later
(Six months before the Flood)

With the approach of dusk, soft dwindling rays of golden light pierced the forest clearing. The meal line had already started to form back near the kilns, with the voices of a hundred laborers rising above even the shrill words of Noah's wife. She issued a dozen commands, as if Mariah, Tamari, Nouhad and the others had never before prepared for such a gathering.

For once, Gravas wasn't pulled toward the line by the smells of cabbage stew and vegetable pie, nor did his stomach give way to the rumblings with which he was so familiar. Instead, he stood transfixed, with one fat hand on the rising scaffold, staring upwards at the mammoth ship as if seeing its enormous hull for the very first time. The oak timbers, smoothed and lacquered thick with dark brown pitch, sparkled in the dwindling light from the clouds and the light of the low-burning fires of the evening meal in the distance.

All too often, the thundering clang of hammers and the squeaking sounds of lubricated gears and roped pulleys that raised the planed planks to the third story of the completely ribbed ship caused him to forget the reason behind their labors. Most days, their work was just a tremendous task, one that required all their efforts and seemed exceedingly slow with progress passing by unnoticed. But as he stood against the towering scaffolding, which rose the height of the Ark and encircled it as well, he took a moment to notice. For the first time, he saw the Ark as it really was: the most magnificent structure his eyes had ever gazed upon, rising upon its formidable platform, sitting majestically within the center of the clearing.

He understood then how much of their work had been accomplished and how close they were to completion. The thought brought tears to his eyes and moistened the lines around them that had deepened from the heat of many days and his own passing years. The uppermost story was nearly completed, as was the towering walkway that ran atop the full length of the craft. Certainly, finishing touches were needed within the ship, and another coat of bitumen would do nicely within and without, but with the exception of gathering the animals, every major duty was behind them. He couldn't help but wonder how much time remained for the peoples of the earth.

The scent of dried bitumen, mixed with huge measures of chopped hay for strength, enticed the red hairs of his nostrils to stand on end as he leaned closer to the ship's platform. Habitually, he reached up and inspected the seams of neighboring planks. The smell of painted gopher-wood was something he had been forced to grow used to but even when dry the odor of the sealant was overpowering.

That was one of the reasons that the fields had been planted with so many acres of hay. The stalks would be cut and spread out upon wooden floors of the ship, absorbing odors of both sealant and animal alike. Behind him and a short distance from the scaffolds, great stores of hay were stacked in neat rows, each clump banded together in clusters that could be easily chopped with a single hand ax. The hay was used in the sealant as well as in fodder for the horses, the cows, and the sheep and goats from Aghri Dagh. It grew with hearty abundance, then was scythed low with tools formed by the skill of Tubal-cain or one of his craftsmen. As the grasses dried (before being mixed with the kofer for pitch), they gave off a pleasing aroma and absorbed some of the foul-smelling fumes that permeated much of the clearing. Bales of cut hay had been scattered throughout the area: around the craft and the cottages, and near the tents, to help diminish the stench of sweat, bodies, and other common offenses.

Aboard the Ark, two storage rooms had been fashioned within the belly of the ship solely to hold quantities of the fresh-smelling crop. Another massive holding area was located aft and surrounded by thick, hollow walls that were to be filled with hay. The room had been Traibus's idea, for they had no way of knowing how long they would be aboard the vessel and the need of such a place to discard garbage and manure from the expedition was a certainty.

Gravas's chubby fingers traced the line of wood for a few cubits. When satisfied, he stood back a step and nodded approvingly. As his eyes focused on the hull, taking up his entire line of vision, he wondered how long he could stand being cooped up inside the craft. Despite the fact he had been an experienced tradesman, long sea voyages had never appealed to him. And the thought of being unable to move beyond the sound of Naamah's voice for any length of time appealed to him even less.

As he turned his head and looked along the starboard wall, he saw how the full length of the craft spread out on either side. Though he could not see either end, from his countless daytime measurements he knew the distance to be the full 300 cubits. The distance had proven so great that Noah had taken to using doves (the only pair remaining anywhere near the lake) to carry messages from bow to stern. The white creatures, not much bigger than Noah's hand, carried papyrus script from their master to Anon, or to Gravas (who was often in a meal line) when the foreman needed to be summoned. At night the birds nested high in the branches of oaks on the edge of the clearing, using broken twigs, leaves, and strippings of the field's olive trees—far away from some of the less sensible Mixtures who wouldn't think twice about whether or not such winged creatures were suitable for food.

Under Noah's leadership and the engineering skill of Anon the craft's design was box-like and immensely angular in shape. It had been designed for floating. The master builder swore the project was seaworthy, although it was well known that the ship could not possibly reach the shoreline of even the closest body of water.

As he eyed the structure and the smells of food came to him again, Gravas wondered how much food Lapeth, Tamari, and his nieces planned to take aboard. The idea of having only dried fruits and vegetables for fare caused a great rumbling within his belly. He could not begin to guess how long Traibus's own list of food supplies for hundreds of animals had grown. And on occasion, he could not help but wonder whether or not the fifteen really intended to barricade themselves inside the Ark, waiting in fear for rivers of moisture to fall from the vapors and great pools to surge forth from the ground. Was the vision really going to happen after all?

Just as he began to doubt his own faith, Gravas heard the low sounds of breaking twigs come to his ears. As the noise moved closer, he thought it the sound of footsteps breaking scattered stalks of hay. His heart began to beat faster, for it was unusual for any member of the fifteen to be so near the ship after darkness had fallen over the clearing—and he was aware that a number of the laborers were not to be trusted. He felt the small hairs on the back of his neck stand on end as the crunching continued, and he had almost decided to spin around and face whomever approached him, when the sound stopped moving any closer—though it persisted. The steady, crisp snap of small stalks being crushed continued. Slowly, Gravas turned around, looking past the large framework of lashed beams and crossed planks and stared at where the noise arose.

Immediately, his eyes recognized the intruder as Curtis, one of the shaggy young goats from Aghri Dagh. Somehow, the goat had taught itself to jump the fenced enclosure behind the barn. The creature, whose hide was spotted with equal streaks of gray and brown, had made it clear with stubborn determination that it would not be penned. Pretending to be oblivious to the presence of the man, the goat continued to graze between two bales of hay, refusing to pay Gravas any heed. The sight caused the fat man to begin his familiar chuckle, with hands pressed firmly against the girth of his enormous waist. His laughter increased until tears came to his eyes.

Gravas shot a fat finger at the goat in jest. "Sneak up on me like that again, and I'll make certain the Ark leaves without you."

Although Curtis's ears perked inquisitively into the air, the goat continued eating, while tufts of his small, bearded hairs continued to bob up and down with every chewing motion. When Gravas moved closer to grab hold of the rope collar, the creature stopped eating and raised his dark eyes to look stubbornly at the foreman. As soon as it became clear that Gravas was holding the collar, Curtis tried to back away. However, because of the man's weight and the fact that he gripped the rope between his fingers, the young kid could not budge.

Gravas began walking toward the barn, dragging the four-footed creature behind him. The animal pressed its hooves firmly into the soil, making the journey quite difficult. Still, Gravas chuckled and continued along his way, in spite of the stubborn creature's efforts to free itself. Curtis swung his head wildly back and forth in an effort to dislodge the man's grip, but still Gravas's strength and girth proved the stronger.

The laughter of laborers in the meal line began to join with the foreman's as he neared the kilns. A call went up for Mariah to run to Gravas's aid before his arm tired from the goat's frenzied movements, for she alone seemed to be able to control Curtis. Nouhad took the occasion to comment that the goat's disposition and that of Noah's wife were very much alike, and she called out Naamah's name as though she summoned one of the sheep: "Naaaaaa'mah."

Mariah set down her ladle and wiped her palms on the fresh apron before running to help. At the sight of the woman, Curtis gave his collar one final tug, forcing Gravas to pull even harder and then ran forward in the direction of the fat man. The act caused the foreman to fall flat on his face, and a loud "ugh" arose as Gravas's massive belly slapped the damp earth. When the goat was satisfied with his feat, he pranced toward Mariah, flicking his tail with affection, and nudged his muzzle against her bare arm.

Tubal-cain leapt over the short fence by the kilns and ran to help his fallen friend, while his wife led the contented creature back around the barn to the goat pen.

"Are you all right?" Tubal-cain asked, containing his own smile for fear Gravas might be injured.

"I will be," Gravas said after a moment, "as soon as you do me one small favor." He raised himself from the dirt, letting Tubal-cain help him to his feet. When the cooks, the laborers,

Methuselah, and Lapeth (Noah was at the lake with Shem) saw that the foreman could rise, their howls filled the air. The scene was just what they had needed in order to break the tension that always mounted prior to the payment of wages—a date less than two weeks away.

"What is this favor I can do for you, my friend?" Tubal-cain finally asked above the roar of the crowd. Although a smile had spread across his face, he contained his own laughter.

"Tomorrow, I want you to make a small bell, one with a rather large clapper. When you get it finished, have Mariah tie it around Curtis's collar." Gravas's hands were cupped together as he illustrated the approximate size he thought suitable. He rubbed the dirt from his hands and breeches, then laughed with the others. "I won't have that goat sneaking up on me again."

Tubal-cain simply nodded and asked the portly man to join him in the meal line. Gravas did not require a second invitation.

Early the next morning, when Tubal-cain had skillfully crafted a shining copper bell and Mariah had tied it around the goat's collar, Curtis trotted proudly up and down the length of the wooden enclosure, sporting the glistening object. The animal made certain that all the other creatures saw what it was wearing, going so far as to call out—with a guttural "baaa"—to some of the Mixtures and laborers who passed by.

Lapeth sat before the door of the wooden shed that had been constructed near the lowest conglomeration of rocks behind Naamah's cottage. Common sense demanded—at least in the minds of the crews—that there had to be a place from which payment could be dispensed. For that reason, the tall structure of pine stood near the rocks and was used only on the days when Methuselah, Traibus, and Gravas passed out the wages. On those mornings, Noah walked through the levels of the Ark with the master builder, checking the quarters, the stalls, and the granaries. The crews were too keyed up with excitement over their wages to perform any labor, and their absence and the Ark's emptiness allowed for a thorough examination of the work's progress.

Because of the activity and the noise in the clearing, the moist morning air was filled with anxious anticipation. Since the first rays of light had pierced through the vapors, the crews—men, women, and children alike—had gathered in lines spreading out in reckless patterns from the shed. A clamor arose as Mixtures grunted to one another and men with countless needs on their minds spoke enthusiastically about what their wages could buy this very day in the city. Few listened to one another, paying attention instead to the endless chatter of their own words or the jumbled thoughts passing through their own heads.

As had been true at the close of every other contract, some of the laborers would be leaving. Many were not accustomed to long stretches of employment, nor did they wish to become so. A number of those in line spoke of the journeys they would begin back to their homelands in Syria, Sheba, Dodanim, Persia, the mountains, or even the Gangem. Regardless of whether they planned journeys, however, it was certain that gold coins weighed heavy on their minds.

Those with proper judgment would take their generous salaries back to families who awaited their return to begin anew. Others would squander what they had worked so hard to obtain before even reaching the cities from where they had come. A few would inevitably be cheated or robbed within the first days of their travels. Still, they all ignored such realities, not wishing to dampen the pleasure they would have when heavy golden coins were placed in their palms and the thought of what might be procured with such a sum was easily brought to mind.

When the numbers in the clearing had dwindled in the past, Gravas had simply issued a proclamation with the agencies inside the city for more crews. This time, however, Noah ordered that no new crew be hired; there was not enough work for them to do because the task neared its final stages. All they needed were numbers enough to raise the fence posts to contain the animals, several dozen trappers to aid Traibus in stalking the creatures, and a handful of carpenters to finish the Ark and its stalls and the cages that Tubal-cain and his craftsmen had begun, following the suggested designs of the giant.

The laborers fidgeted about in uneven and haphazard rows. Lapeth watched the people with compassion, wondering why so many were beyond reach of the ancient Law and its tenets. She had even begun to give up the idea of continuing their work in the city after the completion of the mighty vessel. Noah still cherished the hope of returning one day to Shinar and using what time remained to indoctrinate any who might listen. However, she no longer shared his optimism. For the most part a blankness covered the eyes of most of those before her, and even in those few where any sparkle of life remained, the light of the soul grew ever dimmer. The people had forgotten their heritage, and their souls slept. Even death of the physical would not bring immediate resuscitation of the Light. Lapeth had finally accepted the disinterest of the people. She had reached the latter part of her middle years, and with them came the resignation to accept whatever she could not control.

She sat on one of the smaller rocks, her thin robe draped about her and her slender ankles crossed beneath the smooth cloth. Her worn, leather sandals pressed firmly against the ground. The soil remained damp from the pressurized water beneath the earth, as well as the moist air above it. Her watchful eye had been relieved to find that the massive platform supporting the craft had finally ceased its sinking (although it had sunk an entire cubit). The pressure below the ground acted as support for the weight of the gigantic ship.

Lapeth's hair fell down around her face and shoulders, framing the elegance that had been hers for decades. It retained the color of her youth; her beauty continued to rival that of her daughter's. Although her life had changed a great deal since the giant and Methuselah had found her, she had never forgotten Basil. She often revived her memories of him and reminisced when she was alone.

Her vigil was staged for the benefit of the laborers. Meanwhile, Methuselah and Traibus were hastily gathering pieces of gold upon the rocks in another dimension. She knew Methuselah's physical form would be posed in the silence within the shed, while Traibus's body—much too large for the enclosure—was seated on the floor of his own cottage. Gravas was in the shed, as well, sitting patiently on the small chair behind his counting table, waiting for the two to finish their task. Although he had become adept at the silence of meditation, he had never quite mastered movement through dimension.

The shed's door was locked when not in use, though Lapeth was aware of a number of occasions when the iron latch had been jimmied open. However, the intruding culprits had been disappointed to find nothing upon the pine floors save a few chairs and the wooden table. The gold would not be safe, unguarded, for even a few hours, so the coins were not collected from the rocks until the very morning of distribution.

What little patience the laborers possessed was beginning to fade. Some men with great, furry chests and tanned shoulders grew restless and were on the verge of pushing from line those they found disagreeable. The smells of sweat and thick hides of flesh were sometimes disturbing to some but many of the men and baboon-faced laborers had grown used to the aromas.

Wild children with dirt-smudged faces and dangling hair ran naked, while a group of mothers discussed at length what stage budding breasts and boyhood members demanded clothing. From inside her bedroom, Naamah listened to the racket and the screams of youths and the sounds of their mothers and longed instead for the sharp clang of hammers and hoisting timber she usually found so irritating.

The laborers believed their foreman and Methuselah were methodically counting out coins from behind the pine door, though the delay proved to be quite irritating. Shouts of many made it obvious that their frenzied composure had reached its limits—the payment was rightfully theirs and they had need of it quickly. Many a wager was planned for the day.

Lapeth looked up and finally spotted Noah. His presence relieved her greatly. Even the crowd began to calm with his approach. His rope belt dangled outside a garment of dazzling white, and each graceful step brought him closer to the woman he called "sister." The waves of his hair and the soft wisps of his eyebrows sparkled as brilliantly as the woven cloth of his garb. He appeared magnificent, and as he reached her, Lapeth rose, and the two embraced. The tone of her words betrayed her growing apprehension.

"I am grateful to see you," she whispered quietly in his ear.

"There is no reason to fear," Noah assured her tenderly. "These people will have the well-deserved fruits of their labor momentarily."

"Has Anon stayed behind on the Ark?" she asked, looking about for him. "I've been told Mariah and Tamari prepare quite a feast for those who remain in the clearing this day."

"His Atlantean appetite will not let him miss the repast, I assure you. He said he needed to see my sons but Rezepatha and Japheth have slipped from the fields to be alone, and I'm certain that Shem is with Shelobothe. You can be confident Ham and Maran have disappeared as well." Noah smiled knowingly.

"Those two are bound to be vying wits somewhere." She shook her head and remembered the vastly different days of her own courtship.

"No doubt but Maran uses the Sight and I can't believe Ham proves much of an opponent."

"Then your son may challenge her to wrestle," Lapeth said, watching an infectious smile come over his face.

"They may be betrothed after this day," he said, glancing over his shoulders at the rocks, "if my sons have found their nerve."

"Should their delay prove intolerable, the girls may find it for them."

Noah hadn't the chance to agree before both heard scuffling within the pine structure. The racket seemed to suggest that Methuselah had startled Gravas from the seat of his chair. No doubt such had been the mystic's intent.

The noise caused the workers' uneasy excitement to increase. All had long waited for any sound to emerge from the counting house. As the door swung outward on its hinges, laborers with human voices began to cheer, and others raised warm, sweaty limbs into the air with wild enthusiasm.

Methuselah stood in the doorway, leaning heavily on his staff, and was ready to begin carrying out the proceedings in the manner with which he had greeted every other closing of contracts.

He nodded dramatically for the crowd. The cheers grew even louder, though those of the fifteen present knew it was for the gold and not for the old man.

Most who roared with excitement believed that the hunched figure before them was just one of many forms the magician could assume. Tales of his power had grown as favored as those stories of Naamah. Oftentimes, whenever a solitary creature appeared on any path in the forest or was seen flying upwards in order to clear oak treetops, and Methuselah was not to be found, a new tale of his power spread throughout the city of tents. Although many of these supposed sightings had occurred while the mystic was fast asleep within the confines of his room or in the quiet rejuvenation of the silence, in recent months, the number of fables of the man's magical powers had only grown.

No one could be certain why the sage chose to assume the appearance of such an old man, with deeply-lined flesh and tired eyes that had known more days than nearly a dozen of their numbers put together. They didn't understand why he allowed the long bristles of his grayish beard to grow thin when any form might be his. Why he let his step take on that of one who was aged seemed beyond comprehension. For some reason he chose to inhabit a body that seemed to be growing increasingly weary. The laborers couldn't begin to guess the reasons behind this mystery, nor did they have any idea how closely the tales of his power had come to resemble the truth.

Methuselah stepped from the shed and onto the ground at the same moment that the giant's head was spotted coming around the far corner of Naamah's cottage. With his approach, the crowd began a unified cheer. In the fingers of his very large hand, Traibus carried parchments that listed the names of every laborer in the clearing. He would check the names off the list with a small charcoal stick, while Gravas and the others dispensed the gold. Part of his duty was to keep a record for the foreman of those individuals who were leaving the project, as well as of those who planned to stay.

"Again, the day has arrived," Methuselah said casually as he patted Traibus's arm. He stared up into the giant's eyes and saw clearly for the first time the signs of age he himself was beginning to feel. "It would seem that each day of payment arrives more swiftly than the last."

"Then you have forgotten one of the first lessons you taught me." The enormous features wrinkled with the thought of getting the best of his companion of so many years. "The time about us is no more real than a dream." The old man simply nodded in agreement, not quite feeling up to the wit of word games.

"Someone had best decide to help me with these coins," a voice chuckled from the opening of the shed, "for it will be quite a dream indeed when five score men lose patience with your ramblings."

Traibus tucked the parchments beneath his robe and went to the doorway. He bent down, almost dropping completely to his knees, and reached in to grab the thick canvas bag that sat on the floor next to Gravas's sandaled feet. Even for a giant it was heavy but with both hands he managed to carry it over to the lowest flat-topped rock behind Methuselah and the others. The size of the canvas bag made the eyes of several, including Boland the dwarf, bulge with imagination.

Gravas remained merry, though he just barely managed to squeeze between the posts of the doorway. The red curls on his head bounced with eagerness as he hurried toward the rocks. As he threw open the sack, sighs came from many. The crowd pressed in close to see the coins that sparkled as brilliantly as any light piercing the vapors. Overhead, the doves returned from a morning journey and spotted their gentle master; only the closeness of so many laborers kept the birds aloft.

Lapeth dipped her palm into the coins and withdrew a handful to begin passing out; Noah, Gravas and Methuselah did the same. Traibus towered among the four, making certain to mark off names and list those who would be staying. As each of the laborers reached the front of one of the lines, which had lost all semblance of order, one of the four called them by name and inquired as to their plans.

Those who could speak (staring wide-eyed at hands that cupped gold) answered the question, often without even knowing who had asked for the reply. Finally, the payment they had eagerly awaited for six months was dropped, coin by coin, into eager fingers and claws. All received the same, regardless of the duty they performed; it was taken for granted that each would receive the promised bonus, bringing their total wages to seven brilliant pieces. As payment was made, Traibus scribbled the laborers' plans onto thin parchments.

It was no secret among the laborers that the fifteen eventually planned to board the mighty Ark. To those who were leaving, an invitation was issued: They were welcome to return and join the fifteen upon the craft. Some seemed thankful, although they had no intention of ever sitting aboard the enormous ship, waiting like fools for rivers to flow from the sky. An equal number scoffed at the idea as soon as the gold was safely within their grip. A few appeared saddened at the thought of leaving—though not one suggested they might return.

Boland signaled to Methuselah that he would be staying for the remainder of the day as well as for an additional term. He held his tiny arms outward, small hands cupped together, so that the old sage could press seven coins into his palms. As the dwarf walked away, he appeared unable to remove his eyes from his outstretched hands that carefully balanced the gold.

As the counts continued, it appeared that at least half the workers would be staying—including the Black warriors who had been with the project since the beginning. Fizel stood before Lapeth, grinning, when she asked if he would be staying.

"I have nowhere else to go," he said. "No woman awaits my return, and I left no task undone before my arrival."

"Shall you be staying with us for good?"

"Though I owe your family much," he said, after a moment, "I can not claim your beliefs as my own. There is a task for me to do, that is certain, but when it is done, I shall be leaving as well."

She shook her head sadly, knowing it was too much to hope than any of the laborers would be going with them. Of course, none but the fifteen (or at least fourteen of the fifteen) believed the Ark would be going anywhere at all, and even they weren't certain when the journey might be or where it would lead.

Lapeth dropped the coins into Fizel's shiny palm and called out the man's intent to Traibus, who recorded it. Fizel grinned once more as the gold was his and then went to join one of the few who regarded him as friend. Friendship was not easy among the laborers, and Fizel had experienced more than just a difficult time; many remembered him as one returned from the dead, and his presence made them uneasy.

Other than pushing and a few angered voices, the payment of wages was carried out without incident. Some were quick to exchange a single coin for fifty minor shekels, and the games of tables, shoe-toss, and even marbles-for-wager were set up in tent doorways or along scattered sections of the clearing. Others simply readied to leave as soon as the coins were in hand.

Women and children hurriedly gathered the few goods they had brought with them, for their men-folk were anxious to begin long journeys home. Those with carts loaded up all that they owned, including that won in sport throughout their tenure. Some still had goats and horses penned behind the lengthy fences of the barn that were hitched to small wagons or loaded down with the weight of goods strapped to their backs. A few creatures remained behind with the mules and horses and cows. No one claimed Curtis, the stubborn goat from Aghri Dagh, though Tubal-cain was quite certain that none among the fifteen had ever traded for the creature. Each animal leaving the clearing did so in much better health than that in which it had arrived, often with brighter coats and more body weight. Japheth's grain and mixed feed for the stock along with Shelobothe's care at making certain the creatures received proper exercise had brought many back from near death. Throughout the commotion of carts being hauled away and creaky-wheeled wagons being pulled behind clomping hooves of horses and goats alike, Naamah stayed safely in her room.

Nouhad, the Syrian cook, packed to leave, making certain she had stored Naamah's brass stewpot among her belongings. In exchange, Nouhad handed Tamari a few jars of spice to pass on to Naamah.

By midday, the noise of departure had subsided, for those whose evenings were planned for the taverns of Shinar had already left. By the giant's tally, sixty-three laborers planned to remain in the clearing—about half of the number Gravas had hired from the first.

Tamari bustled between the kilns, helping Mariah with the feast they had prepared single-handedly. Both women wondered whether the Syrian's departure was causing Naamah sadness, for

Noah's wife had witnessed many a departure without incident, but neither had gathered enough nerve to broach such a question. Instead, they baked pies, sliced vegetables, and boiled thick bean-and-potato soup until its aroma filled the air about the kilns and the cottages.

Shem returned from his lengthy absence, holding Shelobothe tightly by the hand; Ham and Maran (who couldn't contain her smile) followed the two shortly thereafter. Rezepatha and Japheth were the last to arrive, as though they were newlyweds, and were quick to join the game of horseshoes that Tubal-cain had set up between the cottages. The toss was for fun—no wager at all—yet even some of the laborers joined in for the sport.

Gravas decided there would be no harm in serving some of the ale he had hidden beneath the floorboards of his cottage. With the help of Traibus, one of the barrels was removed from the pit and carried out-of-doors. The horse-trader saw to it that everyone received a fair share of the draft, though none was more fair than his own or the giant's.

Grapes and fresh fruit were passed around in wooden bowls even before Tamari and Mariah began serving the meal. The smells of cooked squash and honey-baked pumpkin mingled with the scent of the pies, finally bringing Naamah from her hiding place. However, she was not at all like herself until she discovered Nouhad's deed and the fact that her stew pot had been stolen. Afterward, the large woman waddled about in her flower-patterned dress, joyfully nibbling on olives and nuts and happily reciting the tale (again and again and again) of how the Syrian had bested her by stealing the pot. She was quick to hide the jars of spice within the folds of her apron, secretly sprinkling a few grains of the herbs on her own plate when no one was looking.

Noah joined Anon against the low fence near the kilns and

spoke of his joy, often looking over his shoulder at the Ark. The red-skinned man simply nodded, though obviously pleased with Noah's praises, and briefly mentioned his need to be off for the Gangem. A new project awaited the master builder, and a great deal of money was to be made in the process.

Lapeth stood with her arm around Methuselah. He leaned on his staff, watching his family and the laborers, and tried to see beyond what physical eyes would reveal. There was much for him to do, and his thoughts became so crowded with these tasks that Lapeth was forced to repeat her own observations to him.

But his mind was elsewhere: the lessons of healing he had neglected to show Noah, great reams of hay he had yet to chop. There were talks he wished to have with Traibus before all that Noah had seen came to pass. He had walks to take, duties to perform, and periods of silence he wanted alone with the One. There were animals to gather and food to store for preservation, and Shem had long waited to be initiated into the ancient priesthood. In the old sage's eyes, he could see that many of the laborers needed to be cautioned against returning to the lands of their birth, for there were dangers. All over the earth, the places of man had changed for the worst. Time was short indeed—and still there was so much to be done.

And while Methuselah glanced about the clearing, from the Ark to the kilns, and in among the cottages, the tents, and the barn, two things became quite clear as he stood beneath the misty sky. The thought of Malock was beginning to fill the air, and time drew near for a wedding. Ham would marry Maran, and Shelobothe would marry Shem—just as Methuselah had known all along.

31 Days Before the Flood

It had not been easy, especially with the numbers involved, the fences to be raised and the gates to be hung but the clearing filled with the sounds and the cries of more than 200 species of animal—though the number was just a fraction of the total Traibus had written upon his ledgers. The giant had been quite careful in going over his lists not to miss any creature with which he was familiar but the sum of his totals had grown so staggering that even Noah was becoming concerned as to whether they had the ability to keep the animals they had already captured penned, watered, and fed until the remaining numbers on Traibus's list could be acquired.

If Naamah thought her family crazy due to the construction of the Ark, the continuous building of fences, wire cages and pens now caused her to consider them insane. She had seen Traibus's charts, figures and estimates. By the giant's estimates, the animals would require twenty times their own body weight in food storage upon the Ark. Traibus had listed 714 types of creature they needed to capture and as if that wasn't bad enough the calculation of pairs more than doubled the total.

There were to be seven pairs of each "clean" animal and one pair of each "unclean," according to Noah's guidance. Forty-three species were designated "clean" and would have seven pairs; the total number equaling 602. The 671 "unclean" creatures fared far better in the giant's figures, totaling 1,342. And after the fifteen had seen the ciphering, Noah stated that before any of his family could board the craft they would have to load the 1,944 animals first. The totals also included dozens of species of birds—some that members of the fifteen had never even seen before.

The pairings had been figured according to the ancient writing of the Law. Clean animals were non-flesh eaters and their numbers would be vulnerable to many of those that were unclean. They would need the extra advantage of seven pairs for survival. Generally, those creatures that chewed a cud and had a divided hoof were labeled clean but many non-predatory birds of the air were included in the category as well.

The clean animals were the cattle, the deer, the antelope and the sheep; each fourteen in number and all fenced behind the large gates that had been raised upon deeply buried posts near the aft of the Ark. The creatures were kept near the bow and far from the tent city but still the smells of manure lingered throughout the clearing despite the fresh hay and the distance of the animals. There were sand grouse and guinea fowl and turkeys within pens and tall wired cages to hold songbirds, canaries, hummingbirds and even doves behind the tiniest strands of mesh. However, the two white doves that belonged to Noah were free to roam the heights of the treetops as before.

Pigeons remained in cages, while ducks waddled about and geese seemed content to nibble upon scattered grasses of the forest. The largest of those to be counted clean animals had not yet been taken, for their numbers included the giraffe and the gazelle and none of the long journeys organized by Traibus had taken any of his trappers as far south as the jungle. Although they had reached the gulf and returned and had journeyed north to the primary foothills of Aghri Dagh, there remained far more journeys to be planned and many more animals to be taken.

The unclean animals were caged far enough from the gentler creatures to keep the latter from continual nervousness. They had scavenger birds like the raven and small furry rodents like the mouse and lizards from the mountains. They had a pair of wild bears, dark as ebony, captured deep within the forest and held in the sturdiest of cages against the farthest trees bordering the expanse; the creatures slept for the most part and were content as long as meals were delivered on time—consisting of great numbers of fish and large eggs provided by the geese. Traibus and his men had yet to obtain the lions, though all hoped the large cats would prove as docile as the bears.

Naamah hadn't always understood the pairings, and she gave up all hope of ever doing so when Gravas told her that squealing pigs were considered unclean: though they possessed a divided hoof, they didn't chew a cud. Camels were unclean, as well: they chewed a cud but lacked the divided hoof. Often, with the addition of a new species, the division between those needing a single pair and those that required seven became all the more confusing to her. She was thankful that the pair of camels had yet to be captured, for there wasn't a fence with which to keep them enclosed and the creatures were large and would require a great deal of looking after and Naamah had more than enough to do to stay occupied.

Each time some of the hired trappers returned from a journey, Naamah wondered how much longer their foolishness would last. Surely, they wouldn't carry out the giant's plan until all 714 species, nearly 2,000 animals, had been secured in the clearing? Not only had the giant grown too old to lead the expeditions but there just wasn't room! Already, the laborers were running out of space to raise the fencing. The damp smells of animal hides and hair and the overpowering scent of manure was everywhere, and the crews themselves did not find the work of feeding creatures, carting away great loads of excrement and listening to the unending chatter, snarls, cries, coos, and whines at all agreeable. Gravas's laborers had dwindled until only fifty worked for the promise of gold. The rest had become quite confident that there was an easier way to earn what they wanted (or that it was easier to go without). Naamah still clung to the hope that someone else in her family would eventually awaken to the ridiculousness of their labors.

Rarely did she see Noah anymore, except from a distance or as he stood among the faces of hirelings who waited their turn in the all too familiar food line. He kept lengthy hours, coming to bed long after she had fallen asleep and rising at least an hour before the first radiance of light. Sometimes she wondered if he had even come home at all. During the day, she avoided him. She was convinced he had become lost in a commitment he believed above all else and no longer had time for her. Yet, in spite of her loneliness, she would not allow herself to become lax in her responsibilities within the clearing. Though she lacked faith, she never neglected her duties, nor had she ever told her husband how she really felt. After awhile, she decided Noah wouldn't care anyway—it seemed as if he had forgotten she was even alive.

She stepped outside her front door and pretended not to see Tamari waving to her from the window of Gravas's tall cottage. She kept her eyes focused downward and shuffled her feet slowly in the direction of the only place she felt comfortable. Of late, she had built her life around her cottage and the kilns and rarely ventured beyond either. Although there were far fewer mouths to feed, there were also far fewer people to help. She shook her head in disgust at the thought of what they were doing.

Naamah had heard there would be elephants and hippos and rhinoceroses inside enclosures before the gathering of creatures was complete. Eventually, the cages and fencing would be laid out into the forest itself, for the availability of cleared space neared exhaustion. Two months earlier, Traibus had told Anon just prior to master builder's departure that their trapping might well last the better part of two years.

Naamah was trying to resign herself to two more years of foolishness, two more years of pungent manure and two more years of feeling like an outcast when the call rose up among the laborers for Mariah to come to their assistance; Curtis had jumped the fence again.

This time, Tubal-cain ran after the bearded creature, around and among the posts of scaffolding, while a few Mixtures cheered from the massive opened doorway in the side of the Ark. It was unclear to Naamah whether they cheered the goat and its clanging copper bell or the aged bronze man who hurried after it. Curtis's scurrying steps were precise, always staying just out of reach.

The intricate system of towering posts and heavy planks, banded together by dried leather and iron nails, rose thirty cubits into the air. Each of the planked walkways at each of the three levels came within a cubit of the ribbed sides of the vessel. Curtis took calculated turns beneath overhead walkways and between the posts and the platform of the ship. Often, Tubal-cain was forced to grab hold of a gopher-wood pole as his feet threatened to give way upon piles of dried hay that were scattered over trampled soil.

Gravas laughed so heartily at the sight of Tubal-cain's uneven footing and the way the long-stained apron kept flapping around the man's waist that his sides began to ache. The old horse-trader leaned against the worktable, gasping with laughter while his eyes moistened with tears. Only when his olive-skinned companion slipped and fell and landed hard against one of the posts did Gravas contain himself and run the dozen steps to Tubal-cain's side.

"Have you hurt yourself?" Gravas asked, with a look of real concern on his face. He squatted down, for he was much too large in girth to lean forward, and rested a hand on Tubal-cain's shoulder.

Tubal-cain ran his fingers through his graying hair and shook his head in denial. He raised his eyes to look at the goat about five cubits away watching him. The goat was calmly chewing cud and splintered hay. Tubal-cain took a moment to catch his breath. The goat seemed as tranquil as ever, though the creature's eyes remained fixed on the humans. "Have you ever wondered if that goat might be in liege with Malock?"

Gravas slapped his companion between the shoulders with renewed amusement. "I would wager no overseer would permit such a rebellious beast to be numbered among his flocks." He rose to his feet and extended an arm for Tubal-cain to grasp. When both men were standing and the craftsman had thoroughly brushed the hay and dust from his garments, Mariah walked casually forward in the direction of the goat.

Immediately, Curtis turned to look at the woman and began to prance, his four thin legs moving toward her. When the creature reached her, he nudged his head forward and allowed her to slip her hand around the collar; a few strands of hay remained stuck around the goat's jaw, which Mariah gently brushed away from his whiskers.

She looked up to see her husband and Gravas both staring in confused amazement and smiled at them. "I think Curtis would be more content with a mate. Ask Traibus to have his crews fetch a young she-goat; otherwise, he'll never consent to be confined aboard the Ark." She walked away toward the barn, with the shaggy animal following contentedly beside her.

"There remains some question as to whether the goat will even be going," Gravas said, loud enough for the amusement of Tubal-cain. He turned his eyes from Mariah and happened to stare in the direction of Naamah and the kilns. When Naamah saw him looking at her, she diverted her eyes and reached down for one of the largest stew pots. Gravas sensed the woman's mood and shook his head in dismay, leading Tubal-cain to the worktable.

"Have you spoken with your sister of late?" he finally asked, unable to disguise his concern. "She seems quite withdrawn from the rest of us."

"I have tried many times, my friend," Tubal-cain said sadly, "and she hears me not."

"She cannot bring herself to believe?"

"Although I would venture to guess we have all had times of doubt, Naamah has had nothing but. She lives each day much as the last."

"With words as sharp as ever," Gravas interjected, remembering anew the reprimand he had received the day before while helping himself to the pot of soup that simmered (seemingly unwatched) in the open air.

"Her words hide sorrow over what her life has become. I think her heart battles between disbelief in this work and love for her husband. Neither of these does she take lightly."

"Has she spoken to Noah?"

"Would you? The few times you have lacked faith in what we

do or the vision that began it all, could you find the nerve to tell him? I could not even bring myself to tell Methuselah."

"Or Traibus or Lapeth," Gravas added quickly. "There are those among us who have been mightily blessed."

"Which is to have the greater blessing, he who cannot share in the conviction of another's faith or he who lacks disbelief and is unable to see why another does not? The answer is not as simple as we might suppose."

"What does Naamah say about all your labors within the vessel? Surely one needn't believe to appreciate the craftsmanship and design of you and your men."

"She has never seen it."

Gravas spun around and looked at him with bewilderment: "What?" he asked loudly. "She hasn't been inside the Ark?"

"Never."

"Has she not asked how the work proceeds? The living quarters? The cages? The distribution shoots for food and water? The granaries? The storage bins? The chapel?"

"Never."

"She is as stubborn as your mother," Gravas said wryly, in disbelief.

Tubal-cain shook his head in agreement. "I think she's convinced herself it will be a very long time before any of us board the craft—a very long time indeed."

"She may be in for a surprise," Gravas said forebodingly as he waved to Shelobothe, Rezepatha, and Maran. The three women hurried toward them from the direction of the fields. In a short while the women would be meeting with Tamari and Lapeth regarding their accomplishments at food storage and the old horse-trader prayed fervently that his favorites would be numbered among the successes.

Only a few remaining rays of light illuminated the forest ground. Dusk fell quickly with long shadows that descended from the sky, dancing and growing beneath the mighty white oaks and tall timbers of pine. Even the scattered fronds of ferns became shaded by darkness and disappeared from casual observance.

They walked in silence, the old sage and Maran, each waiting for the other to speak. The direction of their footsteps led to Shinar but neither had any intention of going that far or leaving the safety of their clearing behind. Methuselah had chosen the path to escape from the sounds and the smells of 600 caged animals—irritants that lasted without interruption throughout the long night. It had been quite an adjustment for him to learn to sleep through the racket of snarls and whines and coos and the endless chatter that assaulted his ears, not to mention the overpowering stench that continually rose to his nostrils.

The two had left the clearing immediately after eating the evening meal. Each was beginning to feel a sense of urgency, though its reason remained just beyond the vision of Sight. Perhaps they would see it together, yet neither was certain what it was they were looking for. In the past, they might have ventured to the lake and sought the silence of the One upon the shores of water but the lake no longer appeared as beautiful nor as rejuvenating as it had when they first came to the clearing and Maran grew depressed just by looking at it. Besides, they needed to be away from the others for awhile and the path to Shinar was the most obvious choice.

Their work proceeded as planned, although the taking, feeding, and exercising of the animals was much more time consuming than any had supposed. All that remained to be done on the outside of the Ark was the application of a single coat of pitch from the base of the vessel to the uppermost walkway—well over thirty cubits above the ground. When the kofer had been brushed properly over every outer seam of the ship, the lumber to the scaffolding would be taken down and used for additional fencing. Already, Gravas had made plans for the remaining laborers to begin the task later in the week.

Their steps were slow as they moved along the deeply scarred path that no longer resembled the tiny trail that had once led to Lemech's solitary cottage. Methuselah leaned heavily on his staff as if carrying a tremendous weight and Maran couldn't help but wonder why the mystic appeared so ill. She, too, felt weighed down by a hundred different concerns, from Naamah's depression to whether or not Malock still posed a threat. She looked at the bearded man, almost hobbling along beside her, and wrapped a slender arm around his robed sleeve before she spoke.

"It is time we rested." Her husky voice tried to sound out of breath. Methuselah merely nodded and let himself be led away from the path toward the huge base of the first oak they came to some distance from the trail. She watched him carefully as he lowered himself to the ground with the use of his walking stick and a great deal of effort before sitting beside him with her back against the tree.

Although the shadows continued to darken, she could see the features of his wearied face. His eyes were closed and she watched as he took a couple of deep breaths. Slowly, the color seemed to return to him so that when his eyes finally opened she stared into the pupils she had come to know so well.

"So you think I've grown old?" He grinned at her and then leaned back to peer at the thick, white clouds through the branches of the trees. The long hairs of his beard dangled softly atop his chest. When Maran made no move to reply, he reached out his aging spotted hand and grasped her own beside him. "Is this so great a crime?"

"What?"

"Is it so great a crime to grow old when one has lived out his purpose?"

She paused for a moment, looking at him inquisitively before speaking. "You sound as though you've had a choice in this—to will yourself to be an old man." He turned his head and smiled, gently squeezing the fingers of her hand. Even in the darkness, she caught the knowing look in his eyes and her face grew alarmed. She couldn't help but lash out. "Why?" Her voice rose to such a level that Methuselah winced. "What are you doing?"

"I haven't decided yet," he said mysteriously. "But it should come as no surprise. I have known myself to be an old man for a very long time. It is time my family acknowledged it as well."

"To what purpose?" she asked. Even in anger, she wondered if he was up to some kind of riddle. "Why would someone make such a choice?"

"Sometimes it's easy to forget the reasons behind choices made. There are also some," he said softly, "who forget the choices themselves and fight against them when they come to pass."

"But I don't understand what . . . "

He interrupted, "A choice made in wisdom should not be refuted by ignorance."

Maran moved to speak but Methuselah waved his hand for quiet and posed a question of his own. "Why is it we both feel something, yet neither can put it into words? What is ahead in the days to come? It is so close to consciousness, so very close." He stopped speaking and waited.

She leaned back, staring up through the treetops where he was also looking. She breathed in deeply, trying to sense what was happening. One by one, she pushed the worries she felt from her mind and concentrated on nothing but the air around them. It was somewhat cooler than the heat of day, yet just as moist. She pushed even these sensations aside and tried to verbalize what it was she felt.

"It is something visible to the mind one moment, yet what it foreshadows is not visible. Without anger or malice or even harm, it comes as surely as tomorrow. Yet for the few who feel its approach, it brings a sense of dread so overpowering that it cannot easily be shaken. Of itself, none could label it good or evil, though throughout our history it has moved humankind in either direction. I cannot welcome its presence, nor do I shy from its arrival." She closed her eyes and paused, as if to grasp something that lay just beyond range. When it would not come after many moments, she sighed in defeat. "At times, I feel as though the knowledge it draws near may be more crippling than the dawn of its arrival. But beyond the undiscovered darkness of what it brings, there is a ray of hope and the presence of Light."

Having revealed her thoughts, she waited patiently for the sage to comment. When he did not, she turned to look at him, wondering where his own mind had taken him. His eyes were opened and fixed with perception—glossed over in moisture as if he had forgotten to blink. He stared between the boughs of the tree for such a long while that Maran began to wonder if the old man had fallen asleep. When she could bear the silence no longer and had nearly decided to shake him to consciousness, he finally nodded as though he had seen beyond the barrier she had described.

"What is it?" her voice broke the silence of night in husky impatience.

"Something so obvious," he said softly, "that we've been

blinded by its simplicity. What approaches makes not for the unknown. The unknown is merely what it brings."

"Methuselah!" his name was spoken with exasperation, "For once, let your words be clear."

"What else could it be?" He shrugged his shoulders, a grave look of seriousness overcame his features. "What inevitably comes without malice or benefit, although it may be used by some for either? Maran, the answer is simple. That which draws near is change—a change so monumental that humankind has never seen the likes of it."

When his words stopped, she moved to speak but Methuselah had not finished. His next remarks seemed to be an added thought to himself, rather than for the benefit of her understanding. "The planet will be transfigured. The children of God have misused their bounty and by their own doing it shall be taken from them. None can even fathom all that is to come. And none have fully realized that were it not for the One, were it not for His grace, were it not for the endless bounty of His forgiveness, were it not for His intercession to save His children from what they have brought upon themselves, all would be lost."

"Why must this be?"

Methuselah pondered the question for only a moment before responding. "What child may ever learn aright, if its parents continually protect it from the consequences of its own actions? The Spirit of Life was breathed into our souls and free will has been bestowed upon each of us. Yet, there is not a one who possesses the right to destroy that destiny which has been ours from the first. The darkness has grown so deep. For our own salvation, we must begin again."

Maran wondered if her question bordered on sacrilege: "Why did God not save us from self-destruction? Surely, He has known since the beginning where our steps would lead?"

"When His children stray purposefully from Him, the One does not wish to know what their wills have chosen in opposition to His own. Else would not the Creator have long ago grieved that He made the human creature? Though He waits in anticipation ever willing to aid when welcomed, He will not be the uninvited guest to those who bar His presence."

She could not stop herself from becoming depressed. She began to feel sorry for the One, although she was quite certain that it didn't make any sense. She could almost imagine the face of a loving father with his arms outstretched to his children while they—the most important things in his life—turned their sight in another direction. Her heart ached as she felt the father's ache and she wondered if it was much the same for the One. Never before had she sensed that the Creator might feel sadness and the thought grieved her to the depths of her very soul. She began to understand, finally, what must lie behind Noah's compassionate blue eyes, for far better than anyone else he seemed to know the One.

"It grows late," the mystic finally said. "Before we return to the clearing, let us both seek the silence. It comes much easier without the endless squalls of Traibus's menagerie." Maran looked terribly distraught so Methuselah added with a grin, "Three times, thus far, I have grown convinced that our friend, the giant, has scheduled the loudest and most nocturnal creatures to be taken first. What better way to irritate an old man who has spent a good number of years trying to get the best of him?"

She was unable to smile in return but her head nodded in agreement. She sat comfortably, closed her eyes and slowly removed all cares from her mind. Her breathing became deep and relaxed, while the tenseness gradually began to leave the muscles of her body. Her hands, which had been clenched in distress, became limp, and she grew calm and at peace and completely indifferent to her surroundings. For a time, there was only the peaceful quiet of the silence. Soon her forehead began to tingle with warmth, and through closed eyes she began to see sights of which no imagination had yet dreamed—for nowhere in the world had they come to be:

The lands of the earth stood before her and she knew what Noah had foreseen had come to pass. She witnessed in amazement what was revealed to her, for the world she looked upon little resembled the one she had known before the deluge.

The trees of the soil had been struck down, and those tiny seedlings that struggled to replace them seemed frail and dry and undernourished in comparison to those of the past. The new plants would never share in the same magnificence. Nor longer did everything that sprang from the ground bear fruit, nuts, seeds, grains, roots, berries or leaves that were palatable to the taste. There were new crops of thistles and thorns and trees that bore neither nut nor fruit nor leaf that might be steamed into broth. There were sickly sprouts and weeds and acres of dried grasses, appearing too pitiful even for fodder. Plants she had never seen before appeared as vines, reaching up from the ground to suck life from the few trees and vegetation that continued to bear nourishment. Even the scattered crops she remembered from the clearing's own garden no longer yielded harvests as rich as those in the past, nor could the size of the fruit ever begin to approach the bountiful offerings which had once been plucked from sturdy branches and leafy, green limbs with two outstretched hands.

And even in the silence she became fearful at the sight of vast wastelands: great stretches of barren ground where no berried shrub or nutted tree or fruited vine or leafy fern could ever grow again. Rivers, lakes, seas, and puddles had all dried with the heat or had suddenly stilled because of a cold air that she found difficult to comprehend. The planet, once warm and humid beneath the water vapor canopy and covered with rich, green vegetation had been altered. Something had happened to the temperature of the planet and Maran didn't know why.

There were continents on the earth where heat boiled, scarred, and burned the land into nothingness, until only granules of sand stretched out before her eyes as far as she could see. One moment, she was in the presence of the heat, trying to understand what had happened and in the next her mind saw a cold so thick that all moisture solidified into permanence. In countless places, white-watered crusts covered mounds where there had once been towns, forests, people, and rivers and soil soft to the touch.

She felt coldness lash out and strike the soft skin of her face, as if the air had a breath of its own and as it blew around her, great quantities of the white, frozen particles were lifted from the ground and whirled about in every conceivable direction. The breath of the air could be warm or cold and it moved in countless storms all over the globe. Where there was heat, the motion of the air added to the warmth but where the soil had become frozen, the harsh movement of air captured a coldness near the ground and kept it imprisoned so that the temperature never changed.

And in a flash, she saw what only Noah had seen before her: droplets of water falling from the sky and striking the ground, cascading with such force that huge mounds of earth were washed from the sides of hilltops, exposing roots of scattered trees, until oaks and evergreens and the cedars themselves began to be ripped from the soil. Though what she saw wasn't the vision of Noah (for that was a part of the past), she knew that what her mind now witnessed would become commonplace for the planet: Huge drops of moisture would fall with regularity from the heavens.

Through closed eyes, she realized the rich humidity of moist air that had once fortified the greenery of the planet was gone. There were stretches of soil so dry that cracks reached out for vast distances and plummeted into the ground for several harsh cubits. And yet, without seeing, she knew of swamps and marshes and boggy terrain so saturated with stagnant waters that little growth could survive. Lands had changed so drastically that one place rarely resembled another and even crops of one continent refused to take root somewhere else.

And as she scanned the devastation and the changes from which there could be no turning back, her eyes began to burn, itch, and ache. Yet, it was neither the sight nor the tears that caused the discomfort. She felt something in the air that had not been there before: rays of invisible light charred, scorched, and beat down upon the globe continually, radiating upon the waters, the hills, and the land, and deep into the soil, regardless of the warmth or the coolness of the continent that she stood upon. She lifted her head to look at the clouds, but the brightness of unseen light so burned her vision that she became as one blinded and then her eyes saw nothing but darkness. And the darkness carried her back to Methuselah's side.

As her breathing quickened and consciousness returned to her, she gradually began to shake with fear because of what she had witnessed. Her eyes shot open and she turned quickly to look at the old man next to her. She wondered how she could wait another moment to tell what she had seen. But his breathing was slow and steady, the gray strands of his hair and beard were held quietly in place and she knew better than to disturb the remainder of his silence, a silence he needed far more than she.

So as she waited, she kept her mind busied on all that must be done: the crops they would need to choose—hearty enough to withstand that which would come to pass; the extra food they would need to sustain themselves in the stinging bitter cold; garments of thick wool, cured hides, and woven fibers that would keep them warm when simple robes proved inadequate. While Maran's mind raced with the pictures she had seen of changing weather and its effect upon the earth, Methuselah began to awaken.

The old man's eyes remained closed for a time, as he allowed the peace he had found to permeate his entire being and his surroundings. Only in the silence was he able to feel like his old self again but this time there was something new as well. He finally grasped the last great mission of service that was his to perform. He accepted it willingly, without thought of changing his mind. It would help more of the lost children of the One than he might have dreamed possible. And he felt gladdened in his heart, for it was a most worthy mission for one as old as he. The opportunity made him feel humbled.

And as the silence began to leave him and his mind regained its consciousness (and the tired ache of old bones returned), he suddenly realized the task was far too large for him to accomplish alone; there would be one more from the fifteen to assist him. The knowledge made him as proud as any father, for although she had yet to realize it, Lapeth had chosen the same purpose for herself.

Methuselah smiled in wisdom.

Forty-nine hours later

Even the soft, filtered light of eventide was unable to illuminate the dark shadows of the forest below. The faint wisps of fresh moisture were pushed aside by the intruders as they stumbled toward their destination; instead of heading back to the overseer's fields, they had taken the route as an afterthought. None had yet decided what it was they were going to do; two of their number still snickered and orders were sure to be wasted on the pair.

The clumsy movements of the patrol—the last fading effects of an earlier drunkenness—were kept hidden by the blackness of twilight. And the sounds of the five Mixtures as they stepped upon thick, tangled vines or the few remaining fronds of ferns were covered by the restless noise of hundreds of creatures penned within the safety of the distant clearing.

As the five left the refuge of the surrounding trees, the smells of hides, moist fur, cracked hay, and fresh dung rose to flaring nostrils and overpowered the scent of gourd liquor which had long been on their breaths. Dachnid, with his long hair, greased back with sweet-smelling oils, led the way, for he had once been familiar with the area—though many changes had come to pass since his time. His large, blank pupils stared momentarily in wonder at the two caged bears that paced the confines of their cell, back and forth in nervousness. He walked cautiously along the fence surrounding sleepy cattle and passed the wide-eyed, frisky sheep in the enclosures next to them. The fences were the same: sturdy, well anchored, and made of pine, but the ground each of the animals trampled had become quite different. Even in darkness, the Mixtures could see that sheep had nibbled the scattered grasses to the very roots and had consequently killed all vegetation within their domain.

Dachnid almost couldn't believe what stood before them: the closeness of the cages, the angry snarls of a fox, the frenzied chatter of countless winged birds and the high pitched cries of the purple-colored male peacock that spread his fan-shaped feathers in arousal and scurried around his dull-colored female like an enraged chicken. There were turkeys and floppy-eared rabbits that cuddled together in slumber (though their eyes were quick to open at the sounds of footsteps), all behind iron mesh cages. A small gray kitten, eyes glowing like yellow fire, scampered off toward the cottages as Dachnid, Baird, Ceron, Hermann, and Lars—the latter two being the most inebriated—made their way past the menagerie of quacking ducks and yawning llamas, in the direction of the mammoth platform which Dachnid had helped build. They heard the whinny of horses (though some distance away) and Baird, whose ears were much better than the rest of the patrol's, caught the steady tinkling of a small clanging bell, though he had no way of knowing it belonged to a goat.

When the Ark lay before them in the darkness, Dachnid's angry frown was replaced by a look of disbelief. He raised his eyes in order to take in the dimensions of the enormous structure. It was as if the immense platform he remembered so well had grown tenfold, and the vessel's height towered upward, until it finally disappeared into the dark of night.

"It's unbelievable!" Baird lisped in amazement, but even the excitement of his words could not rise above the clamor of caged creatures.

Hermann nervously fingered the black whip that encircled his waist before turning from the massive ship to his companions: "Do we all see . . . this same . . . craft?" His voice was unsteady, as though he feared his eyes were playing tricks on him.

"We all see it," Dachnid said disgustedly, "and all the gold that has been wasted on this foolishness."

Lars stood silent for a moment, for the sight was sobering. He became awestruck by the Ark's fine craftsmanship. He longed to look upon the structure during the light of day and see the inner design of the ship but his patrol was scheduled to return before daybreak and he didn't care for Malock's correctional measures. Besides, they had neither candle nor lantern to peer inside the belly of the craft.

"Beautiful," was all that Lars managed to say, though, at the same moment, he was quite certain Malock himself would want to look upon the sight; such a vessel belonged under the overseer's jurisdiction.

"It's unbelievable!" Baird repeated as he spotted the huge dimensions of the ship's open doorway, at least twenty square cubits.

Ceron's eyes scanned the intricate scaffolding system that completely encircled the ship and stood next to the huge, gopherwood planking which had been sawed, planed, and hammered into place. Ceron suddenly remembered Sterba and growled with pleasure. "Let's burn it!"

Baird and Hermann looked at each other fearfully, though they remained quiet. Both thought of Methuselah, yet neither was certain anymore whether the sage possessed as much power as they had been taught to believe.

"No!" Lars argued angrily, when it became apparent that the others were hesitant to speak. "Malock would wish to see such magnificence."

"The Ark won't burn," Dachnid said positively, "not unless you managed to build an enormous fire against its side and such a blaze would be quick to awaken everyone. Can't you see the vessel has been painted with pitch? Even now they prepare to add an additional coat," he pointed a crooked finger at the covered stone jars of kofer that had been gathered near one of the posts of the scaffolding.

"We could try," Ceron replied, ignoring the hateful look of Lars's scowl.

"I tell you it won't burn!" Dachnid said truthfully. "However it would be a shame not to take back some story to strike Malock's fancy. I have an idea."

He assured Lars that the ship would not be harmed and after convincing Baird and Hermann that Methuselah was no match for the might of the overseer's patrols he put them to work. With little difficulty they found the necessary tools and acted as quickly and as quietly as the task allowed. The squawks and clamor of the restless creatures suppressed the few noises the patrol made, and in less than two hours, they had finished. Afterward, Dachnid made certain that no signs of their presence in the clearing remained; the sawdust was buried and the tools returned to their place.

In the end, their single action that night in the clearing under the cover of darkness would completely alter the course of events that Noah had foreseen for the work.

Tubal-cain had risen before daylight with the strongest desire to recapture the days of his youth but they were days that had long since gone and seemed far removed from the present. Simple memories of the way life had once been in the clearing flashed through his head and he remembered how the oldest cottage had appeared when it stood alone and was occupied solely by himself, his father, and his father's wives, and how the tall oak trees of the forest had surrounded them in comfort and solitude. The unhappiness he vaguely remembered from his youth no longer was as real to him and even the arguments of Adah and Zillah had all but faded from his mind, so that the days of his childhood suddenly seemed to be some of the very best he had ever lived.

The olive skin of his bare arms and face gave him the appearance of one who was decades younger. He wished for an hour of quiet contemplation but the continual noise of the creatures seemed to prohibit all but the thought of it. He sat comfortably on the petrified stump (something he had not done for a very long while) and waited for the rest of his family to awaken. He realized it would soon be time to begin the labors of another day and the thought both thrilled and saddened him. He was excited because he loved the work and the skill of the craftsmen who assisted him but he regretted that the day's labors would entail leaving behind his reflections of the past. And he didn't know when he would have the chance to pick them up again.

He thought of his sister as a young child, and how she had changed. It was almost as if Naamah had grown in unhappiness as she had grown in years. He pictured his half-brothers, Jabal and Jubal, and wondered if they had ever found what they had been looking for or if they had ever again thought of their homeland or their family. He drew to the present and thought of Mariah, whom he had left in the comfort of their bed, and of her loving gentleness. It did not seem to matter that they had never had any children, for their lives were rich with love. Both were the other's best friend and though they spent long hours apart—she with Naamah and he with the craftsmen—they were constantly on each other's mind.

"Is it the stump that has grown smaller or has the man who sits upon it changed in size?" the question rang out like a riddle and Tubal-cain lifted his head to see Methuselah leaning heavily on his staff and Traibus towering next to him.

The giant's huge teeth were exposed in a smile and he spoke quickly before Tubal-cain could greet either of them. "Refuse to answer the question!" The movement of Traibus's enormous arms caused his robe to ripple in animation, "For if you do, my friend here will find something mistaken with the content of your words, regardless of what you choose to say."

"Then tell me, Traibus, how would you respond to the question of a sage such as this?" Tubal-cain asked happily, remembering how often in his youth they had played the same game around the stump.

Traibus's enormous features drew together in concentration for the challenge. He patted his huge palm gently on Methuselah's aged shoulder and looked to the billowy clouds to collect his thoughts. Methuselah looked back and forth between the two men as his long beard dangled from his chin and his eyes sparkled with anticipation at the fun he was about to have.

"When responding to a wise one," the giant said finally, "you must often answer as a fool. To the question, 'Is it the stump that has grown smaller or has the man who sits upon it changed in size?' there can be but one reply. If you say it is the man who has changed, then Methuselah will retort: 'Only his body has changed, for the man is ever the same. The man is a soul within a body, not a flesh body with a soul.'"

"And to the changing of the stump?"

"He will say that the stump is of the earth, and the earth is of the flesh. Yet, the dimension of materiality is only a tiny reflection of all that is really there. It does not exist as we think we see it. Therefore, our physical sight has blinded us to the truth and the stump is an illusion of that which cannot be."

"Then the only answer," Tubal-cain replied, for he was certain he had it, "is that our perception of both has changed, and neither of the objects themselves."

"Very good," Traibus said, smiling. "In fact, the same would have been my response as well—in the past, but not today." Methuselah's gray eyebrows suddenly slanted upward as his forehead lined with surprise.

"To the wise answer of perception," the giant continued, "the sage will only comment that he posed the query in order to bring to mind events of the past. Our old friend was merely thinking of long ago when you were a boy sitting on that very stump and the three of us were together in a world that didn't appear so fated. So the answer to the question, Tubal-cain, is 'Yes, Methuselah, those were carefree days indeed—days of freedom and of youth and of times when it seemed easier to know what we should be about. I too wonder if the world will ever be as young again.'"

Methuselah shook his head in bewilderment, leaning with both hands wrapped around his sturdy support. "It would seem," the tired old man said honestly, "that the student has outgrown the usefulness of his teacher. Your wisdom rivals my own."

"That may be true," the giant said eagerly, "but your foolishness continues to surpass any I could hope to possess."

All three laughed heartily at what they knew to be true.

Later in the day, when breakfast had been served to the fifteen and the hirelings and Naamah had complained bitterly about the fact that someone had chipped her ceramic mixing bowl in the wash water (though she knew perfectly well she had done it herself), Traibus and Methuselah returned from the short walk that they had taken to oversee the conditions of the animals. As they walked along, unknown to either of them the tiny gray kitten with three black paws stalked the hems of their lengthy robes in fascination. He stayed close to the fence line, with his fluffed hairs pressed low to the earth, and tried to find the courage to attack—though both moving objects appeared far too large for an assault.

Traibus motioned to the enclosure which contained the deer: seven spotted females and the same number of majestic bucks, one of which boastfully carried eleven point antlers. "If we extend the fence back into the trees," Traibus said, trying to keep the tired man's attention, "there should be room for the giraffes. We'll have them within the month. Of course, we're going to need some of the lumber from the scaffolding for materials. Isn't Gravas supposed to schedule the last coat of pitch sometime soon?"

"The job is being done as we speak, my friend," Methuselah said wearily. He hobbled along, with the help of his staff, trying to keep up with the lengthy steps of the giant while the tiny kitten scurried after them.

Overhead, Traibus caught sight of the doves circling and decided Noah must have entered the Ark to inspect the latest work on the stalls and storage bins. He turned his eyes toward the vessel, proud to see what they had been able to accomplish. Its dark gopher-wood planking glistened from the light and the layers of sealant that had already been brushed over the beautiful wooden surfaces. The top of the craft had the general form of a whaleback deck, with the exception of the raised walkway that ran the entire length of the ship. The sloping roofs would easily shed water if it became necessary.

The enormous doorway lay open, while its massive portal was stored beneath the wide planking that rose at a gentle incline from the compressed soil to the ship's entryway. The door would be pulled in place, when everything and everyone had entered the ship, with sturdy ropes and interlocking pulleys, then bolted from the inside with iron locks and wooden wedges hammered on either side of the seams. The portal's design had been cut to fit snugly; once the wood was saturated with water and the connecting joints began to swell, the doorway would be impenetrable.

What had pleased Traibus all along was the fact that he could walk upright on all three levels and move comfortably down the corridors of every hallway within the Ark's interior. Not only would the wide-open space provide them all with room to move about but it also allowed for the best possible circulation of air. And the giant was quite certain they would each long for fresh air throughout their confinement in the craft. In spite of the fact that the scent of crushed hay still rose nearly five-and-a-half cubits to reach his nostrils, the smell of the animals proved much stronger.

They checked on the sheep, the cows, and the caged birds of yellow, orange, blue, and green—singing cheery songs from the bare branches of the replanted birch within the cage as though the brilliantly feathered creatures had become oblivious to their surroundings.

Traibus was quick to point out Ham's ingenuity in the design of the gopher cage, though the mystic was certain Maran's suggestions had been incorporated as well. It had been erected right next to the high-standing coop of singing birds. The enclosure was not exceedingly large, for it held only two creatures, a female and her male, but a good deal of compressed soil had been stacked in the shape of a hill in the center of the cage. The wire mesh safely surrounded all four sides, as well as the roof and flooring, thereby preventing the gophers from burrowing themselves free. The mound of soil had given them freedom to dig three intricate tunnels within the confines of their pen. One of the bobbing brown heads, cheeks fat and full with a fine store of acorns, watched the two men curiously as its tiny nose poked at their lingering scent in the air.

As the men walked past the cages in the direction of the worktable, the kitten finally saw a chance and bravely leapt upon the hem of the giant's robe with two tiny, black front paws. The kitten's paws snagged deep into the fabric—the length of the material was more than five cubits to the giant's shoulders, but the little furball of a creature was so light that Traibus failed to notice the extra weight he was dragging. As a result, the kitten's hind legs and end were whipped left and right over the soil. When the creature finally became aware of the garment's size and decided it had had quite enough, it quickly retracted its claws and bounded off to hide in the tall grass around the cottages.

Already, a half-dozen laborers stood on the mighty, three-tiered scaffolding, rising above the worktable, painting the seams with the thick, brownish paste. Gravas leaned against the table, checking his scattered diagrams with one hand while wiping a woven kerchief (a gift from Tamari) with the other.

"I shall never grow used to the aroma of pitch," he chuckled nasally. "Far better are the odors of the animals around us."

"You may change your mind quickly, once we've gathered all these smells within the Ark," Traibus said matter-of-factly. He towered over the fat man, who was half his height.

"That may be true," Gravas said joyfully, "though it is certain I shall be grateful to have the presence of nostrils as bounteous as yours to filter the air around me." Gravas noticed the mystic's eyelids growing heavy for sleep, so he directed his question at the old man, knowing perfectly well of Methuselah's loathing for the thick smells of compost which forever hung in the air. "Which would you choose, Methuselah," Gravas asked, holding the handkerchief over his nose, "great buckets of pitch or the smell of a hundred caged animals?"

Methuselah merely shook his head tiredly as he spoke. "I would choose a rest. Even in all this racket, I would choose sleep." He looked gently into Gravas's eyes and tried to grin in response to the man's joviality. His weak hand extended to grasp the horse-trader's bare arm. "I believe our friend, the giant, has worn me out on purpose." His gray eyes held only a hint of their former enthusiasm. "Would you come for me when I am needed?" The foreman gave a simple nod and watched for a few moments as the old sage relinquished his hold and then limped off in the direction of his worn mattress.

When Methuselah was safely out of hearing range, the giant peered into Gravas's eyes. Without saying a word, each knew what was on the other's mind. They had begun to worry about Methuselah's deteriorating health, though they feared to speak aloud what might be true. "I guess he's just been very tired of late," the foreman managed to say. "He'll be all right after a rest."

Gravas diverted his gaze to the second tier, where Boland worked silently (and as speedily as the Black man next to him). The dwarf's small hand brushed the planks of the Ark so rapidly that Hollis, a warrior from Cush, kept glancing down at his small companion to make certain his own momentum was as timely.

"If you were as active, my little friend," Traibus joked, as he patted the foreman gently on the back, "you would shrivel up to the size of a mere man in no time at all."

"Yes," Gravas laughed as the sound of tinkling moved closer to them. "It is a good thing that I find hard work as distasteful as old giants appear to." They spun around to see Curtis's shabby face dashing madly back and forth in order to stay out of the clutches of Tubal-cain and Rezepatha, trying to corner the creature between them. The goat had a clump of parsley dangling from its jaws so it immediately became apparent to all that Curtis had sneaked into the garden. Tubal-cain, work apron flapping behind him, managed to cry out for Mariah, who had not yet come into view.

The commotion of the chase and the shout of the iron maker brought all labor within the clearing to a complete halt. The men and the Mixtures and even the fifteen stopped what they were doing and turned to look at the familiar sight. Gravas's laughter proved infectious to those around him. Laborers on the scaffolding dropped brushes into paint trays and buckets and followed the comical movements of the bronze man, the striking woman with dark hair flapping on her shoulders, and Curtis, who refused to drop the clump of parsley he was positive the two were after.

Rezepatha had the hardest time retaining her balance. Her sandaled feet frequently slipped on the earth and the countless strands of drying hay. Her robe grew moist from her own sweat, and even her cheekbones began to show the strain as she ran with extended hands, darting back and forth to stay with the pace and the nimble, shifting movements of the four-footed goat. When she had had just about enough and couldn't bear the thought of trying to keep up any longer, she stepped upon a scattered pile of freshly-cut hay, and her legs slid out from under her. She stumbled hard to the ground, about twenty-five cubits from the Ark, and spent a long time rubbing her thigh, while Tubal-cain continued the chase, moisture streaming down his forehead.

Lapeth, Shelobothe, and a bare-chested Ham watched the bronze man's pursuit from a distance, where they stood on the edge of the field. Tamari looked up from her place at the kilns to see Mariah dash out from the cottages and race toward her husband. Naamah simply shook her brightly colored frame in disgust. Shem appeared in the doorway of the Ark and tried to signal to Tubal-cain that his wife was coming but the man's eyes burned with frustration and he saw neither Shem nor Mariah.

The giant was satisfied that the chase was over when Curtis noticed the friendly woman coming toward him. The goat even stopped, allowing the exhausted Tubal-cain a rest, and suspiciously eyed Mariah with his black pupils. Curtis's whiskered snout bobbed hesitantly at the air and he thought for a moment how pleasing the woman's gentle hands might feel, stroking his neck. Of late, however, Mariah also becoming associated with the pen, so the goat chose not to give up the prized clump (soil still dangling from the roots of one end) or to be taken to the fencing behind the barn. In a flash, Curtis sprang between Tubal-cain and Mariah.

Three of the largest Mixtures, including Hollis, who quickly climbed down from the scaffolding, ceased their laughter and clambered after Curtis, amid the excited sounds of hundreds of other caged creatures. Fizel came from around the bow of the ship, carrying a coil of rope and saw the commotion. His pearly smile flashed briefly as he witnessed the goat's stubbornness, but when he realized Rezepatha had fallen, he threw his rope down and quickened his steps toward her.

The goat ran beneath the support of the scaffolding while Mariah and Tubal-cain stood dumbfounded midway between the worktable and the craft. Mixtures attempted to circle the creature, slipping upon spilled pitch and scattered hay as they ran. When Curtis finally appeared to be cornered against one of the mighty wooden posts, two laborers jumped for the goat, slamming hard against the bracing of the scaffolding, just as Curtis slipped between their legs, and pranced in the direction of the ship's aft end. Rezepatha began rising to her feet.

Fizel had not yet reached her when he heard the tremendous sound of splintering wood. He peered over his shoulder to see a hundred cubit segment of the scaffolding wavering on its sawed base. The horizontal beams had been cut as well, and the entire section began to fall toward him. He heard Tubal-cain shouting to Traibus and Mariah's screams as he sprinted forward, yelling for Rezepatha to move out of the way.

Tubal-cain was struck down by the walkway of the second level falling against his chest, just as the entire vertical post collapsed with the force of many tons against the portly form of Gravas. Boland managed to jump free of the scaffolding before its first thundering impact. The horrible noise of crashing timber drowned out the shrill noise of those nearest the Ark. Fizel gave one final leap, knocking Rezepatha several cubits away, just as the third-story platform slammed against the back of his head, pinning him to the earth and breaking his neck.

Tamari saw her husband go down, and her screams rang out as she hurried toward the Ark, calling out his name. The sky filled with dust from the ground and clods of earth and bits of hay hung almost motionless in the air for a few moments before settling back into place.

Naamah threw her cooking pot to the ground, waddled forward as fast as she could (falling far behind Gravas's widow) and called first for her husband, who couldn't possibly hear her above the screams of the others, and then for her brother. Shem jumped down from the Ark's doorway and hurried to where Traibus had fallen, just as Japheth and Ham bounded out of the fields and over to where they had seen Tubal-cain and Mariah go down in each other's arms. Shelobothe turned and buried her head in Lapeth's breast; the woman had frozen in place at the sight. Rezepatha began to sob just as Maran appeared around the corner of Lemech's old cottage, dragging Methuselah by the side.

Suddenly, a figure dressed completely in glimmering white appeared in the doorway of the Ark. The shock of what lay before his eyes caused Noah's legs to buckle, and he fell to his knees in horror.

The Preparation

When Boland's leg was set in a tiny cast fashioned by Shem and Japheth, when Curtis finally gave in to capture, when the laborers began to remove what remained of the fractured section of scaffolding under the direction of Ham, when Fizel was buried along with Alki, Martin, Hollis, Gravas, and Mariah and his lifelong friend and cousin, Tubal-cain—all near the old stump, not far from Lemech's resting place—and when his heart could bear the pain no longer, Noah walked in solitude to the lake to find answers to questions he didn't even know how to ask.

Part of him wanted to lash out at a God who would allow such a catastrophe; part of him blamed himself for what had happened; and there was a portion of his being, one that had never existed before, that just wanted to die. He wiped the moistness from his eyes with the fingertips of his hand and stepped wearily along the path he had not traversed in much too long a time. Even the thought of seeing the golden face of Enoch or finding peace along the shoreline of the lake did nothing to comfort him.

More than anything, he just wanted one more chance, a brief moment, to reach out and embrace his cousin, the chuckling horse-trader, and Mariah who had never spoken unkindly of anyone. But it was too late, for they were all gone. Noah felt saddened, sorry for himself. He would never have the chance to say goodbye.

He had come from the clearing in search of guidance. They would all look to him for direction and the weight bore heavily upon his shoulders for he had none to give. Worse yet, Traibus still lived but was suffering and even the healing arts of the ancient Law could do nothing to save him. Four of the giant's ribs had been broken; one had struck the tissue of his lung. There would be no getting better; it was merely a matter of time. Traibus lay, delirious, in his own enormous bed, with the shaken Methuselah huddled over him in sadness and frustration: There was not anything the old sage could do. The giant was going to die.

Noah's steps moved over the scarred path with sadness. He headed away from the clearing, the Ark, the tents, and cottages, as well as from the people he was not yet ready to face. Repeatedly, he lifted his hand to his face to rub away the tears that ran over his cheeks. He was engulfed by memories of friends he would never see again.

He saw Mariah and the unending patience she had always given Naamah. He beheld Tubal-cain's smile as he had shown the work of the craftsmen on the stalls and the cages and in the galley of their enormous ship. He was filled with thoughts of Gravas and tried in vain to recall the last words spoken between them. He remembered, instead, the day they had first met—outside the peaceful stables of the horse-trader's barn—while there had still been so much hope. He was forced to direct his thoughts elsewhere, for fear he was going to cry.

He tried not to notice the numbers of dying ferns, the broken limbs of trees hanging from bows of oaks and pines nearest the trail or even the sparse vines of thinning underbrush. Despite his sorrow, he couldn't help but be aware of some of the changes. No longer did the scent of pine permeate the air, nor was there any fragrance of wild blossoms nor ripening fruits. In their place, the humid odor of rotting leaves and wet mildew rose throughout the forest. Red melons, soft-shelled nuts, and yellow-flowered seeds had disappeared from everywhere except the cultivated fields in the clearing. No sound of chirping bird nor hopping rabbit nor startled buck broke the heaviness of his movements.

He felt the anguish of Tamari, who lay bedridden in one of the cottages and in such a state of shock that she wouldn't even respond to Shelobothe or Maran. She had become immobile, staring upward at the ceiling of Lapeth's room, and would neither speak nor eat nor give any indication that she was conscious of another's presence. Since the tragedy, she had uttered only a single sound, a cry of alarm, when they had tried to help her to her own bedchamber—the sight of the mattress she had shared with Gravas had moved her to collapse at her nieces' feet.

Noah knew his own wife was deeply distraught over the death of her brother. But Naamah, of late, seemed to shy from his presence, and Noah had not yet recouped his own strength nor had he found the strength to go to her.

After he passed over the last length of trail and the trees of the forest spread in either direction to encompass the expanse of water and its surrounding shoreline, he stared mournfully at the tremendous contrast between the surface of the lake and the sky above. The water had grown gloomy and green and murky—so dark as to be unable to reflect the brightness that fell from the overhead vapors. And although the purity of clouds remained steadfast, as if the disease that had entered the forest could not reach the innocence of the heavens, he wondered for the very first time if the vision of the flood could be avoided.

He sat upon a patch of dead earth, once rich with wild grass, plush beds of lavender buds, and tiny field mice that scampered for cover at the approach of all but the gentle white-haired man. He looked out over the lifeless water and thought of a time when beauty had been the lake's sole concern. He tried to inhale deeply in order to relax but his nostrils found the scent offensive. His heart ached for the peace and restfulness of the silence. He had not found sleep since the tragic deaths of the seven; he was weary and longed for relief from the weight of his own thoughts. His eyes were closed in stillness and he tried to free his mind from all that had transpired. Only in the silence might he find the rejuvenation he needed to help the others. Yet, as he relaxed and began to shake from his reflections, the heaviness of sorrow, and the pain of death, the exhaustion within him grew stronger and his mind turned instead to sleep.

And while he slept upon the barren shoreline of the lake, Noah dreamed of a place he had seen only in his dreams:

It was the most beautiful continent in the world, with rolling hills and sparkling blue lakes, wide-open valleys and trees laden with their bounty, just ripe for the picking. Fields of plush grass surrounded magnificent gardens: tulips of pink, daffodils of yellow and the lavender flowers he had once loved so well grew plentiful. Walkways of cobblestone and red-tiled trails opened up onto terraces and encircled scented fountains or led to massive temples of marbled columns and polished stone. Statues of alabaster carved in the finest detail told the history of the people from the dawn of recorded time. The sculptures lined pathways or stood like sentinels beneath the arches of towering facades. This was the land of possibilities, Poseidia, with its irrigated valleys, scientific wonders and ancient structures that housed the most advanced civilization in the world. Above it all rose Mount Alta, the tallest peak on the continent, overlooking the splendor of the people's traditions.

On a smaller peak, not too distant from Alta, a woman stood against the railing of her terrace, peering down onto the greenery of the valley beneath her. She wore the finest silken robes, woven together with thread of spun gold. Her hair, once blonde but now filled with highlights of silver, had been combed with the greatest of care by one of her house servants. Her husband was on the Ruling Council and there was nothing his influence (or money) could not buy. And yet, she was deeply troubled. For many long months, her life had been filled with worries that seemed neither rational nor possible to overcome.

She had every reason to be content: a loving husband, two intelligent children and an elegant marble home with one of the finest views of the valley and of the rising majesty of Mount Alta before her. Even her father remained in good health, living under the same roof, often doting upon her and the children when he wasn't in city temples on business with her husband. There were servants to wait upon their every need but none of these things were enough to bring her comfort. She felt something unseen all over the land and in the air about her and it was something she had come to fear.

Although the land, the peaks, the valleys, the gardens, and the sparkling city of columned architecture and rising pyramids—symbolizing the ascent of souls of the children of the One—retained the beauty and lavish grandeur found nowhere else on earth, there was something evil going on. She felt it surrounding her, at times so thick she could almost reach out and grasp it. More than anything, she had come to believe its presence threatened the very existence of the faithful.

Her fears had been spoken frequently to her husband but he pushed them aside with a few calming words and tried to give reassurance. Yet, his denial caused her even greater concern, for she had often seen his eyes fill with a fear greater than her own, as if he knew something far too foreboding to mention.

There were rumors of uprisings throughout the nation and of the mysterious deaths of some who had been faithful to the tenets of One. She had heard whisperings regarding the children of darkness—Mixtures and half-breeds who hoped to overthrow the Children of the Law—and how the rebels had gained strongholds all over the land. Even her servants had spoken of plots to overtake Alta and thereby control the continent.

And as she thought of these things from her terrace and of her concerns and worries for her family, she had no way of knowing that the very struggle the people feared most between the rebels and the faithful had begun—and the rebels were winning.

Atop Alta, where mammoth crystals and a firestone harnessed the power of the atmosphere, channeling energy to every part of the continent, the children of darkness had overtaken the power source. In less than an hour, the victors had taken control of the crystals, the source of Atlantean wonders. They planned to create a display that would prove them the victors but in their ignorance they had tuned the firestone too high and something no rebel had ever imagined had begun to occur.

The woman stood with her hands grasping the railing and turned to look at the lofty mountain peak on the other side of the valley. She sensed a change in the air, as if the moist humidity that kept the rolling hills so green had suddenly become heavier. For a moment, she thought it only her imagination but tiny bumps of flesh began to break out all over her body and breathing became more difficult. She started to feel dizzy. Still the air grew heavier with a thickness so intense that she was nearly overwhelmed by the sheer weight of it. She felt faint and her fingers wrapped tightly around the protective fencing for fear that she was about to fall. As she grew dizzier and her throat began to gasp for breath, her body grew weak and she imagined she saw tiny bursts of flames spark through the overhead vapors, as if the sky itself had started to burn.

Suddenly, the mountainside rumbled, and the entire continent shook with a tremor so powerful that alabaster statues toppled to the ground, falling from ancient bases that had stood for centuries before shattering into countless fragments. With a deafening roar, a bolt of lightening exploded from the top of Alta and shot straight up into the clouds, striking the motionless purity of soft, white vapors.

Through her blurred vision, the woman witnessed the beginnings of a chain-reaction—one that would take nearly a year to complete. The misty vapors of the cloud cover began to shrivel away, concaving into themselves as white turned to gray. Slowly, the earth began to expose its beautiful landmasses, stable oceans, and sparkling seas to the radiation put off by an entire galaxy.

The woman fell down, prostrate upon the tiled floor, as the oxygen began to disappear. She passed out just as Noah began to realize in sleep that the vision he had looked upon would indeed come to pass. He understood, as well, that the elegantly clothed woman upon the terrace had been Waila, daughter of Raki'el.

Noah stood outside the towering doorway of the giant's cottage and hesitated before entering. He had found neither relief from his tremendous sorrow nor the rejuvenation he had so desperately sought at the lake. The waters were spoiled, and the trees, the grasses, and the flowers had either disappeared altogether or were beginning to die. In such a place, renewal could not come easily and Noah had left the shoreline, much more troubled than at his arrival.

He lingered for a time, standing completely still, listening to the faint sounds of sorrow that still rose through the clearing.

Muffled cries and low whispers came from the cabins and even the words of the remaining Mixtures were soft-spoken, as many paced about, not knowing what to say in condolence nor what to do, except to continue their tasks, feeding and watering and exercising the animals.

As he found time to gather his own thoughts, leaning in anguish upon the doorpost, he could not help but feel a sense of fear growing within his own body over what was to come. Yet he wasn't thinking about the Ark or the vision or his guidance, or even the dream about Waila. Instead, his heart grew heavy, his eyes became moist, and his shoulders felt weighed down with the most difficult burden he had ever faced. There was nothing anyone could do for Traibus; he couldn't last much longer. The time had come to tell the giant goodbye.

After Noah attempted a few breaths to calm himself, he entered the cottage, walked through the narrow but tall hallway and came to the darkened room. The giant wheezed with short, harsh breaths that shook the stillness of the room with their severity. And although Noah had tried to ready himself for the sight of his friend lying on his back with his pale, large features grimacing in pain and the sweat of his brow rolling down his forehead and neck, soaking the fresh linens that Naamah had laundered, he was not prepared for the sight of his grandfather. Methuselah's haggard appearance caused Noah to fear that the old sage himself had finally decided to die.

Methuselah looked much older than ever before, with drawn, sagging flesh and thin, spotted hands that shook nervously. The old man seemed ill as he sat weakly by the side of Traibus's bed in a varnished oak chair once fashioned by the hand of Tubal-cain; Methuselah's feeble legs had grown weary from standing. Upon the ground lay his staff, a long-ago gift from the giant. For hours he had sat immobile, just staring at the form of his friend. His hair and beard were tangled and unkempt. His cheeks had become reddish and chafed from the tears he had continually wiped away with the crumpled, damp cloth gripped tightly in his fist. He turned slowly to look at Noah, and his grandson's sudden presence caused him to sob anew. Noah was the last one who needed to bid farewell.

Noah saw Methuselah's pain and walked over to place his hands on the mystic's shoulders, squeezing gently as he spoke.

"Has he been conscious?" The words nearly choked in the back of his throat, and he moved to brush tears away from his own eyes. He watched the giant closely, feeling pain every time Traibus's body trembled uncontrollably, as the gurgling noise rose from the man's gaping mouth. It was the sound of a man drowning, and neither of them could do anything to help.

"He has been delirious for nearly three hours," Methuselah said helplessly. Earlier, the sage had fashioned a compress of warm oils that was tied about Traibus's chest but it provided only minor relief. The old man reached out with a quivering hand and placed it lightly on top of the saturated compress. "I do not know what else to do."

"There is nothing we can do."

Methuselah bowed his head and let another tear roll down his face without bothering to wipe it away. "Noah," he uttered weakly (and softly lest Traibus might hear), "I do not want this one to die."

Noah could not speak. He merely pressed his grandfather's shoulders in affirmation.

"It is not fair," the aged mystic said aloud, more to himself than to Noah or to the giant, "It is not fair to grow old and yet to watch those we love pass before us, though our age surpasses their own: first Anna, then my son, then my family, and now . . . my friend. Only a fool would wish such upon himself. It is not right to live so long."

Traibus groaned, gradually moving his head in the direction of the voices. Slowly, his eyes fluttered open, and he attempted to reach his arm toward Methuselah. The mystic's hand moved quickly to grasp the giant's. "I am here, Traibus." A tear fell from the wrinkled corner of his eyes and he leaned forward to be as close as possible. He felt a little pressure upon his own hand as Traibus acknowledged his nearness. The giant's lips moved to speak but all that came forth was a whisper.

"I wish to thank you." The hushed words caused him much pain.

"To thank me?" Methuselah's hand trembled in the giant's weakened grip.

"You have shown me," Traibus winced as the pain in his chest grew stronger and the delirium crept upon him, "a most wonderful way to live—and of death; there is no fear." Traibus stopped suddenly and cried out with such agony that his body writhed upon the mattress and the old man shook with fear.

"Do not try to speak," Methuselah managed to say, "for speech is not needed between us."

"I . . . must." Traibus's words were slurred, "Where is Menahem . . . Noah?"

Noah moved forward, laying his soft hand upon the giant's arm. He watched the haziness take over the giant's eyes and realized Traibus was losing consciousness. Through blurred vision he managed to say, "Beside you."

Traibus's throat gurgled with the sound of liquid and the giant was forced to cough in order to continue. When he was certain both men were near, his eyes began to close, and his words were voiced with great difficulty.

"It comes . . . ," Traibus managed to say with one breath. "I have seen it."

Both Noah and his grandfather pressed close to hear, holding onto each other as they gently touched the giant's feverish form.

"It comes . . . ," he repeated in delirium, "sooner than we expected. Gather the food for the animals."

In horror, Noah immediately understood what the giant's words implied and he spoke out: "It is too soon! We have not yet finished the task you began."

Traibus could not hear but in his last moments of life, as his mind witnessed the scene before him, he faintly whispered four final words: "The vision draws near."

At that moment, the old sage knew it was over. He leaned his head in surrender upon Traibus's limp body. "Oh, my friend," Methuselah cried aloud, "I love you."

Though none thought it possible, with the passing of Traibus, the emptiness and sorrow within the clearing became even heavier than before. Idle words were not spoken, for many even among the Mixtures, held back such powerful emotion that tears would likely burst forth with the slightest provocation. Not far from the cottages, the moistness of the soil enabled them to dig, in a few hours' time, an enormous resting-place for the giant's body. When it was done, Methuselah had a disturbing thought as he walked alone over the freshly tilled ground: Nearly as many of their numbers had passed from the earth as now remained behind.

Lapeth, too, had a revelation as she watched the horror and confusion of the laborers over yet another loss. She understood their grief but their actions and hushed tones also revealed an intense fear of death. With so many among the fifteen now gone, the Mixtures found plenty to be frightened about. Although she understood their sorrow, she could not understand their fear. When the deluge finally occurred and death for so many became inevitable, that fear could trap them in the confusion of their own thoughts and prevent them, for a time, from passing into the Light. As Lapeth worked at the task of food preservation, she comprehended the greatest service she could perform: With her own passing, she could lead countless others into the Light, preventing them from being trapped by their fears of the unknown. Sometime later in the day, as she sealed the lid of a stone jar with wax, she finally understood that Methuselah had chosen the same thing; his aging appearance merely reflected his choice.

In the days that followed, as Lapeth and Methuselah confessed to the other what each had come to know, and as Noah and his sons supervised the gathering of food for the animals (and worried about the creatures they would never have time to catch), Naamah tried desperately to shake the sadness from her breast and replace it with an irritation that proved difficult to find. At the same time, Shelobothe, Maran, Rezepatha, and Lapeth dealt with the enormities of vegetable, fruit, and grain storage, while Tamari pined even further away over Gravas. She never rose from Lapeth's bed nor ate to retain her strength. She never listened to the promptings of her family—nor their pleas—nor chose to quench her thirst. In less than two weeks, Tamari, too, had made the transition.

Because of the way Gravas's passing had affected her, Tamari's death came as a surprise to no one. In her youth, she had been used to his long absences but she was no longer young and in the past there had always been a promise of his return. After Tamari's death, a handful of laborers began to view the latest tragedy as an omen of tremendous significance. The thirty score caged creatures had grown more subdued because of recent events—except for a single goat and a tiny gray kitten, each intent upon stalking new territory. Late one night, as the darkness and quiet seemed almost natural, some workers fled to other regions where their fears might not need to be confronted so directly. That morning when daylight broke through the vapors, the clearing contained less than fifty, counting Mixtures, men, and women. It was in order to raise the mood of the people that Noah and Methuselah chose that day to schedule a diversion that both had long foreseen.

Ham wasn't quite certain how it had happened. The corners of his mouth were turned down in confused annoyance. The clean, woven shirt he had been forced to wear irritated the muscles of his neck and forearms. His back was not used to the confines of any cloth garment against his tanned flesh. He gripped his callused palms together nervously, wondering how Shem was managing to bear up so well. He couldn't believe they were both going through with it (he didn't want to go through with it). He was still very much a young man—had not yet seen his first century—and was certainly not ready to get married.

His curls of light-blond hair quivered as he shook his head in disbelief. Somehow he had been tricked but between Maran, Methuselah, and his own father, he didn't know where to place the greatest blame. It wasn't that he hated the idea of getting married to Maran. If he had wanted a wife at all it would have been her but who said he wanted a wife? A woman wasn't really necessary. He was quite able to care for himself. His gruff features pinched together in exasperation; now he would have a female looking after his every move—and one gifted in the Sight at that.

Beneath the cover of towering oak and ancient pine, and a stone's throw from the kilns, Methuselah leaned heavily on his staff (appearing more hunched than usual) and conducted the double ceremony. Ham tried desperately to find a pair of eyes that sympathized with his plight. He turned first to Maran to see if he could tell what was really going on in her mind but her thin smile and glistening pupils made him think she felt the victor in some unnamed game they began playing the day she stepped from the horse-trader's carriage. She took one of his rough hands in her own and squeezed it tightly before looking back at Methuselah. Now, more than ever, Ham felt trapped.

He glanced about the gathering, the shirt irritating the ruff of his neck as he turned and became disgusted when Rezepatha and Japheth nodded knowingly at him. He didn't want his marriage to be like their own. His brother and sister-in-law had grown ever too much alike. Sometimes Japheth was soft, like a woman and too often Rezepatha forgot her place, just as Maran had done on occasion. After the ceremony, he would have a talk with his new wife. (It would have caused him even greater concern to know that Maran planned a talk of her own.)

The sight of Shelobothe and Shem staring dreamily into each other's faces was incomprehensible to him. Ham had no doubt that Shelobothe was a wonderful woman. She knew a thousand different entertainment diversions and Tamari had taught her a great deal about cooking—though it was rare that Naamah allowed anyone else to cook, especially when it was something she didn't know how to prepare herself. Even Shelobothe's fascination with the care, feeding, and exercising of the animals (undoubtedly the work of a man) could be excused as harmless interest, but what cause did Shem have to marry her? After all, he had dreamed of becoming a member of the ancient priesthood—

even a prophet of the Law—and Ham couldn't understand why his brother needed a wife. In fact, he found it hard to imagine why anyone needed a wife, unless it was to be cared for when old age had taken away a man's ability to look after himself.

A couple dozen workers, including Boland with his mending leg and the only remaining warrior from Cush stood around, waiting anxiously for the old sage to finish blessing the unions. There was much to be done. Three of the Mixtures, with elongated features and confused, wide-opened eyes, were bewildered by the event, for they had believed the foreman's beautiful nieces wedded to Noah's youngest sons all along.

Noah stood motionless in his brilliant white robe, watching the ceremony proudly. He was able to forget the work that lay ahead of them. Lapeth, too, had pushed from her mind the purpose she had discussed with Methuselah. She was quite taken by the marriages and the happiness she hoped for both couples. She wished them as much joy as she and Basil had found for a time, as much joy as her daughter and Japheth seemed to share. And as she looked at Rezepatha and the way her daughter stood by her husband, Lapeth's eyes were opened and she suddenly realized something that Rezepatha had not yet revealed to anyone.

As Ham let his eyes complete their wanderings, only Naamah seemed unchanged by the event. He was sure his mother understood more clearly than anyone how he felt about the marriage, for her own life had turned out far differently than she could have imagined as a young woman. Of course, Ham didn't notice that his mother stole glances more often at Noah than she did at either of the couples exchanging vows.

The final pronouncement of his vows from his own lips surprised Ham more than anything. And years later, on those rare occasions when he'd regret the day he ever wedded (for a few fleeting moments anyway), he'd look back and wonder if Methuselah hadn't somehow bewitched him, for out of his own mouth came the binding words:

"To be together as one," he said without hesitation, "I take thee as mine."

When he had kissed Maran, and Shem and Shelobothe had finally parted lips, and they all took time to embrace, Methuselah came over and patted him on the back. "From this day forth," the old man grinned joyfully, "you just might find yourself under new supervision."

"We shall see, grandfather," Ham whispered quickly, "we shall see."

Although they had been constantly occupied with their duties, the work of each day continued to last for as long as any glimmer of light fell from the sky. Though the craftsmen had nearly finished the structure within and completely without (and Naamah had yet to see their handiwork inside the vessel, save what could be spotted by peering up into the massive doorway when no one was looking), and ladders had been erected and the last layer of pitch had been brushed over solid gopher-wood planks and beams, the enormous task of storing the rations aboard the Ark began.

Lapeth spent hours with the younger women, filling stone jars and metal tins with dried fruits and vegetables and uncooked oats, flour and rice. Maran's vision of the uncertainties of their first harvest prompted them to fill countless containers with foodstuffs, while heating many of the storage vessels to remove all possible moisture before sealing them with bee's wax. They gathered wheat, honey, corn, nuts, lentils, peas, barley, beans, millet, salt, hominy and great stores of seed, hay, fodder, and dried cereals for the animals.

Noah ordered food to be gathered for every creature on Traibus's list, even the hundreds of species they would never have time to trap. He had grown convinced that his family would one day encounter each of the animals. Perhaps when the Ark came to rest on the side of a mountain range, they would find giraffes, elephants, camels, and a mate for Curtis, all waiting hungrily above the water level. Surely the One had no intention of letting any creature vanish from off the face of the earth. Certainly, there was an ample surplus of crops to carry out Noah's intentions. Japheth's and Rezepatha's fields had been planted with the idea of feeding more than 200 and nearly six months had passed since half that number had inhabited the area.

At the end of one very busy day—after a regularly scheduled wagon arrived and was unloaded of its huge barrels of fish taken from the gulf (for the meat eating creatures), the crew prepared to leave for another journey of food gathering. The darkness gave way to low-burning fires scattered among the abandoned tents and one near the kilns. Noah assembled the faithful together. It was their first meeting without the entire fifteen, and even with Boland's presence, the five they lacked were sorely missed.

They encircled the tiny fire and huddled closely together, not for secrecy or in order to hear but that they might find comfort in the nearness of one another. The three youngest couples held hands (Maran held Ham's in her lap), while Lapeth and Methuselah sat side by side. Boland was squeezed between the old sage and Naamah, who was infuriated with her family for continuing the foolishness in spite of all that had transpired.

All faces turned to Noah. Even Naamah was no longer afraid

to look straight into his eyes. His firm hands were placed gently on his knees, while his deep-blue eyes looked upon each of them with compassion. The small flickering flames of the fire caused shadows to dance behind their backs but none present paid any heed, waiting instead for Noah's words. When he finally spoke, it was with a great deal of emotion:

"My dear friends," he began slowly, "much has happened that we did not foresee. Things that even the Sight could not expose have befallen us." He glanced quickly at Methuselah and then Maran. The brightness of the fire illuminated his features as he turned. "The task we began, our work here, has been deeply wounded but not mortally so. The time has come for us to complete that which the One would have us do and we are almost done. So much depends on our success. So much rests upon our shoulders."

"It is difficult to put aside the thoughts of those who are gone, when so much of our surroundings can't help but bring them to mind. Which of us takes a meal without seeing Mariah smiling from the kilns? Who can lift an ax or raise a hammer to a nail or see the polished woodwork of craftsmen without shedding a tear for Tubal-cain? Who is able to laugh or chuckle and not feel empty inside for Gravas? When looking toward my grandfather or walking beneath the mighty height of cottage doorways or watching the animals we have captured, who does not miss Traibus? And now, Tamari, too, has been taken."

"But we are forced to put aside our grief. There may not be time for even an idle thought or a moment unspent upon this task. We have chosen a service. Who among us could turn back after the call?" He paused for a moment, looking at his sons, their wives, his own wife, his grandfather, Lapeth, and the dwarf. Without trying to alarm them, he spoke the words that had been on his mind all day: "In a very short while, a morning will dawn when we must board the craft. At long last, our time has come."

The silence was unexpected. Although all eyes turned to each other for signs of reaction, there was not a sound but the crackle of burning wood, the whisper of the laborers back by their tents, and the restless noise of creatures, off in the distance digesting an evening meal.

Finally, Naamah was moved to speak. "Are you trying to tell me," she asked, her words unsteady at first (but as she thought of Zillah and the way her mother's bright red lips had often issued a challenge, she regained her bravery), "that you expect us to get inside that monstrous ship and wait? For what?" Her large breasts shook with defiance, the firelight shining on a myriad of colored flowers. "After all the time we've wasted on foolishness, you're still convinced that water is going to fall from the sky?" The others became uncomfortable and moved uneasily in their places as she continued:

"This is incredible in itself, but if you now propose that, out of the countless people upon the earth, we, alone, would be chosen to be spared—why, this is more unbelievable than your threat of a flood. I can't accept it and I won't!"

"Look at the ten—I mean eleven—of us gathered here, just waiting like children to hear whatever you say next. I've been patient much too long, waiting to speak my mind but no longer. Your belief that rivers will flow from the clouds can be disproved with time—when nothing happens. But if you've grown to believe that somehow we're set apart from the rest of the world, then there's nothing I can say that will convince you otherwise."

Naamah's words had been spoken quickly. The group had always known Naamah's feelings but to speak them aloud in front of Noah—well that was another matter.

An eerie and uncomfortable silence fell upon the circle, while the three younger men tried to avoid their mother's gaze (and wondered what their father would do next). Only Methuselah seemed amused by the tension and tried repeatedly to keep from smiling; finally lifting a hand to scratch a nose that didn't itch in order to allow a grin to hide behind his sleeve.

"Naamah," her husband began, undaunted, "I assure you the waters are coming. However, you have raised a most valid concern, though I'm uncertain whether my reply will comfort you: I find us neither worthy to carry out this task—though it is ours nonetheless—nor do I believe that survival will be ours alone." He accepted a nod from Lapeth as support. "We are not alone. All over the world, some may prepare even as we for the inevitable. Yet, our work is as important as theirs. Without us, they would be lost; without them, our toils would come to naught. All souls possessing some aspect of divinity in the earth shall be spared, whether that divinity be of body, mind, or soul. How else might the One's plan succeed?"

"It is our lot to be among this group, assuredly not due to worth—as it is measured by the illusions of men—for, my wife, all have been called. It's just that so very few have chosen to listen. Some of us here may possess the beauty of the divine in the flesh," he explained, looking at Rezepatha, whose face glowed in the light put off by the flames, "and hence the call. Though I say to you, many may be seemingly pure in body but wicked in heart and will not accept the call. Others may be pure in heart and ideal, though deformed in body. They, too, shall be spared. All who strive to manifest some aspect of what is perfect in the earth shall hear the voice of the One and be saved."

"We alone may be left from Shinar, or from all the lands from the Great Sea to Persia, even from the entire continent—none but the One knows for certain. We might be the only ones in the clearing who choose to board the vessel." Lapeth moved to speak but Methuselah stopped her words with a motion of hand. "Perhaps Boland and others," Noah said hopefully, "will decide to join us but it must be a matter of free choice."

"Then I would choose," Naamah interrupted definitely, "not to board the vessel, waiting upon a ship that merely travels deeper into the ground!"

Shelobothe squeezed Shem's hand and gasped with disbelief at Naamah's outburst. Methuselah moved to speak, calmly, before any of the others. "Naamah," he said wearily, in the voice of a very old man, his spotted hands grasping the staff outstretched on his knees, "It is true, you think you've made your choice but what the choice really is you do not remember. In time you will see, I assure you. Perhaps better than any of the rest of us, you will come to understand."

Naamah shook her head and rose to leave, although her enormous bulk caused her much strain. Noah nodded as well and smiled at the group in a way that showed he had not been offended. "It grows late," he said, and the fire began to die down, as if by command. "Tomorrow begins a new day and we shall go on as planned from the beginning. There is yet much to be done."

A short while later, Noah tried to talk to his wife in a way he had not attempted in a very long while. It had become so rare for them to rise together or even drift to sleep at the same hour. He wanted to know her fears, her concerns and her beliefs about what they should do. He even pleaded with her but she merely lay in bed with her back turned toward him and refused to speak—though her eyes continued to leak tears late into the night.

10 Days before the Flood

With the dawn—a few hours before Malock would rise to wax his mustache and begin making plans for an assault on the clearing—all of the craftsmen and laborers had completed all work on the Ark. The time had finally come for every remaining stone jar, iron container, watertight firkin (packed full of wrapped goat cheese and butter) and every tiny seedling of pine, fruit tree, oak sapling, and grape vine (each stored in buckets) to be loaded into the ship.

Noah, as foreman, stood majestically in the center of the Ark's massive doorway, helping the laborers pass the boxes, smaller barrels, and earthen receptacles up from the ground nearly four cubits below, and up the ramp, through the doorway, and into the proper storeroom in the belly of the enormous craft. Standing side by side, the craftsmen and workers and Noah's sons formed a human and Mixture chain, passing the cargo crates one to another. Boland, with bare feet and the tiny breeches of a boy, dashed about with a large piece of chalk, marking the jars, containers, and stacked boxes for the proper storeroom.

The wispy vapors of the sky hung motionless overhead, yet the activity and excitement on the ground seemed as productive and energetic as ever. Everyone in the clearing was working around the Ark, either with the animals or as a link in the chain that quickly moved supplies up the rampway. The rows of tents had been abandoned by the laborers, and the cottages, shed, and the area surrounding the kilns all stood empty. Naamah's outburst more than a week before had caused her such embarrassment that she volunteered for all sorts of tasks—though she had neither changed her mind about the possibility of the flood nor ventured a single step up the ramp leading through the Ark's doorway.

The rich smells of manure, sweat, and damp animal hides hung in the air and even the great stores of scattered hay could do little to camouflage the odor. Flies as big as a man's thumb buzzed atop the hind ends of horses and cattle—as tails swooshed away their footing—then alighted on deer, sheep, or llamas, or flew in the direction of men rhythmically lifting cartons of supplies or bales of fodder up the massive rampway. Some of the insects found laborers with coarse flesh too leathery to notice their presence but most were waved aside.

A bare-chested Ham stood midway up the ramp between his brothers. One after another, he hoisted object, crate, jar, or bucket from Shem's arms and passed them to Japheth, who handed them further along the way. Meanwhile, Naamah waddled nervously about (twice, almost running into the dwarf), all but forgetting her task of inventory as she made certain that her dishes, pans, and pottery cooking pots were being handled with care. She felt it quite a waste of time loading all the items but she wasn't going to say anything. They would only have to unpack when the waters never came. Although visibly irritated and flustered, she held her peace (and failed to notice the tiny, gray kitten stalking the hem of her colorful dress).

Methuselah waited on the ground, leaning with one hand against the rising rampway and the other placed upon his staff. To the laborers, it appeared as though he were resting, which they accepted because of his age. However, he was not resting. Since rising early that morning he had felt a change about them, as if in the air itself. The lines of his forehead were creased together in thought as he tried to pass beyond the limits of consciousness to see what approached the safety of the clearing. He pushed aside all thought of the tremendous stores being loaded upon the craft, including the oil and wicks for the ship's lanterns. He forgot about all of the foodstuffs that had been loaded. He even managed to remove from his memory the sight of the enormous water casks, so large that their construction had taken place within the walls of the vessel itself.

As Methuselah pushed these pictures of the Ark and the laborers and his family from his thoughts, he attempted to reach out with his mind to discover what moved toward them but he was blocked from the attempt. Something powerful, with a strength that dwarfed his own, stopped him and that something was moving toward the clearing. He turned his eyes to look at Noah, then toward Lapeth, to see if either noticed it as well, but there was nothing. He moved to speak but found he could not, nor could he release his grip from his staff, nor move his sandaled feet from their stance. Whatever he had felt now held him in place, so that all he could do was wait and he knew the wait wouldn't be long. Whatever it was that approached just beyond the veil of Sight was coming. The distance was closing and only a few moments remained.

Lapeth was impervious to Methuselah's discomfort; her mind was focused elsewhere. While Shelobothe and Maran scouted the fields for the next crops to be plucked and dried, Lapeth walked alongside her daughter, each woman carrying a small box to the stacks where Boland stood impatiently with his chalk. When they dropped their load and turned to fetch another (and Lapeth was quite certain no one was listening), she placed her palm under Rezepatha's chin and turned her daughter's eyes toward her own.

"In a short while, you should refrain from work such as this," Lapeth said, lowering her proud, green eyes to catch signs of her daughter's swelling.

"How did you know?" Rezepatha asked in surprise. "Though I have wanted to share my happiness, I have told no one."

"Even Japheth?"

"No, lest he worry about me while this task demands his greatest attention. Besides, he will know soon enough, once we've entered the craft. Noah grows more certain the time swiftly approaches. Then I will have my husband and you as my time comes." She reached out to touch her mother's face.

Lapeth looked toward her feet, finally managing to speak what had long been on her mind. "Neither Methuselah nor I will be going." The reply almost knocked Rezepatha to the ground but before she could cry out in protest, the power Methuselah had felt moved into the clearing.

The ground along the north end of the fields began to rumble and the soaring treetops of oak and pine away off in the distance began to shake violently enough for all to see. The penned animals within the clearing grew hysterical. Bears awoke from complacent slumber and growled while nervously pacing the confines of their cage. Sheep scurried from one corner to another, running tightly together as a single group, looking frantically for a place of safety. Behind mesh enclosures, dozens of feathered wings took flight as high-pitched calls rose through the air. Shouts of men and Mixtures mingled with the whines and snarls of animals, and all work came to a halt.

Noah dropped a wooden crate to the floor and turned in amazement to see what approached. Before long, all eyes stared fearfully in the direction of rustling leaves and the splintering sounds of shattered branches and crisp broken vines. Curtis remained behind the barn but the bell clanged apprehensively and the goat pondered jumping the fence or remaining with the other goats. Near the stacks of piled crates, the kitten froze for an instant before diving beneath the hemline of Naamah's dangling dress. Suddenly, all sensed the power Methuselah had awaited and a hush descended upon them. The old sage felt a sensation rise up his spine just as several of the gopher-wood trees on the outermost edge of the north end fell forward. Two enormous heads with leathery skin and deep-set eyes appeared among the trees and lifted trunks in the air simultaneously, issuing a trumpeted roar announcing their arrival.

Most of the humans and Mixtures had never seen elephants, with their legs as massive in girth as some of the tallest trees, their curving tusks of pointed ivory and their footsteps that vibrated the very ground beneath them. As the creatures strolled forward between fence posts on either side of the trampled dirt leading to the Ark, moisture dripping from their tusks, the laborers witnessed an even greater surprise: The elephants were not alone.

There were other creatures, dozens of them—hundreds! Creatures followed behind the elephants in rows of twos, as if it was the most natural thing in the world. Fourteen graceful gazelle, seven on either side, followed close behind the elephants. Behind the gazelle walked great, woolly buffaloes, with broken leaves and pieces of fern still clinging stubbornly to their brown, matted coats. Tigers and spotted leopards pranced forward along with oxen that seemed oblivious to surroundings and even to the spider monkeys gripping tightly to their backs. Fourteen lofty giraffes, with curious long necks that whiplashed left and right above the fenced enclosures, tried to take in everything inside the clearing with a single swirl of their towering heads. There were hunching gorillas and three-toed rhinoceroses sporting armored flesh—the male had but one upright horn on his snout; the female, two.

The rows of creatures seemed unending, extending double-file far back into the heart of the forest. The animals came, led on by the elephants, squeezing into the trampled aisle until it was filled. They entered the clearing and took up what space they could find near fenced deer, caged bears, or the sniffing foxes. There were lions—an enormously maned, golden-red male and his solemn mate—and curious orangutans. Two chimpanzees waddled back and forth with the footsteps of tiny children, holding hands so as not to lose each other; their hairy backs were nosed on by zebras following right behind.

Noah couldn't believe what he saw. He stood dumbfounded in the doorway of the Ark and waited, noticing neither the looks of amazement on his grandfather's wrinkled face nor the tear-stained cheeks of Rezepatha, whose stare moved repeatedly from the menagerie to her mother, who remained by her side. Noah's eyes scanned the long rows until he suddenly realized that every animal inscribed upon Traibus's papyrus was accounted for. So many had entered the clearing that there were more creatures waiting on the outside of pens and cages and fencing than had been captured since their first expedition. Amazingly, none seemed to fear the presence of any of the others.

There were hyenas and rams standing next to each other and to wide-eyed ostriches, whose plumes bounced as they walked. Overhead, there were birds—the eagle and raven—both of which had continually outsmarted the skills of the trappers. There were dogs and more cats and cud-chewing camels—more animals than Noah's soaring doves, afraid of neither eagles nor scavenger ravens had ever seen in flight. And bringing up the rear was a solitary, white, female goat.

Noah's sons and the laborers on the rampway moved out of his way as Noah walked down the plankway to greet the two massive creatures leading the entourage. The elephants came to a halt at the base of the ramp and the white-haired man reached out his hands to pat the creatures gently on their thick trunks. He shook his head in amazement at the procession behind the enormous pair and his eyes grew moist at the thought of such a miracle. The laborers and the Mixtures were convinced that the gathering of animals was some kind of magic and many stole glances at Methuselah to see what he was doing. But even the old mystic was as surprised as they were—and was made even more so by what followed.

As the elephants looked into the deep-blue eyes of the man before them, they seemed to recognize him. In unison, both creatures let front legs buckle so their heads dropped low. And the other creatures followed their example so that, one by one, every animal in the clearing (save the male lion) bowed down in the presence of its new master.

It was while the creatures prostrated themselves before her husband and voices of awe filled the air that Naamah began to wonder if water really could fall from the sky. She lifted her eyes to the heavens, looking at the misty vapors for signs of a change. She was relieved (and quite thankful) to find there was none.

Seven days before the Flood

Rays of filtered light broke through delicate wisps of vapor and cascaded upon the moist soil surrounding the Ark. In a matter of moments the earth was illuminated. And just as quickly, the massive gopher-wood structure appeared larger than ever before, its towering thirty-cubit height reflecting from dew-covered pitched surfaces the brightness of the clouds. The craft rose among open gates and scattered fenced enclosures, amid empty mesh cages and animal pens, each dwarfed by the vessel's enormity and all abandoned by the creatures that had once been contained.

The rich smells of hay and animal waste still rose from the damp earth, but the corrals and the bird perches, the rabbit hutch and the area behind the barn, even the chicken coop and the single mound of gopher holes stood vacant. The empty surroundings caused the ship to appear even larger as it sat atop its resting place in the middle of the clearing.

The muffled cry of a rooster rang out from somewhere within the Ark. Unseen from the cottages, the conceited fowl cocked its bobbing comb and issued another cry as its sharp, clutching nails marred the kofer-coated plank of the white oak floor. A moment later, the waking sounds of scuffling and crunching, neighing and hissing, flapping and barking, growling and mooing, and collar-ringing passed through the immense doorway of the craft.

It had taken more than two days to load the animals upon the ship—two days of hauling squealing pigs, coaxing stubborn mules, dodging nipping geese and forcing giraffes to crouch low enough to fit lengthy necks through the doorway. Part of the second level in the stern had been cut away so that adult giraffes standing on the first floor would be quite comfortable dining from a row of troughs on the second. For those two days, Naamah had argued with herself over the miraculous happening that seemed to support the inevitability of a flood. During the same period, Rezepatha had grieved over her mother's insistent, unalterable decision. For Shem, there had been the final evenings of instruction—long into the wee hours of night—before Methuselah had finally welcomed him into the ancient priesthood of the children of the Law of One. (In Malock's domain, there had been two days of arguments within the overseer's household over whether an aged magician could stand against the might of every patrol in the legion, and every volunteer in Shinar who could be mustered for a price.)

Maran sat impatiently propped against the oak tree and waited as she watched the trail in the direction of the clearing. She had been told to meet Methuselah, yet had apparently misjudged the time it would take to dispense the final payment of wages. Without the help of Traibus to gather the gold and Gravas to distribute the coins and because the old sage so loved dramatics, the task might well take several hours.

Their own meeting had to be brief, however. With all the creatures boarded upon the Ark and with so many laborers planning a departure to Shinar or scattered homelands, the work she needed to accomplish had multiplied tremendously. Not only was she expected to assist Noah and his sons in feeding and watering the animals (and somehow, she could foresee a number of competitive wagers Ham was bound to propose) but Shelobothe, in her enthusiasm had volunteered all of Noah's daughters-in-law to make certain every animal received ample exercise. Constrictive movement would encourage sluggishness and depending on the length of time the animals were shut up in the Ark, inactive limbs could atrophy. Maran's greatest desire was that their imprisonment might be short in duration—several weeks at most.

Golden strands of wheat mingled with the wild grasses and reminded her how pleasant the air had once been in their clearing. Once Noah made his decision to board it would be a long while before she could inhale such a fragrance again. As long as their confinement endured, she would miss the freedom of the forest. But more than that, she could not bear to think of leaving Lapeth and Methuselah behind. Her entire family was treating the final stage of their work the same as always: they mentioned the food, its allocation and storage; the animals, nearly two thousand in number; even the construction of the massive ship, but never once did they mention that only eight of the original fifteen would be going.

All around her was silence. Not one sound came to her ears nor had she spotted even a single insect crawling along the bark of a tree or darting frantically above the ground. No birds whistled from above nor did she hear the rustling movement of squirrels scurrying along the leafy branches overhead. Not even a lone black cricket chirped in the grass. She was beginning to wonder where all the creatures had gone, when more than a dozen figures approached from the clearing, walking into her line of sight.

The Mixtures' steps were brisk, kicking up small waves of dust in jovial anticipation. Some carried a few belongings slung over shoulders but most hadn't bothered with the added weight. They had been offered as much as they might pick from the fields, though none had gathered even a single cob of juicy corn, for there were victuals and drinks aplenty to be had in the city and everyone in the group seemed anxious to pay the price. Three of the males spoke of companions to be found before nightfall. Some among the group wore the breeches and bare backs they had grown accustomed to working in, while others had changed into Syrian stripes or woven rags or the simple garments of the plains people.

These were the first to leave after collecting their wages—Mixtures heading for engagements they had long planned in Shinar. There would be gourd liquor and laughter and table games of chance and skill, with high stakes to be won (though the odds were weighted in favor of the house). They would tell stories of magic and mystery, of the Ark and of the unusual people for whom they had worked and the actual size of the fifteen's hoard of gold would be cause for frequent speculation.

As the laborers passed by Maran, she lifted an unblemished arm to wave, but each pair of blank eyes was too intent on the path ahead. No one saw her, and not one would be passing this way again. After they disappeared from sight, she expected to see Methuselah but her wait continued.

In time, others passed by, some pushing carts of belongings, or carrying a tomato or cucumber to eat on the way, as liquid from the vegetables dripped over clammy hands and fingers. Some scratched themselves as they traipsed along or spoke to themselves excitedly over schemed adventures of the night, or simply tottered in silence along the trail. Others let robes hang sloppily, dragging clods of earth behind them. Some of the Mixtures waved as Maran gestured goodbye or acknowledged her with voices or grunts or shouted a farewell.

Those who left last seemed to have taken the greatest care in departing from the clearing. Many carried extra tools. Some had baskets or pushed rickety carts that had been stored in the barn and were now laden with vegetables and covered with damp cloths. Others coped with the awkwardness of metal buckets in either hand and filled to the brim with fruit. The final two leaving the clearing pulled a wagon loaded with canvas tarps, wooden stakes, ropes, and tent poles behind them. They were dark-skinned traders with a plan and enough tents to make them even wealthier. A short while after the final two had wandered from Maran's sight, Methuselah made his appearance.

He walked slowly, though with less effort than in days past, gripping his staff with one hand and carrying a shiny brass box under his other arm. The long, gray hairs of his beard swung back and forth as he moved toward her. The brass box reflected the light of afternoon. She started to rise, but he motioned her to remain where she was. A few moments later, he sat down beside her and gathered his breath before speaking. He placed the ornate box in the shade of the tree on the ground before her. Methuselah savored the young woman's curiosity, grinning as she stared at the object, less than a cubit square but covered with curls of twine and handles on either side, all made of the finest polished brass.

"The work of Tubal-cain?"

"That without is of his making. That within is partially mine," Methuselah said mysteriously, "mine and a few others."

"I see, and what riddle are you proposing just now?"

"No riddles, my child. There is not enough time," he answered. "My delay was not intended. A matter of counsel lay before me. The others prepare, even as we speak. This day, by the order of Noah, you shall enter into the Ark."

The silence was long before she finally managed an agonized reply: "It comes so soon."

"Were it a decade hence, too soon would it be to say goodbye."

"Is there not a way to make you change your mind?" Her husky voice was heavy with emotion.

"There may be many ways," he said honestly, "but I wish not to be tempted. This I must do." He lifted a withered finger to her soft face and wiped away a tear. "You wouldn't have me cramped aboard that craft, unable to venture beyond the smell of animals and their unceasing racket for weeks on end, only to disembark, when all was finished, in this tired body of a very old man?"

"You are not aged."

He chuckled and patted her robed knee, as the wrinkles in the corner of each eye deepened and accentuated his twinkling pupils. "There are few as old as Methuselah and fewer still who would wish to become so. Yet, even in this failing body, there remains one final task I'm empowered to do."

She closed her eyes so as not to look at him. "I do not wish to think of you suffering through what is to come."

"Then set your fears at rest, for neither Lapeth nor I intend to."

"But you will die, surely as the Mixtures!" Her eyes remained closed, and a tear rolled down either cheek.

"Look at me," he commanded softly, waiting for her to see the truth in his gaze. "How can that which is eternal ever die? Or when does forever see an end? There can be nothing truly temporal for the everlasting; that which appears to be is like a dream."

"Is it an illusion that I will not see you again?"

He smiled and shook his head in disagreement. "As long as you are blinded by consciousness you shall be unable to see, but each day, in this world of shadows, you will think of me."

"What will it be like for you?"

This time, Methuselah closed his eyes wistfully for a few moments before speaking. "As if I have suddenly awakened from a deep sleep. I will know myself to be myself, throughout. A single instant will not pass without true consciousness. One by one, the shadows will be lifted and I will come to know, to remember, who it is I really am. And what it is I am to be about. Much more than this, I will rediscover that the old man before you is simply an illusion as well, a mere reflection, a tiny fragment of the soul which has always been."

"In this state," she asked, feeling sad and confused, "will you be able to think of me?"

He smiled, grasping both of her youthful hands between his own. "As long as forever. Besides, my child, I assure you, our work in this world of shadows is far from complete. Shortly, even as man measures time, we will be together again. I promise you."

"But until that time," he continued, "if you need someone to talk to, if you need someone to listen to your words, if you need a very old man at your side, simply speak as we do now. Though you may not see me, I will be there."

She couldn't help but cry and as she laid her head in his arms and sobbed, she thought of all the times they had been together and imbedded them in her mind, to be taken out and dwelt upon whenever she might need them. He let her alone a long while before speaking again. "We must return to the clearing," he said, wiping the moisture from her cheeks, "but before we leave, I wish to give you this." He tapped the brass container with the palm of his hand.

"What is it?" She rubbed her eyes so they would clear.

"Inside is the work of a lifetime. I can think of none worthier to have it." He pushed the shiny box toward her. "All that I have come to know has been passed on, either by word or in script. Your children's children and their children for generations will have need of these things; but more important than the ramblings of an old man may be the story of our beginning—written by Adam's own hand."

Her eyes opened wide in wonder as she grasped the box by its handles. "Why give it to me?"

"Who better? History should be in the hands of those who might learn from it. My dream has been to save these things for those who come after; in them is the hope of the world. There was a time when I wished to send this to the land of our forefathers, but such would have been a mistake. It belongs on the Ark, with you. For myself, I have a simple request."

"Anything you would name."

"When this has passed, read what is inside. Many things may surprise you, not the least of which that you will find Adam's papyrus sheaves as smooth and supple as the day he took reed in hand, whereas the sheets of Methuselah have already begun to yellow with age."

"What does it mean?"

He grinned. "Only that he knew far more than I could hope to. But, nevertheless, I want you to continue what I have started. Write all that transpires from this day forth. Our people will one day need to know it for themselves." Maran could only nod.

"I have one more request," he added softly, "to embrace you once more before we leave on our separate paths." She wrapped her arms around his small frame and squeezed him gently, though both fought back the tears that threatened to blur their vision. When the time came, she helped the old man to his feet, took the brass box under her arm and turned in the direction of the Ark. They traveled the distance in silence.

When the trail came to an end, the sight surprised her. The clearing seemed emptier even than before. The tent city was gone, though a handful of dwellings remained in place, scattered unevenly over the same ground where there had once been many rows. Only a score of laborers had not yet decided where their travels would lead (some favored the idea of following after Anon and looking for hire). For the first time, though, not a single pottery flask or mixing bowl was left lying in the wash water near the kilns. The few curtains had been taken from the cottage windows, making the cabins appear deserted. Even the door to the shed had been left ajar so all might see there was no gold inside.

Her family was waiting by the rampway, wiping tears as they kissed Lapeth or looked to Noah for support. Only Naamah stood off by herself, staring upward at the sky, shaking her head in disbelief—Zillah would have thought they had all lost their minds.

"Where have you been?" Ham asked. He gave his wife a look of real concern before reaching to take the brass case from her hands. She didn't want to let it go, but had to so she could part with Lapeth. She walked to the dark-haired woman and kissed her.

"I will miss you," she cried, as both Shelobothe and Rezepatha looked on and sobbed.

"And I you," Lapeth said sweetly, and then repeated again in a whisper, "and I you."

As Methuselah embraced the others, ending with Noah (with whom he remained the longest), Maran bent to kiss Boland on the cheek, for the dwarf had decided to remain with Methuselah and Lapeth. Finally, Naamah felt prompted—though uncertain why—to bid Lapeth and Methuselah farewell. "From the looks of things," she said stubbornly, taking one final glance at the heavens, "I will see you both shortly."

"Perhaps a lot sooner than you think," Methuselah replied gently.

Then, the old sage took Lapeth by the hand and walked out of the way of the ramp. One by one, the eight headed up into the ship, Naamah being the last to finish her waddling ascent before

Ham, Shem, and Japheth hoisted the massive planking up through the doorway.

Methuselah, Lapeth, and the somber-looking dwarf remained still, waving up to them from the ground only when the rampway had been secured in place. The three provided quite a contrast: tiny Boland, with suspenders and fluttering ears; the mystic, leaning heavily on his staff, moving his head slowly to take one final look into each of their eyes; and Lapeth, whose gaze rested longest with Rezepatha as she thought of the day they had hidden together in the forest. Rezepatha sobbed as Japheth wrapped his arm around her. Each of the newlyweds stood close together for comfort and Naamah had to stop herself from what she felt was senseless crying.

Lapeth released one final kiss from her fingertips before Methuselah spoke his parting words: "Above all else, do not lose faith."

Noah wiped a tear from his eye and turned, beckoning his sons to help with the pulleys. Slowly, as the four men rotated the cranks—and the animals grew restless with the noise, and echoes began to reverberate with Rezepatha's hurried footsteps to new chambers—the solid oak doorway was lifted into place. Soon, iron bolts were thrown shut, the wood splints were hammered into place, and by the light of candles and lanterns, Noah and his sons painted the seams of the doorway with pitch.

At long last, the eight were sealed within the Ark.

Three days later

Naamah couldn't believe she had been so foolish. To submit to being locked inside the ship for three days was complete insanity. Three days of waiting and sitting and hearing the scuffle of creatures on two decks below her and the groan of the ribbed vessel as it sank even deeper into the soil had to be the stupidest thing she had ever agreed to. Already, she was sick of the heavy odors of pitched gopher-wood and the growing stench of animals that drifted up through water and grain chutes. She was tired of the burning smells of oil put off by the lantern and the way the room always appeared filled with shadows regardless of how high she turned the wick. She loathed being left alone while everyone else attended to the animals (there was no way they were going to get her down there again by any mangy lions or growling bears), joining her only when it was time for a meal or passing by on the way to their own chambers, when the need for solitude weighed heavily on their minds (Rezepatha still could not shake her sorrow), but more than anything, Naamah hated the way they had designed her kitchen.

The room was huge, located on the starboard side of the bow, measuring twenty cubits long by ten wide. The galley fire, constructed in the manner of the kilns, was much too squatty for her liking. Though Shem had pointed out that the weight of the bricks was more evenly distributed by lengthening the ovens and that her cooking surface on top would be larger (and that Tubal-cain had been responsible for the design), she was not at all crazy about the idea of bending over a dozen times a day to check on what was inside. Besides, now that the interior of the oven was different in proportion, Naamah had no idea how the heat might be distributed or how long breads or pie shells or vegetable stews took to cook.

The heat was vented to the outside through intricate metal pipes that fit snugly through the wall of the vessel. Each of the vents could be closed from the inside, just as could all of the airshafts, scattered at strategic and invulnerable positions throughout the ship. A long, rectangular-shaped smoke collector, fashioned of hammered iron, was suspended above the length of the kiln. By stamping a pedal on the floor with her foot, Naamah could draw any smoke from the galley into the outside air. Although she thought the device quite ingenious and used it when no one was looking, she had let her temper flare when the fan was first pointed out to her. When was the last time they had ever seen her burn a meal?

On the left side of the ovens, the side leading to her and Noah's bedroom, was an oblong pine counter (theirs was the only chamber with two doorways: one to the hallway, like the others, and her own private entrance directly in to the kitchen). She liked the counter—there was plenty of working space—and the way her pots and crockery could either be stored above on the shelving, or below behind carved cabinet doors. But after her countless objections about everything else, it didn't seem quite right to voice a sound of approval.

She also thought the pine table and benches were unsightly—surely the work of crudely skilled laborers—much too long and bolted to the floor too far from where she'd be serving. There was no way to get enough light into the room (how was she supposed to see what she was doing?), the sink on the opposite end of the kiln was much too small, the barrel of water overhead would not last very long, and filling it would be a great inconvenience; she'd have to get the stepladder out of the storeroom. The hardwood floors were painful to the soles of her feet; she had spent years cooking out-of-doors beneath the shade of trees, where it had been much cooler than the galley was obviously going to be. These were just a few of the things she found need to relate to

Noah first, and then to Shem, Rezepatha, Shelobothe, Ham, Japheth, and, finally, to Maran. She told each of them individually, cornering a listener when no one else was around, with words that she eventually knew by rote.

Their living quarters, four compartments of similar design (though Naamah's was closest to the kitchen wall and had the extra door), were built in the front of the craft, as well, though on the port side. There also were additional living compartments, those intended for Gravas and the others, which had been hastily converted into storerooms.

On the outside of the Ark, the bow and the stern appeared identical (although, in truth, the bow was slightly narrower for direction). Each had a ladder built against the ribbed surface leading up to the walkway that ran the length of the ship. The catwalk could be accessed from inside the central uppermost storeroom but as a precaution, Noah had sealed the hatch with a thin layer of pitch. Nevertheless, on the inside, the front and the rear of the vessel were quite different.

Toward the back of the craft, on the same level as the compartments, were housed nearly all the birds. Though they were separated from the living quarters by more than 200 cubits, Naamah swore she could hear the racket continuously. Some birds were penned in large latticework cages, but the majority flew freely about the huge room dotted with hay for nest-work. More than six and one-half cubits above the floor, within the narrow expanse of the ceiling inside the catwalk, long windows covered with thin, wire mesh could be slid open for fresh air when the danger had passed.

Noah's doves sat contentedly on one of the white oak sills, while the ravens remained below in a cage, in close proximity to the vultures and the buzzards; Noah had not known how long the creatures would remain peaceably together, so some had been contained. There were long-tailed pheasants and gay-flighted swallows, blue jays and crows, robins and meadowlarks, doves and canaries, starlings and sparrows, parakeets and whippoorwills, chattering mockingbirds and wrens, dozing owls and bright red cardinals, and horrified gobblers who hadn't yet realized where they were.

Many clung to branches, or perched on sills, or swooped effortlessly from one rafter to another, or splashed about carelessly in the shallow water tub near the doorway. There were nearly 450 feathered creatures together—not counting the chickens, roosters, ducks, and geese that were happiest on the second level, away from the ceaseless chirping and the constant bombardment of bird droppings from the air.

Naamah had been having a difficult time sleeping. There were many thoughts spinning in her head and she spent long hours every evening tossing and turning next to Noah, wondering what to do—he remained peaceably still, as if in another world. She wanted to put an end to this foolishness. If they hadn't been sealed inside the Ark (by their own doing no less!), she would have left after the first day. She had only agreed to follow the others after the animals had made such an incredible appearance in the clearing. Then, for a short while, it had even seemed reasonable that water might fall from the vapors. But now, it all looked as foolish as before. Surely the One hadn't called them inside the craft, where they waited without reason, Rezepatha crying, though she tried to carry on her tasks to feed and tend to hundreds of animals that could have easily fended for themselves in the forest; Naamah's sons working long hours with the creatures, figuring food rations, proper diets (Traibus' sheets had most of it written out anyway), and stall cleaning schedules that would never be used. Zillah would have never put up with what was going on, and Naamah wasn't about to either.

"Well, I will not keep my peace for long!" she said, as she angrily chopped a zucchini squash into small pieces for the vegetable pie, her large frame bouncing beneath its flowered dress as she worked in quick movements. She would give her husband a few more days (just to make certain) to let him realize how wrong he had been about everything.

And then, she would demand to be let off the ship, sealed doorway or not.

Seventh Day aboard the Ark (four days later)

While Naamah talked to herself in the galley, cleaning up the plates from a hastily eaten breakfast and tried to work up the nerve to confront Noah about her release, Methuselah walked from behind the cottages and stared upward at the sky, searching for signs of a difference that he was beginning to feel inside his weary bones.

He was tired, though he had slept the night long, and walking proved extremely painful. His staff helped him move over the ground but it failed to ease his discomfort. He knew their time drew near, although he had yet to see what direction it would take. As he stood for a moment and stared at the overhead clouds, his gray robes hung motionless about his body. Suddenly, through squinted eyes, he thought he could see a change: the vapors appeared to be in motion! At first the movement was gentle but there was movement. And as the motion continued—so faint at first that the old man had difficulty seeing it—the pure white wisps of the heavens seemed to fill with ash, softening the brilliance of the light. The change was slow but something was happening. A moment later, Methuselah realized that it wasn't the clouds that were in motion but billowy fingers of gray creeping through the vapors like a shadow.

"It is nearly upon us," the soft-spoken voice of Lapeth stated as she reached his side.

"They are nearly upon us, as well." Methuselah said, looking toward the north end of the clearing, where elephants, rhinos, buffaloes, and giraffes had once trampled a patch of fallen gopher-wood trees.

"Malock and his legion?"

"Even as we speak. Nigh on four thousand. Are you afraid?"

She smiled faintly, her fair-skinned features beautifully framed by once-fully black hair. "Of two things, only: that there are those we cannot help from the blindness they have brought upon themselves—and that an old man might try to take on more than he is able."

His bony fingers briefly touched the soft skin of her arm. "I have you to assist me," he said, though his mind seemed to be filled with other concerns. He looked around the clearing, focusing for a time upon the magnificent Ark that remained completely still.

"They will be all right," she voiced, more as question than as fact. A small pool of water oozed from the crumbling soil, moistening the rims of their sandals. "Even the earth has come to know the hour."

Methuselah nodded before speaking. "Then we must prepare to meet it." He closed his eyes, leaning with both hands upon his staff, while his lips moved silently in prayer. Lapeth watched him for a moment, until the appearance of his face became less worried and the wrinkled skin partially regained its color, before closing her own eyes to gather the strength of the silence.

Boland watched them both curiously from his seat in the doorway of the wooden shed (ears twitching without his notice). His tiny, moccasined feet were placed squarely on the damp ground for support as his hands busily arched a small bow so that his fingers could connect the cord end to end. He did not know what weapons his two companions were using but he had no desire to be unprepared. For five days, he had whittled slender-shafted arrows, feathered for perfect flight with leftover pitch still bucketed against the hull of the Ark. Although the two had claimed it quite unnecessary, he couldn't expect them to stand alone. There was no doubt he would fall in battle but it would be after many of the enemy had ceased to take breath. And he felt quite fit for the task at hand. His leg, finally free of the splint and wrapped in a simple, poulticed cloth, had healed quite nicely.

He plucked the bow with dwarfed fingers, until he was satisfied with its tautness, before gathering together the remaining arrows that had yet to be piled with the surplus on the other side of their barricade. From behind the kilns, they would take a stance—surrounded by thick, wooden benches overturned and stacked between brick ovens, a washtub lying on its side and the towering oak that had watched over nearly five thousand meal lines. Their place of hiding was camouflaged with limbs of gopher-wood, encrusted with leaves and withered fronds of fern that kept the bricks, the wooden planks, and the metal washbasin out of plain sight. The area had been chosen far enough from the Ark to keep most reaches of the clearing's boundaries within easy view, something that wouldn't have been possible inside one of the cottages.

Boland positioned himself between the kilns, where their barricade had been constructed of pine benches. Spaces through which he could peer or shoot quite well separated each of the planks. When he had readied a handful of pointed shafts for flight, Lapeth and the mystic joined him behind the barricade. The dwarf was quite troubled to find neither of his friends had brought anything with them, save Methuselah's staff, and he quickly urged them with hand motions that they had better become prepared.

"Oh, but we are quite ready," Methuselah said positively.

The little suspendered man signed, "Then what is your weapon?" with a curious glance on his face.

"Time," the old man said without hesitation. "Though my Sight is not as clear as it used to be, I believe events will unfold in our favor."

"When do we act?" Lapeth asked, placing her palm on the dwarf's shoulder to bring him comfort. She leaned forward to peer between the planks of one of the benches and the hundreds of leaves that attempted to obstruct her view and saw only the Ark and the dozens of abandoned enclosures and opened cages.

Methuselah raised his eyes to the clouds and watched as the shadows in the vapors lengthened throughout mists of pure white. Boland kept his face turned toward the mystic's lips in order to understand what the old man might say. "We can do nothing," Methuselah replied truthfully, "until the fear within Malock and his men—the fear that physical sight brings them—rivals their dread of the unknown; else, the hold they have upon life will be too great to overcome."

Boland appeared confused and Lapeth only nodded. She spoke so that the dwarf could see her words. "Do not worry. Together we should be without harm." Her hands touched the curve of his bow and pointed to one of the arrows. "Do not use your weapon if it can be avoided."

His ears flapped anxiously as a frown passed over his brow. He had great respect for them both but found it difficult to believe they planned to die without a struggle. He started to sign in protest but Methuselah waved his gestures aside. "They're here." His words were spoken softly, though his eyes had not peeked through the barrier that surrounded them. Boland got down on his haunches and looked through the lowest spacing of slats. Between the shed and the cottage on his left and the mighty vessel on his right, he saw all manner of men and Mixtures way off in the distance.

Malock was mounted on a dark, mammoth steed with hoofed front feet, its legs rippling with muscular anticipation as hot breath snorted through its slightly whiskered nostrils. Deep cracks lined the giant's cheeks, as jowls pulled tight with nervous expectancy. He prepared himself to see the form of the magician at any moment. Despite the many reports his ears had been privy to, he had never laid eyes on Methuselah firsthand. A finger smoothed his thin, dark mustache as he looked cautiously about.

All about him, the sounds of guards and preparation and those of mercenary merchants, limping slaves, and his personal patrol, were hushed by the sight of the Ark. Only those men who had yet to enter the clearing still clamored with anticipation or growled with confusion regarding the sudden halt. Horses whinnied in bewilderment, tugging at reins gripped tightly by Mixtures who had forethought enough to ride. Countless eyes turned to see the wonder before them: fence posts, hanging gates, baking animal chips, intricately crafted pens, and a structure of gopher-wood grander than even their master's finely built manor. The vessel proved even more beautiful to Malock than Lars had found the words to describe.

"You spoke no exaggeration," Malock voiced aloud, as Lars dismounted next to him.

"It's incredible!" Lars uttered. "It is a prize worthy of your dominion."

Basil and Hermann stood nearby, fearfully watching for the old man. The giant's authority and the thought of gold had prompted their participation but they had yet to shake their fear of Methuselah.

Although Malock's uneasiness was equal to theirs, the giant appeared quite in control. His dark brown eyes pieced together the message of the surroundings as much as possible: Why would the magician seek protection aboard such a vessel? Was it defensible? Were the animals, hundreds of creatures whose scent still clung stubbornly to the ground, inside the craft as well?

"Do you suppose they have loaded the gold with themselves?" Dachnid asked disgustedly from behind, just as the same thought entered Malock's head, but no response was offered since much of the legion had become restless and shouted for them to move forward.

Following Hermann, Lars, Dachnid, and Baird, and eager Ceron, whose horse pressed closely to the giant's, were thousands of other men less prone to talk than action. The army advanced cautiously, causing the narrow road between the corrals and leading up to the vessel to fill to capacity. Then the crowd widened, toppling fencing beneath the weight of burdened stallions and ape-like creatures ripped posts from the moist earth, which gave way with a 'plop.' From behind, the entire legion pressed forward.

There were men of every manner of dress and nation: Syrians and Mixtures from Mizraim and idle youths from the city and half-crazed beasts that broke through fences and use bare hands to split pine trees with ease, as leathery snouts grew moist with sweat and sniffed at the air for humans. Shopkeepers stood amid horsed warriors and baboon-faced guards, wondering if the exchange of a month's rent had been worth the price of conscription and if the overseer would hold true to his bargain. Human forms and all manner of men stared at the Ark and its remaining scaffolding, while relishing the account of the five whose sabotage had felled a section.

The clearing filled with the ranks of countless soldiers and hired men, most on foot, while Malock dismounted his steed and strolled forward. Some of his warriors followed, passing bridles to serfs or captives from the giant's own fields. Slaves had been rounded up (those still fit to walk) with the promise of freedom once victory was assured; yet bargains made prior to combat might easily be forgotten.

Plains bandits moved among robed merchants and city dwellers dazed with assurances of gold. Scattered throughout the troops were a number of Malock's field patrols, excited by the prospect of diversion, though they had yet to see any real action. There were men in breeches and tattered garments heavy with soot; some wore the hides of trappers or tanned vests stolen from the marketplace. Mercenary soldiers, whose allegiances changed as frequently as coins dropped between purse strings, comprised the remainder of Malock's legion.

Soon, the crowds grew restless with inaction and the mysteries posed by the sight of the craft. A thousand voices rose as one as lances were taken in hand or weapons were unsheathed, and a half-dozen arrows swished in the direction of the Ark. Ceron, still riding atop his mount, leaned to speak in the giant's ear, while unnoticed in the heavens, the sky continued to fill with particles of gray.

"Do we have your permission?" Ceron growled with eager pleasure.

The overseer hesitated for a moment before granting the request. If Methuselah was to be feared, it might be good to let Ceron feel the mystic's wrath. Finally Malock agreed, "If you must set your flames, do so, but keep them from the vessel. We may draw them out and let the ship go unscathed."

Ceron let loose a joyous cry before charging toward the cottages on his steed. A hundred more, those who had never heard the name "Methuselah," rushed forward on foot, sending clods of earth into the air, while the rest of the troops looked on, weapons readied at their sides, waiting to see what the magician might do.

The shouts rose to such a clamor of excitement that animals grew still inside the Ark and the human occupants ran to the galley behind gopher-wood walls to find comfort in the words of their leader. Outside the craft, the woman, the old man, and the vigilant dwarf, remained perfectly still behind the barrier of greenery. Lapeth and Boland watched the attack on the dwellings, while Methuselah turned his eyes to the vapors—and watched as the tint of the sky grew darker.

In his excitement, Ceron jumped from the horse and bounded toward the cottage that had once belonged to Gravas. Before even peering inside, he happily worked the pieces of flint, allowing sparks to lash out at torn curtains. Dozens of Malock's men shouted at his actions, some with encouragement, while others screamed for him to stop until they had a chance to ransack the structure. Though a flame began, ten of his companions hurried through the interior, smashing Tamari's antiques and overturning woven carpets in their hurried search. Loose floorboards were removed, and a large keg of ale, half-drenched by rising water in the pit, was hoisted from the earth. Though not the gold, they had found something of value.

When no hand moved against the aggressors, Baird and

Hermann grew bolder from their place in the distance. While the shouts of a legion surrounded them (and Hermann remained somewhat stunned by the beauty of the ship), Baird found his nerve: "Shall we draw them from the craft?" he lisped bravely.

"How?" Malock asked, as the fear he had once felt toward the old magician began to appear absurd. Even Methuselah was no match for an entire army.

"With fire!" several throats growled with excitement, seeing the fascinating work of Ceron before them.

Hermann's dirty claws picked at his belted waist as he turned to hear Lars voice the objection he had considered: "No! Such a vessel belongs within Malock's domain."

"Can it be moved?" the giant wondered aloud.

Shouts of men and Mixtures too removed to hear the debate went up, calling for action, as javelins and arrows struck the Ark before falling back to the earth: The lacquered surface had become nearly impenetrable, although a number of lances clung to the posts and walkways of the scaffolding.

Hooves tore at the soil of trampled corrals as dozens more gathered their courage and raced toward the cabins. Some of the first drank what was left of the ale, while Naamah's kitchen quickened with fire and the vines of centuries turned loose of the cottage as leaves withered to ash and dropped away. And while three structures burned and maniacs shattered clay pots against the huge rocks (and whooped with glee over the ease of their ambush), not a set of eyes noticed the barricade of greenery beneath the massive oak or how the illumination from the clouds was beginning to fade in a darkening sky.

"With ten thousand in servitude, it might be done," Dachnid pondered aloud in answer to Malock's question. He nodded in affirmation and ran a palm through his oily hair, as the giant looked at him from above. "It could be done," Dachnid stated positively.

"How would you empty the ship of its cargo?" Malock asked, relying on the man's knowledge of the craft.

A few of the warriors began to chant, "Gold!" when they heard the craft would be opened.

"With fire against the starboard to remove the doorway." When he saw the giant's displeasure over harming the ship, he quickly added, "Twenty cubits of portal might be easily replaced."

The overseer thought for only a moment before agreeing. "Direct them as you will."

Dachnid shouted instructions to those who could hear above the clamor, his arms motioning wildly as he directed some to fetch tools. Bare-chested men strong enough to yank scaffolding posts from the ground gathered together the wood for burning. A few gathered sticks and hay and what remained of the tents for kindling, while hundreds joined Ceron in his madness, dashing amid the flames. The majority surrounded the Ark and took positions upon the surviving scaffolding that might prove advantageous when the inhabitants disembarked. The strongest stacked logs against the hull, along with a generous supply of hay and kindling, piling them upward to reach a doorway still several cubits above the earth. Dachnid decided to let none but Ceron torch the pile of wood. Let him, alone, finish what he had begun, just in case the magician possessed more than a few meager tricks.

Finally, Boland had seen enough and could wait no longer. While Lapeth peeked through the slats and the old man was deciding what to do about the sky, the dwarf—with a handful of arrows tucked behind front suspenders—grabbed bow in hand and limped from hiding. If only he could stop the fire-happy Mixture waving the burning stick from reaching the Ark.

As he emerged from the greenery, the dwarf was spotted immediately. Just as Boland let loose an arrow that flew true to its mark—barely a moment of physical pain broke through Ceron's blind euphoria before a final grunt passed through parted lips and hairy knees stumbled to the soil. A spear of iron pierced Boland's own shoulder and pushed him back, pinned and bleeding to the earth.

Methuselah acted swiftly, before Lapeth could voice her horror. He hobbled quickly from concealment in order to assist the little man, so quickly, in fact, that his staff was left at Lapeth's feet and the pain in the old man's legs was excruciating. When he reached the dwarf, he dropped to aging knees, leaning close while bony fingers touched the spot where the spear stood upright. Boland moved his mouth to cry out but voice eluded him; his small body writhed in pain.

In one swift movement, Methuselah placed his shaking hand upon the tiny chest while the other ripped the iron weapon from flesh. The noise that jumped from between Boland's lips was audible. His face quivered, showing an uncertain hold upon consciousness. Quickly, Methuselah placed both his hands on the wound, while his fingers massaged a gaping hole through which blood began to stain the hem of each sleeve.

Suddenly, warmth began to permeate the tiny shoulder Boland had thought broken and instantly the dwarf regained his fleeting senses. When his shoulder had grown so hot that he could stand it no longer, he bolted to his feet. In amazement, his hands searched the place where his shirt had been torn, his small fingers searching for a wound that was no longer there.

"I had hoped we could do this without any pain," the old man said, grinning just as Malock and a thousand others saw his form rising from the ground. (Overhead, the shadows grew even darker.)

Lapeth jumped up to warn the old man and the dwarf, just as a hairy-faced guard, standing among what was left of the cottages, took spear in hand and aimed with precision at the mystic. The guard let loose his weapon at the same moment Lapeth reached down for Methuselah's staff and threw it toward the mystic as hard as she could. The staff sailed steadily from the barricade of greenery and headed straight for the javelin flung by the enemy; wood, without breaking, dislodged iron from flight, and both objects fell with a clatter to Methuselah's sandaled feet. Immediately, Malock began to charge, with his army behind him.

"We shall give them something more interesting to look upon," Methuselah shouted to the dwarf, who knew not whether to run or to turn and bravely face the assault. For the very last time, the mystic bent down to take his staff and thought meaning into the words which came from his lips: "That they might see."

Without wasting another instant, Methuselah hurled his staff toward the rocks that rose near the place where Naamah had once kept her kitchen. Birch rattled against stone before settling in a crevice. While Methuselah and Boland scurried back to their place in the barricade, a faint glow encircled the ancient boulders, and the air in the forest began to grow cooler. The glow set off by the staff gave way to sparkles of yellow light, and suddenly the great heaps of coin that rested upon the rocks came into full view. Suddenly the overseer and a thousand others were stopped in their tracks. Malock and his legion could see the gold.

In the blink of an eye, thousands of coins became visible. They were scattered haphazardly in immense piles atop stone and rock, heaping over level slabs and jagged edges alike. Immediately, the patrols forgot the burning cottages or dropped their logs far short of the stack being placed against the Ark's hull. Fellow soldiers were pushed aside and broken pine fencing was kicked down as more than a thousand hurried toward the gold. When Dachnid and the others ran forward, Malock was left alone.

As the legion clamored for the gold, Methuselah and Lapeth led Boland away from the kilns. They walked slowly, hand in hand, without fear, and moved toward the place where a tent city had once risen upon the soil. Repeatedly, Methuselah looked from the Ark to the sky to the confusion of angry fists and scattered coins and bulging pockets of greed. The three were unnoticed by all but Malock, who finally stared upward to see what the old mystic kept looking at, and the sight which greeted the giant nearly felled him.

Black clouds swelled in visible motion and the appearance of a sky he had never seen brought fear into his heart. As men and slaves continued their struggle, each pushing the other aside (and the weakest being trampled to death in the process), the air in the clearing grew even cooler. Beneath the smoky vapors, Malock believed the magician had finally let loose his vengeance. Suddenly, the clash of a thousand drums broke the heavens and a streak of yellow-fire shimmered through the clouds. As the rumble from the clouds echoed throughout the forest, the legion begun to come to its senses.

Men stared in open-mouthed terror as the first drops of water fell from the sky. As the water fell, Mixtures ceased their groveling for coins. Screams mixed with shouts as droplets descended from the vapors with rapid intensity. All at once, the legs of a legion ran in all directions, for many believed the liquid, thick with ash, would burn as it touched flesh. Some ran for the cover of trees but the majority ran straight toward the Ark.

Inside, the eight huddled to find comfort amid the confines of the galley, as the drops sounded like pebbles being thrown against wood and voices from the outside passed hollowly within. Only

Maran realized how the water would look, how the air had grown cool, how the sky had darkened, and for a brief moment she felt as though she glimpsed the entire scene through Methuselah's own eyes.

Guards and merchants slipped or tumbled on their way to reach the doorway of the ship, struggling to scramble over stacked logs. Shouts grew louder as they shrieked to be let into the craft, and horses broke roped confinement to find safety. Malock simply watched the three off in the distance and stood, drenched, beneath the sky, as the downpour increased in intensity and pools of water began to form upon the already soaked earth.

Fists and claws pounded on gopher-wood planks, begging to be allowed inside. The eight in the Ark huddled against each other as eerie screams (made softer by the ship's walls) called for help. Still, the falling water continued and the water level rose to Malock's ankles. Rezepatha wiped a tear from her eye, and Naamah whispered a prayer for forgiveness, as the cries became more horrible than any could have imagined, save for Noah, who had seen the vision.

"I am ready," Lapeth said above the racket of the falling waters, as she and the old man closed their eyes. Their hair, garments, and flesh had become saturated. Boland joined them as well, suddenly knowing what to do.

Methuselah and his daughter become quiet and focused upon the silence. Each took a deep breath, as their spines began to tingle. Finally, when the time had come and they were ready, Lapeth and Methuselah raised palms overhead and pushed through themselves a power from on high. As water fell from the heavens, as the lands of the earth were flooded, and as the air grew energized with their presence, the two called forth the souls of an entire legion.

With regulated precision and without pain or struggle, the bodies of Mixtures and men, one by one, splashed to the ground. The Law moved its way outward, as spines tingled and foreheads grew warm, so that nothing, neither creature nor beast nor fowl within Shinar's forest, would face the horror of having to drown. Methuselah also passed to the other side at the same moment an explosion shattered his staff into particles of dust upon the rocks, dust quickly washed away by the splashing waters.

Within the galley of the Ark, still safe from the storm, the eight heard the voice of Lapeth surround them in comfort:

"Hold fast to love," the gentle words were spoken.

The Flood

In the six hundredth year of Noah's life, in Marcheshvam, the second month, the seventeenth day of the month, the same day were all the fountains of the great deep broken up, and the windows of heaven were opened.

All over the earth the children of the planet acted as though the day was much like another, though the white vapor of clouds continued to grow ominous. Few gave thought to anything but the lives they had known. They planted and they reaped their harvests, they bought and they sold, they built and they destroyed, they ate and they drank, they married and they were given in marriage. Yet, there remained some, those touched by the prayers and the work of the faithful, those following after the promises of the One, who harkened after the call and entered vessels they had crafted. But as the sky grew darker and filled with bright flashes of crackling light and as a thunderous roar shook the very foundations of the globe (the sound of a thousand huge boulders crashing headlong into each other), and as the dew of the heavens sizzled into the scent of sulfur, the people of every nation crouched in fear from that they had brought upon themselves. Physical eyes saw sheets of water pour from the sky in mighty torrents that crumbled mounds of clay into rivers and lakes, swelling them until their shorelines disappeared and they became one with the rising tides of oceans and seas. Shrieks of terror rose in rhythm with the waters, as minds believed the heavens fell down without reason or design (though none faced anything for which they were not accountable).

The earth was broken up in many places. If not for the prayers of those who followed the Law, all things might have perished. Waters from the deep poured forth from chasms and fissures and stable crusts of valleys erupted into motion. Towering sequoia, willow, and ebony alike tumbled beneath the force of quakes, as roots of eons severed instantly into lifelessness. Castles and cottages and mighty tents fell upon foundations or vanished in the blink of an eye beneath the movements of hillsides and buttes of stone that erupted upwards toward the heavens. Lemuria disappeared forever beneath the rush of the ocean.

Sea floors built mountain ridges or dived into deeper depths and waves sixty cubits in height rose in response to alter coastlines and sweep away islands that had never been named by man. Volcanoes boiled ancient lagoons of shimmering blue surfaces into pits of steaming mud while black obsidian crystallized, creeping in hardening ripples over the endless reefs of colored coral. An explosion atop Alta—the mountain of Poseidia—divided the continent into three islands, as the waters of an ocean crashed into valleys and aftershocks shattered temples and pillars and marble fountains into dust.

The Tigris and Euphrates spread beyond ancient banks, until

neither river was distinguishable from the other. Shinar's alleys and roadways became swift streams, as new currents filled abandoned markets, tore brick from the walls of tenements and enabled unattended gaming tables to float past third-story windows of lifeless apartments. Forest trees appeared shorter as lakes rose from trampled trails and scattered hay and water quickly swallowed up posts and planks and discarded timber of a mighty scaffolding.

Rain lapped forcefully against the sides of lacquered gopherwood, while droplets beat down upon the rooftop of Noah's solitary craft within the center of the clearing. Chasms from the deep split open and loosed the moisture of centuries and the height of the flood waters surged upward. Tremendous groans sounded from the saturated soil as the vessel's buoyancy finally pulled it loose from the ground. As the bottom of the ship jolted free from the moist earth, the eight in the galley were jarred from their places around the wooden table. The floodwaters continued to fall from the sky without interruption, as the waters of the deep continued to break free from pressurized caverns—and through it all, the misty vapors of the clouds began to dissolve.

In time, towering oaks and pines surrendered their loftiest branches, limbs, and leaves to submergence and Noah and his family, within the safety of the Ark, began to float above even the trees.

And the waters prevailed, and were increased greatly upon the earth; and the Ark went upon the face of the waters. And the waters prevailed exceedingly upon the earth; and all the high hills, that were under the whole heavens, were covered. Fifteen cubits upward did the waters prevail . . .

19th Day of Rain; 26th Day upon the Ark

In less than a month's time, Shelobothe had already forgotten what it was like to breathe air that lacked the scent of burning oils or the odor of animals. She had almost grown used to the curious mixture of pitch and hay and manure and fur, and to the gaseous remains of flickering oil lamps that illuminated the central passageways with eerie shadows. In a corner of her mind, she could only vaguely recall how the light from the heavens had once felt as it brushed down upon her face with dazzling fingers of warmth. And there were times when she began to wonder if her memories had their basis in fact or if her mind had simply imagined a place of beauty far beyond the confines of the ship.

She walked aft on the second level, though her destination lay at the midpoint between the stern and the bow. The walls of the hallway were dimly lit by the slow-burning glow of lamps, wicks kept low in an effort to conserve fuel. She felt dwarfed by the magnitude of her surroundings: the long, empty hallway dotted with tiny blazes of light disappearing off in the distance, the hollow sound of footsteps echoing across the floor for her human ears to take note of before being swallowed up by the steady sounds of the downpour, and the scratching and scuffling sounds behind walls which held the wealth of a kingdom in livestock.

She heard the early morning call of the rooster, whose waking cry grew more erratic, squawking two and three times a day—or not at all—before being drowned out by the water. She often anticipated the strained sounds of excitable creatures rising for a meal as her footsteps passed by side corridors that branched off from the main passageway. Yet, because of the enormity of the ship, she often felt completely alone.

The day loomed before her with countless tasks still left undone and responsibilities that could never be completed in time. Hours might pass before seeing her husband or even another member of the family. The vessel was huge, and seven of the eight (Naamah remained in the galley or tended to the birds, never complaining—except at mealtime, when there was someone to listen) rotated responsibilities throughout the different areas of the craft.

Shelobothe's feet passed over the hardwood floor, littered with pieces of fine straw and hay—some strands scattered freshly by hand, others falling from the hides of creatures who traipsed the length of the passageways during scheduled exercise. Sheep and horses, ostriches and deer, camels and zebras, even elephants on the floor beneath her were released from pens or cages or larger rooms as often as once a week and allowed to stroll on their respective levels, save the giraffes, which, out of necessity, were led around the confines of their two-storied enclosure. For this reason, each of the three central passageways running the full length of each level, for the most part, were about twelve cubits in width. And in Shelobothe's opinion, it was the wideness of the hallway before her, the shadows cast by the lamps, and the continual sound of water beating down upon the Ark that made the long corridors appear so gloomy.

Something was happening to a number of the animals aboard the Ark that even Traibus had not foreseen. Conditions within the ship—reduced light, restricted movement, and even what appeared to be a slight decrease in temperature were creating extended periods of sleep for some of the creatures. It was not unusual for the bears to sleep seven days at a time, though when they awoke they heartily consumed in an hour's time enough food for two days' rations. There were others as well, burrowers mostly, that took naps for days on end, lying hidden within the safety of tunneled mounds of earth piled high upon planked floorboards or snuggled in furry balls deep within beds of drying hay. The prairie dogs, marmots, squirrels, hamsters, hedgehogs, lemmings, skunks, woodchucks, and even the tiny dormouse seemed subject to regular episodes of extended sleep.

But despite those in slumber, Shelobothe and her family each had to care for over 400 species every single day. And they were days little different from one another, and even hours that became indistinguishable one from the next. Inside the Ark, with windows sealed tightly to keep out the storm (though air vents with shafts leading to invulnerable positions on the outside were essential), there wasn't any way to differentiate night from day—though never once did Noah forget to scratch a mark on the wall of his bedroom immediately upon awakening. Each morning, as it was measured by their schedule, he paused at the doorway leading to the galley, took a dangling nail between thumb and forefinger, and made an inscription to the right of the door post: a single mark for the start of another day, underlined if he had awakened to the sound of falling water. So far, only the first seven lines lacked the sign for water. And later each morning, when no one was looking, Naamah never failed to run her fingers through the scratches that her husband had etched in the paneling (though she paid them no heed when he was nearby) and wondered, from the depths of her confusion, how much longer a confinement that she had not expected could possibly last.

Though the Ark's inhabitants had no way of discerning whether time within their craft was measured identically by the outside world, it became the guiding force in their lives. Shelobothe had her schedule and her own duties to perform. And as she neared her first destination and thought of those tasks—of the cows that needed milking (for hay remained plentiful); of the hens that needed to be checked, regardless of sharp claws and frenzied beaks (for eggs still arrived, on occasion); of mules that demanded fodder, and goats as well, if Curtis's attentions could be pried from his love interest for half an hour—she also thought of the task she dreaded most of all. Before mid-afternoon, all of the horses and sheep needed their exercise and both kinds of creatures seemed to make it a point to mark their movement through the enormous hallway. Cleaning up stalls was one thing but carting the wheelbarrow and shovel through a passageway that ran the entire length of the ship was quite another. She turned into the wing that led to the gentle farm animals, just as the rooster cockled a cry that startled her, and wished, much as Rezepatha and Maran had done before her, that she wasn't always so quick to volunteer.

Her final thoughts were centered on those she could not help stop missing, and for a moment she allowed her mind to picture each of their faces: Lapeth, Methuselah, Gravas, Traibus, before turning, once again, to the tasks that lay before her.

Since Shem's initiation he had all but given up wearing the tight breeches of the laboring class, sporting his former attire only for the most unsavory of tasks, such as the mopping of stalls or carting manure to the enormous storage compartment in the stern of the lower level. He sat on the floor of the chapel with a lightweight robe flowing around his crossed legs and bent knees, on feathered cushions that had been stitched with the greatest of care by Naamah, who had never once mentioned the long hours involved. As the silence came to an end, Shem sent out prayers to those who he was certain continued to survive the storm, and as his conscious mind returned to him, he began to wonder if anyone on the earth knew how much longer the waters would prevail or even if the downpour had affected every continent of the globe.

He rose to the bare soles of his feet and walked across the piles of scattered cushions to the doorway. The small room was comfortable enough in size for the four couples to spend devotional time together, amid beautiful, draperied walls of soft blues and shaded pinks, although it had yet to happen. There always seemed to be something else of greater import to do. However, the place of solitude was on the starboard side of the uppermost level, halfway between Naamah's galley and the huge chamber that provided a haven for all manner of perched or caged or flighted birds. Perhaps when the eight became more accustomed to hectic schedules, they could find a few moments to come together.

He turned the brass-handled latch and stepped out into the hallway leading across the width of the ship that was joined at midpoint by the central passageway. His sandals were waiting upon the lacquered, hardwood floor, and he slipped them on in a single step. Afterward, he headed toward one of the storage rooms. The smooth skin of his face had given way to a thick growth of whiskers that covered his angular features.

To his left, stood the entrance to the enormous cereal and grain storerooms where wheat, barley, oats, millet, corn, and rye were all stored inside tightly sealed containers in long rows. On his right rose the portal through which he could find the large barrels of water bolted to the floor and arranged end to end and side to side in magnificent lines. There were water stores on every level, enough for cooking and drinking and all of the Ark's occupants for a very long time to come. The old mystic himself had calculated the amount necessary, though it appeared there was much more than even eight humans and nearly 2,000 creatures could consume, almost regardless of how many weeks they were aboard the vessel.

Shem turned aft down the main passageway. The ramp leading to the lower stories was situated against the furthermost wall. Behind the wall was the enormous aviary but instead of going straight through the single doorway, he stepped to the right and began a gradual descent to the next level.

The incline was certainly not narrow, although only a single lamp at the halfway point illuminated the surroundings of lacquered gopher-wood and pine panels. He could have taken one of the sets of stairs by the water barrels or next to their quarters just as easily but the ramp came out nearest the storage room where he was headed. As he walked, his robe lightly touched the hardwood floor, statically picking up a few pieces of straw behind him.

The storeroom was on his right: an open portal leading to great mounds of twigs and leaves, tender pieces of bark and plains grass, piles of hanging moss and soft lichen, sealed bushels of countless berries and tender fruit, kept fresh in wax-sealed bins. Though much of the food would have been suitable for the eight humans, all of the tremendous stores before him was strictly for the animals. For the most part, Naamah's supplies were located next to the galley.

At first, Shem was nearly overpowered by the scents of mineral-rich bark and cut greenery, although he found the aromas much more agreeable than the smells of animal droppings, which permeated the air throughout much of the Ark and crept into his conscious awareness most of the day. In the beginning of their confinement, he had thought there might come a time when nostrils no longer took notice of the odors of creatures or their hides or their wastes. He had found, however, that though one grew accustomed to the smells of the ship, each of the scents retained its own distinctive aroma; he could still tell when animal compost was lying around, waiting to be carted away.

He grasped the iron handle of the four-wheeled cart and pulled it toward a pile of leaves. Their schedule called for a rotation in which only the outermost portion of each of the stacks—a hearty mixture of fronds, oak, and yellow-seed leaves with vines—was used. By alternating piles, the roughage beneath the outer layer stayed fresher. There would come a time, after the greens had spoiled, when the creatures' diet would consist solely of grains, cereals, dried fruits, and the ever-present hay. Until then, however, the ruminants and other herbivores would be provided with what they liked best.

With the pitchfork he had left in the cart, Shem walked in between the huge piles, some nearly as tall as he, and gathered a selection of feed. The cart was eight cubits long and nearly as wide as the double portal. It took him a half-hour before the cart was brimming with leaves, twigs, and a good supply of berries, all neatly organized within the wagon. He tossed the pitchfork atop the greens and walked to the back of the cart. Each end had its own handle, allowing the wagon to be pushed (though it was much more difficult when full) or pulled, for it was too lengthy to be turned in all but the main passageway.

It took a great deal of initial strain, and though his robe was littered with an assortment of plant fragments and his whiskered chin flinched with the effort, he managed to pull the wagon through the portal with only the barest clearance on either side. The iron axle squeaked through half a dozen revolutions before he heard the distinctive sound of hooves scratching the floors of stalls in hungry anticipation. When he finally brought the wagon to a halt, he unconsciously lifted a sleeve to his forehead and wiped away the moisture. His daily feeding schedule had begun.

The cart was positioned in the central passageway. On either side, iron fencing rose from the floor to the ceiling with only a cubit's space between Shem's wagon and the enclosures. On the left, the ship's starboard side, twenty-eight deer awaited his arrival (two distinctive species—some with spotted hides; others with hair-fluffed white tails). On his right were the antelope and the gazelle. Fifty-six sets of eyes stared at the man and his wagon, as each of the creatures pressed toward the front of the enclosures, bumping graceful limbs and raising splintered straws and clouds of dust. On either side of the passageway, there was room in the front for about twelve creatures (fifteen, if the males with the largest antlers remained at the back). Unfortunately, each of the quadrupeds insisted on a chance to press a snout firmly against the iron-linked barricade, with wide-eyed looks of dumbfounded excitement. Some even allowed thick lips to smack lightly against the fencing, as if it were edible.

The stalls had been the handiwork of Tubal-cain and his craftsmen and were ingenious in design, with a long row of troughs running perpendicular to the outer fencing. Instead of one of the humans having to press against a doorway trying to get in while the animals pushed toward the front, the troughs bordered the creatures within their enclosure, keeping them away from the entrance. Shem, or Ham or Japheth, as the schedule cited, could fill up the lengthy, triangular-shaped trough from one side while the animals grazed from the other. A second gate within the stall was opened when the time came to take the gentle creatures around the feed troughs and into the outer passageway for exercise.

Taking the pitchfork in hand, Shem headed for the deer and unlatched the door. When the animals saw what he was doing, they began moving toward the feed chute; the youngest were pushed aside, though all would eat shortly. As Shem worked, a few pieces of vines, leaves, and strands fell to the floor between the wagon and the trough, yet he was incredibly skilled and swift at the process. The creatures' large ears remained erect, as brown-eyed deer watched the man fill the chute with a great quantity of greens.

Lips moved swiftly, sucking in large amounts of leaves and twigs, barely chewing the morsels, often swallowing entire portions whole. Although the creatures lacked upper front teeth, possessing thick growths of skin instead, they had teeth on the bottom and sides. However, it appeared as though each of the deer preferred to use teeth solely for chewing their cud; four-sectioned stomachs could digest nearly anything.

The antelope and gazelle came next, and though the animals were similar in appearance (save for the slender, spiral horns protruding straight from the gazelle heads, while the antelope horns shot upward and then backward at the midpoint), Shem preferred the temperament of the gazelle to that of his shy cousin. There were also tiny tufts of hair on gazelle knees and both creatures had huge, soft black eyes but the gazelle rubbed muzzles against the man's hand if he extended his arm over the trough. The creatures' diet was much like the deer, though Shem did shake a generous quantity of red berries from the bushel basket to mix with their feed. As a final chore, he eyed the level of the water barrels in each of the stalls and made certain there was enough—from the appearance of the water level, the gazelle rarely drank at all.

The barrels were strategically placed below a single pipe poking through the ceiling and were filled from the water storeroom on the level above. The Ark had been constructed with its own system of tiny canals running to a majority of the stalls. Anon had called it a waste of time; Noah had voiced it a necessity.

Within the cart's hold, there remained an ample supply of forage for the giraffes: leaves and vines, fruits and the soft twigs they chewed complacently while grazing beneath wired-basket feed troughs, teeth and lips pulling fodder through the containers which hung two cubits above the second-story floor while the animal's hooves remained upon floorboards ten cubits below.

Shem hauled the cart further down the hallway with much greater ease than when he had first left the storeroom. He came to a halt barely three arms' length from the giraffes, whose eyes were nearly level with his waist, and watched one of the symmetrically-patched creatures with two rounded horns beneath a covering of skin and hair stare up at him from the huge enclosure. At forty cubits across, the length of the stall was the largest pen in the craft. Because of its size and placement, a small passageway encircled the enclosure before opening up into the continuation of the hallway on the opposite side.

He pitched a plentiful supply of greens and what fruit remained into the five baskets and shoveled a generous heaping over the railings to the floor below. Several of the animals that were not fully grown had become accustomed to eating by squatting forward, limbs and barely bendable knees outstretched to the side. For a moment, he watched them move rhythmically about their stall, legs stepping forward on one side and then the other, before he tossed the pitchfork into the empty wagon and returned the entire cart to its storeroom.

The rest of the morning passed swiftly; he circled around the giraffe stall, leaving piles of leaves, vines, and twigs behind, and headed toward the port side of the bow. There were zebras to feed, wildebeest to look after, and an ostrich pen to deal with (a stall was not easy to clean while long, two-toed feet stumbled over the intended directions of shovel and broom alike). On his way to the ostriches, Shem nearly ran into Shelobothe coming from the direction of the farm animals. Husband and wife stared momentarily in surprise before embracing—bits of her splintered straw traded places with the spindly tendrils his vines had left behind. He laughed before kissing her.

"You are beautiful," he said, pushing Shelobothe's hair back behind her ears.

"I only appear so," she smiled, wiping a smudge of dust from above his whiskered cheek, "for you've been alone with the animals all morning."

They kissed again, lips lingering for a long while before Shem looked into her sparkling eyes. "Do you know the soft hay in the bow's storage?" She nodded, completely forgetting about how she looked, or the horses, sheep, and cattle that came next on her list (and neither remained conscious of the noisy patter of water beating against the outside of the Ark).

"What do you think the others would say if we were late for the meal?"

Through forty days and forty nights did the heaviness of the clouds allow waters to descend from the heavens, covering Gallia and Tarshial, Numidia and Macedonia, Scythia and Libya, Gangem, Ophir, Mizraim, and all lands to the West—including Poseidia and the Yucata jungles. Beneath darkened clouds the entire Armenian range was flooded . . . until, finally, even the mountains were covered by the rising tides.

47th Day upon the Ark

The waters had stopped! For the first time in many weeks the vessel's occupants listened to the sounds of settling planks and weighted crossbeams and the creaking murmur of the ship's hull as it was propelled ever so slowly toward the north (though none inside could discern its true direction). The chatter and movements of creatures continued as before, from the tiny mice, nosing whiskers through scattered sesame seeds, to the trumpeted blast of the elephants, who had grown quite used to the attention of humans and were not beyond calling out for it. Meanwhile, the racket of Naamah clanging pots together and the frequent bickering of Maran and Ham were even more audible without the background noise of falling water. (A full two days would pass before any of the eight grew accustomed to speaking normally again.)

Though there had been a great deal of excitement when all had arisen and immediately noticed that the sounds of the downpour had stopped (and Noah had marked his wall accordingly), Naamah had been quick to point out during breakfast what everyone including her husband had apparently overlooked. Much time would yet pass before anyone could disembark. Until the level of floodwaters began to dissipate and the ship came to a rest upon solid ground, there would be no leaving the vessel. Still, even Naamah couldn't totally undermine their anticipation. There were countless reasons for wanting to be on the outside again, including being able to roam over plains of soft grass and through fields of wheat and corn and lush groundlings. They missed the beauty of the vapored sky and the towering limbs of birch, pine, and white oak. In their imaginings of the way the earth would appear upon their release, they longed for rolling hills and the gentle sparkle of lakes and clear springs.

After having lived so many days aboard the craft, all yearned for the simple luxury of moving about freely. Although the Ark was immense, everyone felt the constraints of the ship's dimensions, the stifled flow of air (in spite of the vents) and the incredible lack of light. The feeling of being trapped with no end in sight was also difficult to bear. However, none of these things proved as irritating to Maran as the mere presence of her husband.

Rarely could she even speak to him without being annoyed. Meals were spent with eyes and comments deliberately averted from the man. She could not stomach sitting next to him in the galley, though she took her place on the wooden bench nonetheless in order to maintain peace with the rest of her family. Despite the excitement over the cessation of falling water, lunch had almost been spoiled. Watching Ham eat was akin to watching the animals, with his moist smacking lips and teeth that chewed enormous portions, his grinding crunches rising above even the clicking noise of his tongue and saliva (her own tiny morsels were carefully chewed before swallowing). Whether one glanced at him (which was a mistake) or merely listened to the sounds he made, or heard the clang of his utensils scratching against pottery plates, mealtime was disgusting. There was no longer any doubt in Maran's mind—she had married a barbarian.

Perhaps if his ignorance of manners had been his only fault, it could have been overlooked. If only Ham were as refined as Japheth or as wise as Shem, but he was not. Her thoughts to the contrary were simply useless. She had begun to see so many little things she didn't like about him and it surprised her that she hadn't noticed some of them before. He never listened, even when she was trying her best to explain something in words simple enough that even he could understand. Another constant challenge was the way he attempted to answer her before she had even finished speaking her mind. His pretending to know everything (even when she knew he did not) nearly drove her insane. He was always late for meals and when he did arrive, he was unwashed and barebacked. He was so immature that it often seemed as if she had obtained a child before Rezepatha (who would give birth in less than three months' time). Sometimes Ham could be so conceited, as if he felt superiority for having been born a male. Sometimes, just looking at her husband made her feel sick.

To make matters worse, the day's scheduling paired them together in less than an hour for what had to be the single most repulsive duty aboard the vessel. It seemed only fitting, somehow, that Ham would be a part of it. The two were to clean the stalls of the larger creatures—all located in the bow at the lowest level (of course, manure had to be carted the entire distance to the stern)—which included the rhinoceroses, the buffalo, the oxen, and the elephants. A simple shoveling of animal chips and distribution of fresh hay wouldn't suffice on this occasion; they needed to swab down the entire area. However, rather then leaving immediately, she tarried behind at the meal table, sipping a steamed brew of chamomile and spearmint leaves. There wasn't a shred of doubt in her mind as to who had upset her digestion.

She happened to be alone in the spaciousness of one of the few rooms constructed large enough for its intended purpose. Naamah was at the other end of the Ark, attending to birdseed and grubs and the water trough (her mother-in-law had developed quite a routine of complaining about her duties). Everyone else had assigned tasks they needed to be about as well, so it was no wonder—as her eyes remained glued on the grain of the wooden tabletop and her hand wrapped around the porcelain cup—that she was startled when Noah sat down across the table from her.

"Did I frighten you?" he asked softly. The gentle touch of his hand reached out to pat her arm.

She glanced momentarily into the vivid blue of his eyes before returning her own to the direction of the table. She hoped he couldn't see what she had been thinking. "I have been lost in my thoughts." Her husky voice cracked as she spoke to him.

"Well, that is why I am here—to hear what is on your mind."

She tensed for a few seconds before realizing he hadn't come to hear about Ham. "What would you have me say?"

"Exactly what you see."

Maran heard the hopefulness in the tone of his voice and was saddened, though she couldn't bear to look at him again and face the intensity of his stare. Only in her mind did she allow herself to see how he appeared, with the white wisps of his hair and his pale, woven robe that lacked the smallest stain or blemish.

"What of the waters?" he finally asked, in order to break the silence.

"I saw not the end of the downpour; neither do I foresee when we might leave this vessel."

He simply nodded and looked down at the tabletop. "Who remains among the people of the earth?"

"I see nothing," came the swift response.

"Will the Ark come aground?"

"There is nothing."

"What heading does the ship take?"

"Nothing."

He paused for a long while before posing the final query. "Shall

Rezepatha birth a boy or a girl child?"

"Father, I cannot," Maran cried out, as she pushed the cup away in exasperation. Noah had never seen her so upset. "Though I have tried, I cannot."

"It's of no matter," he said quickly, in an effort to calm her.

"It does matter!" The reply came in the tone she normally reserved for Ham. "The Sight eludes me."

There was silence. Maran kept her eyes focused downward as Noah tried to sense exactly what was bothering her. He watched his daughter-in-law quietly for a few moments. Their captivity was beginning to weigh heavily upon them all. She appeared quite stern; the way her hair had been pulled back behind her head, and the tightness of her forehead and cheekbones gave the appearance of one who was both deeply sorrowed and angry at the same time. There should have been some excitement over the cessation of water, yet there was none. He had noticed tension between her and Ham lately, but that was certainly natural for newlyweds (though Shelobothe and Shem seemed even closer). He pushed from his mind the thought that they were having problems, just as Maran moved to speak.

"I miss him, Noah," she said with a great deal of sadness.

"Methuselah?"

She nodded her head, allowing him to see her eyes for one brief moment. "I miss him very much."

"We can't help but miss them all."

"But Methuselah most of all," she stated aloud, mostly to herself. "He could have answered your questions."

Noah was silent, for the thought had been on his mind as well. Finally, he spoke, "I have come to believe that it is not always so important to realize what the One has in store. The knowledge that there is a plan—though we know not what it might be—

should suffice to gladden our hearts."

"Perhaps," she spoke in her deep voice, "but this does not console me."

"Then find comfort in the love another shares with you," he said matter-of-factly. "Go to your husband and find the peace you seek."

Maran looked up at him. Suddenly, her eyes gave Noah such a stare of contempt that she betrayed her silence. In an instant, he felt her emotions.

"My child," he began softly, "why war with the one who is capable of helping you?"

"In what?" The words nearly choked in her throat.

"In allowing your soul to come to realize itself." She looked both upset and confused as he continued. "What would you perceive as Ham's greatest fault?"

She nearly said the number would be difficult to choose from but the truth came to mind and she spoke it: "He acts as one who possesses the knowledge of all things, though I know this not to be true. He would have me follow his every lead but he has yet to become certain of his own steps, and," she continued, becoming agitated with the thought, "he refuses to believe that I might have the answers he lacks."

"Then know this," Noah said softly, hoping she was ready to hear his words. "You have a wonderful opportunity. Use each other just as you would peer upon the surface of a lake. Look at one another without judgment, and see if you can't find a glimmer of your own reflection staring back at you. In this way, both may become whole."

"I wish I had the time," the voice of Naamah interrupted from the galley's doorway, as she shook her head in utter disbelief, "to sit around and entertain company." Dozens of tiny pieces of birdseed clung to the fabric of her massive chest; she clicked her tongue in disgust. Her hair was mussed, and the bright red color of her lips was beginning to streak in a single line down her chin. “If you think I’m about to prepare another meal after what I’ve just been through, well then you have another . . . ”

Maran shot up from the table before the older woman could finish. Her face was red with anger and her hands were clenched together in fists. “I am nothing like Ham!” she said hotly. She turned and pushed her way out of the room, bumping into Naamah as she left.

Noah did not hear his wife’s complaining, nor the way she inquired about Maran’s manners. He watched the young woman leave and thought about following her but decided she needed to be alone. At that very moment, he spotted a movement on the floor next to Naamah’s skirt. The gray cat had somehow found its way to the uppermost story and as the furry creature began to purr and rub up against the flower pattern of Naamah’s dress, Noah braced himself for the inevitable.

It was evening, after the lamps on every level had been turned to their lowest positions. Though the Ark’s inhabitants had bedded down for the night—three couples had fallen swiftly to sleep after the day’s events—something was to occur amid the silence of the night that would affect the people of the earth for generations to come.

Maran couldn’t stop thinking about what had been said to her. She could contain neither the anger she felt toward Noah, nor the disgust she felt in the back of her throat as the callused hands of her husband began to caress her. Her eyes became moist with the thought of what she had done with her life.

Ham, too, was upset. Never before had he been so infuriated with her outbursts. Her scene down in the stalls, screaming as one gone mad, had frightened even the animals. He was enraged and his jaws were tightened in anger by two things: his marriage to Maran, and the fact that he hadn't been able to shake his desire for her.

A day would come when both had only love for the other. Many would perceive their gentleness toward the other as the source of a perfect relationship. Yet, though the evening and the anger and the loathing would one day be forgotten, it would influence them both for the rest of their lives. For uppermost in their minds, as they lay together as one, burned a deep-seated hate.

And on that very night, Maran conceived a son.

And God remembered Noah, and his wife, and his sons, and his sons' wives, and all the cattle that were in the Ark, and every living thing: And the One made a wind to pass over the earth, and its stagnant waters. Thus, the wind created movement upon the surface of the waters, causing the Ark to journey northward as the vessel propelled its bow into the waves. And ever so slowly the waters began to assuage.

126th Day upon the Ark

Though the torrential waters had ceased, there were afternoons when the sound of water droplets was heard pattering against the hull or the vessel's catwalk. At times, the craft was gently tossed about upon the surface of the waves. The motion of the ship caused a number of creatures to stand uneasily. Twice, the oxen had managed to stupidly tumble over their own hooves. The wolves howled in rhythm to the waves, while other creatures bellowed in voices that irritated the male lion (who became more ill-tempered with each passing day). Once in awhile, the large maned-mammal even raised a paw in defiance and let out a threatening roar; only Noah remained brave enough to continue feeding him. Naamah was frustrated with the racket as well, and she was far from delighted with the tiny cat that wouldn't leave her alone, nearly causing her to trip on a dozen occasions.

For his part, Japheth was extremely tired and yet he was as joyful as he had ever been in his life. At any moment, he was to become a father, and the thought made his few remaining duties even more difficult to complete. He was anxious to return to his wife's bedchamber for he was quite certain Rezepatha would birth the child before evening; her pangs had commenced in the early hours of morning.

His months inside the Ark had caused his skin to become lighter, and his thick, black hair had been allowed to grow almost to shoulder length. A slight growth of whiskers covered his face and upper lip, though he clipped it back every few days. (Conversely, Shem had been fully bearded for some time now.) For many weeks, Japheth had worked harder than any of the others, for he had taken upon himself the greatest number of Rezepatha's tasks as her time drew near. Sometimes, he managed to get only a few hours of sleep, but he was not nearly as weary from the chores or his lack of sleep as he was of waiting to see the child. In his excitement, he never once regretted the fact that his baby would be born within the confines of the Ark.

Again and again, he imagined all of the things a baby might mean to his entire family. He might finally see a smile on his mother's face when she took a grandchild into her arms. He knew for certain that Noah regarded the entire event as a blessing, Shem and Shelobothe would contemplate having one of their own, and there was even hope than an infant in their midst might somehow bring Ham and Maran back together. For himself and Rezepatha, he saw only the same happiness they had always shared but somehow it would be more special and their lives would take on an even greater meaning. Raising a child between them was a gift from the One—an amazing adventure that he and Rezepatha would share.

The dampness of the large room caused Japheth's open shirt and loose-fitting breeches to cling to his skin. The air was rich with moisture and the crisp smells of life in Shinar's forest. Japheth believed the vaulted chamber situated on the lowest level between the giraffes and the water storage room was his favorite place in the entire Ark. Here, between walls of pine lined with flickering lamps (the flicker a result of both the irregularities in fuel consistency as well as the scattered air passageways) he could recapture some of the same love he had felt for the gardens, the fields, the moss, and the trees back in their clearing.

All about him were buckets of bushy fern that had been lined among soil-filled crocks of shoulder-high pine, cypress, birch, and gopher-wood. There were sturdy, open crates filled with rich earth and prickly brambles of raspberry. Scattered pots of tomato vine sat next to tiny trunks of wooden sprouts that would grow to become apricot trees. Japheth walked among the plants—buckets and crocks arranged in intricate patterns, though he had long since memorized the maze—checking soil with fingers or tasting a few granules with his tongue. Small cans held grape vines, but it would be a very long while before he tasted any raisins other than those which were among the dried fruits of Naamah's inventory.

The water can was still half full as he carried it to examine the moistness of potted ivy and felt the leafy foliage of the massive philodendrons reaching toward the ceiling. The scents of growth and rich plant life were everywhere, covering even the smells of the giraffes that filtered through the meshed windows, allowing for the circulation of cleaner air. The longest leafy vines had been tied against the walls as they climbed and dangled from the beamed ceiling.

Japheth didn't expect the plants to bear fruit while in captivity, nor was he upset when leaves refused to reach proper maturity due to a lack of light. He wasn't discouraged that some of the ferns seemed dwarfed or that a few of the potted trees had lost a number of their leaves. His single hope was that shrubs and sprouts, seedlings and vines, trees and groundlings, even tiny trunks, might somehow survive the journey. The sight of abundant greenery made it clear that there was a chance.

His inspection was thorough but more speedy than usual. Already, he had completed Rezepatha's scheduled duties, including feeding the snakes and the smallest caged creatures and the tiny rodents—animals in wired-iron coops in lined rows from the floor to the ceiling (and removable trays beneath each cage for easy cleaning). The rabbits (separated by males and females, for there was no room for more) had been fed a mixture of grains with a few leaves, carrots, and sugar beets thrown in for good measure. The lettuce had long been used up before spoilage took its toll, though there were seeds aplenty stored in sealed canisters on the uppermost level.

Japheth had already fed Curtis and Dina, along with the other goats. Curtis continued to sport a tinkling bell about his neck but instead of attempting escape, the goat spent long days following the waddling she-goat in utter devotion, licking her floppy ears or nibbling the hide of her back. Japheth took a few moments to scratch the pairs' jowls before moving on to his other chores.

When the expectant father had done all that was urgently required of him and set aside those tasks that could be completed on the morrow, he scurried down passageways and halls, around corners, and up three flights of shadowy-lit wooden steps (nearly half the distance from the old cottages to the freshwater lake), and headed toward the galley. He cleaned himself up in a hurry and went inside the bedchamber to sit by his wife.

Rezepatha lay on their divan, surrounded by stuffed pillows she had tossed about in an effort to find comfort. A thin weave of fabric covered her until the time came. Though her face appeared strained and moist, she was beautiful. For a long while, Japheth sat on the stool next to her, and she held his hand, squeezing his fingers when the pains returned, releasing her grip as they subsided. After a short time, he unknowingly began to follow her patterns of breathing.

Through it all, Naamah took charge. The older woman ran about the room in a frenzy, calling for the rest of the family to stay out or to take the cat back to where it belonged. She just couldn't fathom why everyone was in her way—there was boiled water, soft rags, and a blanket to fetch (she had stitched it herself)—and even Noah had been underfoot. There was far too much to be done, and dinner was out of the question. She issued orders to everyone (save for Rezepatha, whose forehead was frequently wiped) and demanded compliance, for she had birthed three children of her own and certainly knew how it was done. Her orders continued to pour forth right up until the moment came—and Rezepatha gave birth to a baby girl.

The infant was placed on her mother's naked belly and all but Japheth was chased from the room. Both parents watched the tiny, slippery baby in wonder as she wriggled ever so gently. They were filled with awe. Naamah made certain the three had plenty of time to be alone; she blocked the doorway with a threatening glare. Rezepatha stared at the child with the same piercing look her mother had first directed at her. Japheth's eyes teared with emotion, for even imagination had not shown him an infant so perfect in every detail.

The child came to be called Miya, and descended from her would come one who looked on as Pharaoh's daughter reached down and pulled Moses from the river.

267th Day Upon the Ark

And the waters prevailed upon the earth one hundred and fifty days, and after the end the waters were abated. And the Ark rested in the seventh month, on the seventeenth day of the month, upon the mountains of Aghri Dagh. And the waters decreased continually until the tenth month: in Tammuz, on the first day of the month, were the tops of the mountains seen. And it came to pass at the end of forty days, that Noah opened the windows of the Ark.

Naamah had taken it upon herself to serve one of the largest breakfasts since their confinement. To any who would listen, she detailed how much exhausting work had been involved, but in reality she undertook her labors because the day promised to be special. There was plenty of food, so much that even Ham had been unable to consume all that had been prepared for them: wheat bread and honeyed muffins, milk and cheese, nuts and olives (Nouhad had loved olives), eggs, and the last of the oranges. Even the gray cat, who Naamah had named Uzal—for he was a wanderer—had been given a saucer of fluffy cooked eggs. Each of them finished the meal with a choice of raisin or fig cakes or both. At the end, everyone had eaten their fill.

When the meal was cleared away and the men went about their long-anticipated task, the women remained behind in the galley, sipping hot mugs of spiced beverage, picking at the last crumbs of cake, and waiting patiently for a turn to hold the children who had finished nursing. With the passage of time, Noah now had two grandchildren upon the Ark. The four women laughed and praised Miya, who tried eagerly to imitate their sounds. They brushed back her silken hair and covered her small, perfect cheeks with kisses. She giggled at their attentions and grabbed for noses and didn't mind in the least being passed about. Through it all, she seemed to relish their attentions and frequently stared in fascination at the ever-present cat.

Grandmother, mother, and aunts were as attentive to Maran and Ham's son, Canaan, as well. (The couple's relationship had also improved tremendously since the birthing, for watering and feeding challenges had taken the place of bickering.) Their attentions, however, appeared to be for naught. The little boy never uttered a sound in response to their coos; his lips never turned up in joy; his eyes remained dark and glaring, never sparkling with light as his cousin's did. He seemed so beautiful and yet acted so very angry, even since the day of his birth. Nonetheless, the four women, as well as his grandfather, father, and uncles, showered him with love and were certain he would grow out of it in time.

While the women attended to the needs of the two children, Noah, Japheth, Shem, and Ham readied themselves with chisels and iron hammers and prepared to remove the coverings to the windows of the Ark. Though they were extremely anxious to see what lay beyond their captivity and finally glimpse how the earth had fared, none allowed themselves to be overcome with unbridled excitement. They had learned to restrain emotions that often led to disappointment. Although the torrential downpour had ceased after forty days, they had yet to be freed. Although the light patter of falling water did not occur with the same regularity as it had for the first 150 days after the downpour, it continued. Although the sound of air moving beyond the walls of the craft seemed to hold promise that the waters would diminish, and though the Ark felt as if it had become lodged and no longer drifted upon the waters of the deep, it was impossible to ignore the fact that, when water fell from the heavens, a careful ear pressed against the planking of a storeroom wall could hear droplets from the clouds striking water still prevailing upon the ground. The earth remained flooded.

The hardest part of their confinement was that none of them had any idea how long it was to last or how much longer they would need to be upon the Ark. Their excitement over removing the window coverings that ran the full length of the catwalk was checked by caution. The women went about their regular duties (when they could pull themselves away from the children, for they watched them in shifts), knowing their husbands would come fetch them if there proved anything at all to see. Naamah, however, spent a great deal of time peering out into the central passageway, waiting to hear from someone.

The first plank proved much more difficult to remove than any had supposed. After the sliding wooden panels had been opened on the inside, Ham and Japheth clung to the ladder within the central storeroom of the uppermost story, wedging tools between gopher-wood planking and the vertical ribs, and attempted to push the solid sheet of white oak out, toward the outside. After a great deal of pushing and groaning and grunting, and the realization that the wood had expanded and that the bitumen pitch had gotten between some of the joints, Ham spoke a few cross words before he and Japheth pushed and pried again. Finally, the wood gave way and tumbled down noisily against the outside hull of the Ark until there came a splash. Japheth and Ham crawled out the opening, hoisted themselves onto the roof, and were quickly joined by Shem and Noah. For a very long while, the four stood silently upon the catwalk and stared in awe at the sight that had awaited them.

As far as eyes could see there was only water. Off in the distance, there was neither land, nor tree, nor hovel, nor branch. The smoothness of a giant ocean covered all that lay beneath their craft. It appeared deep and dark and lifeless, save when wind rippled tiny waves into motion, and even then there was nothing to see but water. All about, a darkened horizon surrounded them. The sight caused them to blink incessantly, for they were not used to the movement of air, when there had been only stillness within the craft.

When the four had taken in their surroundings, they took turns looking down over the side of their mighty ship (holding each other's ankles so as not to fall) to stare toward where the ground should be. The reason for the Ark's lack of movement became immediately clear, for it appeared as if the Ark had lodged itself between enormous rock formations. Although the rocks were surrounded by water at least a cubit in depth, farther away from the craft, the reflection of the waters showed much greater depths. As tiny wisps of Noah's hair fluttered in the breeze, he pointed out to the others that they had landed upon a mountain, or rather a mountain had gotten in the path of the Ark.

Overhead, the thick, dark clouds were in constant motion, billowing shapes and massive puffs moving in multiple directions. Each man pointed in awe and wonder at the movement; it showed little resemblance to the motionless cloud vapors they had always known. Because of the darkness around them, Japheth was the first to wonder aloud whether the light from the sky had been dimmed by the deluge.

In spite of the grim appearance of their surroundings, being on the outside after such a lengthy confinement was beyond description. Legs were stretched, laughter was exchanged, and excitement grew to a point they had vowed not to allow. None of them had imagined how wondrous it would feel to breathe in fresh, cool air (although their deep breaths made them light-headed). Noah and Shem led a prayer of thanksgiving before the three sons raced the length of the roofing. While his sons shouted back and forth for joy, Noah wondered how many other people remained alive upon the earth and were staring toward an unrecognizable sky, or remained huddled within the confines of a boat. Finally, the four remembered the magnitude of their task, and they began to pry loose the planking that covered the windows of the Ark.

The windows were a cubit wide and lay beneath the catwalk. They ran nearly the full length of both sides of the ship, and were divided at regular intervals by the ribbed beams of the craft. The remaining panels pulled free much easier than the first one had pushed out, for it was not difficult to carefully stand upon the sloping roof and pry wooden sheets loose with four or five movements of a strategically placed chisel and hammer. Underneath the panels, sliding partitions were opened to allow in air (and to allow the stuffiness inside to seep out). The calls and chatter of countless birds broke through to the outside as the planks from their windows were pulled free and placed upon the Ark's roof. The bird windows were covered with wired mesh that could be slid aside but for the time the mesh was kept in place.

The four worked eagerly in order to complete the job before what light there was disappeared from dark clouds. They were much too excited to take lunch, preferring instead to finish their task. It lasted late into the afternoon, as plank after plank was removed and then stacked for safekeeping—they could build a shelter with the wood later, although a few planed timbers slipped between fingers and fell overboard, striking the waters below with a splash.

They completed the job while light yet remained in the darkened heavens. The women gathered from inside the craft and climbed out onto the roof to see the emptiness and solitude that surrounded them. Naamah used the children as an excuse to remained grounded (someone had to keep watch on the little ones, and she was certainly used to attending to their needs by this time), which suited her own children quite well, for it was doubtful that the dimensions of the window could accommodate their mother's frame. Although Noah was not alone in glimpsing the sadness in his wife's eyes over not being able to see what had so excited the others. At last, their confinement upon the vessel seemed to be nearing an end.

When the adults finally finished their frivolity and the noise of shouting out to one another from opposite ends of a three-hundred-cubit ship abated, it was the last lingering hour of daylight. Ham's empty belly rumbled a call for supper, and the sons found their way to the ship's galley. Noah, however, journeyed the catwalk toward the aviary and slid open the mesh-wired windows of the chamber. He descended the ladder inside the window to fetch one of the birds.

He passed over sparrows, grouse, cranes, and wild ducks, wanting a creature that wouldn't be afraid to venture into a sky that hadn't existed before. He thought about using either the doves or the ravens, for both were known for their bravery. In the end, however, he chose one of the ravens, for its haggard appearance and dark color more closely resembled the sight surrounding the Ark.

The raven was released through the window in the Ark, and circled, for a time, around the massive vessel, though it returned in quick order, for it had not taken such a flight in a very long while, and the air felt cool against its feathered-breast—and there was no place at all, save the Ark, for the raven to rest its feet.

293rd Day upon the Ark; in Elvi, the sixth day of the month

Noah was always the first to rise, checking to make certain the kitchen barrel was amply supplied with water before taking the few moments he allowed himself for his morning period of silence. If it hadn't been for his markings next to the door post—dozens of weeks already accounted for—he would have surely lost track of days, for each was so very much like those that had gone before. He ventured out onto the catwalk to peer at the sky, the water, and the darkened clouds, and the horizon in hopes that he might see another ship passing in the distance but there was none, and he couldn't stop feeling a little disheartened as he returned to the galley. Somewhere upon the earth there had to be more survivors but he had no idea where or how or when he might begin looking for them.

There were other thoughts on his mind, as well, including one that made him especially nervous to contemplate. Nonetheless, something had to be done that he had been putting off for much too long a time. Later, when his sons and their wives were fully occupied with the day's chores (and Miya and Canaan were in Shelobothe's care), he would spend some time with Naamah. At long last, they needed to talk about their life together. They had grown much too far apart and he felt the greatest blame was his own. Their conversation could wait no longer, though he had planned it for several months in hopes that an end to confinement might return their lives to some degree of normalcy. The waters were descending much slower than he had anticipated and all the while Noah and his wife continued as though they were physically isolated one from the other.

He managed to keep these thoughts to himself as he ate with his family, even doting over his two grandchildren when the meal was finished. His own duties were verified on the schedule, though he knew the tasks by rote and he managed to find a moment to listen to Maran about the script she was recording, to be placed along with Methuselah's in the brass box. For much of the morning, he glanced at his wife out of the corner of an eye and managed to see the essence of the girl he had married so very long ago. He only hoped that Naamah might come to see him as he had once been then their marriage might begin anew.

Naamah had sensed something in the air immediately after spotting Noah returning from the outside. She began each day with the first chore of breakfast (later, she had to take care not only of the birds but also of the scouring of a bathroom as well), but she had a hard time keeping her mind focused on the meal she had planned (they had not eaten creamed oats in a long while). Her husband kept watching her in a way that made her most uncomfortable, and she couldn't help but wonder what she had done or said in the last few days to upset him. No one else seemed to notice the change in his behavior, although it certainly had its effect on her because the morning passed much more slowly than usual. There was a tremendous feeling of uneasiness inside of her and it was growing.

When the others finally left the table and the day's tasks were underway, Noah lingered behind. Once the two of them were completely alone, he finally spoke to her.

"Naamah," he said softly while taking one of her hands between both of his, "we need to talk."

Without reason, she suddenly became conscious of her enormous size and her heartbeat began to quicken. She stared down at the floorboards, one hand nervously gripping her waist, wishing she could remember what she had done wrong, and shaking her head in confusion, "Whatever it is, I can only be sorry."

His voice filled with much concern. "Naamah, I do not wish to reprimand you." He put his palm under her chin and raised her eyes to his own. She saw his smile, his gentleness, his beauty, and the sparkle of his glance and wished, more than anything, that he would go away. "I just want you to know," he continued, hoping to calm her discomfort, "that I love you."

She looked away and managed to respond matter-of-factly (much as her mother would have done): "I love you too."

"No, Naamah," he said, turning her head back to face him, "I really love you. We've played this game much too long already and I wish for it to come to an end." She appeared confused as his words continued. "The time has come for us to share what each has to offer. No longer can we go about separate paths, each of us stumbling because we lack the partner we need to help us along the way. I will not go about my life alone any longer while you go about yours. From now on, we shall have a life together, as husband and wife."

"What is it you suggest?" she asked, with as little emotion as possible, though she was quite thankful not to have been scolded.

"Our children share the labor of their days whenever possible; perhaps we should try the same."

"You mean you plan to help me in the kitchen?" She was confused.

"And you would assist me with the creatures; our days should be shared."

She shook her head in complete amusement. "Why you don't know the first thing about preparing a meal!" Her tongue made a clicking sound against the roof of her mouth. "And I will not have it said that I can't take care of my family. I managed for more than a hundred; I can certainly handle ten!"

"That's not the point, Naamah, for no one doubts your abilities. Though you have never brushed the mane of a horse, or gathered hay for the elephants—who prefer to be fed by hand—I would find joy in showing you."

"To what end?" she asked harshly, "for I certainly have enough tasks to demand my attention as it is."

"By working together we can accomplish the same chores but they may take on greater meaning. Do you not think it would be fun to try?"

"I think it would be nothing but foolishness. You don't belong in the kitchen anymore than I do with the animals."

Noah nodded gently and turned to leave the room but not before Naamah had seen the sadness and disappointment upon his face. Yet, what she considered to be her common sense remained with her. Although he had appeared unhappy about their conversation, she couldn't bring herself to feel the same way, and part of her could not be sad that Noah finally felt the same way she had felt so many times before.

It hadn't taken Naamah long to regret her reaction to Noah. Before she had even finished with the birds—making certain they had been replenished with seed and water—she wanted to tell him that she had changed her mind. At first, she thought it best to wait for his return to the upper story at lunch but then they wouldn't be alone. In the end (though she tried to argue herself out of it), Naamah decided to follow him. It would certainly come as a surprise to him that she knew his schedule as well as he. And although she had never wandered beyond the confines of the third level, she knew her way around the vessel as well as anyone. She had spent many hours staring over Gravas's shoulder at the plans for the craft; she had heard much of the discussion between Anon and her husband; and, of course, mealtime often brought with it tales of the happenings throughout the entire ship. But, unbelievable as it was, she had never descended the ramp or used one of the stairways to either of the levels below. It was an act of extreme bravery (and, she thought, possibly one of stupidity) for the whole while she pondered the decision her head filled with pictures of spotted leopards—though she had never seen one up close—and growling bears and snorting bulls who were quite capable of crashing through wooden barriers at the slightest provocation. She finally made up her mind, pushing Uzal out of the way with a foot, sending his paws sliding down the passageway for nearly three cubits before he regained his balance and darted into the storeroom. For some reason, she felt a sense of urgency in the air.

Naamah took the stairs closest to their bedchamber, gripping the railing tightly as she began her descent. It had been a long while since she had attempted to move her girth in such a manner and she found neither the darkened walls nor the shadows thrown off by the flickering lamp (not to mention the fact that she couldn't see her feet) at all conducive to movement. She waddled downward, the hips of her patterned dress nearly bursting at the seams, observing that a number of the steps below were littered with strands of straw and a fine layer of sandy dust. She took note of the conditions and would be quick to mention it the next time they were all together, for surely someone had been scheduled to sweep.

When she came to the doorway exiting at the second floor, her breathing was hard and fast. She leaned against the wall and tried to stop the wheezing sounds in her throat. Even if she hadn't been familiar with the placement of animals upon the vessel, she would have known her nearness to farm creatures; she could tell the scent of a sheep without any difficulty at all. Her eyes remained shut in an effort to calm herself, opening only when a picture of a snarling tiger jumped into her mind.

When she finally regained her composure, she attempted the next flight, as dark and dreary as the last. As she continued further along the way, it became even clearer that she was going to have to show someone the proper way to work a broom; her feet stepped carefully around patterns of dust that she was doing her best to memorize.

With her descent, the air about her grew ever damper, so that Naamah had to pause twice in order to wipe moisture from her forehead. By the time she reached the end of the stairway, her face was completely wet, her hair was a mess, and her dress (having ridden half a cubit up her hips) clung to a layer of dust. Because of the way she looked, she didn't know whether to cry or to scream (she was certain that the lines on her face had been accentuated by the dirt). She began to have second thoughts about whether her place was in the galley after all.

Naamah took great pains to pull her dress back in place, but the damp fabric refused to cooperate fully. When it became apparent that she looked as good as she possibly could after such an ordeal (and when she had wiped her chin carefully just in case the color from her lips had started to run), she stepped out onto the lowest level and followed the short hallway into the central passageway.

Immediately, she felt torn between turning back the way she had come or calling out to her husband. It had been an insane idea to begin with and she shook her head nervously at the thought of her own stupidity. Behind thick-barred cages on her left were the massive bears, sound asleep. Their muzzles sniffed at the air in unconsciousness, though they still appeared dangerous and would be as tall as any giant upon their hindmost paws.

Further down toward the bow, she saw a massive chamber organized in much the same manner as her aviary but with magnificent bars anchored into both floor and beamed ceiling. A huge elephant, bony-gray forehead covered with a mixture of short hay and particles of sand, watched her in amusement before sounding a trumpeted blast. She stopped herself from screaming and turned aft. According to Noah's schedule, he would be somewhere nearby.

She paid little attention to the buffaloes, for she thought them such stupid-looking creatures. The oxen were nearly as bad and she had never cared for the sight of cud-chewing camels, for they smelled like damp musk. The passageway was obviously in disarray, with its cluttered pieces of withering vines and chunks of discarded fodder lying alongside the paneled walls. She made a disgusted sound in the back of her throat as one hand pulled her dress back in place and decided that Ham must have been the last one to clean the area.

Finally, she thought she heard the soft-spoken voice of her husband and managed to push all other thoughts from her mind (though later she would be quick to tell the rest of her family some of the things she had spotted). As she walked along, she peered into storerooms and looked at giant water casks that closely resembled her own on the uppermost level. Again she heard Noah's voice but this time it was followed by a growl so terrifying that her legs froze in place, her palms grew moist, and her lips clenched tightly together in an effort to keep any sound from escaping. She wondered how far away it was to the nearest stairwell.

The growl continued like a deep-throated rumble, and the woman's eyes widened in fear as she began to imagine that the flesh-eating creature watched her from a darkened portal and readied to spring. She forced herself to take a few shuffling steps, almost deciding upon the urgency of a hasty run, when her movements brought her into view of the lion cage. It was then that she saw her white-robed husband, standing trapped behind bars against a cell wall while the enormous, maned lion guarded him closely.

Noah stood still. A metal tin of goose eggs and salted fish lay at his feet. Though he spoke in soothing tones, not seeing his wife, the huge, male lion shook its golden-red mane from side to side in defiance and snarled with white teeth and moistened gums exposed. The lion had long believed the man its captor and had had enough. The lioness (quite used to her mate's temperament) busily ate from her own large dish—her silken coat glimmering in what light there was. The lioness gave Naamah's white-faced presence only the quickest of curious stares before returning to her tin.

Naamah wanted to scream but could not and part of her was

uncertain whether such a reaction would be dangerous. She hurriedly searched her memory in an effort to remember if one of her children was close by with their duties but she could not recall, nor could she have brought herself to leave her husband's side for even a moment. As she watched his gentleness, and the way he spoke without fear and how his palms turned outward to assure the snarling cat that he concealed nothing, Naamah remembered her love for him.

Cautiously, Naamah slid her feet sideways in the direction of the cage door, erected in the same manner as that for the gazelle, the antelope, and the deer. She planned to go inside, divert the creature's attention, perhaps providing her husband with a chance to get away. Her pace was slow, as Naamah couldn't take her eyes from Noah. Even in her fear, she couldn't help but notice the dazzling purity of his white hair and robe, the smooth-skinned softness of his face, and the way not a single strand of hay clung to the weave of his garment. While her eyes remained riveted upon him and her steps inched slowly toward the doorway, the lion—with one single swift motion—raised a paw and swung at the man. Sharp claws ripped through white weave, splitting the flesh of one thigh. Noah gasped in pain as he was thrown to the ground, his blood splattering upon floor and robe. In the same moment, he tumbled to the floor, unconsciousness, and Naamah screamed.

She ran for the door of the cage and flung it open, fingers clenched in panic. In spite of her size, her tears, and the sound of the growling lion in her ears, she moved swiftly. She had just passed through the second doorway, giving no thought at all to danger, when the massive-shouldered beast backed away from its felled victim. Naamah's shouts and the straw she kicked from underfoot frightened both cats into moving even further away. With some difficulty, she lowered herself to her knees as she reached Noah.

Her eyes stared in horror at the sight of the gaping wounds, four across, permanently marring his flesh. The flow of blood caused her to feel weak as the red liquid flowed from deeply-gashed cuts, pouring over his skin until a red stream ran onto the hay and dirt and upon broken threads of Noah's perfect gown. Ever so gently, Naamah reached to touch the exposed flesh of his leg while her other hand wiped away the moisture from her eyes. She tried to call out for one of her sons, though her throat choked with sadness.

Suddenly, the light inside the cage grew brighter. It seemed to fill the cell, as if a hundred lanterns had been lit at the same time. She rubbed her eyes, which were obviously playing tricks on her but the radiance of her surroundings became almost overpowering. She started to blink incessantly and even the lions began to squint at the glow that encircled them. However, none of the illumination was as bright as that which surrounded Noah's body. The air around him began to sparkle with a thousand tiny crackles of flashing light, and the sound of rushing air swirled about them both. It was then that Naamah heard the voice of a man, though she saw no one, and his words melted the harshness she had long made a part of herself:

"Let thine eyes be opened, so you might see," the voice thundered inside of her head.

Slowly, as the radiance of the light surrounded her husband's body, the blood stopped flowing from his wounds, and the deep gashes began to shrink to become tiny cuts, before turning to scratches, then fine lines. Before Naamah's eyes, Noah's wounds diminished until they were gone.

She sat still by his side, and listened to the gentle sounds of his breath as both felines looked on in confusion. Before the sparkle of lights had subsided, she remembered the One and Methuselah's words, which had come to pass. In an instant, she was completely transformed, and her mother's personality was buried once and for all.

And as the light in the cell returned to its normal intensity, the male lion humbly bowed down as if in reverence to them both.

Aghri Dagh

As the waters began to subside, Noah and his sons saw the twin peaks of the mountain range upon which the Ark had come to rest, settling upon the side of an incline atop the highest peak, and they knew the place as Aghri Dagh.

And again he sent forth the raven which went to and fro until Noah had released its mate, and the pair circled in an effort to find a place where the waters had dried up from off the face of the earth.

Also, he sent forth a dove from him, to see if the waters were abated from off of the ground.

And the scavenger ravens stayed afloat while perched upon drifting planks from the window covering, cawing and splashing about the water's surface, eating the fish which were beginning to return, and flapping wetted wings in complete contentment over their release—they returned not again unto the Ark anymore.

But the dove found insufficient rest for the sole of her foot, and she returned unto him into the Ark, for the waters were on the face of the whole earth reached in flight: then he put forth his hand, and took her, and pulled her in unto him into the Ark.

And he waited yet another seven days; and again, he sent forth the dove out of the Ark; And the dove came in to him in the evening; and, lo, in her mouth was an olive leaf pluckt off, the likes of which caused such joy upon the Ark which had not been seen in a very long while. Thus, the green leaf of the olive showed the lower elevations were exposed, and new life had begun on the earth. And Noah knew the waters were abated from much of the ground.

And he stayed yet another seven days; and sent forth the dove and its mate, which returned not again to the craft to nest but built anew within the grove upon the greenery of the hillside.

And it came to pass in the six hundredth and first year of Noah's life, in the first month, the first day of Tishri, the waters were dried up from off the earth; and Noah and his sons removed the door to the Ark, and looked, and, behold, the face of the whole mountain was dry.

With the darkness of evening they returned to the craft, for the time of their departure had not yet arrived. Their days became spent as in the past, though each came forth from the Ark to behold the mountainside and its surroundings. When light began to dwindle from the overhead clouds of gray they returned, for a time, to the safety of the Ark, after the advice of Noah.

And in the second month, on the seven and twentieth day of Marcheshvam, was the earth dried.

And God spake unto Noah, saying, "Go forth of the Ark, thou, and thy wife, and thy sons, and thy sons' wives with thee.

"Bring forth with thee every living thing that is with thee, of all flesh, both of fowl, and of cattle, and of every creeping thing that creepeth upon the earth; that they may breed abundantly in the earth, and be fruitful, and multiply upon the earth."

And Noah went forth, and his sons, and his wife, and his sons' wives with him:

Every beast, every creeping thing, and every fowl, and whatsoever creepeth upon the earth, after their kinds, went forth out of the Ark.

373rd Day upon the Ark

Noah was certain that he heard the voice of the One upon awakening. In the last lingering moment of idleness, as he stared up at the beamed ceiling with Naamah's sleeping form lying next to him, he had heard It register inside his head not in spoken words but just as clearly as when It had come to him upon the shore of the freshwater lake. He knew the time had come. At long last, they could leave the Ark!

He reached over and stroked Naamah's bare shoulder, smiling at her when her eyes finally opened. She understood completely when he spoke the words. "It is time."

Her lips, a shade of soft pink, turned up in joy, while her eyes moistened at the news. Noah wiped away a small tear with the thumb of one hand, kissed her gently on the side of the mouth and swung his legs out from under the thin blanket.

He got up out of bed and walked immediately to the doorway, where he took the iron nail in hand and etched the final day into the paneling of their room; more than a year had passed, from the first mark to the last. Noah found himself grateful that they had not known beforehand the length of their confinement, for such knowledge would have been difficult to bear. He journeyed to the chapel to say a silent prayer of thanksgiving before awaking the rest of his family.

When all had arisen (the news had been quick to bring them to their feet) and the news of their release had been shouted with excitement back and forth among chamber doors (Miya had giggled in her mother's arms but Canaan's expression remained the same even while Maran and Ham spoke gleefully to him in baby tones) they gathered around the galley table and made plans for the release of the animals. Flesh-eating creatures could not be released at the same time as the gazelle, the rabbits, or the sheep (though the lions had seemed more content since the attack on Noah).

In the end, the others listened to Shelobothe for her knowledge of how quickly each creature could move was surpassed by none; she had been exercising each species even before anyone else had entered into the craft. Japheth was quite certain some of the animals would attempt a return to Shinar's forest (if there remained such a place)—a distance of nearly 300 leagues to the south. Others would require time to establish bearings before taking journeys into a world that had never before existed. Already, the air grew cooler as wind continued to whirl in sporadic gusts around the mountain peaks.

It was decided that each of the clean animals had to be released from the craft first; the unclean could follow three to seven days later. Some, like Curtis and Dina would remain part of the family, as well as Uzal (who was delighted to find that Naamah now let him lie in the warmth of her decreasing lap, while her firm fingers scratched beneath his chin and perked ears).

Save for the hawks, the vultures, the eagles, and the like, Noah and his sons removed the covering to the aviary and released the birds. Most were unused to the freedom of extended flight and returned again and again to the safety of the craft before setting off once more. The parakeets, the cockatoos, the parrots, and the toucans spread their wings immediately and soared in the direction of warmer climes.

Naamah stood on the outside of the mammoth ship at the base of the sloping ramp in order to see her cares take flight (though she had lost a great deal of weight, she still didn't want to take chances by venturing out onto the catwalk). She stared toward the whirling-clouded sky and watched countless birds soar far above the enormous height of the Ark. There were such numbers that the sounds of flapping wings could be heard from the ground. There were song birds and sparrows, starlings and blue jays, canaries and pheasant, ducks and hummingbirds, which she couldn't see until they came closer, honking geese and red cardinals, spotted wrens and singing swallows, and cranes and the remaining doves that quickly joined the others upon the hillside. She would feed none of them again to encourage them to look elsewhere for seed; however, she would make quite certain that the birds of prey had their fill and then some before being released.

Not long after the nearly 300 birds had tested flight, soaring around the lofty mountain peaks, Noah, Japheth, Shem, and Ham bolted the Ark's rampway firmly against the ground with thick gopher-wood stakes and iron hammers. Although the ship was sinking gradually, settling into the damp earth (already, the stern was slightly elevated above the bow), it would remain in place long enough for their purposes. Once the craft was entirely emptied of its cargo, the tremendous decrease in its weight probably would allow the enormous vessel to stabilize upon the slopes of the mountain; though no one had any intention of remaining on the Ark beyond what was required for the animals. As Maran had long foreseen, the weather was changing. Nights were becoming much too cool in the face of winds that refused to cease altogether and the mountaintop was no place to raise a family. They had decided to begin anew with fields and cottages and open expanses for the children to play at the base of the mountain—a descent of nearly 11,000 cubits.

The creatures came forth from the Ark through the massive doorway much as they had entered: walking side by side with mates when there was room, or following one another closely when there was not. Fourteen giraffes, some with necks longer than when the journey had begun came from confinement one at a time. Ropes had been tied loosely about their necks in order to persuade the animals to bow low and clear the height of the exit. Deer hooves clicked eagerly against planking as pairs were persuaded by Naamah, who held before her clumps of alfalfa in either hand to come down the ramp. Antelope looked in wonder at the grayness of the clouded sky and scattered tufts of grass making an appearance all over the ground.

After the bolts were removed, Rezepatha and Maran spent the entire morning hoisting small cages from the ship's inner walls and carrying them outside. The pair set loose field mice and squirrels, guinea pigs and furry lemmings, and floppy-eared rabbits that scampered beneath the shade of the ramp's incline for safety, twitching bobbed noses, as if shivering, until some of the larger animals were out of sight.

Ham, Shem, and Japheth began to lead the camels and gazelle to the midpoint of the mountainside with the assistance of two husky dogs nipping at hooves which fell out of place. Though neither antelope nor deer required such help (being used to such heights), the gazelle and the camels fidgeted in fear and needed to be led down the slopes, avoiding the steepest inclines, the rocks, and the narrow ravines. Not only would the journey provide Noah's sons with immeasurable knowledge for use when the family made its own descent but none had wished to risk broken limbs or animal life when all of the creatures had fared well on the journey thus far.

When the time came to bring forth the sheep from out of the craft, Shelobothe took charge of the great woolly creatures with black muzzles (except newborns), slow wits, and bleating voices that called out endlessly without waiting for reply. The men making the mountain's descent would be gone for more than a day. The lead animals appeared in no hurry, for there was much confusion while the flock crowded together on the sloping rampway before finally coming to a halt upon the ground on the outside. Noah fetched great bales of fodder and fed them in the level clearing of the Ark's starboard side. He planned that his sons would become the keepers of a great herd, allowing himself and Naamah to begin searching for any who remained of the children of the earth.

On the afternoon of the second day, after the unclean creatures had been fed and watered (which was no easy task with three of the men still away down the mountain slope), they released yawning llamas, heads held proud while eyes squinted, as well as the flightless birds. The high-pitched screech of the male peacock preceded its exit into the open air. Turkeys came next (no one doubted the senseless birds would require an escort down the mountain, as well), bumping into one another, claws scratching planked gopher-wood as heads bobbed, feathers ruffled, and scaly legs tripped over themselves. Chickens flapped wings that could not take them into flight and scurried over damp soil, looking for the insects that had not been a regular part of their diet for many months (though there had been flies and spiders, and an occasional centipede). Some chased after baby chicks that still looked like yellowed puffs. The rooster was so thoroughly confused by this time that Rezepatha made it a point to feed grain to him from the palm of her hand in an effort to bring reassurance. (In a matter of weeks, the creature's internal time would match that of the earth, and the ten could look forward to being awakened at precisely the same moment every single day.)

Wide-eyed ostriches passed through the portal, followed by squealing pigs (though they were unclean) and piglets that hurriedly slid down the sloping incline, running beneath the cautious feet of the birds. There were chimpanzees and orangutans (the gorillas came later), chattering back and forth in excitement while both used hairy limbs to pick up the small crates against the ship's side that Shelobothe had taken from the supply rooms. Monkeys shook boxes playfully while toothy smiles tried to draw the attention of one of the women (for Noah wandered the central passageways, deciding which animals came next). When the primates realized the sport was for naught, they chased after one another, ambling about swiftly on knuckles and feet, or terrified the turkeys, or hunched upon all fours to look beneath the rampway in utter fascination at rabbits and dormice almost hidden by the shade. When Noah's sons finally returned, the orangutans and chimpanzees had found the Ark's outer ladders, located on either end, and had taken over the towering catwalk. Though they playfully hooted down for a chase, none of the men had any energy to begin such a pursuit.

With the dawn of the third day Curtis and Dina (four months heavy with kid) were finally released from their pen. Neither seemed pleased, however, with having had to wait so long, yet the open freedom of the hillside soon convinced both to forget the irritation of their confinement and Curtis's bell was heard tinkling from many directions around the Ark throughout the day. The other goats followed close behind.

It wasn't long before there were cattle (and calves), zebras, and stubborn mules scattered about the slopes, munching on grasses or exercising limbs that had grown tired of walks through one of the dimly-lit hallways. Horses galloped about excitedly, their tails whisking in the air at nothing and their nostrils and flabby lips blasting out breaths in an effort to hear the sounds of freedom. Sleek ponies chased after mares on unsteady limbs that had become used to hardwood floors. Scrawny kittens rolled about the ground, entangled with tiny claws while teeth chewed playfully on one another's ears.

Naamah wore one of her simpler-patterned dresses and carried Uzal outside in her arms, while the cat lay on its back purring noisily. Clutched under her other arm, she carried the inventory sheets she had compiled with Boland; the sight of the dwarf's scribbled marks still brought her sadness. Many of the notations on the papyrus pages had been struck through as the items had been exhausted, though all of the seeds, the plant starts, the bucketed vines and the tiny sprouts remained intact.

While her husband and her sons released the remaining nonpredatory animals—the buffalo, the rams, the oxen, and the mammoth elephants who looked for a long while into Noah's sparkling eyes before blowing one final farewell salute into the air—Naamah and the other women began the tremendous task of gathering together everything they would take from the Ark: plants, clothing, tools, supplies, Maran's papyrus records (along with the rest), linens, food, the smallest water containers (the largest barrels would have to be left where they were), and the pieces of lumber which were not too awkward to carry. All were to be taken to the base of the slopes of the mountain, which was to become their home.

For the next several days, while herbivores roamed to lower elevations, finding homes in the valley, and the predatory creatures were kept amply fed and contained within the ship, Noah and his wife and his sons and his sons' wives began carting supplies, boxes, small barrels, and crates, to the midpoint of the mountain. Saddle bags of dried foodstuffs were tied to the backs of horses and camels, leather packs were flung over shoulders, and carts were filled with lumber and plant life (and monkeys who wanted a ride) and pulled upon sleds. It had taken Mixtures and hirelings a fortnight to load the Ark, and though many of the supplies had been used, it would take Noah and his family twice as long to move all they planned to keep with them halfway down the slopes of the tallest peak.

Seven days after the first creature had stepped foot from the Ark, the rest of the unclean animals were released (though each had been well fed in the early hours of morning). The eagles were let loose with the hawks into a sky that no longer fluttered with the wings of more than forty species of bird (many had already begun new nests far to the east and south). The hyena and the bears (who had been quite difficult to wake) came forth with the red-tailed fox (the male making certain his coat was well primped before the outing). In pairs, or by species, the remaining creatures left pens and cages and cells, until inner walls within the ship echoed with the sounds of footsteps or the movement of cartons and bins or hushed voices that spoke in whispers to prevent words from reverberating throughout the vast emptiness.

The leopards and the panthers darted out of the ship as swiftly as possible in an effort to find cover (Naamah stood behind Noah, watching with her hands wrapped tightly around his waist). The large cats would spend a full day upon the rocks of the second peak before making a journey in search of a jungle. The armor-coated rhinoceroses waddled through the portal doors after the big cats, the two-horned female going first. Though the pair weren't predatory, they hadn't been released earlier for there hadn't been any danger (what could eat a live rhinoceros?). The tigers followed and were quick to sprint in a direction opposite that of the leopards.

The very last to leave the Ark were the golden-maned lion and his somber mate. The pair remained for a long while, in the open doorway of the ship and looked below at the men and women (and two children) standing around the rampway. Noah stood the closest, his white hair and long robe rustling in the breeze. Naamah was right behind him, though still somewhat afraid; Japheth (with two days' growth of beard) held Miya as though he were the proudest father alive, while his other arm wrapped firmly around Rezepatha; Shem (wearing a gray robe and leaning upon a wooden staff that he appeared much too young to use despite the full beard) was next to Shelobothe, who held Canaan (for Maran and Ham had released the lions) with both hands as the boy was in the midst of a tantrum. The lions took one last turn with their noble heads, staring for a brief moment at the sheep grazing beneath the starboard hull of the enormously-planked ship, and then strolled down the incline in the direction of the valley. When the pair had vanished from sight, Maran's husky voice was the first to speak.

"It is done," she stated, as she and Ham came out of the Ark. She went to take Canaan from Shelobothe, though the child's angry stare did not change at all.

"There remains yet one task left undone," Noah said softly, as his children drew near to him. "We shall make an offering unto the One in thanksgiving, for He has delivered us from the blindness of a world that lost its way and has given us the chance to begin anew."

He took Shem, Ham, and Japheth with him to gather stones from the peak in order to build an altar unto the One. Meanwhile, Naamah, Rezepatha, Shelobothe, and Maran gathered enough stalks of wheat and fibers of grain (and a jar of tangy spice from the galley) out of the ship's hold to build a tremendous fire, one sufficient, Noah hoped, that the offering might be seen by any who survived beyond the valley.

Shem wanted to kill one of every clean beast still grazing around the Ark and of every clean fowl that remained on the hillside, such as the dove, and add their carcasses to the offering as well. Noah swiftly refused and pointed out that the One would not wish them to sacrifice the creatures they had taken such great pains to keep alive. In the end, Shem agreed it was just as acceptable to gather each of the clean animals and a few of the clean fowls as onlookers, so they, too, might surround the altar in one large circle, together with his family.

When the fibers and stalks had been piled high and the spice had been sprinkled generously throughout, the offering fire was lit. A few moments later, flames leapt from the surface of stone and a sweet savor of smoke rose throughout the air. The scent gladdened their hearts (save for Canaan's), for they felt as though they had successfully completed their enormous task. The family stood around the altar in a circle, surrounded by sheep and horses and cattle and sparrows, and Noah's doves, all scattered upon the hillside, and watched as the wind grew in intensity and caused the entire offering to become engulfed. Then, as one voice, they began the psalm that had been taught to them in the old world by Methuselah:

"Thou art maker of the heavens and all worlds. Thou hast preserved thy servant, this day, for a purpose in the earth. All silver and gold, and the cattle on a thousand hillsides are Thine, lent only that we might glorify Thee. Thou has set before us choice, that we might further come to know Thy Ways. Help us ever to choose the right path, that we may truly be a channel of Thy will and ever point the way to Thee."

The gray clouds overhead began to swirl through the sky at such speed that Noah feared the winds might blow out the flames, yet the wind upon the mountain did not increase. Suddenly, the air became heavy with moisture, and dew began to form upon the soil, the stones, and the few blades of grass. The offering flames began to die down, and as the fire went out, each person felt a tingle of warmth race up their spine; in their sincerity, they had been heard. The thundering Voice brought them, one by one, to bended knee:

Behold, I establish my covenant with thee.

The words prompted heads to bow low and eyes to become filled with tears.

And with thy seed after you; and with every living creature that is with you, of the fowl, of the cattle, and of every beast of the earth with you; from all that go out of the Ark, to every living beast upon the earth: neither shall all flesh be cut off any more by the waters of a flood, nor shall there any more be a flood to destroy the earth.

Though, even now, the vines and the trees and the limbs of the earth shall not give forth their bounty as before the flood. Every moving thing that liveth, then, shall be meat for you in accordanst with thy needs; even as the green herb have I given you all things. And the fear of you and the dread of you shall be upon every beast of the earth, and upon the fishes of the sea; into your hands are they delivered. But taking life thereof when flesh is not sustenance is forbidden, and with mine own words do I

condemn it. And beast shall not sheddeth man's blood: for within each man lies the image of his god. Neither shall man sheddeth the blood of man, or his own blood shall be shed in the same manner.

And as the One spoke, the light upon the hillside grew brighter, and their shoulders became warm; while overhead, the thick clouds of ash dissolved even further the words continued:

This covenant I make is with Me and thee and every living creature that is with you, for perpetual generations. Out of thy love did thou maketh the Ark with thine own hands and did set it before Me; out of my love for thee do I set a sign in the clouds as an everlasting token of my covenant with thee.

Without their willing it, each of the ten felt their eyes turn to the heavens, and they blinked at a brightness of sky that had never existed before. The few remaining clouds were swept aside as shimmering bands of colored light formed as a mighty arch between the peaks of Aghri Dagh, dwarfing even the Ark. The bands were red and orange and yellow and green and blue and indigo and violet, and the tingling sensation of warmth continued up their spines. The One spoke again:

I do set my bow in the clouds as a sign of this promise. And it shall come to pass, when I bring clouds over the earth, that this bow shall be seen in the clouds. And I will remember my covenant, between me and every living creature that is in the earth, and no more will a flood come to destroy all flesh.

The rays of the arch, though transparent, glistened in the moisture of the sky, as the One blessed Noah and his wife, his sons and his sons' wives, before speaking the final words:

Be ye fruitful, and multiply, and replenish the earth.

The children of the earth stared upwards at the first rainbow, at the pure blue sky which filled the heavens and at the dazzling ball of yellow fire they would come to call the sun.

A Brand New World

Against the backdrop of Aghri Dagh, beneath the pure blue firmament above a brand new world, they began again. Their new home was to be a place of peace in a world unlike any they had ever known—one that Noah had longed for and Methuselah had only dreamed about. They decided to call the place of their dwelling Erivan, for it was there that humankind first made an appearance in the world after the deluge.

The uppermost reaches of the great mountain towered far above the mighty expanse of level plains and was often hidden from view by the billowing, white clouds moving through the air of a brilliant, blue sky. Four cottages were constructed in the manner of those in the old clearing (save there was no need to take into account the height of a giant), along with a barn and great lengths of fencing that divided off the food crops from the fields for the animals. The majority of lumber came from the window coverings of the Ark, which remained intact and had settled a lengthy distance down the slope of the tallest peak. From cottage doors they looked out at the beauty of the plains: the scattered growths of wild grasses that had overtaken their surroundings, the trees, the vines, and the groundlings. The Ark's seeds and produce had been planted and everything and everyone worked hard to adjust to a new climate.

The massive ferns that had once been covered with enormous, tear-shaped leaves fared the journey worst of all. Fronds that had grown as large as a man before the Flood were now no bigger than that which could be contained in a medium-sized pot. There appeared to be changes in the rest of the fruits and vegetables as well. The harvest was no longer year round, as it had been in Shinar's fields. Each crop appeared to have its own season and time for growth. Though many of the vegetables were readily available in the months of Tammuz or Ab or Elvi, apples couldn't be plucked (and they were much smaller than they had once been) until late in Ethanim or even in Marcheshvam; pumpkins reached maturity in Kislev, along with the wheat. There was another crop of wheat in Sivan, just as the brightest flowers began to appear in the tiny garden beds outside the door stoops of each of the cottages. Corn was at its best in Elvi; and though melons were ripe and full of sweet juice in Marcheshvam, berries were usually gone by the first weeks of Tammuz.

It took several seasons of plantings before they became used to the fact there would be no new potatoes until Tishri and that walnuts were not fully ripe until Tebet. On more than one occasion, Maran, Rezepatha, and Shelobothe were grateful that Lapeth and Tamari had gone to such lengths to show them the proper methods of food preservation and storage. The talents each had acquired while preparing foodstuffs for the Ark's storerooms were quickly put to use so they could have fruit preserves in Adar and bottled tomatoes in Shebat—the two bleakest months for harvest.

Japheth saw to it that the fields benefited from methodical crop rotation, while Ham and Shem concentrated on keeping the flocks well fed, healthy, and sheared when the time came. The soil was rich with minerals (because of the waters of the deluge) and cultivated with compost (because of the labors of Noah's three sons) and would be a place of healthy vegetation for generations to come. Although the peaks of Aghri Dagh were often blanketed with white from the end of Ethanim to the first of Iyar, their place at the foot of the mountain was not covered with snow (as it would come to be called) during that entire time due to the lower elevation. However, they had plenty of frost and breath that smoked the morning's air on more than enough occasions for their liking.

When spring came with the days of Iyar (or Veadar when that month was added), the melting snow runoff from the other areas swelled the banks of the river. The headwaters of the Euphrates were at the foot of the mountain and provided the fields with complete irrigation. Though there were fish throughout much of the year (and Naamah tried diligently to prepare them with all manner of spices, in stews, baked, broiled, fried in a saucepan, steamed in crockery, or smoked in a kiln), it was a very long while before they could put more than the smallest of morsels in their mouths without becoming ill by the very thought of eating animal flesh. The deluge had caused the weather to change and along with it the abundance of crops, making food scarce for much of the year. And yet, the idea of even attempting to eat anything else besides an occasional freshwater trout was completely out of the question, which made canning and preserves all the more important. It would be a generation, indeed, before Noah's descendants could eat meat without revulsion.

The women used a great deal of wool in making warmer garments for each of them. Naamah needed a completely new wardrobe anyway, for she had become more slender than she had been at any other time in her life (which came as a great surprise to her, for their diet consisted of many different cheeses—goat and cow milk was always abundant—and breads often took the place of fresh vegetables). Perhaps the greatest change of all, however, was in her outlook. For Naamah, life had become a pleasure instead of a burden.

For the most part, the first years after the Flood were a time of immense joy. There were minor squabbles among Noah's sons and their wives, for they lived in close proximity and spent the greatest part of each day with one another but they were happy. Noah and Naamah became the closest of companions and were inseparable. They took long walks together, watching the beauty of their valley change with the seasons. They shared lengthy discussions about the One—Naamah seemed to know as much as her husband—and wistfully planned to venture from the mountain to seek out other children of the earth who might somehow have survived the deluge. They watched Miya grow into a beautiful child whose smile could cheer the saddest of gloomy countenances. She sang with the songbirds and spoke to the other creatures with such joy that Curtis and Dina followed her around incessantly when she was outdoors, and stared into the panes of cottage windows when she was not. She excelled at the game of true vision that the old mystic had taught the giant many centuries before, in spite of the fact that no one had ever taught it to her. She was gentle in manner, and radiant, and perfect in every detail. In all respects, she embodied everything that Noah had ever hoped would be a part of their new world.

And then there was Canaan.

With each passing year, he grew more bitter and angry. Though perfect in form as well, an unsteady gait gave him the walk of a Mixture, and his eyes lacked any sparkle whatsoever and were accentuated with a brow that became darker with the passage of time. His face was continually gloomy and even Miya's and Noah's and his grandmother's determined attentions could do nothing to move him. He refused to be held or kissed or coerced into listening to stories of the One, nor did he take any interest in what the others were doing. At four, he went out of his way to squash worms, frogs, crickets, and ants with his small feet (regardless of whether or not his toes were bare), and twice, he deliberately broke the neck of a baby chick. Ham never found it in his heart to tell Maran, though she saw these things and worse when her Sight returned.

As Canaan grew older, he finally found something that gave him immense joy. Maran and Ham had three additional sons after the landing at Aghri Dagh, and Canaan found it his duty to command them. As often as he could, he tormented his younger brothers, Cush, Phut, and Mizraim (who came to be called Jeurepth when he became a counselor to others), with both his words and his deeds.

At the age of seven, one hot afternoon, Canaan's stomping feet and angry fists ripped entire root systems from the soil, destroying many of the vines, groundlings, and plants that Japheth had taken such pains to keep alive upon the Ark. There would be no yellow-seed flowers that season, nor would they have dried grapes for raisins in the fall. Despite his wisdom and knowledge of living things, Noah could save only a few of the growths and the remainder were tilled beneath the earth. Because of Canaan's misdeed, Rezepatha, heavy with her fifth child (besides Miya, there were Gomer, Magog, and Tiras, who they called Pelus), sobbed aloud, and Japheth wiped moisture from his eyes. There was much sadness at Erivan, except in Canaan's mind, for many days to come.

The four grape vines that Noah managed to salvage (and they were pitiful in appearance, with bent limbs and broken leaves) were carefully planted along the fencing which lay at the edge of the fields—far from the cottages for their safety. Nearby, Noah raised a small tent where he might find quiet with Naamah for their periods of the silence. Those moments away from the bustle of cottage life were necessary for them both, for Shem and Shelobothe also had their own sons now: Elam, Asshur, Arphaxad (who was born two years after the Flood), and Lud.

Less than eight years after the floodwaters abated and the first rainbow formed, there were more than a dozen grandchildren at the foot of the peaks of Aghri Dagh—and not a one gave the rising and setting of the sun in a sky lacking all trace of the overhead vapors a second notice at all.

As the size of Noah's family grew, so, too, did the numbers of creatures in the fields, grazing along the banks of the river, and within the fenced confines adjacent to the barn. There were large, cackling chickens with sturdy pronged feet, silken white feathers, and plump breasts that resulted from many calm hours of leisure (save when Canaan sneaked into the hen house) and great quantities of the richest feed. Majestic horses with muscular limbs and gentle muzzles (eager to be stroked) stood readied for the journey that Noah always promised to make beyond the shadow of Aghri Dagh, though he had yet to find the time. There were cows for milk and sheep for wool; dogs and cats to chase after mice or to be chased by the children (Uzal, however, stayed in the warmth and comfort of the cottage, preferring Naamah's lap most of all). There were loud, honking geese whose eggs were tried on occasion, along with those of the hens. There were countless squirrels, prairie creatures, and wild rabbits that hid in the shade and foliage of the spreading grape vines that began to thrive in the solitude around Noah's tent. And then there were the goats.

After the landing at Erivan, Curtis and Dina had their first kid (goats gestated their young for nearly five months) which was born with great mounds of full-bodied hair, and wide eyes eager to see its surroundings. Four hours after being birthed, the young kid could run and jump, through its weak legs gave the appearance of a youngster who could only stumble and trip. It followed around after a very proud mother and a bell-clanging father.

When a year had passed, Curtis and Dina had another kid, a female, and in the next season they brought forth twins, and so it went, until eleven years after the deluge (which happened to be four years after Noah replanted the grapevines). In truth, so many things occurred at Erivan that Maran's written account filled many more pages than all the years that had preceded it.

Dina the goat was sick—far more than just mildly ill—and her appearance made it obvious that she was dying. Her color had become extremely pale, her furry knees were so wobbly that they were unable to support her weight, the whiskers of her chin were brittle to the touch, and whole handfuls of hair fell from her pink hide without apparent reason. No longer could she romp around the cottage, looking for Miya, or run through the fields, catching the warmth of the sun. She could barely lift her head from a bed of soft straw in order to take nourishment. The women of Erivan poured generous amounts of liquid between Dina's cracked lips, while Noah's sons sought out the choicest plants, vines, and medicinal roots for her diet. Nothing anyone did for her seemed to help.

The change that came over Curtis was overwhelming. He refused to leave her side for more than the briefest of moments, though the urge to run free through the grasses and wide open plains was as strong as ever. Instead, he spent long hours standing over her prostrate form, nudging his nose against her neck and side to bring comfort and affection.

Naamah took time to brush down Dina's back, belly, and limbs, though it only made the creature's hair fall out more swiftly. Noah tried to treat the goat's ailment in the manner shown to him by his grandfather but it was useless. It wasn't until Maran had spent an hour in the quiet of the barn alone with the two goats that anyone realized what was happening, and her husky-voiced answer given as they gathered around the cottages was more terrifying than anything they might have imagined on their own:

"Dina is dying of old age."

"But how can that be?" came Shelobothe's quick retort. "She is no older than twelve, for she was merely a kid when she entered the clearing!"

"You must be mistaken," Ham said positively, though his response was spoken without malice.

"I know this with the Sight," she replied, so there could be no doubt, "A she-goat, which has yet to see its second decade, will die within three days of old age."

"Poor Curtis," Japheth said somberly as Rezepatha took his hand.

Naamah shook her head sadly, standing on the cottage door, holding Uzal in her arms, and looked to Noah, "I certainly never heard of such a thing before the Flood. We all know Dina has been lovingly cared for. What has happened?"

As if in answer to her question, the line of shade striking the trampled earth perpendicular to their cottages began to dwindle in the doorway, and the brightness of the heavens peaked over the roof, splattering rays of light upon their faces.

"The sun!" Noah and Maran answered simultaneously.

Shem lifted his fully bearded face to look skyward (after having checked out of the corner of his eye to make certain Elam and Asshur were not being bothered from where they played by Canaan). "Then we shall be affected, as well," he said, positively, "and each of the animals, and our children and our children's children."

"It would appear the vapors held back more than our weather alone," Rezepatha managed to say.

"What does it mean?" Miya's melodic voice asked, as she approached their gathering. Her walk possessed the certainty of one who was much older, and even at eleven, she was every bit as beautiful as Lapeth had been in her youth.

"Shorter spans of life," Maran replied without hesitation.

Miya nodded and seemed to understand without fear.

Japheth watched his daughter's beauty and maturity and was thankful that they were not surrounded by the men and the Mixtures of the clearing. Already, he had caught Canaan looking at her in a manner that should have been beyond a youth of his years. "Perhaps we won't be affected immediately," he said finally, "or even for generations to come. Curtis does not appear harmed, nor do any of the other creatures. The plants have adjusted, for the most part. The melons are ready to be gathered from the vine. The sunflower seeds (as Shelobothe had decided to call the yellow-seed flowers for they had the appearance of the sky's yellow ball of fire) can be roasted in the kilns at any time, and the plumpness of father's grapes indicates they should have been plucked more than a week ago.

"None of us seems to have been injured (he was quite certain that Canaan's surliness had little to do with the disappearance of the vapors), so it may take time before our own lives show signs of it."

"But it will be life!" Noah interrupted emphatically. He turned to each of his children, and their wives and stressed the point they had apparently overlooked. "It will be life as it was meant to be lived! We have been given a new beginning in a world of hope, safe from the deeds of the past. The length of each sojourn matters not, for we have a chance to begin anew. At long last, we might become what the One intended. Surely no greater gift could be ours."

Naamah smiled at her husband's words, taking his hand in her own. Never had they been happier together; truly, they had become companions. They were the best of friends, with so very much to live for—their family, the work they would do beyond the valley (the journey seemed a real possibility now that their children were settled) —and they had much love.

As their children concurred among themselves about what he had said, she whispered up to him, "I do love you."

"And I, you," he answered.

Two days later, Dina was laid to rest beneath the rich soil of the plains and Curtis began a lonely vigil, standing above her graveside, bleating out in sorrow over a loss that would not be consoled. Through it all, Maran couldn't help but wonder whether Dina's passing merely foreshadowed that which was to come for them all.

And Noah never did get a chance, that season, to pick his grapes from the vines before they began to sour.

Noah could have never imagined in all of his long years how completely devastating it would be. No words could explain the way he felt. There was nothing that could ease the pain. No healing technique that could mend the ache that ripped through his body. No one who could bring him comfort. Nothing he might do to help himself. He had neither the strength nor the will to go on with life. Though each hour seemed endless and the endless hours of sorrow gave way to days, and the days amassed into weeks until nearly a month had passed, he still couldn't believe it had happened. Over and over again, he had to tell himself it was true, that it had really occurred, but even then he would forget—in those rare moments when the grief lifted—and some ordinary thought would come into his mind, something he just had to share with her—and then remembered that he couldn't. Then it would start all over again, and he'd have to tell himself more than a thousand times each and every day that Naamah was dead.

It was the hardest, most difficult, most painful thought Noah had ever held inside of his head. Worse even than watching Traibus die. Or the time he had fallen to his knees in the Ark's doorway. More sorrowful than having to say goodbye to Methuselah and Lapeth when they had been still very much alive, and remembering, later, so many things he had wanted to say. The reality of Naamah's death was as frightening (on occasion even more so) as the thoughts he had once had that their work with the children of the One in the city of Shinar might fail. He couldn't shake his sorrow or his fear or his loneliness, and even when his thoughts were his own to control, he didn't want to.

He had awakened one morning—one just like all the rest—when the fresh air of daybreak seemed to dance upon the ground and his mind was filled with thoughts of what might be done with the day—and he had found her gone. Without apparent reason, she had died. Not that a reason might bring him solace but her death had never, ever, been expected, and having no reason left him devastated. The one thought that continued to enter his mind—once the plans for the day were discarded—was that it just wasn't fair; he had done all that the One had asked of him, and yet, his own reason for life had been taken.

Perhaps, she had died like Dina, though age had not stricken her features; perhaps, she had finished her purpose for life, though he believed they had but begun; perhaps, she had known, herself, that her time drew near, for their last days—and those all-too-brief nights together—had been perfect. All he could think of was that she was gone, and his children and his grandchildren—even Miya—could not bring him comfort. In fact, he found himself angered at the rest of them for having gotten on with their lives so quickly, as if Naamah had not been as essential to them all as she had been to him. Only Curtis, it seemed, felt grief as Noah had come to know it.

The two of them—the gentle, white-haired man and the gray-streaked goat—remained apart from the others, eating sometimes when food was brought to them (but only enough to stay alive), and sharing a sadness that only they could understand. Noah sat cross-legged in the flapping doorway of his tent, staring in the direction of the fencing and the clinging vines and the great bunches of soured grapes, but he saw only Naamah. Curtis who had cried out so frequently that his voice had finally left him, rubbed his whiskered muzzle against Noah when he needed to reaffirm their mutual loss. The goat's life seemed as useless as Noah's.

For that reason, it came as a great surprise to Noah one morning to find Curtis prancing back and forth between the fencing and the tent, appearing as joyful as he had ever been in his youth. To Noah's amazement, the goat nipped playfully at tiny moths and wild grasses, kicking hooves against the earth simply to dislodge soil into a cloud of dust, racing his own shadow for entertainment, and rolling upon the ground (his hairy coat already completely covered with fallen leaves, yellowed grass, and layers upon layers of dirt). All the while, though his voice had not yet returned completely, he blurted out uneven noises that did not contain one shred of sadness, stopping only long enough to chomp down another bunch of shriveled, darkened, plentiful, grapes.

Even Noah's sorrow, still heavy on his mind, could not hold back a grin at Curtis's antics. He walked toward the creature, his once flawless, white robe tattered, ripped, and hanging unevenly (his appearance was quite haggard, for he had let himself go much too long) and reached to scratch the goat's neck.

"What's gotten into you?" His voice cracked, for he had not spoken aloud in more than a week.

He continued stroking Curtis, while the animal continued chewing, and looked the goat over thoroughly for any signs that might account for the change. Though the goat was thinner and much more unkempt, the only difference appeared to be the creature's eyes: shiny and widened and glossed over with a look of complete and utter contentment and the fact that the creature's whiskers appeared covered with a purple hue. Something had happened, but what?

After looking about, it didn't take Noah long to pluck one small grape from a cluster himself, tasting it cautiously at first (for its flavor was much like that of a bitter lemon). The second was the same, and the third, and so on, until Noah decided that he had been wrong, and it wasn't the grapes at all that had produced such a state in his friend. But by the time Noah had finished several handfuls—for he had not eaten any breakfast—the flavor was more to his liking, and he continued to feed himself even though Curtis had stopped and was resting from the morning's antics.

Noah couldn't help but feel uplifted; even the thought of Curtis rolling in the grass brought a smile to his lips, and then a laugh. He found himself chuckling and then couldn't stop, reflecting on of what a fool the goat had made of itself without apparent cause. He began to feel full and hot at the same time and quickly wiped his mouth on his sleeve (which was already stained), for he was quite certain some of the purple juice had slipped through his lips and was running down his chin.

It was at that moment, as the cloth of his robe rubbed against his face, that he realized something was wrong; the skin of his face felt quite numb, and yet, it buzzed with warmth. He laughed aloud, slapping the side of his leg with glee—much as Gravas might have done—and realized that the soured grapes were more delightful than any ale he had ever tasted.

He turned to tell someone, anyone, what he had discovered but Curtis appeared to be asleep and there was no one else within sight. And then he realized that the quick movement of swinging around had made him quite dizzy and he walked (stumbled, actually) toward the door of his tent to lie down for a moment. He chuckled again and then began to remove his robe, without giving it much thought, for he was beginning to sweat profusely from the heat, before finally lowering himself with a large measure of difficulty to his mat on the ground. He knew now why Curtis had felt well enough to chase after shadows, and he might have done so himself, had he managed to get up. But he felt heavy, and dizzy, and weighed down, and so very sleepy, for he had eaten far too much.

And although he felt giddy, he began to wonder what good it would be to be alive in a world of constant hope—far removed, forever, from the faults of the past—when the one he wanted to share it with was gone. In his last conscious moments, he understood what was about to occur, for it had happened before. There, all alone in his tent, during the hours of early morning, free for a time from his thoughts of self-pity, Noah received a dream:

Decades had passed, generations of time; children had grown older, bearing children of their own. On many continents, the greenery of the planet had regained its bounty. Creatures of the earth had multiplied many times tenfold. And one of the youths at Erivan had become a man.

There was no doubt who it was, his eyes as dark and glaring as they had been since birth, his gait more uneven than ever, his hands coarse and rough, and the perfect flesh of his body giving way to thick tufts of hair. His scowl was angry—a diseased mind gave life to thoughts of wickedness, surpassed in evil only by his deeds. He was most cursed among all the people of the earth, more hateful and hated than any had been since the days of overseers (and lost souls who found sport only in the torture of other men). He was accursed beyond the sin of Cain—and descended directly from the line of Noah. Canaan had come of age.

Though Maran and Ham had done much to teach their children in all manner of things that were right—the ways of the Law, the truth of the One, and the tenets of old—their eldest son never harkened after the Way. It should have come as no surprise, but as Canaan grew older his influence upon his younger brothers increased. Now Phut and Cush had become much like the eldest and followed his every lead. Jeurepth followed after the ways of his grandfather, and his grandfather's grandfather before him, so that the love of the One might be made manifest in the earth.

It seemed that Noah and Naamah also had been right all along: Those from the Ark were not alone among the surviving people of the earth, for others had come to settle at Erivan—old women with their memories and men with their stories of the past, youths with great dreams, and children with the greatest potential for hope that had ever come into the earth at one time. All were hungry for what Noah's sons and daughters-in-law might teach about what was holy and found favorable in the sight of the One, but over them, as well, Canaan began to exercise his dominion. He became a master of men, a king at the foot of Aghri Dagh. His sovereignty had come to pass. Those who posed threats to his rise disappeared in the darkness of night—man, woman, child, or brother. Those who assisted him became masters in their own right. Canaan hoarded the wealth of the city, the valley, and even beyond, rewarding those he favored, as well as those who offered their favors up unto him.

He longed to number among his possessions all that was beautiful, all that could be had by mortal men. The lust of his loins lacked any discrimination, nor could it be satisfied (there was no doubt in his mind he would lie with Miya). He took into account the life of no one, save his own. In time, the deeds of his kingdom would curse the very ground upon which it was built; his evil influence would be felt for generations. Because of Canaan, the sins of the earth would become greater than ever before. He intended to have dominion over all the earth, and the ways of Noah and Methuselah and the line back to Seth would be no more.

It the dream, Noah became lucid; while still asleep, he realized there could be but one answer: Canaan's life had to become subservient to the rest, else Canaan would make himself master over all, and hope would be lost among the children of the Earth—and the waters of the flood would have been for naught.

From the place of hiding where he often obtained worthwhile information, Canaan had overheard his father and his uncles discussing Noah's state. Not only had it given him the urge to laugh, but he wished exceedingly to see the old man's condition himself. For as long as he could remember—though he was not yet eleven—Canaan had been disgusted by tales of the One, of Methuselah (who sounded even more crazed than his grandfather), and of Noah's senseless ways. The man was an old fool who was forever hearing and seeing things, a man who had deceived himself and others into believing he had spoken with angels. The mere thought of his grandfather's stupidity sickened him.

He couldn't wait to see the disheveled hair, the stained robe (which his mother had once claimed couldn't be blemished), the destroyed appearance of an old man who everyone held in such esteem. His grandmother had been as disgusting, but she, at least, had served a purpose: Naamah's death made his grandfather out to be the hypocrite Canaan had always known him to be; it seemed that Noah had lived for his wife and not "the One" after all.

Canaan moved quietly through the wild grass plains—he had trained himself to sneak up upon all kinds of living things—dragging his left leg as if it were lame, though, in truth, it simply felt more natural that way. His squinting eyes, bothered by the light of the sun, watched for any signs of movement around the lone tent, but there was none. He spotted a bloated Curtis, a fitting companion for any simpleton, lying in a stupor, yet Canaan had no desire to inspect the creature when his grandfather's imagined appearance promised such rare entertainment. He gave a quick thought to emptying his bladder upon the leather tarp or defecating in the old man's doorway and then racing back to describe vividly into what depths Noah had sunk but Canaan hadn't accounted for the whereabouts of the rest of his family and being caught in such an act would serve no purpose (besides, the tent could be spotted from a long way off).

He crouched at the entrance for a moment and listened, finding himself quite pleased. A smirk took hold of his lips when the only sound coming through the doorway was that of deep breathing. With one swift, though quiet, movement, he flung open the flap and peered inside: The sight surpassed his wildest expectations, and he had to stop himself from laughing out loud.

Noah was naked as a babe, save for a gold chain and coin he wore about his neck. Canaan's initial thought was to run and fetch Miya, for seeing Noah thusly (as bare as the day he was born, with flesh aged and creased beyond its youthful vigor) would forever destroy her senseless devotion. However, he certainly didn't want his grandfather to awaken before his father, and Japheth and Shem had seen him. For that reason, Canaan decided to retrieve them first.

One of the greatest tragedies of human nature is when a father can no longer trust his own son; Ham had long been in such a position. When Canaan had left the cottages at the base of the mountain, Ham followed after him in order to halt whatever transgression the youth planned to commit, for the boy's creeping manner made his intentions quite obvious. So when Canaan turned around to go back, he found his father standing behind him.

"What are you doing now?" the elder man asked sorrowfully.

Canaan was speechless and Ham became so after spotting his own father's nakedness through the open doorway. He didn't know how but Ham was certain Canaan had something to do with Noah's appearance. Without wasting any time he took the boy, gruffly, by the arm, and went back to get Japheth and Shem so the three of them might decide how to help their father. When Noah's sons returned to the tent, Shem and Japheth brought a clean robe, while Ham clutched his son's arm, though the youth tried to break free several times. Ham didn't dare let the boy out of his sight.

In honor of and respect for their father, Shem and Japheth took the clean garment between them and went backward into the tent to cover Noah's nakedness. Shem had thought it best, since he had no desire to let the sight of his father's exposure mar the image of the holy man he kept foremost in his mind.

Noah began to rouse from the effects of the grapes and finished dressing himself. He had awakened, knowing all that Canaan, his eldest grandson, whom he had loved, thought of him. He came out of the tent looking his old self; his blue eyes sparkled as they had done before Naamah's death, and he knew without doubt what had to be done. He embraced each of his sons, assuring them he had returned and finally whispered in Ham's ear when the time came:

"What must follow saddens me more than you may ever know." He paused for only a moment, thinking life into the words that had to be spoken and then looked toward Canaan, who stared back at him with complete hatred.

Noah pointed at his grandson and said, "Cursed be Canaan; a servant of servants shall he be unto his brethren all the days of his life." And he blessed Shem and Japheth and proclaimed that, forevermore, Canaan should be their slave, for Noah hadn't the heart to make Ham master over his own son.

Noah was not in the least surprised when nearly thirty settlers with six wagons and supplies and a meager herd of livestock came to their place at Erivan. The caravan was greeted with such merrymaking and laughter—women kissing one another and passing around children, while men jumped about, embracing and shouting in an effort to be heard—that nothing at all, neither Naamah's passing nor Canaan's servitude, could dull the celebration. When it was learned, however, that four of the men and one of the women (with their wives and a husband and twelve children between them) had been sired by Jabal, the tentmaker, Noah's eyes widened with amazement. Two of the women in the group, as blonde in appearance as Adah had been in the marketplace, said their father was Jubal, the musician. The rest were farmers, craftsmen, a leatherworker, and a seamstress, all from the east (not one had ever heard of a masterbuilder called Anon), and all were ready to begin again.

It was not long before they were joined by other travelers as well. Some had wished to climb the highest peak of Aghri Dagh, though it lay buried in snow for much of the year, in an effort to see the entire range. Others had wandered from far away. A few laid claim to having dreamed a dream. It was soon clear that Erivan had not been the sole place of humanity's reappearance after the waters had dried from the face of the earth. Dissension arose (some claimed it had been started by a slave) because the city had been misnamed. After much discussion, the many people decided to rename their homeland Ahora—with its fences, gates, rows of tents, and cottages being raised every day—for it lay at the foot of the mountain.

With the passage of time and with the marriages and betrothals that are worthy of a brand new world, children grew up and begot children of their own and Ahora grew to become one of the grandest cities upon the earth. Had Noah's wish for his sons and their wives and their children and those who came after been fulfilled, there would have been only hope and love at the base of the mountain, but truth fell far short of the dream.

Though the city was grand in size, it lacked the perfect peace for which Noah had always longed. As the population grew so too did dissension, discontent, and opposition among the people—even Noah's sons began to disagree among themselves, threatening to undermine what remained known of the One. But life went on, and in time both Uzal and Curtis passed away.

Japheth and Rezepatha had four additional sons (as recorded by Maran): Madai (who was birthed in the same year as Canaan's destruction of the groundlings), Javan, Meshech, and Tubal (named for his uncle). In the same span of decades, Shelobothe and Shem had only one more son, Aram, who grew to manhood and married in the summer that Miya's sixth child was born; she had wedded one of the youths from the first caravan.

Despite Noah's best efforts, strife continued to worsen among Naamah's three sons, for each held strong opinions as to how Ahora should be governed and organized. Japheth and Shem remained fearful of Canaan's continuing influence upon some of the others, for Cush and Phut had grown into the very image of Noah's feared dream. For decades, Jeurepth took it upon himself to be peacemaker among his uncles, his father, and his many cousins—even trying to settle their many quarrels. But even his optimism could not set all things right, and finally, Noah could find but one solution.

While he yet lived and his sons still harkened after his word, though they had become old men themselves (Shem had witnessed the birth of his grandson's grandson!), the patriarch divided the people of Ahora according to their disposition and in line with which of his sons they wished to follow.

Shem and his people took hold of lands to the south and far east, including Shinar and Sheba, Persia and the Gangem. Ham and his followers claimed as theirs everything south of the Great Sea: Libya and Mizraim, Nubia and the like. Japheth and his own took Ahora and all northern lands, including Scythia and Macedonia, Gomer and Dodanim. Soon, the three sons were separated by great expanses across the continent, for Noah divided the earth among them.

Now these are the generations of the sons of Noah, Shem, Ham and Japheth: and unto them were sons born after the Flood.

The sons of Japheth; Gomer, and Magog, and Madai, and Javan, and Tubal, and Meshech, and Tiras (who was called Pelus).

And the sons of Gomer; Ashkenaz, and Riphath and Togarmah.

And the sons of Javan; Elishah, and Tarshish, Kittim, and Dodanim.

And the sons of Ham; Cush, and Mizraim (who was called Jeurepth), and Phut, and Canaan.

And the sons of Cush; Seba, and Havilah, and Sabtah, and Raamah, and Sabtechah: and the sons of Raamah: Sheba and Dedan.

And Mizraim begat Ludim, and Anamim, and Lehabim, and Naphtuhim.

And Pathrusim, and Casluhim (out of whom came Philistim,) and Caphtorim.

And Canaan begat Sidon his firstborn, and Heth, And the Jebusite, and the Amorite, and the Girgasite.

And the Hivite, and the arkite, and the Sinite, And the Arvadite, and the Zemarite, and the Hamathite: and afterward were the families of the Canaanites spread abroad.

The children of Shem; Elam, and Asshur, and Arphaxad, and Lud, and Aram.

And the children of Aram; Uz, and Hul, and Gether, and Mash.

And Arphaxad begat Salah; and Salah begat Eber.

And unto Eber were born two sons: the name of one was Peleg; for in his days was the earth divided; and his brother's name was Joktan.

These are the families of the sons of Noah, after their generations, in their nations: and by these were the nations divided in the earth after the Flood.

Noah made one final trip to the uppermost peaks of Aghri Dagh the summer before his death. Assisted by only a staff and a few meager supplies tucked inside his sleeve, and with neither tent nor guide nor pack, he ascended the tremendous mountain pass alone. For many years, he had vowed to go back just once more but he had never found the time, dividing the remainder of his days between his sons and their lands. The knowledge that life was about to draw to an end made him finally determined to make the journey.

He was a very old man, with wearied, moccasined feet and vivid thoughts of yesterdays that often felt more real than the present. Only Methuselah had lived so long. But the world had been different then: a place where no sun beat down upon human flesh, scorching skin and creasing lines into permanence; a world where sages dreamed of the very brightest futures and reached out for a hope that seemed near. Instead, old men now looked backward, trying to recapture shadows of promises that had never been realized, and aspired (with little success) to teach their children lessons that should have been learned from the past.

He had told Maran all he could remember of the children of

the One and had long since related everything he knew of the people of the earth and of healing, of life, and of love. She had taken it all down—to be placed with the rest—including his knowledge of crops, of vines, and of herbs and their medicinal properties. He told of ancient wisdom, of faith, and of that which he knew of prophecy—all written down in Maran's script and totaling more than a dozen volumes that combined would become the Books of Noah. He spoke of the tenets of the One, of the Universal Laws he had come to know firsthand, of the world's wonders and the majesty that lay just beyond; he dictated the Sefer ha-Razim—and Maran captured every word.

And, as they had for Methuselah, mystery and wonder surrounded Noah's latter days, and the people constructed stories and tales about his great power. They believed he could take the shape of countless forms or appear to be any age (though he chose that of an old man). Some claimed he had no need of food or drink, though he partook to be among the people; that he conferred with the angels on High; and traveled upon the wings of the wind. On more than one occasion, they noticed how Ham or Shem or Japheth—separated by vast distances—had simply been thinking about their father, and Noah would immediately step foot in their city, or peer out from behind a tree with a smile like that of his grandfather.

The same smile parted his lips when he finally passed over the snow-covered summit with the aid of his staff and knew that it hadn't been a dream after all. He saw the Ark below him, just as he had left it so very long ago. Although it had slid upon its hull further down the slope of the largest peak, it had come to rest in the safety of a small valley. The rocks of the mountain surrounded the ship on all sides, providing a great deal of protection from the wind. The lowest portion of the craft was blanketed with nearly twenty cubits of snow; the rest had melted in the warmest days of spring and summer. From the appearance of things, he was quite certain that the mighty planks, the catwalk, and the windows of the ship had to be buried throughout the long months of the coldest part of the year. He stood completely still to look upon the site before finally convincing himself to venture inside, and when he did so it was through the overhead window of a storage room, for the immense doorway in the ship's hull lay hidden behind a frozen drift.

For a long while, he walked alone with his thoughts through the lengthy hallways and passages of the ship, while the sound of his feet echoed against the silence. With the use of an old lamp left aboard, he looked into many of the stalls and compartments and took time to see the massive water barrels. He walked through storage rooms and stairways and peered over the railing of the giraffe pit—all the while feeling such emptiness. He walked through the aviary and looked, without success, for signs that any of the birds had returned for a time. He paused in the chapel to say a prayer of thanksgiving for having seen it all once more, before heading to the galley and his own chambers beyond.

The greater part of an hour passed as he stood alone in the room he had shared with Naamah, thinking of all the time they had wasted. He ran his fingers over the marks on the wall and tried desperately to recall every event of one solitary day. Finally, by lamplight, he turned to look at the divan—the place he had shared with Naamah—and decided that Methuselah had been right all along:

"A man shouldn't have to live so long," Methuselah had said, and his grandfather's remembered voice broke the silence of centuries.

When Noah had seen all that he wished to and all that he could bear, he journeyed forth from the snowy summit and headed in the direction of the land of Ham, for there remained yet one more tale he wished to relate to Maran.

Noah spent the remainder of his days among his children, and his children's children. There is a tradition that says he saw 14,400 of his descendants, for he lived 350 years after the waters of cleansing had come to the earth.

And all the days of Noah were 950 years, and he died.

The World's Quest for the Ark

And the whole earth was of one language and one speech, though the lands had been divided. The sons of Noah—Ham, Shem and Japheth—led kingdoms in their own right and brought forth nations in accordance with the best each had come to know. For a time, Japheth's people stayed beneath the shadow of the mountain and learned of herbs and farming, of the best methods of cultivating the ground; generation upon generation studied the soil so that the people might bring forth the choicest grasses, produce, fruits, and vegetables. They longed to work with the elements of the earth as the means to improve man's physical state. Japheth wished his people to retain forever their perfection of the flesh and to become more in keeping with the things of the Spirit. In time, his seven sons divided his lands, and the isles to the north and west—and their descendants came to be called the Gentiles.

Ham and his followers took control of an entire continent to the south: a place of great riches and majesty and also of barren wastelands where nothing would grow. His kingdom was one of opposites with its jungles and deserts, its wide-open plains, and with a vastness of minerals found nowhere else on earth. His people were led to become builders and artisans, while his wife instructed them in the ancient teachings and the beauty of the written word, explaining that with the power of the mind, men and women everywhere might develop into that which the One intended.

Shem went into Carpathia and Byzantine, into portions of Arabia and all the Chaldean lands. He studied the laws of his forefathers and established a school of prophets; one day he would know the High Priest Melchizedek. He believed in the awakening of the soul, and taught his people so they might begin to remember from where they had come. He became the father of the Hebrew nation—and Israel was his own.

When the memory of Noah and his wife and of his sons and his son's wives had become simply tales of old in the minds of aged men, the world changed again from what it had been. Though Japheth had loved the One and expressed that love through his labors in the field, the children of his descendants misunderstood and began to worship the soil, the earth, and the like. They offered their praises to the sun, the moon, and the stars, and they no longer had need for a God known only to their forefathers.

Cush, the son of Ham, fathered Nimrod, who was a brave and mighty hunter. And Nimrod built the cities of Nineveh and Rehoboth and Calah, and with his people, began the tower at Babel. With time and greed, his descendants and their many languages conquered all but the Israelites. Canaan, the father of slaves, begat children of his own (for even a slave may take a wife) and taught them hatred all the days of his life. He showed them the worship of idols and all things of selfishness and upon his deathbed, he left them three simple rules to live by: "Hate your masters and never speak the truth; pursue robbery and unchastity; and let there be love only between yourselves." And Canaan's descendants and those of his brothers (save for Jeurepth, who remained in Egypt) founded the cities of Sodom and Gomorrah.

Shem lived a total of 600 years and he fathered both sons and daughters. Peleg, his grandson's grandson (in whose days the earth was divided), lived all of 239 years and fathered sons and daughters. And Terah, the grandson's grandson of Peleg, lived all of 205 years and fathered sons and daughters. And so it went, for the vapor of clouds had disappeared from the sky and the children of the earth might never again live so long. There were those among Shem's descendants who founded Greece and the worship of many gods, but there were others like Terah who remained true to the Law.

And Terah was the father of Abram (whose name means "one being called"), who became Abraham, whose seed was multiplied as the sand upon the seashore and as the stars within the heavens.

Because their hearts had been pure and they had harkened after the One, there were Mixtures and deformities who survived the waters of the Flood and came into Egypt to be healed. Enormous temples were built so that they might be purified of all that hindered, whether of body, mind, or soul. The mighty sphinx was raised upon the sands of the desert as a monument to those who came to be cleansed and as a reminder of that which had existed before the Deluge.

On the coast of the Great Sea in the land of the desert sun, a place of learning began in the city of Alexandria. Sages arrived from the far reaches of the earth to teach and be taught. It was there in a columned library that the writings of Adam and Methuselah and Maran came to rest. For thousands of years, holy men studied the works and left behind knowledge of their own. It was from the material written down by Maran and those who had gone before her that Moses and his scribe compiled the Torah.

The knowledge of healing and medicine, which came from Noah, was handed down to the physicians of Greece and India and the Sefer ha-Razim became the text of ancient mystics. The Books of Noah were read and reread along with the rest at Alexandria—knowledge from the dawn of time. Philosophers, priests, wise men, and novices arrived with unquenchable thirsts for knowledge. There are those who claim that even the Nazarene came to the city to be taught.

In the sixth century after the death of this one called the Christ, the powerful caliph, Omar, gazed upon the ancient library and its books and decided that in light of the Koran the texts were no longer necessary. For six months, in the year A.D. 636, thousands of aged books of wisdom and tenets of old fed the fires of Alexandria's public baths, and the papyrus of Adam, the scripts of Methuselah and Maran, and the Books of Noah were destroyed, along with the rest.

There is an ancient legend among the people of the Armenian range that God now forbids an ascent to the highest reaches of the mountain. There had been a time, for thousands of years, when pilgrims climbed the tallest peak during the warmest months of summer to gaze upon the Ark and to offer worship unto the Lord. But the descendants of Canaan undertook to destroy the craft and the fanciful stories surrounding it. When they neared the summit, however, a mighty storm washed them from their trail and lightening disfigured the rocks; the approach to the lofty valley no longer appeared the same. From then on, the faithful refrained from their journeys for fear of betraying the Ark's location. Yet the stories, the legends, and the tales continued from generation to generation, and on occasion a solitary traveler or a shepherd alone with his flock descended the slopes and spoke of having seen the prow of a ship through layers of melting snow and ice.

In 275 B.C., Berosus, a Babylonian high priest, made reference to the enormous ship and its covering of dark pitch, and claimed that travelers were able to obtain remnants of the wood and its pitch.

Josephus Flavius, the Jewish historian, stated in A.D. 93 that inhabitants of the area could still point out remnants of the Ark to travelers.

Theophilus of Antioch, a bishop of the Church, wrote in A.D. 180 that the Ark could still be seen.

In A.D. 400, a monk called Ephiphanius of Salimas, claimed that the Ark could still be found upon the mountain slopes.

At the base of the mountain, long before the frenzy of the Crusades, a church and a mosque were raised side by side. Each contained holy relics rumored to be from a ship high upon the mountain. Both buildings were leveled in an earthquake during the seventh century and the wood plankings (window coverings from the Ark) that had been held in such esteem were destroyed.

In A.D. 610, Isidore of Seville, a compiler of universal knowledge for one of the earliest encyclopedias, detailed how there were certain times of the year when portions of Noah's vessel could be looked upon by those who sought.

In the ninth century a group of reclusive holy men built their monastery in the saddle of the twin peaks of the mountain and frequented in complete secrecy the place of the Ark, higher up the mountainside.

In 1254, a monk named Jehan Haithon stated publicly that the Ark could still be seen as an enormous, blackened form beneath layers of thick ice.

In 1255, another monk, after years of continuous effort, stumbled upon the entrance to the Ark's valley. He returned from his journey with a piece of aged wood but said nothing. For decades, it was rumored that he had been greeted by an angel and had been asked to turn back—the timber was an offering in exchange for his silence.

In 1647, Boule Legouse made a sketch of the twin peaks of the mountain and the resting-place of the Ark; in 1686, Sir John Chardin did the same.

In 1670, Jans Jansoon Struys, a Dutch adventurer, traveled to the mountain and befriended Domingo Alessandro, a monk. Alessandro gave the adventurer a written testimony of his trip inside the craft, a piece of timber from the Ark and instructions to carry both to Rome. Even to this day, the monk's testimony and the wooden fragment are reported to remain within the Vatican.

For centuries, the Armenians, the Russians, and the Persians claimed it was forbidden for humans to climb beyond the midpoint of the slopes, where they said there was a craft, which was spoken of in awe, reverence and fear.

For generations, it was long-held as an Armenian religious belief that it was completely impossible to reach the top of the mountain, rising 16,000 feet above the level plains and that those who claim to have done so are lying.

In 1829, a highly respected German-Russian physician, Dr. Friedrick Parrot, made the first modern recorded ascent of the mountain but the climb was made with his own team, none of the local villagers could be persuaded to hire on as guides.

Before 1840, it was believed the Ark stood high upon the mountain, in a wooded, valley-swamp—frozen for at least ten months out of every year. However, on June 20, 1840, a tremendous earthquake disfigured the higher peak and altered the shape of the valley. The force of the tremor leveled Akhury, the village at the base of the mountain, covering the ruins of the ninth-century monastery and was followed by a minor quake four days later. There are those who claim the remains of Noah's vineyard disappeared that same year.

In 1856, a major in the United States army insisted he had visited the site of the Ark.

Sometime around 1856, Haji Yearam, an Armenian teenager, set out with his father to find the Ark. His father was acting as guide to three scientists. Each of the three travelers, all atheists, had undertaken the journey specifically to prove fraudulent the biblical account of the Flood. Haji's father decided to lead the expedition, nonetheless—despite thunderous protests from other villagers, for he believed that God finally wished to reveal the truth.

It had been one of the hottest summers on record, and a great deal of the ice and snow atop the mountain had melted into river streams. After much searching and traveling over perilous ground, Haji, his father, and the three men came into the valley and laid eyes upon the bow of an enormous ship. They ventured inside to explore and found stalls, cages, and different levels in the craft. The entire structure was covered, inside and out, with an impenetrable, lacquered finish—there could be no doubt, they had found the Ark.

The scientists were enraged, and Haji and his father were astonished by their reaction. After much arguing, the three men took the only tool they had with them, a small hand ax, and attempted to chop through the planks of the ship, a waste of effort, for the wood had become as hard as stone. They decided to destroy the ship by fire and tried to do so for nearly an hour but the timber would not burn.

Finally, the three took an oath among themselves to never relate what they had seen—else all of their work would be for naught—and they told Haji and his father they would have to die. The Armenians pleaded for mercy and swore themselves to secrecy as well. In the end, the scientists let them go but promised to have their lives if word of the discovery ever leaked out, and for more than fifty years only the five who had made the journey knew the entire story.

In 1863, explorer D. W. Freshfield claimed to have seen the Ark; and in 1876, Sir James Bryce, a British statesman, found ancient hand-hewn timber upon the higher of the two peaks.

In 1883, an earthquake shook the mountain and in 1893 Prince Nouri, archbishop of Babylon, claimed to the Chicago World Parliament of Religions that a tremor had exposed a large portion of Noah's Ark, which he had seen with his own eyes in 1887. The reaction of much of the educated world was one of disbelief, and Nouri's testimony was stricken from the official record and he disappeared amid a cloud of mystery and ridicule.

E. de Markoff, a member of the Russian Imperial Geographic Society, found wood high upon the mountainside in 1888, much as Bryce had done before him.

In 1893, H. F. B. Lynch, a British Merchant, confirmed Nouri's account of changes upon the mountain due to an earthquake.

In 1902, George Hagopian, a twelve-year-old Armenian, and

his uncle made a journey to the Ark. The boy was even hoisted to the roof of the craft. The same journey was repeated in 1904. In 1970 at the age of 80, George worked with an artist to sketch the craft he recalled from his youth, a craft that other Armenian children had seen as well.

Arthur Chuchian, an Armenian immigrant to the United States, confirmed Hagopian's recollection of how Armenian children frequently visited the Ark and detailed how his own father, Jacob Chuchian, frequently told of making his own series of trips to the Ark during the late nineteenth and early twentieth centuries, between the ages of nine and nineteen.

During World War I, Russian expeditions journeyed through blinding snow and reported seeing the outline of an enormous ship off in the distance.

Haji Yearam immigrated to the United States and in his seventies found the courage to relate what had happened to the few who would listen before he died.

In December 1917, 150 Russian infantrymen, army engineers, and specialists made camp in a valley high up on the slopes of the mountain, and took back with them the story of a ship that protruded from a frozen lake.

In 1918, an elderly scientist in London (one of the three who had made the journey with Haji and his father) gave his deathbed confession and confirmed that he had seen Noah's Ark. The story was never distributed by any international press.

In the 1930s, Carveth Wells, a Los Angeles radio announcer, visited an ancient monastery at Echmiadzen and was shown a golden casket purported to contain fragments of the Ark. When he and a crew of his men tried to visit the mountain, admission to cross the Armenian border was denied.

Harwicke Knight, a learned archaeologist, found pieces of

wood upon the mountain in 1936; he reported his belief that the timbers were from the Ark.

There were aerial sightings of an enormous ship upon the slopes of the mountain by both American and Russian aviators throughout World War II.

Ed Davis, a member of the army corps of engineers, was stationed in northern Iran in 1943. He befriended a local family who apparently took him to the very same site that George Hagopian had visited 40 years earlier. The difference between the Davis and Hagopian sightings was that in the intervening years an earthquake had apparently caused the Ark to slide further down the mountain, breaking into two pieces during the fall. Both the Hagopian and Davis sightings were thought to have occurred somewhere around the upper portions of the Ahora Gorge.

In 1948, a Turkish farmer named Resit claimed to have proof that he had discovered the Ark. He was scheduled to announce his findings to the Associated Press, which was to broadcast his story all over the world. Resit disappeared shortly before the interview was to take place. The mystery has never been solved.

On June 17, 1949, an Air Force plane flying near the western summit of the mountain took aerial photographs of an enormous unusual shape that appeared man-made. The shape was curved and appeared to be approximately five hundred feet in length. That photograph was classified and was not seen by the general public for more than forty-five years.

In 1953, George Greene, an oil and pipe engineer took aerial photographs of the northeastern flank of Mount Ararat and obtained pictures of the Ark from as close as ninety feet away. This fact was later verified by more than a dozen people who had seen the pictures. At his death in 1962, the photos could not be found.

In 1955 and again in 1969 with fellow explorer Eryl Cummings,

Fernand Navarra discovered pieces of hand-tooled lumber upon the mountain—wood that he believed to be from the Ark.

Starting in 1970, the late astronaut, James Irwin, made a series of uneventful trips to the mountains of Ararat in search of the Ark. Additional explorations were undertaken by the explorer Ron Wyatt in 1979 and 1984. Many scheduled expeditions to Ararat since 1970 have been canceled due to international conflicts, politics, or the weather.

In 1973, a CIA reconnaissance satellite accidentally took photographs of a boat-like object on Mount Ararat while patrolling the Soviet-Turkish border. When the high-resolution photographs were developed they showed what appeared to be a "heavily damaged bow of some kind of huge ship protruding out of the glacier." The report circulated throughout the CIA about the existence of an object that might be Noah's Ark.

James Irwin and Eryl Cummings made another expedition with a total of 12 others in 1982. Thanks to Irwin's efforts and his political connections, he was able to get eastern Turkey open to expeditions again during the mid-1980s.

In 1991, Kurdish rebels kidnapped five archaeologists near the mountain and the Turks closed Mount Ararat to outside visitors.

In 1995, the Defense Intelligent Agency released the classified 1949 photograph because of the efforts of Porcher Taylor, a professor at the University of Richmond, and Dr. George Carver, a former deputy for National Intelligence in the CIA. The two mounted a campaign through the Freedom of Information Act to release and declassify certain photos of the mountain. The 1949 photograph became known as the "Ararat Anomaly."

In 2001 and 2002, Professor Taylor's efforts led to the possibility of undertaking additional satellite photographs of the mountain hoping to solve the riddle of the Ararat Anomaly. It is anticipated that any additional discoveries in the area will lead to an all-out ground expedition to find the remnants of Noah's Ark.

It is not clear when the people of the earth began to call the mountain by the name "Ararat."

There is a legend that God, Himself, hid the ship high upon the mountain, not far from where Noah left it and there it remains, purposefully hidden, until the hour is right. And when the time comes, God, in His mercy, will let the Ark be found, so that men and women everywhere, all the nations of the earth, might one day have the opportunity, the chance, to believe.

A Remnant from the Library at Alexandria

(From the records of Adam, Methuselah, Maran and their descendents)

"In the Beginning" cannot fully explain that which has always been nor that which will always be, for the eternal can have neither start nor finish. It possesses neither time nor space, nor can it be stilled to pinpoint one fragment of a moment that in infinity consists of nothing more than an illusion. Still, there is a dimension that demands conceptual boundaries. This we have come to call the earth. And it is here that the children of the One entrapped themselves and thus it is here we must begin.

In the beginning, there was Spirit, and It was and encompassed all that was yet to be. It was continually in motion, vibrant and active, constantly rejuvenating itself. In holiest essence It consisted simply of Love—Love manifested as energy in a Universe that had no boundaries, no space, no time. It was everything that ever was and all that could ever be, changeless and yet destined to infinite growth, a growth that could not be measured, for that which is of the Eternal is without dimension. Yet, it was and forever would remain Spirit. And this Spirit was aware of Itself and of Its Love, a Love that was complete, never faltering, never ending, without beginning. This was the Creative Forces; this was God.

And God moved and projected from Himself, in a beginning that consciousness demands, companions, companions who would be like their Creator—eternal. These were his children, aware of themselves and of their oneness with all. These were the souls: individual portions of the Divine, aware of their uniqueness and of their place in the Whole. To each was given free will, to be, to do, and to think whatsoever was wished.

And had there been time and space in this dimension of pure Love, it might have seemed as for an eon of millennia these separate portions of God were indistinguishable from the Whole. The thoughts of all were much like one another. The consciousness was of Love and was complete.

But there came a ripple in infinity when some of the souls took part in an illusion. It was an illusion of their separateness from the Creator's Light, and with the illusion of Light came the perception of darkness. The Light was of the Creator and the darkness was the belief that anything could exist apart from its own Source. The illusion was untrue, yet the souls, with their free will, chose to believe it, and thus made it so. In consciousness, they saw both Light and dark, and their minds believed that which could never be.

And in darkness, there was time.

While in darkness, the children of God were unaware of their oneness with the Whole. Only when they again perceived the Light did the darkness disappear and along with it the illusion of time. As the souls began to experience the descent into time with greater frequency, they began—slightly at first, and then tragically—to forget the real peace that came with at-one-ment with the Divine.

Still, the Spirit of God moved throughout a universe without dimensions, creating and changing that which was of Itself in timeless holiness. The souls, too, were invited to witness and partake of this vibrant act of constant Creation. As companions of the Creative Forces, these children of God were to become co-creators with their Source. So, those portions of the Divine which continued to choose the Light helped create universes, spheres, dimensions, where the Divinity of Love could be expressed. The souls which played in and out of time were able to participate in creation—while in the Light, their acts were at one with the Whole; while in darkness, their creations were mere fragments of that which they had the potential to be. Often, their thoughts in darkness manifested only partially realized conceptions and ideas which were not quite concrete. These became thought-forms, pieces of creation that neither solidified in specific dimension nor rejoined the wholeness of the Source. The thought-forms belonged to neither space nor time, nor did they possess the ultimate potential for oneness in the absence of Divine intervention.

Eventually, there came a wave in the ripple of infinity, when the plane of third dimension manifested in consciousness. The souls, both those of the Light and those of time, saw the beauty of the physical realm and the majesty of the planets. There became countless universes where the Love of the Source was expressed in physical creation. Many of these universes contained planets, suns, moons, and stars, and among these three-dimensional worlds, on a planet which was the third from its sun, many of the souls, in time, came to observe what was occurring. This place came to be called the earth, and it was only a tiny mote in the grand scale of all the universes that had been moved into being.

And it was on the earth that some of the souls, children of God, became trapped. For in their movement through darkness and time they had experimented with their power. They possessed the ability to mingle with the forms of creation and, thus, to feel the consciousness of a limited dimension. These were souls who longed to feel the beauty of the skies, the seas, the forests, the hills, the plains, the flowers, and even of the creatures of the planet which were beginning to make an appearance through the evolutionary process.

So the souls in darkness mingled with the animals of the earth, and in the process, created strange new forms. Some of the animals became Mixtures of creatures that had existed prior to the souls' influx into the plane; others were trapped in forms that resembled nothing that had ever been conceived of in the Light. These souls became entangled in matter and darkness and were trapped until the physical body they had chosen perished with the natural passage of time. Yet, once free from physical confinement, a soul often chose to reenter the material world. In the earth, the children of God had developed appetites and desires, and it was within their power to appease them. Free will had been given to the souls, and God did nothing to take away what had been bestowed in complete Love.

As the illusion of time went on, however, the souls in darkness forgot from whence they had come. In grotesque physical bodies, they only vaguely remembered, in dreams and in stories, their true nature. Their minds had become so completely engulfed by an illusion of darkness that even death of the physical did not necessarily bring with it remembrance of the Light. Their perfection had been lost in the physical, and they could regain that which was rightfully theirs only by perfecting the material bodies in which they found themselves.

But there arose a problem: that which is perfectly Divine cannot be expressed through that which is imperfectly material, so the children of God became completely trapped in an illusion that did not exist in eternity.

The souls which remained in the Light saw that which had befallen those in darkness and were distressed. Their destiny was a return, by choice, to oneness with the Source, but the return was impossible without the whole. As long as there were souls in darkness, the souls in Light would never be able to fully experience the oneness that had been the Creator's intention from the beginning. And so, in this dimension where the expression of Love had been the sole concern, there arose a conflict: If the Children of Light remained there, waiting in infinity for the passage of the illusion of time—hoping that the souls in the earth escaped their confinement—their growth as co-creators would remain incomplete until the children in darkness returned to the Light. Meanwhile, on the earth, the souls in time began to cry out in sorrow for help from a God they only vaguely remembered. Their bodies began to experience pain because their minds dwelt in a place of limitations that wasn't really there.

However, there came an instant when hope finally arose anew in the realm of infinity. One soul, given the name Amilius by the Creator, decided of his own free will to enter the earth and the darkness thereof in order to help those in time escape their illusion. He made the decision out of concern for those who had become trapped, and it was because of this choice that he would become the master soul of the third-dimensional plane. It was his desire to manifest the pattern for perfection of flesh in the earth.

There were others among the souls of Light who volunteered to follow Amilius into the earth and assist him. They hoped to reestablish the consciousness among all souls of their rightful place as companions of the Source.

So, this second influx of the children of God projected themselves into the illusion of being separate from the Light. With the power of their Source, they fashioned bodies which would be able to perfectly manifest the Love of the Creator in the earth. Their bodies slightly resembled that of a creature which already dwelt in the earth—the anthropoid ape. But, man did not evolve from the other creatures of third dimension. He was a completely new form, slightly resembling the ape, yet possessing none of the simian's evolutionary past.

There is no missing link.

It was in this new form of flesh that the soul Amilius dwelt among the creatures of the earth. He took for himself the earth name "Adam" and became the first complete man. His twin soul in the Light became his companion in the flesh and she took the name "Eve." It was their hope to manifest Love and let their example assist all in a return to the Source. The other souls that had followed Amilius into the darkness began projecting themselves into flesh at the same time so that the five races of humanity appeared upon the continents of the earth simultaneously.

And the plan of escape was thus: As the souls which had first entered the darkness left their imperfect bodies in death, they could be born anew as children of the souls of the second influx. Then, they, too, would possess physical forms that had the potential to manifest the Love of their Father in the earth. Flesh could be perfected to possess the Divine, and the illusion of darkness would be obliterated once and for all.

The second influx of souls entered into the earth and mingled with those that had come before, and it was thus that "the sons of God saw the daughters of men that they were fair, and they took them."

So in the realm of time and space, the souls of the second influx began having children who were souls from the first. Adam and Eve had two sons, Cain and Abel, and it seemed, for a while, that the plan of escape would work. Abel remembered who he was and from whence he had come and worshipped his Creator. For a time, Cain, too, began to remember the realm of infinity, but his soul had been in the earth for such a long time that his physical desires were greater than his wish to return to the Source. He saw that many of the daughters of the second influx were fair, and he desired to possess them. His mind retained all those things which were not of perfection and he, like many of the others, experienced emotions which were foreign to the idea of divine Love in the earth. There were those who felt jealousy, rage, hatred, lust, and sadness. Yet, they mistook their sadness as occurring because of the things they lacked in the physical, instead of the fact that, at the level of the soul, they desired—more than anything—a return to the Light. Because a few believed there were those who possessed more than was rightfully theirs, jealousy became real among some of the children of flesh. It was this error that Cain made, and in his blindness, he slew his brother, Abel.

To make matters even worse, there were children of the earth who took some of the other creatures, the animals and the thought-forms, as their mates. They had desires which could only be satisfied by mixing with non-perfect forms. As a result, creatures were born which had one perfect parent and another often more animal than human. No longer did the souls of the first influx necessarily choose to be born in perfect human forms. Eventually there were more Mixtures in the earth than had existed before Amilius and the second influx had entered the darkness.

In their sorrow over what was occurring, Adam and Eve turned again to each other for comfort and gave birth to a son. They called him Seth, and they prayed to God that it might be through Seth that the plan of escape could be realized.

As the illusion of time went on, the greatest tragedy of all finally occurred: The souls of the second influx also began to forget why they had entered the earth. They grew accustomed to life in the flesh and lost any desire to return to the Light. In sadness, the Creator realized what was happening, but because He had granted each of them complete freedom of will, unless they asked for His help, He would not interfere.

The children of earth who possessed fragments of perfection in the earth began to live longer than those creatures who had been parented only by Mixtures. The lifespan was as long as 1,000 years, and during such time, a soul could become completely engulfed with the desires of the physical. It was for this reason that the One decided there might come a moment in the illusion of time when He might intervene. The lifespan of flesh could be cut from a thousand to a hundred years or less, thereby limiting the number of desires that could be accumulated in any lifetime. For it was a law of the universe that all urges acquired in the earth must also be overcome in the physical before the oneness envisioned by Amilius would ever become a reality.

Eventually, Adam, too, made the same mistake as the others and "fell" in the garden. He began to lose hope that his plan would work. He had forgotten that the physical was only an illusion and that the infinite was his true destiny. And once his fall was complete, he, like the others, had to incarnate in the flesh again and again until perfection had been reestablished. This he did, and in each of his physical lives, he made great strides in helping other souls escape the confines of limited consciousness. He was born as Enoch, then Melchizedek, as Zend, as Ur, as Asaph, and as many others who began, more and more, to manifest the Love of the Creator in the earth. He was born as Joseph, beloved son of Jacob, and later as Joshua, scribe to Moses. For thirty-two physical incarnations, he showed the path all souls must follow in a return to their Source. Eventually, this soul, Amilius, was born into his final lifetime. He became the perfect pattern—the Christ—and in his perfection, he raised his own flesh from the illusion of death, time, and darkness, and returned to the Light.

However, a great deal had occurred in this illusion of limitations between the time Amilius fell as Adam and then rose again as the Christ. Something had to be done with the imperfect creatures that were making the manifestation of Divinity in the flesh impossible. Something had to be done to cleanse the earth.

And as the Lord God heard the prayers of Adam, He decided to use the boy, Seth, as a channel for the continuation of the human form that could embody the divinity of the Creator. All over the earth, the children of the first and second influxes began to mix with the other creatures of the planet—except for those who were of the lineage of Seth. For nine generations, the children of Seth married other children of God who had not mixed with the imperfect forms of the earth. Yet as the Mixtures spread, the opportunity to find mates who remained true to the perfection of Adam dwindled. These were the generations of Seth: Seth begat Enos, who begat Cainan, who begat Mahalaleel. There were others—children of Seth and Enos and Cainan and Mahalaleel—who were born, but they did not marry perfect human vessels through which the Love of the Creator could be totally expressed.

And in time, Mahalaleel begat Jared, who begat Enoch, who

begat Methuselah, who begat Lamech. And Lamech became the father of the one who would assist God in saving the people of the earth from themselves. Lamech's son took the name Noah; and Noah was a carpenter and a builder in the land of Shinar, now know as Mesopotamia.

And as the time for the Flood drew near, fewer and fewer souls remembered that the fall of humankind was simply a descent in consciousness, from infinity into the realm of space and time. The souls forgot that their separation from the Light was only an illusion. It never really happened, for that which is one with God is one throughout all Eternity.

References And Recommended Reading

Anchor Bible: Genesis. E.A. Speiser. New York: Doubleday and Co., 1964.

Anderson, Flavia. *The Ancient Secret: In Search of the Holy Grail*. London: Victor Gollanez, Ltd., 1955.

Balsiger, Dave and Charles E. Sellier, Jr. *In Search of Noah's Ark*. Los Angeles: Sun Classic Books, 1972.

Browne, Lewis. *The Wisdom of Israel*. New York: Random House, 1945

Burgess, Gelett. *The Maxims of Noah*. New York: Frederick A. Stokes Co., 1913.

Burrow, J.W. "The Flood." *Horizon*, Summer 1972, pgs. 105-109.

Collected Works of C.G. Jung. No. XX Bollingen Series. Princeton University Press, 1970.

Corbin, B.J., editor. *The Explorers of Ararat and the Search for Noah's Ark*. Long Beach, California: Great Commission Illustrated Books, 1999.

Cummings, Violet M. *Noah's Ark: Fact or Fable? The History of One Man's Search of the Evidences Supporting the Existence of the Ark on Mt. Ararat*. San Diego: Creation-Science Research Center, 1972.

"Did They Find Noah's Ark: Explorers Can't Agree." *Christianity Today*, Oct. 5, 1984.

The Edgar Cayce Readings. Virginia Beach: the Edgar Cayce Foundation, © 1971, 1993-2007.

"Eighth-Century Ark." *Scientific American*, July 1980, pg. 77.

Encyclopaedia Judaica. Jerusalem, Israel: Keter Publishing House. Jerusalem Ltd., 1972.

"Ex-astronaut Plans to Keep Seeking Ark." *The Ledger-Star*. Virginia Beach, Virginia. Monday, Aug. 3, 1987, pg. A2.

Frazer, Sir James George, F.R.S., F.B.A. *Folk-Lore in the Old Testament*. New York: MacMillan Co., 1923.

"The Gilgamesh Epic," Alexander Heidel, trans. *The Gilgamesh Epic and Old Testament Parallels*. University of Chicago Press, 1949.

Ginzberg, Louis. *Legends of the Jews*. New York: Simon and Schuster, 1956.

Hebraic Literature: Translations from the Talmud, Midrashim and Kabbala. Washington and London: M. Walter Dunne, 1901.

Hebrew Literature: Comprising Talmudic Treatises, Hebrew Melodies and the Kabbalah Unveiled. New York: Willey Book Co., 1901.

Heidel, Alexander. *The Gilgamesh Epic and Old Testament Parallels*. University of Chicago Press, 1949.

The Holy Bible. King James Version, 1979. Especially Genesis 4-11.

The Holy Qur-an. Abdullah Yusuf Ali, trans. McGregor & Werner, Inc., 1946.

The Jewish Encyclopedia: A Descriptive Record of the History, Religion, Literature, and Customs of the Jewish People from the Earliest Times to the Present Day. London: Funk and Wagnalls Co., 1901.

Krajenke, Robert W. *Man the Messiah*. New York: Bantam Books, 1974.

Krajenke, Robert W. *A Million Years to the Promised Land*. New York: Bantam Books, 1973.

Jastrow, Morris Jr., Ph.D. *Hebrew and Babylonian Traditions*. New York: Charles Scribner's Sons, 1914.

LaHaye, Tim F., and John D. Morris. *The Ark on Ararat*. New York: Pocket Books, 1977.

Metaphysical Bible Dictionary. Lee's Summit, MO: Unity School of Christianity, 1931.

Montgomery, John Warwick. *The Quest for Noah's Ark*. Minneapolis, Minnesota: Dimension Books, 1974.

Noah and the Flood. Circulating File compiled by Mae Gimbert St. Clair. Virginia Beach: the Edgar Cayce Foundation, 1980.

Oursler, Fulton. *The Greatest Book Ever Written*. New York: Doubleday & Co., Inc., 1951.

Riedel, Eunice, Thomas Tracy, and Barbara D. Moskowitz. *The Book of the Bible*. New York: William Morrow and Co., Inc., 1979.

Rohrbach, Elizabeth C., ed. *Jung's Contribution to Our Time: The Collected Papers of Eleanor Bertine*. New York: C.G. Jung Foundation for Analytical Psychology, 1967.

Ryan, William and Walter Pitman. *Noah's Flood: The New Scientific Discoveries About the Event that Changed History*. New York: Simon & Schuster, 1998.

Smith, W. Robertson, M.A. *The Old Testament in the Jewish Church*. New York: D. Appleton and Co., 1881.

Steiner, Rudolf. *Cosmic Memory: Prehistory of Earth and Man*. San Francisco: Harper and Row, 1959.

Steiner, Rudolf. *Earthly and Cosmic Man*. London: Steiner Publishing Co., ca. 1948.

Todeschi, Kevin J. *The Ark Myth: Biblical, Rabbinical, and Transpersonal*. Virginia Beach: Atlantic University, 1988.

Waite, Arthur Edward. *The Secret Doctrine in Israel; A Study of the Zohar and its Connections*. New York: Occult Research Press, ca. 1915.

Whiston, William, A.M., translator. *The Works of Flavius Josephus*. Philadelphia: David McKay, Publisher, 1865.

8379598R00268

Made in the USA
San Bernardino, CA
07 February 2014